WHY
I LEFT
HARRY'S
ALL-NIGHT
HAMBURGERS

WHY
I LEFT
HARRY'S
ALL-NIGHT
HAMBURGERS

AND OTHER STORIES
from
ISAAC ASIMOV'S
SCIENCE FICTION MAGAZINE

FOREWORD BY

ISAAC ASIMOV

EDITED BY
SHEILA WILLIAMS
and
CHARLES ARDAI

Delacorte Press

Published by
Delacorte Press
Bantam Doubleday Dell Publishing Group, Inc.
666 Fifth Avenue
New York, New York 10103

Grateful acknowledgment is made to the following for the right to reprint their copyrighted material:
Profession by Isaac Asimov, copyright © 1957 by Street & Smith Publications, Inc., reprinted by permission of the author; *The Homesick Chicken* by Edward D. Hoch, copyright © 1976 by Davis Publications, Inc., reprinted by permission of the author; *Still Time* by James Patrick Kelly, copyright © 1983 by Davis Publications, Inc., reprinted by permission of the author; *The Tryouts* by Barry B. Longyear, copyright © 1978 by Davis Publications, Inc., reprinted by permission of the author; *Empire State* by Keith Minnion, copyright © 1985 by Davis Publications, Inc., reprinted by permission of the author; *The Hob* by Judith Moffett, copyright © 1988 by Davis Publications, Inc., reprinted by permission of Virginia Kidd Literary Agency; *Glacier* by Kim Stanley Robinson, copyright © 1988 by Davis Publications, Inc., reprinted by permission of the author; *The Web Dancer* by Somtow Sucharitkul, copyright © 1979 by Davis Publications, Inc., reprinted by permission of the author; *Why I Left Harry's All-Night Hamburgers* by Lawrence Watt-Evans, copyright © 1987 by Davis Publications, Inc., reprinted by permission of Scott Meredith Literary Agency, Inc.; *The Band from the Planet Zoom* by Andrew Weiner, copyright © 1986 by Andrew Weiner, reprinted by permission of the author; *And Who Would Pity a Swan?* by Connie Willis, copyright © 1984 by Connie Willis, reprinted by permission of the author; *The White Babe* by Jane Yolen, copyright © 1987 by Davis Publications, Inc., reprinted by permission of Curtis Brown, Ltd.

Foreword copyright © 1990 by Isaac Asimov
Collection copyright © 1990 by Sheila Williams and Charles Ardai
Design by Margo Hrubec

Library of Congress Cataloging in Publication Data

Why I left Harry's all-night hamburgers, and other stories from Isaac Asimov's science fiction magazine / edited by Sheila Williams and Charles Ardai; foreword by Isaac Asimov.
    p.   cm.
    Contents: Glacier / by Kim Stanley Robinson—And who would pity a swan? / by Connie Willis—The tryouts / by Barry B. Longyear—Still time / by James Patrick Kelly—The white babe / by Jane Yolen—The homesick chicken / by Edward D. Hoch—Empire state / by Keith Minnion—Profession / by Isaac Asimov—The band from the planet Zoom / by Andrew Weiner—The web dancer / by Somtow Sucharitkul—The hob / by Judith Moffett—Why I left Harry's all-night hamburgers / by Lawrence Watt-Evans.
    ISBN 0-385-30044-1
    1. Science fiction, American. [1. Science fiction. 2. Short stories.] I. Williams, Sheila. II. Ardai, Charles. III. Asimov, Isaac, 1920– . IV. Isaac Asimov's science fiction magazine.
PZ5.W625   1990
[Fic]—dc20   89-23675
                                              CIP
                                              AC

Manufactured in the United States of America

June 1990

10 9 8 7 6 5 4 3 2 1

BVG

For our parents

EARTH
IS ROOM
ENOUGH

ISAAC ASIMOV

t is common for science fiction writers to roam the Galaxy; I do it myself. That, however, doesn't mean that it is
absolutely necessary to do so in order to have science
fiction. The essence of the field is to explore new and
strange technologies and to consider the reaction of human beings
to such changes, whether that reaction takes place here or on the
farthest star, and whether it takes place now or in the farthest future.

In fact, sometimes getting too far away from home gives a writer
the temptation of getting too far away from people. And it is the
people, not the setting, that counts in every story.

Once, over thirty years ago, I was accused of spending all my
time sending my characters across the light-years. Naturally, I was
indignant, for though some of my stories lie in the far reaches
(though I try to do this without losing sight of people), many others
are set right here on Earth.

To prove that point, I published a collection of my short stories
entitled *Earth Is Room Enough* (Doubleday, 1957). Every single one
of the stories included was set firmly on earth.

It is, after all, a wonderful world we have here. It has a surface
that is partly liquid, partly solid. It has a variety of climates, being
hot and dry in some places, hot and wet in others, very cold in still
others. It has its flat plains and its rugged mountains. Most important of all, it bears its load of life in unimaginable complexity.

Yes, we might want to picture situations involving stars widely different from our own Sun, circled by planets widely different from our own Earth, with conditions and life-forms on them widely different from those we know. We have the right to do so. But we don't have to. Earth can give us an infinite number of tales as exciting and as marvelous as we can imagine elsewhere.

Another point we ought to make about science fiction is this. Although it is a form of literature that is suitable for all ages, it fits best, somehow, with the young. That might seem an odd thing for me to say, since I have been writing science fiction for over fifty years and have, in the process, grown a little elderly.

Well, that doesn't mean anything now because I was young once and I remember. I started reading science fiction, in fact, at the age of nine; I started to try to write at the age of eleven; and I sold my first story at the age of eighteen.

And why is science fiction particularly interesting to the young? Because it involves change. It involves changes in the level of science and technology; changes in society produced by those changes in science and technology; and changes in human life-style and human ways of thinking produced by those changes in society.

Change is a hard thing to accept. We grow used to things being the way they are. We have an emotional investment in our everyday lives and we don't *want* them changed. The older we are and the longer we've made that investment, the more we don't want things to change and the more strongly we resist the change.

But changes must take place, unless humanity falls back in complete stagnation—a condition which, to my way of thinking, would mean the end of our species. The changes that take place are accepted primarily by young people, whose investment in things as they are is still small, who are newly come to the world, and who are willing to try out new things.

That is why science fiction seems more exciting and less threatening to young people; why they greet it with enthusiasm. After all, it's *their* world of the future that is being described. Thus, when I was young, I read (and wrote) about trips to the Moon, about advanced airplanes and rockets, about robots and thinking machines, about television and new medical procedures, and the time came when I lived it all too.

And, of course, if you *start* young, and continue to read it, as I have done, then constant exposure to the idea of change keeps you aware of its necessity. It keeps you *mentally* and *emotionally* young even if your body ages.

And that, really, is the hope of the world. That people somehow will always be ready to solve problems in new ways and produce new and better things on Earth. So this anthology is largely devoted to science fiction that takes place on our planet, and the stories are chosen so that they will particularly involve the young.

CONTENTS

INTRODUCTION:
MORE
TOMORROWS

Dear Reader:

This book you're holding is a special one. You'll see why in a minute. First, let me tell you a story.

When I was ten years old, living in New York, my father came home after work one day with two books. One was for my brother and the other was for me. Michael's was a novel called *The Caves of Steel,* about robots and humans and life in the future. Mine was a collection of science fiction stories titled *Nine Tomorrows.* Both were by Isaac Asimov.

Asimov had been signing books in the big Doubleday store downtown, my father said. So even though it wasn't one of our birthdays or anything, he had decided to buy us each a book. Sure enough, on the books' title pages were our names *(To Michael, To Charles),* followed by Isaac Asimov's signature and the date: *20 March 1980.*

Michael went wild. He had already read some other Asimov books, and he loved them. I hadn't, so I didn't know what I was in for—but the book looked interesting (it had an orange-and-purple cover with a one-eyed *thing* on it) and I was willing to give it a chance. I lay down in bed, bunched up a blanket under my head, and started reading the first story, "Profession."

When I finished, *I* went wild.

It was wonderful. Not only was it a great story because it made me care about what happened to the characters, but also because it took me on a tour of a world I had never seen before—a world *no one* had ever seen before, because it didn't exist. The story described what the future might be like, and it was convincing. From the moment I picked the book up until the moment I put it down, I believed in the world Isaac Asimov had created. And it was exhilarating.

It's hard to describe the effect that one story had on me. To begin with, I was too excited to go on to the other stories in the collection. Once I calmed down, I finished *Nine Tomorrows*. Then I devoured *The Caves of Steel* as soon as I could pry it out of Michael's hands. Then I read every other Asimov book I could get my hands on, and when I ran out of those I looked for other authors and read everything *they* had written. Not all these books were science fiction, of course, but there was something special about the ones that were: they had a sense of magic, of contact with the unknown, of striving and exploration and infinite possibility.

Michael read many of these books with me, and we divided science fiction up between us. He took the "science," and went on to study robotics and computer programming and artificial intelligence. Today he's a computer engineer, and Isaac Asimov is still his favorite author. I took the "fiction," and became a voracious reader and, eventually, a writer.

And all of this started with "Profession."

That's why this book is so special. First of all, "Profession" is in here. How could we not include it? And there are eleven other stories in here, too, all of them excellent; each one will excite you in a different way.

While you won't necessarily end up a writer or a scientist or an engineer, we hope these stories will help inspire you to conquer your own frontiers, whatever they may be. If there is one thing that science fiction shows, it is that anything is possible.

The stories you are about to read are windows onto a dozen fantastic worlds. They can be the start of a lifelong adventure for you as a reader, as a dreamer, and as a human being. Enjoy them, savor them, and years from now, when you are well on your way to living your private dream, remember them.

Charles Ardai,
August 1989

GLACIER
KIM STANLEY ROBINSON

his is Stella," Mrs. Goldberg said. She opened the cardboard box and a gray cat leaped out and streaked under the corner table.

"That's where we'll put her blanket," Alex's mother said.

Alex got down on hands and knees to look. Stella was a skinny old cat; her fur was an odd mix of silver, black, and pinkish tan. Yellow eyes. Part tortoiseshell, Mom had said. The color of the fur over her eyes made it appear her brow was permanently furrowed. Her ears were laid flat.

"Remember she's kind of scared of boys," Mrs. Goldberg said.

"I know." Alex sat back on his heels. Stella hissed. "I was just looking." He knew the cat's whole story. She had been a stray that began visiting the Goldbergs' balcony to eat their dog's food, then—as far as anyone could tell—to hang out with the dog. Remus, a stiff-legged ancient thing, seemed happy to have the company, and after a while the two animals were inseparable. The cat had learned how to behave by watching Remus, and so it would go for a walk, come when you called it, shake hands and so on. Then Remus died, and now the Goldbergs had to move. Mom had offered to take Stella in, and though Father sighed heavily when she told him about it, he hadn't refused.

Mrs. Goldberg sat on the worn carpet beside Alex, and leaned forward so she could see under the table. Her face was puffy. "It's okay, Stell-bell," she said. "It's okay."

The cat stared at Mrs. Goldberg with an expression that said *You've got to be kidding.* Alex grinned to see such skepticism.

Mrs. Goldberg reached under the table; the cat squeaked in protest as it was pulled out, then lay in Mrs. Goldberg's lap quivering like a rabbit. The two women talked about other things. Then Mrs. Goldberg put Stella in Alex's mother's lap. There were scars on its ears and head. It breathed fast. Finally it calmed under Mom's hands. "Maybe we should feed her something," Mom said. She knew how distressed animals could get in this situation: they themselves had left behind their dog Pongo, when they moved from Toronto to Boston. Alex and she had been the ones to take Pongo to the Wallaces; the dog had howled as they left, and walking away Mom had cried. Now she told Alex to get some chicken out of the fridge and put it in a bowl for Stella. He put the bowl on the couch next to the cat, who sniffed at it disdainfully and refused to look at it. Only after much calming would it nibble at the meat, nose drawn high over one sharp eyetooth. Mom talked to Mrs. Goldberg, who watched Stella eat. When the cat was done it hopped off Mom's lap and walked up and down the couch. But it wouldn't let Alex near; it crouched as he approached, and with a desperate look dashed back under the table. "Oh, Stella!" Mrs. Goldberg laughed. "It'll take her a while to get used to you," she said to Alex, and sniffed. Alex shrugged.

Outside the wind ripped at the treetops sticking above the buildings. Alex walked up Chester Street to Brighton Avenue and turned left, hurrying to counteract the cold. Soon he reached the river and could walk the path on top of the embankment. Down in its trough the river's edges were crusted with ice, but midstream was still free, the silty gray water riffled by white. He passed the construction site for the dam and came to the moraine, a long mound of dirt, rocks, lumber, and junk. He climbed it with big steps, and stood looking at the glacier.

The glacier was immense, like a range of white hills rolling in from the west and north. The Charles poured from the bottom of it and roiled through a cut in the terminal moraine; the glacier's snout loomed so large that the river looked small, like a gutter after a storm. Bright white iceberg chunks had toppled off the face of the snout, leaving fresh blue scars and clogging the river below.

Alex walked the edge of the moraine until he was above the glacier's side. To his left was the razed zone, torn streets and fresh dirt and cellars open to the sky; beyond it Allston and Brighton, still bustling with city life. Under him, the sharp-edged mound of dirt and debris. To his right, the wilderness of ice and rock. Looking straight ahead it was hard to believe that the two halves of the view came from the same world. Neat. He descended the moraine's steep, loose inside slope carefully, following a path of his own.

The meeting of glacier and moraine was a curious juncture. In some places the moraine had been undercut and had spilled across the ice in wide fans; you couldn't be sure if the dirt was solid or if it concealed crevasses. In other places melting had created a gap, so that a thick cake of ice stood over empty air, and dripped into gray pools below. Once Alex had seen a car in one of these low wet caves, stripped of its paint and squashed flat.

In still other places, however, the ice sloped down and overlay the moraine's gravel in a perfect ramp, as if fitted by carpenters. Alex walked the trough between dirt and ice until he reached one of these areas, then took a big step onto the curved white surface. He felt the usual quiver of excitement: he was on the glacier.

It was steep on the rounded side slope, but the ice was embedded with thousands of chunks of gravel. Each pebble, heated by the sun, had sunk into a little pocket of its own, and was then frozen into position in the night; this process had been repeated until most chunks were about three-quarters buried. Thus the glacier had a peculiarly pocked, rocky surface, which gripped the torn soles of Alex's shoes. A non-slip surface. No slope on the glacier was too steep for him. Crunch, crunch, crunch: tiny arabesques of ice collapsed under his feet with every step. He could change the glacier, he was part of its action. Part of it.

Where the side slope leveled out the first big crevasses appeared. These deep blue fissures were dangerous, and Alex stepped

between two of them and up a narrow ramp very carefully. He
picked up a fist-sized rock, tossed it in the bigger crack. *Clunk clunk
. . . splash.* He shivered and walked on, ritual satisfied. He knew
from these throws that at the bottom of the glacier there were pockets of air, pools of water, streams running down to form the Charles
. . . a deadly subglacial world. No one who fell into it would ever
escape. It made the surface ice glow with a magical danger, an
internal light.

Up on the glacier proper he could walk more easily. Crunch
crunch crunch, over an undulating broken debris-covered plain. Ice
for miles on miles. Looking back toward the city he saw the Hancock and Prudential towers to the right, the lower MIT towers to the
left, poking up at low scudding clouds. The wind was strong here
and he pulled his jacket hood's drawstring tighter. Muffled hoot of
wind, a million tricklings. There were little creeks running in chan-
nels cut into the ice: it was almost like an ordinary landscape,
streams running in ravines over a broad rocky meadow. And yet
everything was different. The streams ran into crevasses or potholes
and instantly disappeared, for instance. It was wonderfully strange
to look down such a rounded hole: the ice was very blue and you
could see the air bubbles in it, air from some year long ago.

Broken seracs exposed fresh ice to the sun. Scores of big erratic
boulders dotted the glacier, some the size of houses. He made his
way from one to the next, using them as cover. There were gangs of
boys from Cambridge who occasionally came up here, and they
were dangerous. It was important to see them before he was seen.

A mile or more onto the glacier, ice had flowed around one big
boulder, leaving a curving wall some ten feet high—another example of the glacier's whimsy, one of hundreds of strange surface for-
mations. Alex had wedged some stray boards into the gap between
rock and ice, making a seat that was tucked out of the west wind.
Flat rocks made a fine floor, and in the corner he had even made a
little fireplace. Every fire he lit sank the hearth of flat stones a bit
deeper into the otherwise impervious ice.

This time he didn't have enough kindling, though, so he sat on
his bench, hands deep in pockets, and looked back at the city. He
could see for miles. Wind whistled over the boulder. Scattered shafts
of sunlight broke against ice. Mostly shadowed, the jumbled ex-

panse was faintly pink. This was because of an algae that lived on nothing but ice and dust. Pink; the blue of the seracs; gray ice; patches of white, marking snow or sunlight. In the distance dark clouds scraped the top of the blue Hancock building, making it look like a distant serac. Alex leaned back against his plank wall, whistling one of the songs of the Pirate King.

Everyone agreed the cat was crazy. Her veneer of civilization was thin, and at any loud noise—the phone's ring, the door slamming—she would jump as if shot, then stop in mid-flight as she recalled that this particular noise entailed no danger; then lick down her fur, pretending she had never jumped in the first place. A flayed sensibility.

She was also very wary about proximity to people; this despite the fact that she had learned to love being petted. So she would often get in moods where she would approach one of them and give an exploratory, half-purring mew; then, if you responded to the invitation and crouched to pet her, she would sidle just out of arm's reach, repeating the invitation but retreating with each shift you made, until she either let you get within petting distance—just—or decided it wasn't worth the risk, and scampered away. Father laughed at this intense ambivalence. "Stella, you're too stupid to live, aren't you," he said in a teasing voice.

"Charles," Mom said.

"It's the best example of approach-avoidance behavior I've ever seen," Father said. Intrigued by the challenge, he would sit on the floor, back against the couch and legs stretched ahead of him, and put Stella on his thighs. She would either endure his stroking until it ended, when she could jump away without impediment—or relax, and purr. She had a rasping loud purr, it reminded Alex of a chainsaw heard across the glacier. "Bug brain," Father would say to her. "Button head."

After a few weeks, as August turned to September and the leaves began to wither and fall, Stella started to lap-sit voluntarily—but always in Mom's lap. "She likes the warmth," Mom said.

"It's cold on the floor," Father agreed, and played with the cat's scarred ears. "But why do you always sit on Helen's lap, huh, Stell? I'm the one who started you on that." Eventually the cat would step onto his lap as well, and stretch out as if it was something she had always done. Father laughed at her.

Stella never rested on Alex's lap voluntarily, but would sometimes stay if he put her there and stroked her slowly for a long time. On the other hand she was just as likely to look back at him, go cross-eyed with horror, and leap desperately away, leaving claw marks in his thighs. "She's so weird," he complained to Mom after one of these abrupt departures.

"It's true," Mom said with her low laugh. "But you have to remember that Stella was probably an abused kitty."

"How can you abuse a stray?"

"I'm sure there are ways. And maybe she was abused at home, and ran away."

"Who would do that?"

"Some people would."

Alex recalled the gangs on the glacier, and knew it was true. He tried to imagine what it would be like to be at their mercy all the time. After that he thought he understood her permanent frown of deep concentration and distrust as she sat staring at him. "It's just me, Stell-bells."

Thus when the cat followed him up onto the roof, and seemed to enjoy hanging out there with him, he was pleased. Their apartment was on the top floor, and they could take the pantry stairs and use the roof as a porch. It was a flat expanse of graveled tarpaper, a terrible imitation of the glacier's nonslip surface, but it was nice on dry days to go up there and look around, toss pebbles onto other roofs, see if the glacier was visible, and so on. Once Stella pounced at a piece of string trailing from his pants, and next time he brought up a length of Father's yarn. He was astonished and delighted when Stella responded by attacking the windblown yarn enthusiastically, biting it, clawing it, wrestling it from her back when Alex twirled it around her, and generally behaving in a very kittenish way. Perhaps she had never played as a kitten, Alex thought, so that it was all coming out now that she felt safe. But the play always ended abruptly; she would come to herself in mid-bite or bat, straighten up, and look around with a forbidding expression, as if to say, *What is this yarn doing draped over me?*—then lick her fur and pretend the preceding minutes hadn't happened. It made Alex laugh.

* * *

Although the glacier had overrun many towns to the west and north, Watertown and Newton most recently, there was surprisingly little evidence of that in the moraines, or in the ice. It was almost all natural: rock and dirt and wood. Perhaps the wood had come from houses, perhaps some of the gravel had once been concrete, but you couldn't tell that now. Just dirt and rock and splinters, with an occasional chunk of plastic or metal thrown in. Apparently the over-run towns had been plowed under on the spot, or moved. Mostly it looked like the glacier had just left the White Mountains.

Father and Gary Jung had once talked about the latest plan from MIT. The enormous dam they were building downstream, between Allston and Cambridge, was to hold the glacier back. They were going to heat the concrete of the inner surface of the dam, and melt the ice as it advanced. It would become a kind of frozen reservoir. The melt water would pour through a set of turbines before becoming the Charles, and the electricity generated by these turbines would help to heat the dam. Very neat.

The ice of the glacier, when you got right down to look at it, was clear for an inch or less, cracked and bubble-filled; then it turned a milky white. You could see the transition. Where the ice had been sheared vertically, however—on the side of a serac, or down in a crevasse—the clear part extended in many inches. You could see air bubbles deep inside, as if it were badly made glass. And this ice was distinctly blue. Alex didn't understand why there should be that difference, between the white ice lying flat and the blue ice cut vertically. But there it was.

Up in New Hampshire they had tried slowing the glacier—or at least stopping the abrupt "Alaskan slides"—by setting steel rods vertically in concrete, and laying the concrete in the glacier's path. Later they had hacked out one of these installations, and found the rods bent in perfect ninety degree angles, pressed into the scored concrete.

The ice would flow right over the dam.

One day Alex was walking by Father's study when Father called out. "Alexander! Take a look at this."

Alex entered the dark book-lined room. Its window overlooked the weed-filled space between buildings, and green light slanted onto Father's desk. "Here, stand beside me and look in my coffee cup. You can see the reflection of the Morgelis's window flowers on the coffee."

"Oh, yeah! Neat."

"It gave me a shock! I looked down and there were these white and pink flowers in my cup, bobbing against a wall in a breeze, all of it tinted sepia as if it were an old-fashioned photo. It took me a while to see where it was coming from, what was being reflected." He laughed. "Through a looking glass."

Alex's father had light brown eyes, and fair wispy hair brushed back from a receding hairline. Mom called him handsome, and Alex agreed: tall, thin, graceful, delicate, distinguished. His father was a great man. Now he smiled in a way Alex didn't understand, looking into his coffee cup.

Mom had friends at the street market on Memorial Drive, and she had arranged work for Alex there. Three afternoons a week he walked over the Charles to the riverside street and helped the fish-mongers gut fish, the vegetable sellers strip and clean the vegetables. He also helped set up stalls and take them down, and he swept and hosed the street afterwards. He was popular because of his energy and his willingness to get his hands wet in raw weather. The sleeves of his down jacket were permanently discolored from the frequent soakings—the dark blue almost a brown—a fact that distressed his mom. But he could handle the cold better than the adults; his hands would get a splotchy bluish white and he would put them to the red cheeks of the women and they would jump and say My *God,* Alex, how can you stand it?

This afternoon was blustery and dark but without rain, and it was enlivened by an attempted theft in the pasta stands, and by the appearance of a very mangy, very fast stray dog. This dog pounced on the pile of fishheads and entrails and disappeared with his mouth stuffed, trailing slick white-and-red guts. Everyone who saw it laughed. There weren't many stray dogs left these days, it was a pleasure to see one.

An hour past sunset he was done cleaning up and on his way home, hands in his pockets, stomach full, a five dollar bill clutched in one hand. He showed his pass to the National Guardsman and walked out onto Weeks Bridge. In the middle he stopped and leaned over the railing, into the wind. Below the water churned, milky with glacial silt. The sky still held a lot of light. Low curving bands of black cloud swept in from the northwest, like great ribs of slate. Above these bands the white sky was leached away by dusk. Raw wind whistled over his hood. Light water rushing below, dark clouds rushing above . . . he breathed the wind deep into him, felt himself expand until he filled everything he could see.

That night his parents' friends were gathering at their apartment for their biweekly party. Some of them would read stories and po-ems and essays and broadsides they had written, and then they would argue about them; and after that they would drink and eat whatever they had brought, and argue some more. Alex enjoyed it. But tonight when he got home Mom was rushing between computer and kitchen and muttering curses as she hit command keys or the hot water faucet, and the moment she saw him she said, "Oh, Alex, I'm glad you're here, could you please run down to the laundry and do just one load for me? The Talbots are staying over tonight and there aren't any clean sheets and I don't have anything to wear tomorrow either—thanks, you're a dear." And he was back out the door with a full laundry bag hung over his shoulder and the box of soap in the other hand, stomping grumpily past a little man in a black coat reading a newspaper on the stoop of 19 Chester.

Down to Brighton, take a right, downstairs into the brightly lit basement Laundromat. He threw laundry and soap and quarters into their places, turned the machine on, and sat on top of it. Glumly he watched the other people in there, sitting on the washers and dryers. The vibrations put a lot of them to sleep. Others stared dully at the wall. Back in his apartment the guests would be arriving, taking off their overcoats, slapping arms over chests, and talking as fast as they could. David and Sara and John from next door, Ira and Gary and Ilene from across the street, the Talbots, Kathryn Grimm, and Michael Wu from Father's university, Ron from the hospital. They would settle down in the living room, on couches and chairs and floor, and talk and talk. Alex liked Kathryn especially, she could talk twice as fast as anyone else, and she called everyone darling and laughed and chattered so fast that everyone was caught up in the rhythm of it. Or David with his jokes, or Jay Talbot and his friendly questions. Or Gary Jung, the way he would sit in his corner like a bear, drinking beer and challenging everything that everyone read. "Why abstraction, why this distortion from the real? How does it help us, how does it speak to us? We should forget the abstract!" Father and Ira called him a vulgar Marxist, but he didn't mind. "You might as well be Plekhanov, Gary!" "Thank you very much!" he would say with a sharp grin, rubbing his unshaven jowls. And someone else would read. Mary Talbot once read a fairy tale about the Thing under the glacier; Alex had *loved* it. Once they even got Michael Wu to bring his violin along, and he hmm'd and hawed and pulled at the skin of his neck and refused and said he wasn't good enough, and then shaking like a leaf he played a melody that stilled them all. And Stella! She hated these parties, she spent them crouched deep in her refuge, ready for any kind of atrocity.

And here he was sitting on a washer in the Laundromat.

When the laundry was dry he bundled it into the bag, then hurried around the corner and down Chester Street. Inside the glass door of Number 21 he glanced back out, and noticed that the man who had been reading the paper on the stoop next door was still sitting there. Odd. It was cold to be sitting outdoors.

Upstairs the readings had ended and the group was scattered through the apartment, most of them in the kitchen, as Mom had lit the stove-top burners and turned the gas up high. The blue flames roared airily under their chatter, making the kitchen bright and warm. "Wonderful the way white gas burns so clean." "And then they found the poor thing's head and intestines in the alley—it had been butchered right on the spot."

"Alex, you're back! Thanks for doing that. Here, get something to eat."

Everyone greeted him and went back to their conversations. "Gary, you are so *conservative*," Kathryn cried, hands held out over the stove. "It's not conservative at all," Gary replied. "It's a radical goal and I guess it's so radical that I have to keep reminding you it exists. Art should be used to *change* things."

"Isn't that a distortion from the real?"

Alex wandered down the narrow hall to his parents' room,

which overlooked Chester Street. Father was there, saying to Ilene, "It's one of the only streets left with trees. It really seems residential, and here we are three blocks from Comm Ave. Hi, Alex."

"Hi, Alex. It's like a little bit of Brookline made it over to Allston."

"Exactly."

Alex stood in the bay window and looked down, licking the last of the carrot cake off his fingers. The man was still down there.

"Let's close off these rooms and save the heat. Alex, you coming?"

He sat on the floor in the living room. Father and Gary and David were starting a game of hearts, and they invited him to be the fourth. He nodded happily. Looking under the corner table he saw yellow eyes, blinking back at him; Stella, a frown of the deepest disapproval on her flat face. Alex laughed. "I knew you'd be there! It's okay, Stella. It's okay."

They left in a group, as usual, stamping their boots and diving deep into coats and scarves and gloves and exclaiming at the cold of the stairwell. Gary gave Mom a brief hug. "Only warm spot left in Boston," he said, and opened the glass door. The rest followed him out, and Alex joined them. The man in the black coat was just turning right onto Brighton Avenue, toward the university and downtown.

Sometimes clouds took on just the mottled gray of the glacier, low dark points stippling a lighter gray surface as cold showers draped down. At these times he felt he stood between two planes of some larger structure, two halves: icy tongue, icy roof of mouth. . . .

He stood under such a sky, throwing stones. His target was an erratic some forty yards away. He hit the boulder with most of his throws. A rock that big was an easy target. A bottle was better. He had brought one with him, and he set it up behind the erratic, on a waist-high rock. He walked back to a point where the bottle was hidden by the erratic. Using flat rocks he sent spinners out in a trajectory that brought them curving in from the side, so that it was possible to hit the concealed target. This was very important for the rock fights that he occasionally got involved in; usually he was out-numbered, and to hold his own he relied on his curves and his accuracy in general, and on a large number of ammunition caches hidden here and there. In one area crowded with boulders and crevasses he could sometimes create the impression of two throwers.

Absorbed in the exercise of bringing curves around the right side of the boulder—the hard side for him—he relaxed his vigilance, and when he heard a shout he jumped around to look. A rock whizzed by his left ear.

He dropped to the ice and crawled behind a boulder. Ambushed! He ran back into his knot of boulders and dashed a layer of snow away from one of his big caches, then with hands and pockets full looked carefully over a knobby chunk of cement, in the direction the stone had come from.

No movement. He recalled the stone whizzing by, the brief sight of it and the *zip* it made in passing. That had been close! If that had hit him! He shivered to think of it, it made his stomach shrink.

A bit of almost frozen rain pattered down. Not a shadow anywhere. On overcast days like this one it seemed things were lit from below, by the white bulk of the glacier. Like plastic over a weak neon light. Brittle huge blob of plastic, shifting and groaning and once in a while cracking like a gunshot, or grumbling like distant thunder. Alive. And Alex was its ally, its representative among men. He shifted from rock to rock, saw movement and froze. Two boys in green down jackets, laughing as they ran off the ice and over the lateral moraine, into what was left of Watertown. Just a potshot, then. Alex cursed them, relaxed.

He went back to throwing at the hidden bottle. Occasionally he recalled the stone flying by his head, and threw a little harder. Elegant curves of flight as the flat rocks bit the air and cut down and in. Finally one rock spun out into space and turned down sharply. Perfect slider. Its disappearance behind the erratic was followed by a tinkling crash. "Yeah!" Alex exclaimed, and ran to look. Icy glass on glassy ice.

Then, as he was leaving the glacier, boys jumped over the moraine shouting "Canadian!" and "There he is!" and "Get him!" This was more a chase than a serious ambush, but there were a lot of them and after emptying hands and pockets Alex was off running.

He flew over the crunchy irregular surface, splashing meltwater, jumping narrow crevasses and surface rills. Then a wide crevasse blocked his way, and to start his jump he leaped onto a big flat rock; the rock gave under his foot and lurched down the ice into the crevasse.

Alex turned in and fell, bringing shoe-tips, knees, elbows, and hands onto the rough surface. This arrested his fall, though it hurt. The crevasse was just under his feet. He scrambled up, ran panting along the crevasse until it narrowed, leaped over it. Then up the moraine and down into the narrow abandoned streets of west Allston.

Striding home, still breathing hard, he looked at his hands and saw that the last two fingernails on his right hand had been ripped away from the flesh; both were still there, but blood seeped from under them. He hissed and sucked on them, which hurt. The blood tasted like blood.

If he had fallen into the crevasse, following the loose rock down . . . if that stone had hit him in the face . . . he could feel his heart, thumping against his sternum. Alive.

Turning onto Chester Street he saw the man in the black coat, leaning against the florid maple across the street from their building. Watching them still! Though the man didn't appear to notice Alex, he did heft a bag and start walking in the other direction. Quickly Alex picked a rock out of the gutter and threw it at the man as hard as he could, spraying drops of blood onto the sidewalk. The rock flew over the man's head like a bullet, just missing him. The man ducked and scurried around the corner onto Comm Ave.

Father was upset about something. "They did the same thing to Gary and Michael and Kathryn, and their classes are even smaller than mine! I don't know what they're going to do. I don't know what *we're* going to do."

"We might be able to attract larger classes next semester," Mom said. She was upset too. Alex stood in the hall, slowly hanging up his jacket.

"But what about now? And what about later?" Father's voice was strained, almost cracking.

"We're making enough for now, that's the important thing. As

for later—well, at least we know now rather than five years down
the road."

Father was silent at the implications of this. "First Vancouver,
then Toronto, now here—"

"Don't worry about all of it at once, Charles."

"How can I help it!" Father strode into his study and closed the
door, not noticing Alex around the corner. Alex sucked his fingers.
Stella poked her head cautiously out of his bedroom.

"Hi, Stell-bell," he said quietly. From the living room came the
plastic clatter of Mom's typing. He walked down the long hallway,
past the silent study to the living room. She was hitting the keys
hard, staring at the screen, mouth tight.

"What happened?" Alex said.

She looked up. "Hi, Alex. Well—your father got bad news from
the university."

"Did he not get tenure again?"

"No, no, it's not a question of that."

"But now he doesn't even have the chance?"

She glanced at him sharply, then back at the screen, where her
work was blinking. "I suppose that's right. The department has
shifted all the new faculty over to extension, so they're hired by the
semester, and paid by the class. It means you need a lot of students. . . ."

"Will we move again?"

"I don't know," she said curtly, exasperated with him for bringing it up. She punched the command key. "But we'll really have to
save money, now. Everything you make at the market is important."

Alex nodded. He didn't mention the little man in the black coat,
feeling obscurely afraid. Mentioning the man would somehow make
him significant—Mom and Father would get angry, or frightened—
something like that. By not telling them he could protect them from
it, handle it on his own, so they could concentrate on other problems. Besides, the two matters couldn't be connected, could they?
Being watched; losing jobs. Perhaps they could. In which case there
was nothing his parents could do about it anyway. Better to save
them that anger, that fear.

He would make sure his throws hit the man next time.

*   *   *

Storms rolled in and the red and yellow leaves were ripped off the trees. Alex kicked through piles of them stacked on the sidewalks. He never saw the little man. He put up flyers for his father, who became even more distracted and remote. He brought home vegetables from work, tucked under his down jacket, and Mom cooked them without asking if he had bought them. She did the wash in the kitchen sink and dried it on lines in the back space between buildings, standing knee deep in leaves and weeds. Sometimes it took three days for clothes to dry back there; often they froze on the line.

While hanging clothes or taking them down she would let Stella join her. The cat regarded each shifting leaf with dire suspicion, then after a few exploratory leaps and bats would do battle with all of them, rolling about in a frenzy.

One time Mom was carrying a basket of dry laundry up the pantry stairs when a stray dog rounded the corner and made a dash for Stella, who was still outside. Mom ran back down shouting, and the dog fled; but Stella had disappeared. Mom called Alex down from his studies in a distraught voice, and they searched the back of the building and all the adjacent backyards for nearly an hour, but the cat was nowhere to be found. Mom was really upset. It was only after they had quit and returned upstairs that they heard her, miaowing far above them. She had climbed the big oak tree. "Oh, *smart,* Stella," Mom cried, a wild note in her voice. They called her name out the kitchen window, and the desperate miaows redoubled.

Up on the roof they could just see her, perched high in the almost bare branches of the big tree. "I'll get her," Alex said. "Cats can't climb down." He started climbing. It was difficult: the branches were close-knit, and they swayed in the wind. And as he got closer the cat climbed higher. "No, Stella, don't do that! Come here!" Stella stared at him, clamped to her branch of the moment, cross-eyed with fear. Below them Mom said over and over, "Stella, it's okay—it's okay, Stella." Stella didn't believe her.

Finally Alex reached her, near the tree's top. Now here was a problem: he needed his hands to climb down, but it seemed likely he would also need them to hold the terrified cat. "Come here, Stella." He put a hand on her flank; she flinched. Her side pulsed with her rapid breathing. She hissed faintly. He had to maneuver up a step, onto a very questionable branch; his face was inches from her. She stared at him without a trace of recognition. He pried her off her branch, lifted her. If she cared to claw him now she could really tear him up. Instead she clung to his shoulder and chest, all her claws dug through his clothes, quivering under his left arm and hand.

Laboriously he descended, using only the one hand. Stella began miaowing fiercely, and struggling a bit. Finally he met Mom, who had climbed the tree quite a ways. Stella was getting more upset. "Hand her to me." Alex detached her from his chest paw by paw, balanced, held the cat down with both hands. Again it was a tricky moment; if Stella went berserk they would all be in trouble. But she fell onto Mom's chest and collapsed, a catatonic ball of fur.

Back in the apartment she dashed for her blanket under the table. Mom enticed her out with food, but she was very jumpy and she wouldn't allow Alex anywhere near her; she ran away if he even entered the room. "Back to square one, I see," Mom commented.

"It's not fair! I'm the one that saved her!"

"She'll get over it." Mom laughed, clearly relieved. "Maybe it'll take some time, but she will. Ha! This is clear proof that cats are smart enough to be crazy. Irrational, neurotic—just like a person." They laughed, and Stella glared at them balefully. "Yes you are, aren't you! You'll come around again."

Often when Alex got home in the early evenings his father was striding back and forth in the kitchen talking loudly, angrily, fearfully, while Mom tried to reassure him. "They're doing the same thing to us they did to Rick Stone! But why!" When Alex closed the front door the conversation would stop. Once when he walked tentatively down the quiet hallway to the kitchen he found them standing there, arms around each other, Father's head in Mom's short hair.

Father raised his head, disengaged, went to his study. On his way he said, "Alex, I need your help."

"Sure."

Alex stood in the study and watched without understanding as his father took books from his shelves and put them in the big laundry bag. He threw the first few in like dirty clothes, then sighed and thumped in the rest in a businesslike fashion, not looking at them.

"There's a used book store in Cambridge, on Mass Ave. Antonio's."

"Sure, I know the one." They had been there together a few times.

"I want you to take these over there and sell them to Tony for me," Father said, looking at the empty shelves. "Will you do that for me?"

"Sure." Alex picked up the bag, shocked that it had come to this. Father's books! He couldn't meet his father's eye. "I'll do that right now," he said uncertainly, and hefted the bag over one shoulder. In the hallway Mom approached and put a hand on his shoulder—her silent thanks—then went into the study.

Alex hiked east toward the university, crossed the Charles River on the great iron bridge. The wind howled in the superstructure. On the Cambridge side, after showing his pass, he put the heavy bag on the ground and inspected its contents. Ever since the infamous incident of the spilled hot chocolate, Father's books had been off-limits to him; now a good twenty of them were there in the bag to be touched, opened, riffled through. Many in this bunch were in foreign languages, especially Greek and Russian, with their alien alphabets. Could people really read such marks? Well, Father did. It must be possible.

When he had inspected all the books he chose two in English— *The Odyssey* and *The Colossus of Maroussi*—and put those in his down jacket pockets. He could take them to the glacier and read them, then sell them later to Antonio's—perhaps in the next bag of books. There were many more bagfuls in Father's study.

A little snow stuck to the glacier now, filling the pocks and making bright patches on the north side of every boulder, every serac. Some of the narrower crevasses were filled with it—bright white lines on the jumbled gray. When the whole surface was white the crevasses would be invisible, and the glacier too dangerous to walk on. Now the only danger was leaving obvious footprints for trackers. Walking up the rubble lines would solve that. These lines of rubble fascinated Alex. It looked just as if bulldozers had clanked up here and shoved the majority of the stones and junk into straight lines down the big central tongue of the glacier. But in fact they were natural features. Father had attempted to explain on one of the walks they had taken up here. "The ice is moving, and it moves faster in the middle than on the outer edges, just like a stream. So rocks on the surface tend to slide over time, down into lines in the middle."

"Why are there two lines, then?"

Father shrugged, looking into the blue-green depths of a crevasse. "We really shouldn't be up here, you know that?"

Now Alex stopped to inspect a tire caught in the rubble line. Truck tire, tread worn right to the steel belting. It would burn, but with too much smoke. There were several interesting objects in this neat row of rock and sand: plastic jugs, a doll, a lampbase, a telephone.

His shelter was undisturbed. He pulled the two books from his pockets and set them on the bench, propping them with rock bookends.

He circled the boulder, had a look around. The sky today was a low smooth pearl-gray sheet, ruffled by a set of delicate waves pasted to it. The indirect light brought out all the colors: the pink of the remarkable snow algae, the blue of the seracs, the various shades of rock, the occasional bright spot of junk, the many white patches of snow. A million dots of color under the pewter sheet of cloud.

Three creaks, a crack, a long shuddering rumble. Sleepy, muscular, the great beast had moved. Alex walked across its back to his bench, sat. On the far lateral moraine some gravel slid down. Puffs of brown dust in the air.

He read his books. *The Odyssey* was strange but interesting. Father had told him some of the story before. *The Colossus of Maroussi* was long-winded but funny—it reminded Alex of his uncle, who could turn the smallest incident into an hour's comic monologue. What he could have made of Stella's flight up the tree! Alex laughed to think of it. But his uncle was in jail.

He sat on his bench and read, stopped occasionally to look around. When the hand holding the book got cold, he changed hands and put the cold one in a pocket of his down jacket. When both hands were blue he hid the books in rocks under his bench and went home.

There were more bags of books to be sold at Antonio's and other shops in Cambridge. Each time Alex rotated out a few that looked interesting, and replaced them with the ones on the glacier. He daydreamed of saving all the books and earning the money some other way—then presenting his father with the lost library, at some future undefined but appropriate moment.

Eventually Stella forgave him for rescuing her. She came to enjoy chasing a piece of yarn up and down their long narrow hallway, skidding around the corner by the study. It reminded them of a game they had played with Pongo, who would chase anything, and they laughed at her, especially when she jerked to a halt and licked her fur fastidiously, as if she had never been carousing. "You can't fool us, Stell! We *remember!*"

Mom sold most of her music collection, except for her favorites. Once Alex went out to the glacier with the *Concerto de Aranjuez* coursing through him—Mom had had it on in the apartment while she worked. He hummed the big theme of the second movement as he crunched over the ice: clearly it was the theme of the glacier, the glacier's song. How had a blind composer managed to capture the windy sweep of it, the spaciousness? Perhaps such things could be heard as well as seen. The wind said it, whistling over the ice. It was a terrifically dark day, windy, snowing in gusts. He could walk right up the middle of the great tongue, between the rubble lines; no one else would be up there today. Da-da-da . . . da da da da da da, da-da-da. . . . Hands in pockets, chin on chest, he trudged into the wind humming, feeling like the whole world was right there around him. It was too cold to stay in his shelter for more than a minute.

Father went off on trips, exploring possibilities. One morning Alex woke to the sound of *The Pirates of Penzance*. This was one of their favorites, Mom played it all the time while working and on Saturday mornings, so that they knew all the lyrics by heart and often sang along. Alex especially loved the Pirate King, and could mimic all his intonations.

He dressed and walked down to the kitchen. Mom stood by the

stove with her back to him, singing along. It was a sunny morning and their big kitchen windows faced east; the light poured in on the sink and the dishes and the white stove and the linoleum and the plants in the window and Stella, sitting contentedly on the window-sill listening.

His mom was tall and broad-shouldered. Every year she cut her hair shorter; now it was just a cap of tight brown curls, with a somewhat longer patch down the nape of her neck. That would go soon, Alex thought, and then her hair would be as short as it could be. She was lost in the song, one slim hand on the white stove top, looking out the window. She had a low, rich, thrilling voice, like a real singer's, only prettier. She was singing along with the song that Mabel sings after she finds out that Frederick won't be able to leave the pirates until 1940.

When it was over Alex entered the kitchen, went to the pantry. "That's a short one," he said.

"Yes, they had to make it short," Mom said. "There's nothing funny about that one."

One night while Father was gone on one of his trips, Mom had to go over to Ilene and Ira and Gary's apartment: Gary had been arrested, and Ilene and Ira needed help. Alex and Stella were left alone.

Stella wandered the silent apartment miaowing. "I *know,* Stella," Alex said in exasperation. "They're *gone.* They'll be back tomorrow." The cat paid no attention to him.

He went into Father's study. Tonight he'd be able to read something in relative warmth. It would only be necessary to be *very careful.*

The bookshelves were empty. Alex stood before them, mouth open. He had no idea they had sold that many of them. There were a couple left on Father's desk, but he didn't want to move them. They appeared to be dictionaries anyway. "It's all Greek to me."

He went back to the living room and got out the yarn bag, tried to interest Stella in a game. She wouldn't play. She wouldn't sit on his lap. She wouldn't stop miaowing. "Stella, shut up!" She scampered away and kept crying. Vexed, he got out the jar of catnip and spread some on the linoleum in the kitchen. Stella came running to sniff at it, then roll in it. Afterwards she played with the yarn wildly, until it caught around her tail and she froze, staring at him in a drugged paranoia. Then she dashed to her refuge and refused to come out. Finally Alex put on *The Pirates of Penzance* and listened to it for a while. After that he was sleepy.

They got a good lawyer for Gary, Mom said. Everyone was hopeful. Then a couple of weeks later Father got a new job; he called them from work to tell them about it.

"Where is it?" Alex asked Mom when she was off the phone.

"In Kansas."

"So we will be moving."

"Yes," Mom said. "Another move."

"Will there be glaciers there, too?"

"I think so. In the hills. Not as big as ours here, maybe. But there are glaciers everywhere."

He walked onto the ice one last time. There was a thin crust of snow on the tops of everything. A fantastically jumbled field of snow. It was a clear day, the sky a very pale blue, the white expanse of the glacier painfully bright. A few cirrus clouds made sickles high in the west. The snow was melting a bit and there were water droplets all over, with little sparks of colored light in each drip. The sounds of water melting were everywhere, drips, gurgles, splashes. The intensity of light was stunning, like a blow to the brain, right through the eyes. It pulsed.

The crevasse in front of his shelter had widened, and the boards of his bench had fallen. The wall of ice turning around the boulder was splintered, and shards of bright ice lay over the planks.

The glacier was moving. The glacier was alive. No heated dam would stop it. He felt its presence, huge and supple under him, seeping into him like the cold through his wet shoes, filling him up. He blinked, nearly blinded by the light breaking everywhere on it, a surgical glare that made every snow-capped rock stand out like the color red on a slide transparency. The white light. In the distance the ice cracked hollowly, moving somewhere. Everything moved: the ice, the wind, the clouds, the sun, the planet. All of it rolling around.

*   *   *

As they packed up their possessions Alex could hear them in the next room. "We can't," Father said. "You know we can't. They won't let us."

When they were done the apartment looked odd. Bare walls, bare wood floors. It looked smaller. Alex walked the length of it: his parents' room overlooking Chester Street; his room; his father's study; the living room; the kitchen with its fine morning light. The pantry. Stella wandered the place miaowing. Her blanket was still in its corner, but without the table it looked moth-eaten, fur-coated, ineffectual. Alex picked her up and went through the pantry, up the back stairs to the roof.

Snow had drifted into the corners. Alex walked in circles, looking at the city. Stella sat on her paws by the stairwell shed, watching him, her fur ruffled by the wind.

Around the shed snow had melted, then froze again. Little puddles of ice ran in flat curves across the pebbled tarpaper. Alex crouched to inspect them, tapping one speculatively with a fingernail. He stood up and looked west, but buildings and bare treetops obscured the view.

Stella fought to stay out of the box, and once in it she cried miserably.

Father was already in Kansas, starting the new job. Alex and Mom and Stella had been staying in the living room of Michael Wu's place while Mom finished her work; now she was done, it was moving day, they were off to the train. But first they had to take Stella to the Talbots'.

Alex carried the box and followed Mom as they walked across the Commons and down Comm Ave. He could feel the cat shifting over her blanket, scrabbling at the cardboard against his chest. Mom walked fast, a bit ahead of him. At Kenmore they turned south.

When they got to the Talbots', Mom took the box. She looked at him. "Why don't you stay down here," she said.

"Okay."

She rang the bell and went in with the buzzer, holding the box under one arm.

Alex sat on the steps of the walk-up. There were little ones in the corner: flat fingers of ice, spilling away from the cracks.

Mom came out the door. Her face was pale, she was biting her lip. They took off walking at a fast pace. Suddenly Mom said, "Oh, Alex, she was *so scared,*" and sat down on another stoop and put her head on her knees.

Alex sat beside her, his shoulders touching hers. Don't say anything, don't put arm around shoulders or anything. He had learned this from Father. Just sit there, be there. Alex sat there like the glacier, shifting a little. Alive. The white light.

After a while she stood. "Let's go," she said.

They walked up Comm Ave. toward the train station. "She'll be all right with the Talbots," Alex said. "She already likes Jay."

"I know." Mom sniffed, tossed her head in the wind. "She's getting to be a pretty adaptable cat." They walked on in silence. She put an arm over his shoulders. "I wonder how Pongo is doing." She took a deep breath. Overhead clouds tumbled like chunks of broken ice.

AND WHO WOULD PITY A SWAN?

CONNIE WILLIS

One day when the prince was out hunting, he came upon a pool, and on its still surface sat three white swans, like flowers on a mirror. Two of the swans were large and proud, and they dipped their necks forward, looking for fish in the black water, but the third was small and held its head up bravely on its curved neck, and the prince thought suddenly of a little girl riding before him on a large horse, and he felt a sudden pain, as though an arrow, or a memory, had pierced his heart, and he cried, "Emelie," and would have fallen.

But in that moment, he heard a splash and a sound that was like a swan's trumpeting or a child's cry, and when he looked up, the swans were gone and there were two men struggling with something in the water. The prince thought, with an anger more sudden than the pain, "They have come to steal the little swan," and he leaped off his horse and drew his sword.

"Let her go," he said, but the two men gave no sign that they had heard him. They were bending over a maiden. They pulled her to her feet, and taking an arm on either side, began to wade toward the shore, but she struggled against them so that she went down on one knee with a great splash.

The prince ran into the water and would have fought the men, but when the girl saw him she stood up and looked at him in wonder. She was very young, and her long dark hair hung wet around her face like water weeds. Her white dress was streaked with black mud, but for all that she was very beautiful.

The men still held her arms, though whether to hold her or to aid her, he could not tell, and he saw that they, too, were richly attired, but that their clothes were black with mud.

"Who are you?" the prince said. "What would you with this maiden?"

"She is our sister," the elder of the young men said, and then looked at her as if in wonder that it was so.

"We have been under a spell," the younger brother said.

"A spell?" the prince said.

"We were a king's children," said the elder brother. He spoke as if he were carrying a message that he himself had not understood until now. "A witch laid a spell on us that we should be swans till one remembered us and took pity on us, but we feared we should never be rescued, for who would pity a swan?"

"Swans," the maiden said. "We were swans."

"Who was your father?" the prince said kindly to her. She took a step backward, as if she were afraid of him. "I do not remember," she said.

"We have been swans too long to remember even our names," her brother said.

"Then I shall call her Cygnelle," the prince said, "and I shall call you all welcome. My father's castle lies but a little way from here."

Cygnelle turned and looked back at the black pool. "We were swans," she said, and she stumbled against her brother, who caught her and held her fast against him.

"Our sister has taken a chill," he said. "See how she shivers." He made as if to take his wet cloak from his back. The prince sprang forward and put his own dry cloak about her shoulders.

"Ride with her to your father's castle, and we will follow," her brother said.

And the prince set her before him on his horse and rode with her through the forest until they came to the path that led to his father's castle. The path was wide and straight, and the prince would have turned onto it, but Cygnelle said, "What lies this way?" and pointed toward another path, so overgrown with briars that it was nearly hidden.

"Nothing," the prince said, and turned away so sharply that his horse jerked his head in protest, and Cygnelle shivered. "It is only a ruined castle," the prince said more kindly. "No one has lived in it for years."

And he spurred his horse and brought Cygnelle to his father's castle, and his father the king came out to greet them.

"Father," the prince said, "this maiden and her brothers were placed under a spell by a witch that they should be swans."

"A witch," the king said, and it was as if he spoke to himself. "There was a witch who lived . . ."

"I do not know this maiden's name nor aught of her, but that I wish to make her my bride," the prince said.

"Swans," the king said. "Could it be . . . my child," the king said kindly and took Cygnelle's hand, "I thought that murderers had . . ."

And the prince felt a pain like an arrow, and he said, "She remembers nothing, not even her name. I have called her Cygnelle."

Then the prince had her dressed in rich clothing and her dark hair bound up with flowers, and they were married that very day.

They were taken to the bridal chamber with much merriment and joy, but when they were left alone together, she sat down before her mirror and took the flowers from her hair and looked at them. "One spring when we flew north," she said, "I saw a tree bending over a wall and on the tree white flowers, like these, and I remembered . . ." She held the flowers as if she had forgotten what they were and looked into her mirror and through and beyond it, holding herself still and silent, as if she were treading the dark waters of the pool.

"Forget that," the prince said in a voice he had never used before, not even to a servingman, "come to bed."

She did not start in fear of him, or tremble. She put down the flowers and came and stood before him so that he said more gently, "Come to bed," and she smiled and lifted up her arms to fasten them about his neck.

But the next morning when he awoke, he saw that she had risen early, and when he went out to seek her he found her in the great hall where the wedding breakfast was to be given, talking with her brothers.

"I have remembered something," her brother said. "One spring day, when we flew home from the south, we flew over a path, much overgrown with briars, and a wall and a gate, and I thought, I know this place. It was our father's castle."

"A wall, and a tree with white flowers," Cygnelle said, and took a step backward, as if she were afraid of him. "I remember . . ."

"It is our wedding breakfast," the prince said, and took her arm, though whether to help her or to hold her he did not know, and led her into the feast.

But when they had feasted and the king had toasted the prince and his bride, Cygnelle's brother raised his goblet and said, "May our sister have happy memories always."

Cygnelle smiled and raised her goblet in both hands to return the toast, but her hands shook and her wide white sleeves fell away from her arms like wings, and the prince thought, "She will never forget so long as her brothers are here."

And he said loudly, before Cygnelle had sat down, "Good brothers, when do you depart for your own kingdom?"

Cygnelle set the goblet down carefully, but her hand trembled, and wine spilled out on the table.

"You have remembered your father's kingdom," he said loudly. "My father will give you horses and gold, that you may go and seek it. Is that not so, Father?"

But the king said, as if he had not heard, "Where is this kingdom?"

"May it be so far from here that we shall never be troubled with seeing them again," the prince said, and went out from the marriage feast. His father followed him and put his hand on his arm.

"Where is their kingdom?" the king said.

"I know not. And I care not. I only wish them gone."

"Where did you find them?" the king said, as if he had not heard him. "Was it near King Gudrain's castle?"

"Yes," the prince said. "And would that I had left them there, for all they do is talk to Cygnelle of the days when they were swans."

"What would you have them speak of?" the king said, as if at
last he had heard him. "They do not remember anything else."

"Why must they remember at all? Why can they not forget the
past and go on? That is why I would send her brothers away.
Cygnelle and I cannot be happy until she forgets the past."

"Will you be happy then, when she remembers nothing?" the
king said. "Her brothers mean her no harm. They are only trying to
help her remember who she was." He took his hand away from the
prince's arm. "My son, when King Gudrain was murdered and his
children taken . . . ."

"They talk of the past and you talk of the past. If you will not
help me, I will send them away myself," he said, and he went out
into the garden to find Cygnelle and lead her away from her brothers, but when he came up to her she was standing all alone, and she
looked up at him sadly and said, "I have bidden my brothers depart
for their own kingdom, and they have gone."

"Now we can be happy," the prince said, and took her arm.
"Come and walk with me in the garden."

They walked along the paths of the garden until they came to a
little pond set about with bricks. There was a tree of white flowers
bending over the pond, and the prince stopped and picked a spray
of blossoms for Cygnelle. She buried her face in the blossoms, and
when she raised her face to him, he saw that she had left bright tears
on the white petals.

"Cygnelle," he said, and would have bent to kiss her, but there
was a sudden sound like trumpets blowing, and when he looked up
he saw that it was a flock of wild swans flying overhead, their great
wings spread like wide white sleeves against the sky.

"No," he said, and turned to look at Cygnelle. She had dropped
the flowers and stood watching the swans.

"One day we flew along a wall and I saw a boy riding upon a
horse, and I remembered . . . ."

The prince put his hand under his ribs as if to a wound. "Forget
them," he said, gritting his teeth against some pain. "Forget you
were ever a swan."

"I cannot," she said, and looked at him in despair. "Help me to
remember."

"No!" the prince said.

"Then let me go with my brothers. If you will not help me to remember, perhaps they may."

"No!" the prince said, and took her by the shoulders and shook her. "You say you cannot forget," he said. "Were you so happy when you were a swan?"

"Happy?" she said.

"Did you have swan lovers? Is it they you refuse to forget?" He pushed her from him. "I am going hunting."

The prince stayed out hunting all that day and the day after and the day after that, and when he rode in he found Cygnelle sitting by the pond looking into the dark water. She was holding a white flower in her hand, and her head was bent, so that he could see the curve of her long neck.

"I have been out hunting," the prince said.

She did not look up at him. She held the flower as if she had forgotten what it was, and she looked into the water and through it and past it. "Let me go to see my brothers," she said.

"No," he said. "I have brought you something."

But still she did not look at him.

"You cannot forget your swan lovers," he said, "so I have brought them to you," and he drew forth a pair of wild swans, each with an arrow through its heart, and laid them beside her on the brick edge of the pool.

Cygnelle stood and took a step back away from him and stumbled a little, but he did not reach out his hand to steady her.

"I wish you had not come, that day in the forest," she said.

"So you could be a swan still?" he said bitterly, and went in to find his father.

"I have had good hunting, Father," he said. "A pair of wild swans."

The king had been looking out the window into the garden, and he turned and looked at the prince with great sadness. "Do you think you can kill the past then?" he said. "You cannot. I know. I have tried."

"Would you speak to me of King Gudrain again?" the prince said harshly.

"No," the king said. "For you would not listen. I would speak to you of Cygnelle. You must let her go to her brothers. I have had word from them. They have found their father's castle, as I thought they would." He looked sadly at the prince. "Will you not ask me where it lies?"

The prince gasped, a terrible sound as if someone had tried to pull an arrow from his side. "No," he said, holding his breath against the pain. "I care not where their father's castle is, so long as it is far from here." He took a step back and stumbled, but the king did not reach out his hand to steady him. "You spoke of a witch, Father. Tell me where she lives."

"What would you with this witch?" the king said. "The spell is broken."

"I would have her lay a new spell upon Cygnelle that she should forget she was ever a swan. Tell me where she lives."

"No," the king said.

"Then I will find her myself," he said, and went out and saddled his horse and rode out to find the witch, but when he came to the pool where he had seen the swans, he thought, "While I am gone, she will go to see her brothers," and he turned his horse and went back to shut her in her room and set a watch at her door.

But when he came to the castle again he found Cygnelle lying by the little pond, and his father the king kneeling by her. Her dark hair was wet and lay about her still face like water weeds, and her white dress was streaked with black mud. The king gripped her hand and looked anxiously into her still face. "She has tried to drown herself," he said, as if to himself.

She lay as one dead, and as the prince looked down at her he saw that there were shadows under her eyes as black as a swan's mask. "Perhaps she thought she was still a swan," he said, "and tried to swim away."

The king looked up at him. "The witch lives near King Gudrain's castle," he said. "Take the path that leads from this castle till it meets a path so overgrown with briars it is nearly hidden. You have taken that path before. Take it again, and you will come to a wall and a gate, and at last you will lose the path and come to the witch. Or it may be," he said, holding tightly to Cygnelle's hand, "it may be that you will come to yourself."

"I will go to find the witch and make her put a spell upon Cygnelle that she will forget she was ever a swan," the prince said, "but you must first give me your word that you will not let Cygnelle go to see her brothers."

His father did not answer. He took off his own cloak and wrapped it around Cygnelle, and the prince saw that she shivered.

"I will not go unless you give your word," the prince said.

The king looked up at him and said, in a voice the prince had never heard him use, not even to a servingman, "I give it then, for I would do anything to have you gone from this place," and the prince rode out to find the witch.

He rode along the path that led from the castle and before long he came to the place where it met the path that Cygnelle had asked about. It was half-hidden and overgrown with briars, and when he saw it the prince felt a fluttering of memory like the beating of a bird's wings at his breast.

"No," he thought. "This is a snare of the witch's. She would stop me with memories."

And he put his hand to his side and held it there and rode on, and by and by he came to a wall. It was made of red brick and had once been so tall he could not see over it, but now the wall had tumbled down and briars had grown up around it. But among the briars was a tree of white flowers, and when the prince saw it he felt the knocking of memory in his heart, like the tapping of a bird's beak.

"No!" he thought. "The witch would have me stop here, lost in memories that can only bring me pain."

And he took out a kerchief from inside his shirt and held it to his side and rode on, and by and by he came to a gate. It was rusted, and the garden beyond it overgrown with briars, and the castle tumbling down, and when he saw it the prince felt memory, like the weight of a dead bird, against his heart.

"No!" the prince shouted, and he took off his shirt and tore it into strips and bound it under his ribs and rode on that day, and the day after, and the day after that, till he had lost the path, and at last he came to the witch.

She was standing amid a pile of red bricks, and at first the prince thought it was a ruined castle, but as she moved among the bricks, picking them up and putting them down, he saw that it was instead something unfinished, a stair here, a wall there, a part of an

arch, as if the witch had forgotten what she was making. She was
wearing a white dress, and her dark hair hung about her face like
water weeds.

"Witch," the prince said, "I have come to ask you to help me."

She did not look up. She picked up a brick and carried it over to
the unfinished stair.

"Witch," the prince said. "You must help me."

"Who are you?" she said. She set the brick down on the top of
the last unfinished step. "What are you doing in my forest?"

"A king's children were put under a spell that they should be
swans till one remembered them and took pity on them. I want
you . . ."

The witch sat down on the stair. "To break the spell?" she said.

"No," the prince said. "That spell is broken. I wish a new spell
to be . . ."

"Ravens, did you say?" the witch said, as if she had not heard
him. "I put a spell upon a princess once that she should be a raven
till a prince should love her for her sweet voice."

"Swans," the prince said. "But the spell is broken. I have need
of another spell."

"It was a good spell," the witch said. "She flapped her black
wings and said, 'caw' and 'caw,' but who would say to a raven,
'What a sweet voice!' so she was never rescued. How did you break
the spell," she said, "when you do not remember them?"

The prince felt a sharp and twisting pain, as if someone pulled
an arrow from his side, and he swayed and would have fallen, but
the witch had turned back to her bricks and was piling them now by
the unfinished wall. The prince got down from his horse and went
and stood by her.

"Witch!" he said, "the maiden I rescued cannot forget she was a
swan. I would have you place a spell of forgetfulness on her."

The witch picked up a brick and put it down again. "That she
might forget you?" she said, and looked up at him.

He had thought she would be old, but she was not, and when
he saw her face he thought for a moment that she was younger even
than Cygnelle, but then he saw that her face was only unfinished,
like her castle, the features laid upon it without shape or purpose.

"I would have her forget she was a swan," the prince said harshly. "Will you help me?"

"I laid a spell on a king once," the witch said, as if she could not remember. "I thought and thought what sort of spell to bind him with, for I wished him to be cold and hungry, to huddle against the frost and grub in the mud for worms and mate in a cruel flapping of wings, and I thought, 'I will make him a swan, and he shall never be rescued until someone shall remember and pity him, and who would pity a swan?' "

"And was he rescued?" the prince said.

The witch looked down at the unfinished wall and past and through it, as if she had forgotten what it was. "He had three children, two sons and a daughter, and I made them swans also, and I made them forget that they were ever human, but him I made remember that he might suffer the more."

"What were the children's names?" the prince said.

"I wanted him to live till there was none to remember him," the witch said, "past memory, past pity, to be a swan forever. But as he flew with his children out of their own garden, a hunter passing by shot him through the heart with an arrow, and he fell dead at his own gate."

"What was the king's name?" the prince said, and took the witch by the shoulders and shook her. "Was it Gudrain?"

"I do not know," the witch said. "It may have been."

The prince let go of her shoulders and took a step back away from her. "Why did you wish the king so ill that you would lay such an evil spell upon him?"

"I do not remember," the witch said, and it seemed to him more terrible than the cruel spells that she had told him of that she did not remember why she had made them or even the names of those she had laid them on.

"What of the children?" he said. "Did you lay some spell on those who loved them that they would not remember them?"

She put down a brick and picked it up again. "No. For they lay already under a spell better than any I could devise. A spell of guilt and sorrow, that they would not remember for the pain of it. And refusing to remember, they could not pity, and failing to pity, the children could never be rescued. It is the best spell of all."

And the prince looked at her face and the dark hair hanging about it like water weeds, and he thought of Cygnelle lying nearly dead by the pond because he would not let her remember. "How did you come to be a witch?" he said in wonder.

The witch put her hand to her side, under her ribs, but absently, as if she had long since forgotten whatever wound lay there. After a moment she took her hand away and bent to pick up another brick, and as she straightened, she stopped and looked up at the prince and said, "Who are you? What are you doing in my forest?"

And the prince called to his horse and rode back the way he had come. The way was narrow and choked with briars, so that the prince had to lead his horse by the bridle, and his clothes were torn by the briars, and his hands were cut by the sharp thorns. He could not find the path, and darkness came, and he fell into a muddy pool and let go of the bridle, and when he had struggled to his feet in the waist-high water and stumbled to the edge of the pool, he lay down beside it, shivering with cold under his wet cloak, and fell asleep.

And in the morning his horse came and nudged him gently awake, and he saw that it was the pool where he had found the swans, and he mounted his horse and rode with all haste until he came again to the place where the two paths met, the wide one leading to his father's castle and the other that led to King Gudrain's castle. "I have taken this path before," he thought, looking at the half-hidden path. "My father and I took this path together," and he sat as still upon his horse as a flower on a mirror and tried to remember.

The path had been wide and edged with red stone, and he had been so young that his feet had hardly reached the stirrups, but he had felt tall and proud to be riding with his father. "We go to meet King Gudrain's daughter," his father had said. "She is only a very little girl. You must be kind and watch over her carefully, for she will be your bride one day."

The prince had let fall the reins and sat looking at the path, not seeing it. His horse tossed his head, and the prince came to himself and rode on, and by and by he came to the wall and the tree of white flowers. "I have ridden this way before," he thought, "with Emelie," and he sat and waited on his horse like a swan on the water, trying to remember.

His father had said, "King Gudrain and I have much to talk of," and he had set Emelie before the prince on his horse and bade him take her riding along the path by the wall. She was only a very little girl, much younger than he, but she had sat up straight before him, not touching him, though her little hands clutched the pommel of the saddle, and she shivered when he kicked the horse forward. He had ridden with her as far as the end of the wall, where a tree covered in white flowers bent down, and he had picked her a bunch of the white flowers, and they had ridden back with her clutching the flowers in her little hands.

The prince had gotten down from his horse and was standing by the tree, looking at the white flowers, seeing nothing. His horse stamped its feet impatiently, and the prince came to himself and rode on, and by and by he came to the gate.

"It was here that I found him," he thought, and he sat upon his horse, still as the dead swans on the edge of the pond, already remembering.

"I fear for Gudrain," the king had said. "There is a witch in that forest who means him ill. I must warn him," but the prince had begged his father to let him take the warning to King Gudrain, and at last his father had let him go, and he had ridden hard as far as the place where the two paths met, eager to prove his worth to his father, but as he turned aside onto the path that led to King Gudrain's castle, he heard the trumpeting of a swan, and at the sound of it he forgot his father's warning and he drew his bow and followed it.

Its cry led him deeper and deeper into the forest, though now it sounded more like a man's cry for help, and the way became narrow and choked with briars, so that the prince had to lead his horse by the bridle, and he tore his clothes, but though he listened, he did not hear the swan again.

But at last he caught sight of a gate through the trees, and when he saw it he thought of his father's warning to King Gudrain, and he ran toward it and found King Gudrain lying on the ground, shot through the heart with an arrow. He had sat down on the ground beside the dead king and held his hand, afraid to go and seek for the bodies of Emelie and her brothers, until his father came seeking for him. But when they had gone into the garden they had found the children gone.

The prince had gotten down from his horse and was standing looking at the ground, seeing nothing. And his horse blew and whinnied, and the prince came to himself and would have opened the gate, but his father barred his way.

"I have broken my word to you and brought her here to see her brothers," his father said. "I could not do otherwise. I feared that the next time I pulled her from the pond, I would be too late."

"As I was too late, carrying the warning to King Gudrain," the prince said. And the king looked at his torn clothes and his wet cloak.

"She is in the garden," he said, and opened the gate.

And the prince would have gone into the garden, but her brothers barred his way. "We will not let you take our sister away from here," the elder brother said, and drew his sword.

"Only let me speak to her," the prince said.

"What would you speak of then?" the younger brother said. "The swans you have killed?"

"I would speak to her of her father, and yours. It was I who killed Gudrain," he said. "I did not bring the warning in time." And they looked at his mud-streaked clothes and his cut and bleeding hands, and the younger brother said, "You will find her by the lily pond," and let him pass.

And the prince came into the garden. It was overgrown with briars, and the lily pond was choked with water weeds, but on its surface, like a flower on a mirror, sat a little swan, and on the other side of the pond, looking at the swan, sat Cygnelle. Her head was bent, so that he could see the brave curve of her neck, and she smiled at the little swan, but when she spoke her voice was filled with sadness.

"One day in spring we flew above an open ride," she said, "and I saw a boy riding with a child before him on the saddle, and I thought, though I could not remember why, 'One still lives who will not forget me. And he will come and rescue us.' And you did."

She put her hand out to the little swan, and her wide white sleeve fell away from her arm, "But you did not remember me, or even know my name."

"I know it now," the prince said.

She looked up at him, and he saw that there were black shadows of sadness under her eyes. "I could remember nothing but that I had been a swan, and I saw that the spell was not broken after all, but only changed, and that you would never remember and pity me that I might be rescued, for who would pity a swan?"

"I remember now," he said, and held out his arms to her across the lily pond. "Emelie," he said.

And then the spell was well and truly broken, and she came into his arms and stayed there. And her brothers and the king came into the garden and embraced them, laughing and crying: And the prince set her before him on his horse and took her to his castle, and there they lived lives that only those who remember much may live, and at last they died.

But the witch lived on till all had forgotten her, past memory, past pity, and was never rescued.

THE TRYOUTS

BARRY B. LONGYEAR

The stranger sat cross-legged on the sand, staring at the vent from which the natural fire of the planet Momus illuminated the small wayside depression on the road to Tarzak. His black hood was pulled forward, leaving only twin dancing flames reflected from unblinking eyes as evidence of a face. As a light breeze rose from the desert, bringing the heavy smell of sulphur from the fire, a portly figure dressed in gray robe and apron stepped between the rocks into the firelight. He raised his hand and motioned toward a place near the flames.

"The fire is free," answered the black-hooded stranger. The newcomer squatted next to the flames, pulled a wad of dough from his pack and placed it on a rock close to the fire. In moments the sweet smell of cobit bread drove the odor of sulphur from the depression.

"Care you for some cobit, stranger?"

"For half, two movills. No more."

"Two? Why, it would distress me no more to hand out my bread for nothing."

"In which case, I would gladly take all."

"Three."

"Two."

The man in gray broke the cobit and handed half to the black-robed stranger, who handed back two copper beads. The bargaining hadn't been in earnest; only enough to satisfy custom. Finishing his cobit first, the one in gray tapped himself on his chest. "I am Aarel the mason. Have you news?" Aarel jingled his money pouch. The one in black shook his head. "But, you wear the newsteller's black."

"True, Aarel, but I apprentice only. However, my master will be along directly."

"What fortune! A master newsteller at the fire! Is he known?"

"No."

Aarel shrugged. "I am not one to discourage youth. Is this his first news?"

"No, but only small ones until now. His news tonight will play Tarzak, he thinks."

Aarel raised an eyebrow. "Tarzak? I hope his is the enthusiasm of experience rather than youth."

"My very words, Aarel."

They sat in silence watching the flames until two other men, wearing the tan robes of merchants, entered the circle of firelight.

"Ho, Aarel!" called the taller of the two.

"Parak," the mason answered; then, nodding at Parak's companion, "Jum."

Parak pointed at the fire. "It costs nothing; join us," said Aarel.

The merchants squatted close to the flames, each placing wads of cobit dough on the hot rocks. After some social bargaining and exchange, the four travelers sat munching cobit. Parak produced a wine flask, they bargained further, then passed around the flask while Parak pocketed his movills.

"It has been a weary trek from the Deeplands." He cocked his head toward the black-robed stranger and asked Aarel, "Has he news?"

"His master has news he believes will play Tarzak, and he should be here soon."

"Tarzak, eh?" Parak rubbed his hands together in anticipation. "Has the apprentice introduced it?"

"No."

At that moment they all turned to see another black-hooded figure enter the firelight and gesture toward the flames. "No copper for the flames, newsteller," said Parak. "Are you the master of this apprentice?"

"Yes. I am Boosthit of the Farransetti newstellers." Boosthit seated himself by the flames and cooked cobit, which, after rapid and impatient bargaining, was quickly gulped by the eager travelers. The master newsteller finished his cobit and brushed the crumbs from his robe. Turning to the travelers, he asked, "Is news to your liking tonight?"

Aarel squinted and tossed his purse in the air and caught it. "I can meet a good price for good news, Boosthit. But, I admit, your name is unfamiliar to me. We get few Farransetti this way."

"I agree," said Parak. "Could you tell us a little about it to enable us to judge the fairness of your price?"

Boosthit held up his hand, palm outward, and shook his head. "The Farransetti do not introduce."

"Why so?" asked Jum.

"We believe small glimpses of the whole are devoid of the grace of logical construction."

Aarel shrugged and held up his palms. "How, then, do we judge the price?"

"What would you pay for excellent news?" The mason and the two merchants thought deeply.

"Twenty movills," answered Aarel, "but only for excellent news."

"I would pay twenty-five," said Parak. "That is a fair price in Tarzak for excellent."

"I agree," said Jum, "twenty-five."

Aarel wagged a finger at the merchants. "But, friends, we are not in Tarzak. Do we not deserve credit for trudging out here on the road to hear Boosthit's news?"

Parak smiled. "You are a bandit, Aarel. The newsteller has trudged just as far to tell us the news, and we would be on the road in any event."

Aarel shrugged. "Very well; twenty-five movills."

Boosthit nodded. "Hear me then. I will give my news at that price in advance, but no money back."

"But, what if . . . ?"

"I must finish my offer, Aarel. Twenty-five movills apiece in advance, or hold onto your coppers and pay me double that price at the conclusion of my news if you judge it to be excellent."

Aarel's mouth opened in amazement. "It is an honor to meet a newsteller capable of making such an offer." Parak and Jum nodded in agreement. "We will hold our coppers."

Boosthit arranged his robe, closed his eyes and began. "This news is of Lord Ashly Allenby, special ambassador to Momus from the Ninth Quadrant Federation of Habitable Planets. His mission: one of grave importance to his government, and to the people of Momus. His journey: one of great heroics and high comedy."

"A peculiar opening," said Aarel, "but it captures the attention. The hint of serious events relating to Momus is the true hook, am I correct?"

"I agree, Aarel," said Parak, "and what could it be that interests the Federation in Momus? We have no trade for them, and we refuse to serve them. What could Lord Allenby's mission be? Jum?"

"It is the promise of comedy that intrigues me, but, nonetheless, the opening captures the attention. I had heard the Farransetti were experimenting with openings devoid of prayers and tributes, and many think this radical. But, having heard such an opening tonight, I approve."

Boosthit waited a moment, then continued. "On Earth, the ancient parent planet, high within the tall, gleaming spires of the Federation complex, Lord Allenby was called to meet with the Council of Seven.

"'Allenby,' said the council president, 'you are made special ambassador to Momus, with all of the rights and privileges of an ambassador of the first rank.'

"'I am most honored,' replied Allenby. Lord Allenby stood fair tall as he accepted his charge, his pleasant features composed and dignified, his uniform uncluttered and tasteful."

Jum held up a hand. "Boosthit, is that the extent of the hero's description?"

"Yes."

Aarel scratched his chin. "We are used to lengthier descriptions. Is there a reason for this brevity?"

"Perhaps," Parak interrupted, "it is to let us fill in the description ourselves. Would a mistaken image affect the truth of your news, Boosthit?"

"No."

Aarel frowned. "That is radical, no doubt." He closed his eyes. "But, I can see an image. Yes, I can see him."

"And I," said Jum.

"And I," said Parak.

Boosthit cleared his throat. "Allenby was confused, since a planet of Momus's stature hardly rates an ambassador of the first rank." Aarel, Parak, and Jum nodded.

"This is true," said Parak. "What could the Council of Seven have in mind to make such an appointment?" Aarel and Jum shook their heads.

"Allenby asked the reason for this," continued Boosthit, "and this is the president's answer: 'Momus lies just upon the boundary of the Ninth and Tenth quadrants. In actuality, it is closer to the main population centers of the Tenth than it is to ours. We have learned that the Tenth Quadrant Federation plans to occupy Momus to use as a forward base from which to launch their invasion of the entire Ninth Quadrant.' "

Aarel, Parak, and Jum gasped.

"But Momus has no defense against a military force," said Parak.

"This is grave indeed." said Aarel.

"But," said Jum, "what, then, could the mission be?"

"Lord Allenby asked this question, also," said Boosthit. "The president told Allenby that his mission was to establish relations between the Ninth Federation and Momus for the purpose of mutual defense against the coming invasion."

"A worthy mission," remarked Aarel. "I think sufficient to motivate the hero. What do you say, Parak?"

"It would appear so. Do you agree, Jum?"

Jum rubbed the bridge of his nose. "Allenby is only told of the threat. In the actuality, not the telling, is the real threat, and, therefore, sufficient motivation. I shall reserve judgment."

*   *   *

Boosthit waited until it was silent enough to hear the hissing of the flames. "Lord Allenby could not prepare for his mission; there was no time. He had to make all possible speed to Momus to warn us of the threat, which was difficult since there are no regular routes to Momus. A Federation cruiser brought Allenby as far as the Capella system, but had to turn back because of power problems. Stranded on Capella's fifth planet, awaiting passage on a freighter reported to be heading in this direction, Lord Allenby's baggage was stolen, as well as his money and his Federation transportation pass."

Aarel shook his head. "All he could do, then, would be to wait for the return of the Federation cruiser, is this not true?"

"It would appear so," answered Parak. "A sad day for Momus, except there's something wrong. Jum?"

"Indeed there is, Parak. Such news would be pointless and futile. No newsteller, Faransetti or otherwise, would bother with such a tale, much less inflict us with it. Perhaps the hero is made of stern stuff and will complete his mission?"

"But how?" Parak shook his head. "He cannot travel without money or his pass."

Boosthit smiled. "Lord Allenby, not the kind to be defeated by chance circumstance, set himself the task of continuing his journey. At the Federation consulate, he demanded transportation; but the consul, in turn, required verification of Allenby's mission before he would authorize the release of a ship or money. Allenby was furious, since it would take many weeks for verification to come from Earth; but the consul was within his rights and could not be swayed.

"Allenby haunted the spaceport, the consulate, and even exporting establishments trying to get transportation, but was unsuccessful until he caught wind of an opening on a freighter for a cargo handler. Selling his uniform and medals, he purchased ordinary clothing and secured able-bodied spacer papers from the Federation consulate. Then he signed on with the *Starwind,* which was scheduled to pass near Momus on its way to trade with the Tenth Quadrant."

"I think I see his plan," said Aarel. "It is daring, but it is also dishonest."

Parak shook his head. "The mission outweighs the act, Aarel.

Besides, the Federation would pay for the stolen lifeboat, would it not?"

"Perhaps. What say you, Jum?"

"I will relent on the motivation; I think it is sufficient."

Boosthit leaned toward the fire, spreading his arms. "As you guessed, Lord Allenby took a lifeboat from the freighter as it passed abreast of Momus, but the range was not ideal. After covering the distance, establishing an orbit for pickup was out of the question. He decided to break atmosphere and go for a hard landing as soon as he arrived. To do otherwise would cost both his life and the mission, as he was low on air.

"He had hoped to assume manual control after achieving flight, in order to put down near a large city, but he lost consciousness before reaching our outer atmosphere. As chance would have it, however, the boat's automatic system put Allenby down near Kuumic on the edge of the Great Desert. He wandered the desert for two days until he chanced to meet Garok, the cobit gatherer."

"Hah!" Aarel exclaimed. "I know Garok—the thief."

"I have heard of him," said Parak. "A spirited bargainer, Garok."

"Allenby said to Garok, 'Say, fellow, can you point me in the direction of Tarzak?' " Boosthit smiled and suppressed a chuckle. "Garok tapped his purse and said, 'What is this information worth to you, stranger?'

"Allenby, coming from a rich world where such information is as free as the fire, was very confused. 'You demand payment for such a thing? Absurd!'

"Garok began walking away, but thinking better of it, came back and explained. 'What I say now, stranger, has no value to me and I let you have it for free. I know where Tarzak lies, and you do not.'

" 'So much,' said Allenby, 'could be deduced from my question.'

" 'That's why it is of no value. But, the direction of Tarzak is of value to you, is it not?'

" 'Of course.'

" 'Then, it is of value to me.' Again, Garok tapped his purse.

Lord Allenby had little left over from the sale of his uniform, and he felt in his pocket for the scraps of paper they use for money."

Aarel grabbed his ribs and laughed until he gasped for air. Parak and Jum shook their heads and chuckled.

"Allenby held out one of the scraps at Garok, who took it and examined it closely. 'What is this?'

" 'Money. That's what you wanted, isn't it?'

"Garok handed the scrap back, and said, 'Stranger, how long have you been in the desert? The paper itself might have a value, except for its being covered with ink.' Garok opened his purse and brought forth a single movill. 'This is money, stranger.'

" 'Well, then, fellow, where can I get my money converted into yours?' Garok tapped his purse. Allenby was perplexed. 'You would charge for that information, too?'

" 'Is the information of value?'

" 'Yes, but . . .' Garok kept tapping his purse. As he turned to leave, Allenby had one remaining try. 'Tell me, fellow, would you accept something of value in exchange for the information?'

" 'Barter?'

" 'Yes.'

"Garok rubbed his chin, then fingered a fold of Lord Allenby's utility suit. 'This would do.'

"Allenby was outraged. 'Not that! I landed here in a ship's lifeboat. Would that have value to you?' And, Garok was interested. The boat's fuel and supplies were exhausted, and the ship itself was inoperable, but the furnishings were intact as well as the wiring and other materials. Garok made an offer of one hundred movills, and Allenby accepted."

Aarel snorted. "I said Garok was a thief; I wouldn't have parted with it for less than four hundred. Parak?"

"I was thinking the same thing, although my price would have been higher. Jum, does this make our hero a fool?"

"I think not. The boat had served its purpose and no longer had any value to Lord Allenby. Besides, if I was stuck in Kuumic and didn't know the direction to Tarzak, I might have even taken a lesser amount."

Aarel and Parak pondered Jum's remarks, then nodded.

"Garok counted out a hundred movills," continued Boosthit,

"and handed them to Allenby. Allenby took two of the coppers and handed them back to Garok. 'Now, can you tell me the way to Tarzak?' Garok pointed the direction and reached into his own purse to pay for Allenby's information concerning the location of the lifeboat.

" 'Where is the lifeboat, stranger?' Allenby didn't notice Garok's hand in his purse, and he truthfully pointed the way to the lifeboat. Garok assumed, since no payment was demanded, that the information was worthless. Therefore, he turned in the opposite direction and struck out to find and take possession of his new purchase. It is said that Garok still wanders Momus looking for his lifeboat, and if he maintains his direction, he will eventually find it."

"No more, Boosthit," gasped Aarel. Parak and Jum rolled in the sand laughing. "No more! Let us rest!"

After more cobit and wine, Aarel rose to present and resolve a complicated stonecutting problem in pantomime, followed by Parak's mummery of a wedding ceremony he had supplied with gifts at a price that drew admiration from the travelers. Jum recited a comic poem concerning his efforts to marry the daughter of a cheese merchant. Exchanges were made, and silence settled around the fire as they waited expectantly for Boosthit to continue his news.

"Lord Allenby's journey to Tarzak was one of privation and hardship, not knowing that fat cobit roots just under his feet slept, waiting to be milked. Instead, he visited the fires along the road, buying cobit from other travelers, until he ran out of movills."

"Boosthit, had this Allenby no act?" Parak frowned and shook his head. "Had he nothing of value?"

"He had the news of his mission, Parak; but this he kept to himself."

"Why?" asked Aarel.

"Why, indeed," asked Jum.

"It is curious, but it is the custom among Allenby's people to play information of that sort only before governments. He was waiting until reaching Tarzak," Boosthit laughed, "to play it before *our* government!" The travelers laughed and shook their heads. "Yes, it was not until he hired himself out to a priest as a beast of burden in exchange for cobit and information that he learned Momus has no government."

"A sorry fellow," said Aarel, chuckling.

Parak nodded. "Yes, and can such a character be the hero around which excellent news transpires? I fear for your fee, Boosthit."

Jum held up his hand. "You are too hasty, Parak. Think; would any of us do better, or as well, on ancient Earth, Allenby's planet? As Boosthit said, the information is for no charge, but I have heard that the fire is not! Would we appear any less foolish if someone asked us coppers for fire?"

"But, Jum, is it not part of the diplomat's skill to be versed on where he is sent?"

"Only recall Boosthit's opening, Parak." Jum closed his eyes. "In the second part covering Allenby's trip to Momus: 'Lord Allenby could not prepare for his mission; there was no time.' "

"Ah, yes," said Parak, "I stand corrected."

"And I," agreed Aarel.

Boosthit nodded and smiled. "Allenby carried the priest's pack and paraphernalia, and the priest told him of our freedom. From the priest, and from other travelers along the road, he learned that for Momus as a planet to agree to something, half of each town must petition for a meeting, then half of all the towns must vote and agree, for this is the law.

"Allenby remarked to the priest, 'Momus doesn't have many laws, does it?'

" 'Only one,' answered the priest, 'which is our law for making laws. It suffices.'

"Lord Allenby, coming from a planet which has millions of laws, was perplexed. 'If Momus needed a new law,' he asked the priest, 'how would one go about it?'

" 'To move the people in each town to petition for a meeting, the law must be something the people want. Before they can want it, they must be aware of it.'

"Allenby nodded at this wisdom, and said, 'Since I have yet to see so much as a wheeled vehicle in my travels on Momus, I don't suppose the planet sports anything resembling mass broadcasting media.' "

Boosthit laughed with the other travelers. " 'Ever since the first settlers of Momus were stranded here, we have communicated with art,' said the priest to Allenby. 'It was many, many Earth years before the skies of Momus saw another starship; and by then we were numerous, satisfied with our lot and with our customs.'

" 'And mass media, I take it, is not art.'

" 'I suppose it could have been,' answered the priest, 'except no one knew how to build a radio. In any event, it was not their way.'

"Allenby's doubts concerning the success of his mission grew. 'The original settlers of Momus,' he said to the priest, 'what were their occupations?'

" 'Why, there were many. Acrobats, mimes, storytellers, clowns, razzle-dazzle operators. . . .'

" 'It was a circus ship?'

" 'Not just a circus ship,' answered the priest, 'but O'Hara's Greatest Shows, the finest collection of artists and games in the entire quadrant.' "

Boosthit allowed the travelers a moment of silent prayer. When they raised their heads, Aarel rubbed his chin and thought deeply. "I do not understand, Boosthit, why the hero needs a new law. It would seem sufficient for the Ninth Federation to occupy Momus itself without fanfare. This would serve their objective, and we would be powerless to stop them."

"And," said Parak, "once Momus learned of the threat from the Tenth Quadrant, we would not object."

"The law does seem unnecessary." Jum concluded.

Boosthit held up his hands. "It is complicated, friends, but I shall explain. There is the Great Law of the Ninth Federation, which is actually a collection of many laws. It decrees that the protection of the Federation cannot be extended to a planet that has not asked for it. Because of our one law for making laws, Momus is considered a governed society. If the Ninth Federation occupied Momus without our consent, the Tenth Federation would consider that an invasion, because of *their* laws. This, too, would violate even greater laws that govern all the quadrants. . . ."

Parak held his hands over his ears. "It is clear to me why our ancestors chose to remain on Momus!"

"That is true," Aarel agreed, "Would it not be easier for the Ninth and Tenth Quadrants to change their laws?"

"Impossible." answered Jum. "The objectives of the two quadrants differ. They could not agree. Boosthit, this means that the hero must resolve his mission with the laws that already exist?"

"That is true."

"Which also means he must move the people of Momus to pass another law."

"True, as well, Jum. Allenby asked the priest how this could be done, and the priest told him to wait. 'We will sit at the fire this night, and you shall see how. I have heard a newsteller, Lett of the Dofstaffl, will entertain.'

"That night, Lord Allenby saw the work of his first newsteller. Lett performed well and fattened his purse. Afterward, Allenby asked the priest, 'Is this how the news is communicated?'

" 'Yes.'

" 'Doesn't it strike you as a trifle inefficient?'

" 'Bah! Art is not to be judged by efficiency!'

" 'But, what if there were news that should be communicated to all of the people quickly?'

" 'You weary me with your endless questions! What kind of news could it be that would be of such immediacy?'

" 'I have such news,' answered Allenby, 'would you listen to it?'

"The priest took his things from Allenby. 'Stranger,' he said, 'Your price of endless answers to endless questions to carry my things is high enough. But, to sit and listen to a frustrated newsteller? You take me for a fool!' With that, the priest left Allenby by the fire and hurried off into the night."

Aarel looked into the fire and frowned. "I see the hero's problem, Boosthit, for even I would have acted as did the priest. I would not have listened."

"Nor I," said Parak. "Even though he has news of importance, I would not have listened."

Jum rubbed his hands together, then pointed at his fellow travelers. "The hero is the thing of importance here. Lord Allenby, an ambassador of the first rank, is reduced to a beast of burden in an attempt at accomplishing his mission. Will he continue his struggle to bring his news to the people of Momus; or will he be defeated, letting Momus fall to the evil designs of the Tenth Federation?" They turned toward Boosthit and saw that he had pulled his hood over his eyes. Bowing their heads, they moaned softly.

"For three nights, Lord Allenby stayed at the fire, trying to tell his news, meeting with failure with each new group of travelers. After failing on the fourth night, Allenby was defeated. He bartered his wedding ring for a card trick from a wandering magician, and using this he kept himself in movills until he reached Tarzak, where he planned to find transportation to Earth.

"While awaiting the rare ship that comes to Momus, Allenby purchased two more card tricks and an illusion. With these he paid for his town lodgings, meals and clothing, and began saving for his passage back to Earth. It was during this period that Lord Allenby chanced to hear of Vyson of the Dofstaffl newstellers, playing his news at the Great Square in Tarzak." Boosthit removed the hood from his eyes.

Aarel smiled. "Will the great Vyson inspire Allenby?"

"I heard Vyson play the burning of Tarzak years ago," said Parak. "I was inspired to petition in the town to form the fire company."

"Yes," said Jum, "I heard just an apprentice licensed to repeat Vyson's news, and was inspired to petition for a fire company in my own town of Miira. Yes, that was good news."

"Indeed," said Boosthit, "Allenby was inspired, but not by Vyson's news, which concerned the second eruption of the Arcadia Volcano. What caught Allenby's attention was the number of newstellers and apprentice newstellers among the listeners. After Vyson finished, the newstellers gathered around to bid for licenses to repeat his news. I was among those attempting to get through the listeners in order to bid, when I was stopped by Lord Allenby."

" 'Unhand me, trickster,' I said, for he wore the black and scarlet of the magicians. 'I must get to the bidding.' He released me, but try as I might, I could not get close to Vyson before he closed the bidding. Times had not gone well with me and I was desperate for news that I could take on the road. With this opportunity lost, I turned to look for the trickster to vent my anger. I found him standing behind me. 'See what you've done? News that played in Tarzak, but I can't repeat it because you made me miss the bidding.'

"Allenby pointed at the newstellers clustered around Vyson. 'They will repeat Vyson's news?'

" 'Of course.'

" 'But the people of Tarzak have already heard it.'

" 'They won't repeat it in Tarzak, fool. They will take it on the road and play it in other towns. Some newstellers will issue second licenses to unknown and apprentice newstellers. In days, Arcadia's eruption will be all over Momus.'

" 'Can't you get one of those second licenses?'

"I admit I was exasperated with this nitwit trickster, and told him so, for even children know there are no coppers in a second license. 'I am a master newsteller, trickster. I do not second license, nor do I pick up fireside gossip and play it for news. My news must have played Tarzak!'

" 'News that plays Tarzak will spread, then?'

" 'Of course. You tire me; go away.'

"Allenby stood there a moment, watching the clamor of new-stellers running off with their new licenses, then he turned back to me. 'Newsteller,' he said, 'how much would you charge to hear my story—a story that will play Tarzak, if done properly?'

"I laughed, 'Trickster, there are not enough coppers on Momus to entice me to endure your amateur efforts.' He tossed his purse at me, and when I caught it, I could feel the weight of over five hundred movills in it. As I said, I had been on desperate times. 'Very well,' I said, tucking the purse into my belt, 'but be brief.'

"Allenby told me his tale, and it was raw, clumsy and presented in bad order. But, I saw in it the potential for greatness—possibly news that would play Tarzak.

" 'Can you play this in Tarzak now?' he asked me.

" 'Of course not. It must be worked on, polished, and then taken on the road to see how it plays. If we do well on the road, then we may try Tarzak.' Allenby rubbed his eyes, sighed, and nodded."

Aarel, his eyes wide, turned toward the apprentice newsteller. "But, then . . ."

"Yes, friends," said Boosthit, "I would like to present Lord

Ashly Allenby, special ambassador to Momus from the Ninth Quadrant Federation of Habitable Planets."

The apprentice stood and pushed the robe back from his face. "Oh, excellent, Boosthit!" Aarel exclaimed.

"Yes, excellent, indeed!" said Parak. Allenby turned to Jum.

"And you?"

"Oh, yes. Excellent; most excellent."

Allenby reached within his newsteller's robe and withdrew an empty sack. "In which case, friends, that will be fifty coppers apiece."

As they trudged through the dark on the road toward Tarzak, Allenby said to Boosthit, "We were judged excellent and brought twice the price. I think we are ready for Tarzak. I don't see why we should play any more fires."

"There are still a few things that need to be worked out, Allenby. Your escape in the lifeboat was too easily guessed. I'll have to rework that."

"Humph!" They walked along in silence for a piece, then Allenby spoke. "Boosthit."

"Yes?"

"Since we will be on the road a bit longer, perhaps there is something we could do about my presentation as a comic character. Don't you think if the news were a little more serious. . . ."

"Bah!" Boosthit strode ahead, raising angry puffs of dust from the road. "Everybody wants to be a critic," he shouted at the night. "Everybody!"

STILL TIME
JAMES PATRICK KELLY

Quinn Hutchins was planting marigolds on his roof. For two years he had feverishly built his underground dream house into the south flank of Flatrock Mountain. Now that the place was nearly finished he was squandering a little time on landscaping. Judy and Kitty had chosen the flowers; Quinn had grown them from seed in the solar greenhouse. He firmed the seedlings into the ground and pinched off the growing tips to encourage branching. Come July they would make a spectacular display. If July came.

Since the crisis had begun Quinn had seldom been out of earshot of a radio. His multiband portable Sony was propped against a bale of peat moss. It was tuned to an all-news station in Boston.

"This just handed to me." The news reader paused maddeningly. "The Associated Press reports that the president has left Washington. This unconfirmed—repeat, unconfirmed—report states that the president was flown by helicopter from the White House and arrived at Andrews Air Force Base at ten thirty-one Eastern Standard Time. There he boarded the National Emergency Command Post, a specially equipped 747 jet often referred to as Kneecap. His destination is unknown. To repeat. . . ."

"Son of a bitch!" said Quinn. He threw his tools into the wheelbarrow and muscled it down the side of the house to the garage. "Goddamned idiots!"

He had hoped for more warning: a parting volley of words in the Security Council, orders putting all available Tridents to sea and dispersing the bombers to auxiliary airfields, perhaps even evacuation of the cities. Kneecap was the penultimate step and Quinn Hutchins's little family was scattered all over Strafford County. If he had not spent most of his sleepless nights planning for just this situation he might have panicked.

Even so, his finger slipped as he dialed Judy's number and he had to start over. Seconds lost.

"Dr. Davidson's office," said Becky the receptionist.

"Judy Hutchins, please."

"Quinn, is that you? How've you been, haven't talked to you in ages. She's with the doctor, you want me to take a message?"

"Get her. Now."

There was a rude clatter on the other end. Becky had always thought him peculiar. Now he did not care what she thought.

"Quinn?" said Judy.

Finally. "Come home." He tried to sound calm. "It's starting."

"Are you sure?" She sounded wary of another false alarm. "It'll mean trouble with Davidson. He's got a full schedule. . . ."

"Damn it, Judy!"

"And the car has been acting up again. I was going to stop in at Smitty's on the way home and have him look at it."

"There's no time. Just come home. I'm going for Kitty now."

"It's really starting?" Her voice trembled. "All right, I'm coming."

"I love you." He tried not to think about the junkyard water pump in her decrepit Vega. "We're going to make it, sugar."

It was only ten minutes to the Merrymeeting Children's Center; Quinn decided to secure the house before he picked up Kitty. Although the south facade was glazed with sheets of three-quarter-inch unbreakable acrylic, it was designed to withstand vandals, not the searing gusts of a thermonuclear windstorm. There were winches concealed in the wall; he thrust a handle into each and cranked furiously. Rolling aluminum shutters reinforced with steel rattled down their exterior tracks and locked shut.

He hurried to the master bedroom, pulled all of the clothes out of the closet and piled them on the bed. The closet was built of reinforced concrete; it served as the airlock for the Hutchins's shelter, a four-hundred-square-foot bunker equipped with hand-operated air and water pumps and a six-month supply of dried food. At the back of the closet, surrounded by old shoes, was a green overnight suitcase. Quinn carried it to the kitchen table and unlocked it. Inside were three respirators, a radiation counter, several personal dosimeters, some canisters of mace, and two guns. He loaded the thirty-eight special, slipped it into its shoulder rig, and strapped it on. The semiautomatic twenty-two caliber lightweight rifle was knocked down and stored inside its waterproof stock. Quinn had trouble reassembling it; he had not practiced for a long time. Judy hated guns.

In his haste to leave he could find nothing to wear over his revolver but an old yellow rain parka. The day was clear and hot but he pulled on the heavy parka anyway. He hid the rifle under the seat of his rusty Toyota pickup, swiped the sweat from his eyes and backed down his dirt driveway onto Flatrock Road.

Once Quinn had owned a Porsche. He had lived within walking distance of Boston Common, bought Medoc wines by the case, and earned his luxuries designing shopping malls and corporate headquarters. But Quinn only got to initial the working drawings while the senior partners ate lobster with the clients. His insomnia was just starting then. The nightly news made it worse. When his mother died he sold her house for one hundred and seventy-three thousand dollars—enough to buy his freedom from the unnerving city. He proposed to Judy that they move to New Hampshire. She could finally go back to work; he would stay with the baby and build a house. A house with his name on it, a single-family fortress secure from the madnesses which men were wreaking on the world.

The Merrymeeting Children's Center was located in the basement of the Congregational Church. Quinn was one of its founders; it had been under his direction that a group of parents had worked over several weekends to transform the place with secondhand rugs, temporary partitions, and buckets of bright paint. He had also served on the committee which had chosen Rachel Kerwin as director.

She had shoulder-length red hair and bad teeth. Her wardrobe consisted of a variety of floppy men's clothing culled from secondhand stores. Although she was thirty-seven years old, time had yet to crack her boneheaded idealism. She was a marcher, a letter-writer, a collector of causes. It had not bothered Quinn at all to find out that she had been arrested several times while protesting; it was good for little children to be around people like that.

He had no time for her today. "Where's Kitty?"

"Out." She stooped to pick up a snuffling infant, Billy . . . somebody. "We sent the big kids out on a nature walk. Should be back soon." She tugged at his rain parka and chuckled. "Where you been getting your weather reports from, the Amazon?"

Quinn stepped to the window and scanned the nearby woods. "Damn!" He patted the revolver hidden beneath the parka; it helped steady him. "Do you think I could find them?"

"Why, Quinn?"

"No other parents have come in yet?"

"Why?"

Now she was scared; everyone in Merrymeeting knew that he was a survivalist. "The politicians are scurrying out of Washington like rats leaving a sinking ship."

Billy started to fuss; she jiggled him. "So?"

"So it's coming!" Her obtuseness made him angry. "Turn on the radio and wake up, Rachel! The bombs, don't you understand? We're set to blow ourselves to hell."

"I can't believe. . . ." She shook her head numbly. "There should've been more demonstrations. If people like you had marched instead . . . instead of. . . ."

"Jesus." He glared at the woods. No sign of his daughter. "I'll wait outside."

She barred his exit. "What's going to happen to these children, Quinn?"

"If we're lucky there should be time for everyone to go home." Quinn liked Rachel Kerwin; when he saw that she was crying he almost fell into the trap of pity. "Look, the nearest target is the Air Force Base in Portsmouth. Forty miles away; the blast effects shouldn't be too bad here. Just start filling every container you have with water. Your biggest worries are fire and fallout. . . ."

The phone rang. Billy Somebody began to cry too. Rachel answered. "Hello. Oh God, Judy. It's horrible, I can't believe it; yes, yes, he's here."

Quinn grabbed the phone from her. "What?"

"Thank God I caught you." Her voice trembled. "The car is dead. I'm at Miller's Drug in Farnham."

He could hardly hear her over little Billy's caterwauling.

"I don't know, I don't know what to do, Quinn. The traffic is all going north; no one is taking the turnoff for Merrymeeting. Should I try hitching anyway?"

"No, don't hitch." He did not want her riding with some panicky loser on a blind run. "Can you steal a car?"

"Quinn!"

"Look, sugar, everything is falling apart. Nothing, nobody matters but us." Rachel tried to butt into the conversation and he turned away from her, twisting the handset cord around his shoulders.

"You're wrong, Quinn," Judy said firmly. Despite all their arguments, she had yet to accept the first law of survivalism.

"Daddy!" Kitty scooted through the door. "I saw your truck, Daddy, look what I found." She waved a blue jay feather at him. "Why are you here so early, can we stop for ice cream on the way home?"

Quinn was momentarily dizzy; he shut his eyes. He was at the edge of control and unless he could slow down he would certainly make the mistake that would kill them all. "Kitty, go to the truck. Now!" There was no time; he wished that someone would strangle little Billy Somebody so that he could think. "Judy? Stay where you are. I'm coming for you. Twenty minutes." He hung up.

Kitty was dawdling by the door. He scooped her up and carried her to the truck. Rachel followed him like a watchdog nipping at the heels of a mailman. She lectured him as if he were responsible for the war.

"It's not fair. You can't just leave these children to die. You'd better stop and think about what you're doing, Quinn Hutchins. You'd better hope that everyone who survives isn't as selfish as you."

As he loaded Kitty into the truck he saw that her chin was

quivering. Although he had been able to ignore Rachel, his daughter
had been wounded by her rage.

"Will it be worth it?" Rachel grasped the door handle to keep
him from leaving. "Do you think Kitty will thank you tomorrow for
saving her life?"

Quinn unsnapped his parka and pulled out the thirty-eight; he
did not release the safety. "You want to save those kids inside some
misery, Rachel? Shoot them. Now." He offered the butt end of the
revolver to her. "You're so damn sure it's not worth living anymore?" He shook it at her and she shrank from him. "Go ahead!"

She turned and ran back to the church.

It seemed quieter than it was inside the truck. The engine
boomed, the suspension clattered, the wheels shrieked at the corners but nobody spoke and the radio was broken. Quinn had forgotten the Sony in the wheelbarrow.

Farnham consisted of a boarded-up brick schoolhouse, Ben's
Bait and Fruit Stand, Miller's Drug and a scattering of musty cot-
tages. The most direct route climbed over the mountain and passed
Quinn's house on Flatrock Road. A tourist from Ohio might finish
this scenic drive in forty-five minutes; a drunken teenager with a
death wish could do it in a half hour. Quinn thought twenty minutes
was about right.

Kitty had tucked her legs beneath her and was scrunched into
the far corner of the cab. She was chewing on strands of her long
black hair, a habit which usually annoyed Quinn. But she was so
pale and wide-eyed that he did not bother her. At least she was not
crying. Her father's daughter.

They were about a mile from the house when he finally broke
the silence. "I'm letting you off at the driveway, honey. Get into the
shelter as fast as you can and wait for us. I'll be back with Mommy
in two shakes."

"I won't."

"Kitty."

"I don't want to stay all alone with the bombs."

"I'm not arguing, Kitty. You do it." He downshifted as the truck
approached the driveway. "I'm letting you out."

"I won't go in. I'll stand by the mailbox until you come back."

He had slowed enough to glance at her and gauge her determination. She stared back fiercely, her jaw set. She was six and a half years old and already she had all the pluck she would ever need. He stepped on the accelerator and the truck shot past the driveway.

"Am I going to die, Daddy?"

"Of course not."

"Are Grammy and Grampy going to die?"

"I hope not."

"Lisbeth? Maggie?"

"I don't know."

"How about Rachel?"

"Kitty, anyone who wants to live and tries hard enough will make it."

She considered. "But some people are going to die?"

"Yes."

As they crossed the southern ridge of Flatrock there was a flash of light that overwhelmed the sun. Quinn felt the mountain tremble beneath him. The truck veered toward the shoulder and he slammed it to a skidding stop. Below them were the tidy orchards surrounding Farnham, less than three miles away. In the distance to the southeast was what had once been Portsmouth, New Hampshire.

He had a glimpse of hell out of the corners of his eyes. The fireball was dazzling; it rose with the stately grace of a hot air balloon at a country fair. It seemed to draw the land directly beneath it toward the sky; farther out it cast a shadow of flame. In four thousand million years the dull stones of the planet had never witnessed quite so ravishing a spectacle.

But one glimpse was enough for Quinn; he was nearly blinded. He made a screeching U turn and raced back the way he had come. He hoped that the top of the ridge might afford some protection from the shock wave. He saw a dirt track running into a rock-strewn pasture and pulled onto it, crashing through the wooden gate. Safe from falling trees.

"Out!" He flung open his door and, dragging Kitty with him, flopped face-down behind a desk-sized boulder.

The thunderclap sounded as if the shout of an angry god had split the sky open. Immediately afterward came a terrible pressure on Quinn's back, as if that same god meant to squash him into the dirt for the sin of being a man. His ears popped; he could not breathe.

He was not sure how long he lay there; he was revived by Kitty's crying. ". . . hurts."

"What hurts?" He rolled her over. "Kitty!"

"The air hurts."

She had to shout to be heard. A roiling black cloud had filled the sky and a gale blew from the north, stripping the trees. A white birch toppled onto the road as he watched. But his lightweight truck was still upright.

"Let's go."

He opened the green suitcase and they both slid respirators over their faces. He clipped a dosimeter to Kitty's blouse and pushed another into his shirt pocket. Kitty hooked her canisters of Mace to her belt without being told. Quinn marveled at his calmness as he waited for the counter to warm up.

Click, click. Of all his survival gadgets, he trusted this one the least. The instruction booklet, translated from the Japanese, had been nearly incomprehensible with its jabber of phosphors and photocathodes. *Click.* The liquid crystal display read four-tenths of a millirem per hour, thirty times the normal background. Nowhere near lethal levels yet; still an hour, maybe two, before the killing dust began to sift out of the sky. *Click, click, click.* Either way he went, the road might be blocked. A dose of four hundred and fifty rems kills half the population; at six hundred, everyone dies. *Click.* Even now, a few of Quinn's cells were shriveling, exploding, spewing poisons. Judy. The invisible seeds of cancer.

Even though Quinn's grip on the steering wheel was painfully tight, his arms trembled. He was sucking huge amounts of air through his respirator and still felt out of breath. The wind shrieked at the truck. He blinked, blinked again, and realized that he was crying.

"What am I going to do?" He was thankful that the respirator filtered the sob out of his voice.

Kitty slid across the seat and hugged him. "First we have to get Mommy." She spoke impatiently, as if she thought he had merely forgotten the plan. "Then we stay in the shelter until it's safe to come out."

He pulled back from her so that he could see her face. The rubber mask concealed her nose and mouth but her eyes . . . the eyes. He drew strength from her ignorance.

"Buckle your seat belt." He pulled onto the highway, swerved around the fallen birch and headed for Farnham.

It took twenty minutes to reach the end of Flatrock Road. Quinn had to ram one tree out of his way. He passed a wrecked station wagon without stopping. The count was up to six rems an hour and was climbing rapidly.

Route Sixteen was a two-lane highway with big shoulders; four lanes of northbound cars now spilled across it. Most were creeping along; a few had stopped, smoke and steam hissing from under the hoods. Quinn saw one angry driver crash his Trans Am into the rear of a stalled Rabbit. He repeated the attack several times until he had nudged the crumpled Volkswagen down an embankment into an apple orchard. The driver of the dead car scrambled onto the road with a rock, leaped onto the hood of the Trans Am, and started smashing the windshield.

Farnham was less than a mile south of the junction of Flatrock Road and Route Sixteen. As luck would have it there was just enough room for Quinn to squeeze by near the southbound shoulder, two wheels on gravel, two wheels cutting through tall weeds. He ignored the chorus of honks and curses from the refugees and sped on.

He quickly discovered, however, that it was the state police, not luck, which had kept the lane clear. A patrol car was blocking his way into town; an angry trooper waved for him to stop. The man had a cut over his right eye and a spatter of dried blood matted to his face. He kept his hand on the butt of his pistol as he approached the truck but he seemed dazed, like a fighter waiting to be knocked out.

"Where the hell you going, Mr. Gas Mask?"

"Farnham, officer. My wife. . . ."

He had already turned away, not listening. He held up his hand to stop a blue van in the nearest lane of traffic. Slowly a space opened in front of it. Northbound.

"You, in there." He waved Quinn toward it.

"Please, officer, my wife is in Farnham and I. . . ."

"Burning." The wind whipped at his hair. "Everything. Get your ass turned around right now."

The space the trooper had created expanded to two, three car lengths and those behind the van began to honk impatiently. The trooper spun away from Quinn's truck and shook his fists at the faces staring from behind closed windows. "Shut up, *shut up!*" The gale overpowered the hoarse voice; only Quinn could hear. "It's too late, damn you! You're all dead anyway."

The revolver seemed to jump into Quinn's hand. He released the safety and held the gun in his left hand just under his open window so that the trooper could not see it.

He did not want to shoot. He was not turning back.

"No, Daddy." Kitty slid across the seat and tugged at his shirt. The look on her face scared him; he thought she might try to interfere. Get them both killed. He shoved her to the floor on the passenger side. Again she reached out to him, offering her mace. "Please."

"Listen, buddy, I'm not going to tell you again. . . ."

Without thinking, Quinn closed his right hand around the canister, thrust it at the trooper and sprayed a burst into his eyes. He screamed and clutched at his face as if trying to tear it off. Quinn fired another burst, and another, until the trooper had staggered out of range.

Quinn whipped the truck through the space in front of the blue van and managed to scrape between it and the patrol car before the refugees could react. He raced down the shoulder toward Farnham.

He knew that he had taken a foolish risk. The policeman had a gun. And a radio. The effects of the mace were temporary. Quinn should have used the thirty-eight. Kitty climbed back onto the seat, slipped her mace canister into its holder and hugged him.

Not a single window remained unbroken in Farnham. The wind carried the acrid smell of electrical fire but Quinn could see no flames. Only the old schoolhouse still squatted intact on its stone foundation; its boarded-up facade and rusty civil defense sign seemed to mock the devastation. Ben's Bait and Fruit was a jumble of broken timbers. Miller's Drug had been a ramshackle Victorian roadhouse just waiting for a reason to collapse. The bomb had provided reasons aplenty. The roof had vanished entirely; the front had fallen back into the building, bulging the side walls out at crazy angles. He was astonished to see two women in street clothes, totally unprotected against fallout, standing next to the ruin.

He parked beside them. The counter read thirty-six rems per hour; he shut it off. According to his own dosimeter he had already absorbed a dose of between twenty and thirty rems. Not much time left.

"Lock the doors; I'll be right back."

Kitty watched him take the revolver from the seat and tuck it back into his shoulder rig. He mussed her hair. "It's okay," he said.

The two women were gazing at a broken window. A paint-spattered step ladder was propped against the wall directly beneath it.

"Anyone in there?"

They looked at him blankly; he could not be heard speaking through the mask into the wind. Reluctantly he pulled the respirator down and let it dangle around his neck.

"We heard shouts before the wind picked up," the younger woman said. "My husband's inside trying to help."

The older woman, who wore a calico kerchief over her mouth like a bandit, approached him as he stepped onto the ladder. "You send my Frank out. He's got a bad heart, you hear? And the traffic—we gotta go."

Quinn slithered feet first through the window and slid over a desk into a tiny office. All the furniture had skidded across the tilting floor to the wall. The office opened onto the wreck of the sales area.

"Hello?"

The room smelled of rubbing alcohol. Shelves had spilled their contents before toppling onto one another. The floor was strewn with candy, broken glass, cheap plastic toys, smashed boxes, magazines and gaudy pills. Greeting cards fluttered in the wind as if in welcome.

"Over here!"

A sweating man stripped to his T-shirt struggled with an enormous tangle of junk: broken plaster, fallen joists and rafters, cotton candy puffs of insulation. A gray-faced man with a paunch sat on a fallen shelf and watched.

"I'm all right," he repeated. "A minute. All right."

The sweating man did not pause in his feverish efforts. "Made it through the shock wave. But the windstorm blew the roof away. They hid in the crawl space. One way in." He kicked at the yellow wooden trap door half buried beneath the pile of debris.

Quinn pried a two-by-four out of the way. "Sure they're alive?"

"Heard 'em. Vent holes in the foundation." Together they flipped a chunk of wall off to one side. "Some of 'em ain't."

"My wife's down there."

He blinked at Quinn. It took just that long for a bond to be formed between them; a fellowship of sympathy and fear, a pact of cooperation. "We'll find her," he said.

Quinn nodded. "Why you here?"

"Neighbor."

They labored with grim intensity until they had cleared away almost everything but a collapsed and immovable assembly of four-by-ten ceiling rafters. They strained at this last mess of wood and plaster.

"Stuck." The good neighbor grunted. "Got a bar in my garage. Pry some loose first?"

"I'll be all right," said Frank.

"Take him." Quinn gestured at the gray old man.

Left alone, Quinn circled the remaining debris, probing for a point of attack. The beams were too massive; there were too many of them. Not without a bulldozer, he thought as he toyed with the dangling respirator. Reason demanded that he walk away. Quinn was beyond reason.

He felt a thumping underfoot and dropped to his knees on the trapdoor. "Judy! Are you down there? Judy?"

He thought he heard someone say "Hello." Or was it "Help?" The yellow door was thick and the wind had deafened him.

"Jud-ith Hutch-ins!" he shouted.

"Open . . . no air . . . soon. . . ."

With a strangled moan, Quinn linked hands around the outer-most rafter and tried to pull it toward him. The rough edge bit into his hands; muscles in his arms, stomach and calves stretched to their limits. He blocked out pain with anger. It was not fair . . . he had prepared . . . his family . . . damned politicians . . . no time . . . not . . . *fair!*

A berserk power tingled through him. Something popped and Quinn thought he had hurt himself. Three more pops followed in rapid succession as the spikes holding the rafter in place released. It came free with a squeal. Quinn staggered backward, dragging it out of the way.

Quinn had never witnessed a miracle before. He did not know whether to praise the Lord or his adrenal glands. Whatever the source, his newfound strength could not be denied. He drew an enormous breath and turned to the next rafter.

The second was the hardest, the third was easy. Only three left on top of the door. He tried to lift them all at once. His back spasmed and he reeled away, stumbling over a twisted light fixture.

"Quinn!" The haze of pain lifted. Someone sat him up. He felt a grinding at the base of his spine. Judy kissed him; her face smelled like tears.

The neighbor helped him stand. "This your wife?" he said, grinning.

The rafters still pinned the trapdoor.

"What?" Quinn swayed.

Judy caught him. "Some people were hurt during the shock wave. They needed help, beds. Mrs. LeBeau opened her house, no one knew much first aid but me. Then this happened." She hugged him. "I tried to watch for the truck but I was busy and I . . . I didn't think you would come . . . after. . . ."

"Not come?" He did not understand. "You weren't trapped."

The neighbor had wedged his crowbar under one of the fallen rafters and was straining to lift it. "Jesus!" He shook his head. "How'd you do it?"

Judy was staring. "Quinn," she said, "let me see your dosimeter."

He thrust it into his pocket without looking and gave her a quick kiss. "Listen," he said, joining the neighbor, "your only chance is the schoolhouse. If it was a shelter it should have a hand pump. But you'll need food: canned, dried—lots of rice, you understand?" He picked up the bar and rammed it deeper into the pile. "Stay put until the fallout passes. I've got a counter in the truck you can have."

Quinn did not want to die but he could not leave until he had given the strangers trapped below a chance to live. The bomb had changed everything—the survivalists had been right about that. Nothing was certain; a chance was all anyone could expect. Maybe he could bushwhack through the orchards back to Flatrock Road. Maybe.

Judy was pale. "This won't take long," Quinn said. "There's still time." He felt the strength returning to him. "Still time."

THE WHITE
BABE

JANE YOLEN

A nd the prophet says a white babe with black eyes shall be born unto a virgin in the winter of the year. The ox in the field, the hound at the hearth, the bear in the cave, the cat in the tree, all, all shall bow before her singing, "Holy, holy, holiest of sisters, who is both black and white, both dark and light, your coming is the beginning and it is the end." Three times shall her mother die and three times shall she be orphaned and she shall be set apart that all shall know her.—So goes the Garunian prophecy about the magical birth of the White Babe, layering in all kinds of folkloric absurdities and gnomic utterings to explain away the rise of a female warrior queen. These "hero birth" tales arise long after the fact, and it is no coincidence that one tale resembles another. (C.f. the birth of Alta's Anna, or the white one, motif 275f in Hyatt's Folklore Motif Index of the Dales.) This one points to the birth of White Jenna, the Amazonian queen of the Dark Riding, a figure of some staying power in the myth sequences out of the early Garunian period during and after the infamous Gender Wars.

THE MYTH:

Then Great Alta plaited the left side of her hair, the golden side, and let it fall into the sinkhole of night. And there she drew up the queen of shadows and set her upon the earth. Next she plaited the right side of her hair, the dark side, and with it she caught the queen of light. And she set her next to the black queen.

"And you two shall be sisters," quoth Great Alta. "You shall be as images in a glass, the one reflecting the other. As I have bound you in my hair, so it shall be."

Then she twined her living braids around and about them and they were as one.

THE LEGEND:

It happened in the town of Slipskin on a day far into the winter's rind that a strange and wonderful child was born. As her mother, who was but a girl herself, knelt between the piles of skins, straddling the shallow hole in the earth floor, the birth cord descended between her legs like a rope. The child emerged, feet first, climbing down the cord. When her tiny toes touched the ground, she bent down and cut the cord with her teeth, saluted the astonished midwife, and walked out the door.

The midwife fainted dead away, but when she came to and discovered the child gone and the mother dead of blood-loss, she told her eldest daughter what had happened. At first they thought to hide what had occurred. But miracles have a way of announcing themselves. The daughter told a sister who told a friend and, in that way, the story was uncovered.

The tale of that rare birthing is still recounted in Slipskin—now called New Moulting—to this very day. They say the child was the White Babe, Jenna, Sister Light of the Dark Riding, the Anna.

THE STORY:

It was an ordinary birth until the very end and then the child hurtled screaming from the womb, the cord wrapped around her tiny hands. The village midwife echoed the baby's scream. Although she had attended many births, and some near miraculous with babes born covered with cauls or twins bound together with a mantling of skin, the midwife had never heard anything like this. Quickly she made the sign of the goddess with her right hand, thumb and forefinger curved and touching, and cried out, "Great Alta, save us."

At the name, the babe was quiet.

The midwife sighed and picked up the child from the birth hide stretched over the hole scraped in the floor. "She is a girl," the midwife said, "the goddess' own. Blessed be." She turned to the new mother and only then realized that she spoke to a corpse.

Well, what was the midwife to do then but cut the cord and tend the living first. The dead mother would wait for her washing and the mourning her man would make over her, with the patience of eternity. But so as not to have the haunt follow her down the rest of her days, the midwife spoke a quick prayer as she went about the first lessons of the newborn:

> In the name of the cave,
> The dark grave,
> And all who swing twixt
> Light and light,
> Great Alta,
> Take this woman
> Into your sight.
> Wrap her in your hair
> And cradled there,
> Let her be a babe again,
> Forever.

"And that should satisfy her," the midwife mumbled to herself, knowing that to be a babe again, to be cradled against the breast of the eternal Alta, was the goal of all life. She had faith the quick prayer would shrive the poor dead woman at least until the candles could be lit, one for each year of her life and an extra for her shadow-soul, at the bedfoot. Meanwhile there was the child, blessedly a girl, and blessedly alive. In these past years of hard living it was not always so. But the man was lucky. He had only to grieve for one.

Once cleansed of the birthblood, the midwife saw the babe was fair-skinned with a fine covering of white hair on her head and tiny arms. Her body was unblemished and her pale blue eyes looked as if they could already see, following the midwife's finger left and right, up and down. And if that were not miracle enough, the child's little hand locked upon the midwife's finger with a hold that could not be broken, not even when a suck was made for her using a linen cloth twisted about and dipped in goat's milk. Even then she hung on, though she pulled on the makeshift teat with long, rhythmic sighs.

When the child's father came back from the fields and could be torn from his dead wife's side long enough to touch the babe, she was still holding the midwife's finger.

"She's a fighter," said the midwife, offering the bundle to his arms.

He would not take her. It was all he could do to care. The white babe was a poor, mewling exchange for his lusty redheaded wife. He touched the child's head gently, where beneath the fragile shield of skin the pulse beat, and said, "Then if you think her a fighter, give her to the warrior women in the mountains to foster. I cannot bide her while I grieve her mother. She is the sole cause of my loss. I cannot love where loss is so great." He said it quietly and without apparent anger, for he was ever a quiet, gentle man, but the midwife heard the rock beneath the quiet tone. It was the kind of rock against which a child would bruise herself again and again to no avail.

She said then what she thought right. "The mountain tribes will take her and love her as you cannot. They are known for their mothering. And I swear they will bring her to a stranger destiny than her tiny gripping hand and her early sight have already foretold."

If he remarked her words, the man did not respond, his shoulders already set in the grief he would carry with him to his own grave, and that—though he knew it not—soon enough, for as they said often enough in Slipskin, *The heart is not a knee that can bend.*

So the midwife took the child and left. She paused only long enough to cry out to the village diggers and two women to bathe and shroud the corpse before it set badly in the rigor of death. She told them of the child's miraculous birth, the wonder of it still imprinted on her face.

Because she was known to be a stubborn woman with a mind set in a single direction—like a needle in water pointing north—none of them gainsayed her going to the mountain clans. They did not know she was more frightened than even she herself knew, frightened of both the child and the trip. One part of her hoped the villagers would stop her. But the other part, the stubborn part, would have gone whatever they said and perhaps they guessed it and saved their breath for telling her story afterward. For as it was said in Slipskin, *Telling a tale is better than living it.*

And so the midwife turned toward the mountains where she had never been before, trusting Great Alta's guardians to track her before she was gone too far and clutching the child to her breast like an amulet.

It was luck that an early spring melt had cleared most of the paths to the mountain foot or the midwife would never have gotten even that far. She was a woman of the towns, her duties bringing her from house to house like a scavenger. She knew nothing of the forest perils or the great tan-colored cats that roamed the rockslides. With the babe swaddled and wrapped to her breast, she had started out bravely enough and managed surprisingly well, getting to the mountain foot without a scratch or slip. Many a strong hunting man had not done as well that year. And perhaps it was true, as the villagers said, that *Fish are not the best authority on water.*

She sheltered the first night among the twisted roots of a blasted tree, giving the child suck from a milk crock with a linen teat dipped in. Herself, she ate cheese and brown bread and stayed warm with half a skin of sweet wine she carried. She ate unsparingly for she thought she had but a single overnight to go before she reached the holds of the mountain clans. And she was sure the women of the mountains—whom she had long desired to visit, that longing compounded of envy and fear—would give her plenty of food and drink and gold to sustain her when they saw what it was she carried to them. She was a townswoman in her thinking, always trade for trade. She did not understand the mountains or the people who lived there; she did not know that they would feed her independent of all else but her need and that they had little use for gold so never kept it.

The second day was bright and pearly. Clouds lined only the horizon. She chose to walk along the bank of a swift-flowing stream because it seemed easier than breaking a new trail. If she had noticed the scat and could have read it, she would have known this was a favorite run of mountain cats, for trout were plentiful in the stream, and foolish, especially in the evening in the presence of bugs. But she was a woman of the town and she could read print only, a minor learning, and so she never heard the cat on her trail nor noticed its scratchy warnings on the trees.

That second night she stashed the babe in a high crotch of a tree, believing it quite safe there, and walked down to the stream to bathe in the moonlight. Being a townswoman and a midwife she valued cleanliness above all other things.

It was while she was bent over, dipping her hair in the cold water of the stream and muttering aloud about how long the trip was taking, that the cat struck. Swiftly, silently, surely. She never felt more than a moment of pain. But at her death the child cried out, a high thin wailing. The cat, startled, dropped its prey and looked about uneasily.

An arrow took it in the eye, its death more painful than the midwife's. It whimpered and trembled for several moments before one of the hunters cut its throat in pity.

The babe in the tree cried out again and the entire wood seemed to still at the sound.

"What was that?" asked the heavier of the two hunters, the one who had cut the cat's throat. They were both kneeling over the dead woman seeking in vain for a pulse.

"Perhaps the lion had cubs and they are hungry?"

"Do not be foolish, Marjo, this early in spring?"

The thinner hunter shrugged her shoulders.

The child, uncomfortable in its makeshift cradle, cried out again.

The hunters stood.

"That is no lion cub," said Marjo.

"But cub nonetheless," said her companion.

They went to the tree as unerringly as woodsense could lead them and found the babe.

"Alta's Hairs!" said the first hunter. She took the child from the tree, unwrapped it, and gazed at its smooth, fair-skinned body.

Marjo nodded. "A girl, Selna."

"Bless you," whispered Selna, but whether she spoke to Marjo or to the dead midwife or to the ears of Alta, high and far away, was not clear.

They buried the midwife and it was a long and arduous task for the ground was still part frozen. Then they skinned the cat and wrapped the babe in its warm skin. The child settled into her new wrapping and fell asleep at once.

"She was meant for us," said Selna. "She does not even wrinkle her nose at the cat smell."

"She is too young to wrinkle her nose."

Selna ignored the remark and gazed at the child. "It is true, then, what the villagers say, *When a dead tree falls, it carries with it a live one.*"

"You speak too often with another's mouth," said Marjo. "And a village mouth at that."

"And you speak with mine."

They were silent after that, neither saying a word as they trotted along the familiar paths toward the mountains and home.

They expected no grand reception at their return and got none, though their coming had been remarked by many hidden watchers. They signaled their secret names with careful hand signs at every appointed place, and the guardians of each of those turnings melted back into the forest or the seemingly impenetrable rockface without a sound.

What messages, what bits of news were passed to them as they traveled through the night came to them in the form of bird song or the howling fall of a wolf's call, where bird and wolf were not. It told them they were welcome and recognized and one particular cry told them to bring their bundle at once to the great hall. They understood, though no words, no human words, were exchanged.

But before they reached the hall, the moon slipped down behind the western mountains and Marjo bade farewell to her companion and disappeared.

Hefting the child in its cat cloak, Selna whispered, "Till evening, then." But she said it so softly, the child in her arms did not even stir.

THE SONG:

Lullabye to the Cat's Babe

Hush little mountain cat,
Sleep in your den,
I'll sing of your mother
Who cradled Fair Jen.

I'll sing of your mother
Who covered Jen's skin.
Flesh of your flesh
Did sweet Jenna lay in.

Sleep, little catkin,
Perchance you shall dream
Of rabbit and pheasant
And trout in the stream.

But Jenna will dream
Of the dark and the light
Your mother will shelter her
From the cold night.

THE STORY:

There were cradles scattered around the Great Hall, some of oak with the grain running like rivers to the sea, and some of white pine, so soft the marks of a baby's nails could be seen, like runes, on the headboards. But for some reason Selna did not put the child in any of them. She kept it on her breast when she showed it in the Great

Hall and all the rest of the day, hoping the steady beat of her heart would comfort it.

It was not unusual for a new fosterling to be kept, swaddled, at one breast or another. The women of Alta's-hame shared the care of them, though Selna had never before shown any interest in fostering. The stink of the babes and their high, cranky crying had always put her off. But this one was different. She smelled not of sour milk and spittle but of mountain cat, moonshine, and blackthorn, that being the tree she had been wedged in when the cat had struck her mother. She had cried only twice, each time at a death, which Selna thought an omen. Surely the child must be hungry or fearful or cold. Selna was ready to put her away at the first sign of fretting. But the babe had stared at her with eyes the color of a spring sky, as if reading her very soul. And so Selna had kept her heart to heart far into the morning. By then everyone had noticed and commented so that she could not—for fear of being shamed—let her small burden go. Physical abuse had never bothered Selna. Indeed she was proud of her ability to withstand the worst punishments. She was always in the forefront of any battleline, she was the last to the fire, the first into a cold stream. But she could never stand the tauntings of the women in her Hame.

By midmorning, though, the child was hungry and let her know with small pipings, like a chick in the henyard. She fed the babe as best she could with one of the Eastern bottles so prized by the kitcheners. Both she and the babe were thoroughly splattered in the process, and so Selna took the child down to the baths, heated the water well below her usual steaming, and holding the naked child against her own bare shoulder, plunged in.

At the water's touch, the child cooed contentedly and fell asleep. Selna sat on the third step of the bath so that only their heads showed above the water. She stayed until her fingers had wrinkled and the water began to grow chill and her hand around the child cramped. Then she got out reluctantly, dried the sleeping babe, and wrapped toweling around herself for the long walk back to her room. This time there were no comments even though she passed many of her hamemates. Whether she willed it or not, the child was hers.

THE HISTORY:

The women of the mountain warrior clans did not take fostering lightly. Once a child was chosen by her foster mother, the woman had full charge of the child's care. A kitchener's child grew up amongst the great pots; took her first steps on the tiled kitchen floor; ate, napped, and slept out her childhood sicknesses in a special children's nook in the kitchen.

So, too, a child chosen for rearing by one of the warrior/huntresses was carried about in a special pack wherever her foster mother went. Lowentrout finds evidence of this in the famous Baryard Tapestries (his essay "Packchildren of the Western Holds," Nature and History Vol. 39, is especially interesting). There is a leathern pack unearthed from the famous gravemound at Arrundale and preliminary examination leads to speculation that it may be one of the Amazonian child-carriers. (For more about this dig, see Sigel and Salmon's video "Graverobbing Among the Dales.") Such burdens did not hamper the women warriors either in battle or on the hunt, according to Lowentrout, and textual evidence supports his claim. The three scrolls ascribed to the Great Archive of G'run Longbow graphically depict the battles in which the mountain clans took part. One in particular speaks of "the double heads of the amazons" and, in another place, "the precious burden carried by (them)." And most striking, "She fought, all the ways her breast to the foe for as not to expose the one at her back." Vargo argues that the word "at" simply refers to another fighter since fighting back-to-back was a familiar style in swords-battle. She further states that if a pack-child had been meant, the word "on" rather than "at" would have been used. However, Doyle, whose seminal work on Altalinguistics has just been published, points out that in the old tongue on/at/upon *and* by *are used interchangeably.*

THE STORY:

"You will have to name her, you know," Marjo said that night, lying on the far side of the bed. The lantern hanging above them cast shadows on the wall and floor.

Selna looked at the child sleeping between them. She touched the soft cheek with a tentative finger. "If I name her, she really is mine forever."

"Forever is longer than either one of us shall last," said Marjo, her finger stroking the child's other cheek.

"A child is a kind of immortality," Selna murmured. "A link forged. A bond. Even if she is not of my blood."

"She will be," Marjo said. "If you claim her."

"How can I not—now?" Selna sat up and Marjo followed suit. "She looks to me first, whoever holds her. She trusts me. When I brought her into the kitchen at dinner and everyone wanted to touch her, all the while her tiny head swiveled around to see me."

"You are being sentimental," said Marjo with a laugh. "Newborns cannot swivel their heads. They cannot even see."

"She can. Jenna can."

"So—you have already named her," Marjo said. "And without waiting for my approval."

"You are my sister, not my keeper," Selna answered testily. At the sharpness in her voice, the child stirred between them. Selna smiled a lopsided apology. "Besides," she said, "Jenna is just her baby name. I want to name her Jo-an-enna in full."

"*Jo* for lover, *an* for white, *enna* for tree. That makes sense for she was found in a tree and her hair—what there is of it—is white. I presume that *Jo* is because you love her, though I wonder at how quickly such a thing came about. You usually do not *love* so quickly. It is usually your hatred that is quickly aroused."

"Do not be an idiot. *Jo* is for you, Marjo," Selna said, "and well you know it." She reached out to touch her companion across the child.

Marjo's hand met hers halfway and they both smiled.

The child between them cooed.

In the morning Selna took Jenna to the infirmarer, Kadreen, who checked the babe from the crown of her head to the soles of her feet.

"A strong one," said Kadreen. She did not smile but then she rarely did. It was said she had stitched too many wounds and set too many bones to find life amusing enough for a smile. But Selna knew that even as a young woman, before she had chosen her calling, Kadreen had not found much to smile at. Perhaps, Selna thought, the calling found her *because* of that.

"Her fingers grip surprisingly well for a newborn. And she can follow the movement of my hand. That is rare. I clapped my hands to test her hearing and she startled at once. She will be a good companion for you in the woods."

Selna nodded.

"Make sure you feed her at the same time and she will sleep through the night within the first moon's change."

"She slept through the night last night," Selna said.

"She will not again."

But despite the infirmarer's warning, Jenna did sleep soundly through that night and the next. And though Selna tried to feed her on the schedule dictated by Kadreen's long experience with infants, she was always too busy to do so. Yet the babe seemed to thrive on the erratic meals and, in the woods, strapped to Selna's breast or back, she was as quiet as any seasoned hunter.

Selna boasted of her fosterling at every opportunity until everyone but Marjo grew weary of it.

"You are in danger of becoming a bore," said Donya, the head kitchener, when Selna dropped off a fine roebuck and seven rabbits after a two-day hunt. "She is a fine babe, no doubt. Strong and quite pleasant to look upon. But she is not Great Alta. She does not walk across the Lake of Sighs nor ride the summer rainbow nor leap between the drops of falling rain."

"I did not say she was the goddess," mumbled Selna. The child at her breast laughed delightedly as she tickled it under the chin with one of the rabbit's feet. Then she looked at the kitchener squarely and roared. "And I am *not* a bore."

"I did not say you were. I said you were in danger of becoming one," said Donya calmly. "Ask anyone."

Selna glared around the kitchen but the girls all dropped their eyes and suddenly the room was quiet of voices. All that could be heard were the *snick-snack* of kitchen knives at work. Donya's young ones knew better than to tangle with one of the warriors. Selna, especially, was known for her hot temper though she, unlike some of them, seldom bore a lasting grudge. Still, not a one of them envied her fosterling that temper when it roared.

Selna shook her head, still angry, and turned back to Donya. "I shall want the rabbit skins," she said. "They will make a soft lining for the pack. Jenna has fine skin."

"Jenna has a baby's skin," said Donya evenly, ignoring Selna's scowl. "And of course you shall have the fur. I'll also save you the deerskin. It should make a fine pair of leggings and many mocs."

Selna smiled suddenly. "She will need many mocs."

"But not right away," Donya said, with a laugh.

There was a titter around the room as her own fosterlings enjoyed the joke.

"What do you mean?" The anger was back in Selna's voice.

Donya set down the heavy crockery bowl and wooden spoon, wiped her hands on her aprons, and held out her arms. Reluctantly Selna recognized the signal and unstrapped the babe, handing it over to Donya.

Donya smiled and rocked the child in her arms. "This is an infant, Selna. A babe. Look around at my own maids. Seven of them. And once they were each this size. They walked at a year, only one sooner. Do not expect too much from your child and she will grow in your love. When her moon time comes, she will not turn from you. When she reads from the *Book of Light* and calls her own sister into this world, she will not forsake you. But if you push her too much, you will push her away. A child is not yours to own but yours to raise. She may not be what you will have her be, but she will be what she has to be. Remember what they say, that *Wood may remain twenty years in the water but it is still not a fish.*"

"Who is becoming the bore now?" asked Selna in a weary voice. She took Jenna, who was still smiling, back from the kitchener and went from the room.

That night there was a full moon and all the dark sisters were called forth. In the great open amphitheater the circle of women and their children was complete.

Selna stood in the circle's center below the altar which was flanked by three rowan trees. Marjo was by her side. For the first time in almost a year there was a new fosterling to celebrate, though two of the gardeners and one warrior had each borne a babe. But those infants had already had their consecration to the goddess. It was Jenna's turn now.

The priestess sat silently on the backless throne atop the rock altar, her own dark sister throned beside her. Their black hair braided with tiny white flowers, lips stained red with the juice of berries, they waited until the crowd of worshipers quieted. Then they leaned forward, hands on knees, and stared down at Selna and Marjo, but only the priestess herself spoke.

"Who bears the child?"

"Mother, I do," said Selna, raising Jenna to eye level. For her the word mother had a double meaning for the priestess had been her own foster mother, who had grieved sorely when Selna had chosen to follow the warrior way.

"And I," said Marjo.

They stepped together up onto the first altar rise.

"And who bore the child?" the priestess asked.

"Mother, a woman of the town," said Selna.

"She died in the woods," Marjo added.

They mounted the second step.

"And who now bleeds for the child?" the priestess asked.

"She shall have my blood," said Selna.

"And mine." Marjo's voice was a quiet echo.

They reached the third step and the priestess and her dark sister rose. The priestess took the silent babe from Selna's hands, turned, and placed the child upon the throne. Marjo and Selna were beside her in one fluid movement.

Then the priestess dropped to her knees before the child and, taking her long black braid, she wound it about the child's waist. Her sister, on the other side of the throne, did the same. As soon as they were done, Selna and Marjo knelt and offered their hands, wrists up.

Taking a silver pin from a box mounted in the arm of the throne, the priestess pierced Selna's wrist where the blue vein branched. At the same time, her sister with an identical pin did the same for Marjo. They held the warriors' wrists together so that the blood flowed each to each.

Next the priestess turned and pricked Jenna lightly, above the navel, signaling to Selna and Marjo silently with her free hand. They bent over and placed their wrists side by side on the baby's belly so that their bloods mingled.

Then the priestess and her sister drew their twined braids over the steady hands.

"Blood to blood," the priestess intoned. "Life to life."

The entire congregation of Alta's-hame repeated the words, a rolling echo in the clearing.

"What is the child's name?"

Selna could not keep from smiling. "Jo-an-enna," she said.

The priestess spelled out the name and then, in the old tongue, gave the child her secret name that only the four of them—and Jenna in her time—would know. "Annuanna," she said. "The white birch, the Goddess tree, the tree of everlasting light."

"Annuanna," they whispered to one another and the child.

Then the priestess and her sister unwrapped their hair and stood. Holding their hands over the two kneelers and the babe, both priestess and sister spoke the final prayer.

> She who holds us
>   in her hand,
> She who molds us
>   in this land,
> She who drives
>   away the night,
> She who wrote
>   the Book of Light,
> In her name,
>   Blessed be.

The assembled women all came in perfectly on the responses.

When they were done, Selna and Marjo stood together, Selna holding out the infant so that all could see. At the great cheer that arose below them, Jenna woke up, startled, and began to cry. Selna did not comfort her, though the priestess looked sharply at her. A warrior had to learn young that crying brought no comfort.

Back inside, after the magnificent feast that followed, the baby was handed around the table for all to see. She began in the priestess's arms and was handed over to the plump arms of Donya who handled her expertly but "as routinely as a bit of mutton just off the spit," Selna commented testily to Marjo. Donya handed the child to the leaner arms of the warriors. They chuckled and clucked at Jenna's chin, and one dark sister threw her up into the air. She screamed with delight, but Selna pushed aside the circle of companions angrily to catch the child on her downward flight.

"What kind of a misbegotten son-of-a-son are you?" she cried out. "What if the light had failed? Whose arms would have caught her then?"

The dark sister Sammor shrugged her shoulders and laughed. "This late mothering has made mush of your brains, Selna. We are *inside*. There are no clouds to hide the moon. The lights of Alta's-hame never fail."

Selna tucked Jenna under one arm and raised the other to strike Sammor but her hand was caught from behind.

"Selna, she is right and you are wrong in this. The babe is safe," Marjo said. "Come. Drink a toast with us all to forget and forgive, and then we will play at the wands." They brought their arms down together.

But Selna's anger did not abate, which was unusual, and she sat outside the circle of sisters when they threw the wands around the ring in the complicated patterns that trained them for sword-handling.

With Selna out, Marjo could not play either, and she sat across from her sister and sulked as the game went on. It became more and more complex as a second, then a third, and finally a fourth set of wands were introduced into the circle. The flexible willows flipped end over end in the air, passing from woman to woman, from hand to hand, and soon the dining hall was quiet except for the *slip-slap* of the wands as they hit palm after palm after palm.

"The lights!" someone shouted, and a cheer went up from the watchers around the ring. Sammor's sister Amalda nodded and two of the kitcheners, new enough to the sisterhood that they stuck together as close as shadows, rose to stand by the torches that illuminated the circle.

The game went on without stopping, the wands slipping even more quickly through the air. Not a hand had missed since the throws began. The whizzing of the wands as they passed one another was punctuated by the slapping of palms.

Then without warning both torches were doused in the

waterbuckets, and the dark sisters in the circle disappeared. The circle was halved and there was a clatter of wands hitting the floor. Only Marjo, who sat beyond the range of the two doused torches, and the dark sisters of the watchers who stood far from the game, remained, for the lights from the kitchen shone upon them.

Amalda's voice counted out those who had lost their wands. "Domina, Catrona, Marna." Then she turned and nodded for two new torches to be brought.

The relighted circle arranged itself, as dark sisters appeared again. The losers—Domina, Catrona, and Marna and their dark halves—went into the kitchen for something to drink. Playing at the wands was thirsty work. But Selna stood, the child at her breast, and spoke so loudly no one could miss it.

"It has been a tiring day, sweet Jenna, and time we were both in bed. I will put out the light tonight."

There was a gasp heard around the circle. To put out the light was to send your sister back into the darkness. To announce it so, was an affront.

Marjo's mouth grew tighter, but she said nothing as she stood with Selna and followed her out of the room. But Sammor spoke to their departing backs.

"Remember, Selna, that it is said *If your mouth turns into a knife, it will cut off your lips.*" She did not expect an answer and, indeed, got none.

"You shamed me," Marjo said softly when they reached their room. "You have never done such a thing before. Selna, what is wrong?"

"Nothing is wrong," Selna answered, arranging the baby in her cot, smoothing the blanket and touching the child's white hair with a finger. She began to hum an old cradle song. "Look! She is already asleep."

"I mean, what is wrong between *us*?" Marjo bent over the cot and stared at the sleeping child. "She *is* a sweetling."

"There, you see? Nothing is wrong between *us*. We both love her."

"How can you love her after so short a time? She is nothing but a bit of flesh and coos. Later she shall be someone to love—strong or weak, bright-eyed or sad, handy with her hands or her mouth. But now she is only . . ." Marjo's voice stopped abruptly in mid-sentence for Selna had blown out the large candle over the bed.

"There is nothing wrong between us now, sister," Selna whispered into the black room.

She lay down on the bed, conscious of Marjo's empty half for her sister could always be counted on to talk and laugh and come up with a quick answer before they slept. Then she turned over and, holding her breath, listened a moment for the baby's breathing. When she was sure the child was safe, she let out the air with a loud percussive sigh and fell asleep.

THE HISTORY:

The "game of wands" has come down to us in a highly suspect form. It is played today only by girl children in the Upper Dales where the chorus, sung in modal tuning by watchers (usually boys) standing outside the circle goes:

Round and round and round the ring
The willow sword we now do fling.

The concentric circles of players sit on the ground facing one another, wands in hand. Once made of willow (which no longer grows in the Upper Dales though evidence of a different floraculture proves willows may have been plentiful a thousand years ago), the wands today are manufactured of a plastine that is both flexible and strong. At a drum signal, the wands are passed from hand to hand in a clockwise manner for seven beats, then returned for seven beats. Next the wands are flipped between the circles in preset partnerships for seven more beats. Finally, to the accompaniment of the choral singing of the watchers and an ever-rapidly increasing pattern beat out on the drum, the wands are flipped across the circle, first to the partner and back, then to the person directly to the partner's right. The wands must be caught in the sword hand, which gives left-handed players a decided disadvantage in the game. As soon as a player drops a wand, she is "out."

Lowentrout points to the famous "insert piece" of the Baryard Tapestries, which had been found in the vault of the eastern potentate Achmed Mubarek thirty years ago as proof positive that the "game of wands" played by warriors in the mountain clans and the nursery circle game are one and the same. While it is true that the "insert piece" (which has been repaired inexpertly by many Eastern hands—some say as many as thirty times as evidenced by the different colored threads) shows concentric circles of women warriors, they are holding swords, not wands. One of the so-called players is lying on her back, sword in her breast, obviously dead. She is ignored by the other players. Cowan argues forcibly that the "insert piece" has been too mangled over the years to be plain in its correspondences, but that it is more likely a picture of a specific form of execution as the "insert piece" occurs in that section of the tapestry which deals with traitors and spies. Perhaps the true meaning of the "insert piece" will never be known, but Magon's shrill argument that the inner circle consisted of the "dark sisters," or "shadow sisters' " who could be seen by the light of the moon or the heavy tallow candles (still popular in the Upper and Lower Dales) and the outer circle was that of the "light sisters" harkens back to the last century when the Luxophists sought to resurrect the "Book of Light" practices. Those practices had been banned for at least seven generations and the "Book of Light" has been so thoroughly discredited by Duane's brilliant "Das Volk lichtet nicht" I need not reiterate her arguments here.

Some confusion over the intricately engraved silver rings found in the Arrundale grave mound still exists. Sigel and Salmon call them "wand holders," giving credence to Magon's shaky thesis, but there is even more evidence that these artifacts are napkin rings or possibly pack cups for long trips, and that is convincingly argued in Cowan's "Rings of the Clans" in Nature and History, *Vol. 51.*

THE STORY:

Selna's shameful behavior became the talk of the Hame. Though sisters had quarreled before, little fiery arguments that sent a moment of heat and light, and then died down without even embers of memory, what Selna did was unheard of. Even the priestess' records mentioned nothing like it, and the Hame had seventeen generations listed and eight great tapestries as well.

Selna stayed in the bright sunlight with her child during the day and at night, babe bound fast to her breast or back, avoided the well-lighted rooms of the Hame. Once or twice, when it was absolutely unavoidable, and Selna had to come into a torchlit room, Marjo crept behind her, a thin attenuated figure. Gone was the dark sister's robust laughter, her hearty ringing tones.

"Selna," she would cry to her sister's back with a voice like a single strand of sigh, "what is wrong between us?" It was a ghost's voice, hollow and dying. "Selna . . ."

Once, in the kitchen begging some milk for the babe, Selna turned for a moment when Marjo called. She put her hands over the child's ears as if to block out the sound of her sister's voice, though it was so low by now it could scarcely be heard. Behind her, Donya and her own sister Doey and two of the older girls watched in horror. They saw in Marjo's wasting figure their own slow deaths.

Marjo's eyes, the color of bruises, wept black tears. "Sister, why do you do this? I would share the child with you. I have no wish to stand between."

But Selna turned slowly and deliberately away from the pleading figure, back toward the kitchen's light. When she noticed Donya and Doey and the two girls standing there, stricken, she bowed her head and hunched her shoulders up as if expecting a blow. Then she turned and went back without the milk into the darkest part of the hall.

On the thirteenth day of her shame, the priestess banished her from the Hame.

"My daughter," the priestess said, her voice heavy, "you have brought this upon yourself. We cannot stop what you do to your own dark sister. Once you accepted the teachings of the *Book of Light* we could instruct you no more. What falls between the two of you is your own concern. But the Hame is shattered. We cannot continue to watch what you do. So you must leave us and finish out what you have so ill begun alone."

"Alone?" Selna asked. For the first time her voice quivered. She had not been alone for as long as she could remember. She clutched baby Jenna to her.

"You have thrust your own dark sister from you," said the priestess. "You have shamed us all. The child stays here."

"No!" Selna cried, turning. By her side, the gray shadow that was Marjo turned, too. But they ran into a wall of six warriors who pinned them against the wall and took the babe, despite Selna's screams and pleading.

They took Selna out into the bright day, which meant she would be truly alone at the start of her journey, with only the clothes she wore. Her bow, sword, and gutting knife they threw after her, tied in a heavy bag that took her near an hour to unknot. They said nothing to her, not even a word of farewell, for so the priestess had instructed them.

She left Alta's-hame by day, but she returned that night, a shadow among shadows, and stole away the child.

There were no guards by the infant's cot. Selna knew there would be none. The women of the Hame would be sure she would never return, so shamed and low had they left her. They would trust in the guards of the outer gates. But she was a warrior, the best of them, and often she and Marjo had played among the secret passageways. So silently, Selna stole back in, more quietly even than a shadow. She doused three lights along the hallways before Marjo's pale voice could alert the sleepers.

Jenna woke and recognized her foster mother's smell. Giving a satisfied sound, she fell asleep again. It was that small wisp of sound that confirmed Selna's determination. She raced down the secret ways and was at the forest's edge before it was dawn.

As she slipped along the old paths where the rocks were worn smooth by the passage of so many feet, the birds heralded her arrival. She found the large boulder off to the side of the path where she had left her weapons. Shamed as she was, she would still not have raised her sword or bow against her Hame mates. Leaning back against the rock, into a niche that seemed to exactly fit her body, she slipped her tunic down to her waist. Now that she was truly the child's mother, she could nurse it as well. She gave the baby her breast. For a few moments Jenna sucked eagerly, but when no milk came, she turned her head to the side and wailed.

"Hush!" Selna said sharply, taking the child's face between her fingers and squeezing. "A warrior must be silent."

But the baby, hungry and frightened, cried even more.

Selna shook the infant roughly, unaware that tears were coursing down her own cheeks. Startled, the child stopped crying. Then

Selna stood up and looked around, making sure no one had been alerted by the child's cries. When she heard nothing, she sat back down, leaned against the rock, and slept, the baby in her arms.

But Jenna did not sleep. Restless and hungry, she caught at dust motes in the rays of the sun that filtered through the canopy of aspen and birch. At last she put her tiny hand into her mouth and sucked noisily.

It was hours before Selna awoke and when she did the sun was already high overhead and a fox was puzzling on the edge of the small clearing, its sharp little muzzle poking into the undergrowth. At Selna's waking, it looked up, ears stiff with warning, then turned abruptly and disappeared into the shadows.

Selna stretched, and looked at the babe sleeping on her lap. She smiled, touching Jenna's white hair. In the sunlight she could see the infant's pink scalp under the fine hair and the beating of the pulse beneath the shield of skin.

"You are mine," she whispered fiercely. "I shall care for you. I shall protect you. I shall feed you. I—and no others."

At her voice Jenna awoke and her cry was cranky and thin.

"You are hungry. So am I," Selna said quietly. "I shall find us both something to eat."

She pulled her tunic down, and bound the child to her back, slipping the ribands under her own arms, tight enough so that the child was safe, loose enough so that they both could move. Holding her bow and sword in her left hand, she slipped the gutting knife into its sheath over her right shoulder where she could reach it for a fast throw. Then she began loping down the forest paths.

She was lucky. She found tracks of a small rabbit, stalked it easily, and brought it down with a light arrow at the first try. Fearing to make a large fire still so close to Alta's-hame, she nevertheless knew better than to eat a rabbit raw. So she dug a deep hole and made a small fire there, enough to at least sear the meat. She chewed it, then spit the juices into Jenna's mouth. After the second try, the babe did not refuse the offering and sucked it up eagerly, mouth to mouth.

"As soon as I can, I will find you milk," Selna promised, wiping the baby's mouth and then tickling her under the chin. "I will hire out to guard one of the small border towns. Or I will find the High King's army. They like Alta's warriors. They will not refuse me."

Jenna smiled her response, her little hands waving about in the air. Selna kissed her on the brow, feeling the brush of the child's white hair under her nose, as soft as the wing of a butterfly. Then she bound the baby on her back again.

"We have many more miles to go tonight before I will feel safe," Selna said. She did not add that she wanted to stay the night in the forest because the full moon was due and she could not bear to speak to her pale shadow and explain all that she had done.

THE LEGEND:

In the dark forest near Alta's-hame there is a clearing. Under a stand of white birch grows a red-tipped iris. The people who live in Selkirk, on the west side of the forest, say that three ghosts may be seen on the second moon of each year. One is a warrior woman, a dark necklace at her throat. The second is her shadowy twin. And the third is a snow-white bird that flies above them crying with a child's voice. At dawn the two women strike one another with their swords. Where their blood falls the iris spring up, as white as the bird, as red as the blood. "Snow-iris" the folk of the East call the flower. "Cold Heart" say the folk from the South. But "Sister's Blood" is the Selkirk name and the people of that town leave the flowers alone. Though the juice from the iris heart binds up a woman in her time of troubles and gives her relief from flashes of heat, the Selkirk folk will not touch so much as a leaf of the flower, and they will not go into the clearing after dark.

THE STORY:

At the edge of a small clearing, a short run to the outskirts of the town of Seldenkirk, Selna rested. Leaning against a small oak which protected her from the bright full moon, she caught her breath and dropped both bow and sword. Her breathing was so labored at first, she did not hear the noise, and then, when she heard it, it was already too late. Strong, callused hands grabbed her from behind and twisted a knife point into the hollow below her chin.

She stopped herself from crying out in pain, and then the knife slipped down and carved a circle of blood like a necklace around her throat.

"These be the only jewels an Alta-slut should own," came the gruff voice behind her. "You be mighty far from your own, my girl."

She fell to her knees, trying to twist and protect the child at her back, and the movement frightened the man, who jammed the knife deep in her throat. She tried to scream but no sound came out.

The man laughed raggedly and ripped her tunic down the front, exposing her breasts and belly. "Built like a boy," he said, disgustedly. "Your kind be good only dying or dead." He grabbed her by one leg and pulled her out from the forest onto the softer grass of the moonlit clearing. Then he tried to turn her from her side onto her back.

She could not scream, but she could still fight him. But another woman screamed from behind, a strange gurgling.

Startled, he looked over his shoulder, saw a twin of the first woman, her own throat banded by a black line of blood. Turning back, he realized his mistake, for Selna had managed to get her hand on her knife. With the last remaining strength in her arm, she threw the knife at his face. It hit him cleanly between the eyes. But Selna did not see it, for she had already rolled over on her stomach and died, her fingertips touching Marjo's.

The man tried to get to his feet, managed only to his knees, then fell on top of Selna, the handle of the knife between his eyes coming to rest in baby Jenna's hand. She held on to it and cried.

They were found in the morning by a shepherd who always took his flock to that clearing where the spring grass was sweetest. He arrived just before sunrise and thought he saw three dead folk by the clearing's edge. When he got to them, pushing his way through his reluctant sheep, he saw that there were only two, a woman, her throat cut, and a man, a gutting knife between his eyes. A silent infant was holding on to the bloody knife handle as if she herself had set it on its deadly path.

The shepherd ran all the way back to Seldenkirk, forgetting his sheep, who bleated around the ghastly remains. When he returned, with six strong ploughboys and the portly high sheriff, only the man lay there, on his back, in a circle of sheep. The dead woman, the babe, the knife, and one of the shepherd's nursing ewes were gone.

THE BALLAD:

The Ballad of the Selden Babe

Do not go down, ye maidens all,
  Who wear the golden gown,
Do not go to the clearing
  At the edge of Seldentown,
For wicked are the men who wait
  To bring young maidens down.

A maiden went to Seldentown,
  A maid no more was she,
Her hair hung loose about her neck,
  Her gown aboun her knee,
A babe was slung upon her back,
  A bonnie babe was he.

She went into the clearing wild,
  She went too far from town,
A man came up behind her
  And he cut her neck aroun',
A man came up behind her
  And he pushed that fair maid down.

"And will ye have your way wi' me,
  Or will ye cut me dead,
Or do ye hope to take from me
  My long lost maidenhead?
Why have ye brought me far from town
  Upon this grass green bed?"

He never spoke a single word,
  Nor gave to her his name,

Nor whence and where his parentage,
  Nor from which town he came,
He only thought to bring her low
  And heap her high wi' shame.

But as he set about his plan,
  And went about his work,
The babe upon the maiden's back
  Had touched her hidden dirk,
And from its sheath had taken it
  All in the clearing's mirk.

And one and two, the tiny hands
  Did fell the evil man
Who all upon his mother had
  Commenced the wicked plan.
God grant us all such bonnie babes
  And a good and long life span.

THE STORY:

The priestess called off the banishment, for four of the hunters had found Selna's body hand in hand with Marjo. The hunters had melted quickly back into the forest when the shepherd had appeared, waited out his discovery, then taken Selna, the babe, and the ewe back to Alta's-hame.

"Our sisters are once more with us," the priestess said, and she made Alta's mark—the circle and the crux—on Selna's forehead, when she met the hunters with their sad burden at the great gate. "Bring her in. The child also. She now belongs to us all. No one of us shall mother her alone."

"The prophecy, Mother," Amalda cried out, and many echoed her. "Is this the child spoke of?"

The priestess shook her head. "The *Book* speaks of a thrice-orphaned babe and this sweetling has lost but two mothers, her first mother and Selna."

"But, Mother," Amalda continued. "Was not Marjo her mother as well?"

The priestess's mouth grew tight. "We may not help a prophecy along, sister. Remember that it is written that *miracles come to the unsuspecting.* I have spoken. The child will not have one mother here at Alta's-hame hereafter but a multitude." She twisted her long braid through her fingers.

The women murmured amongst themselves, but at last they agreed she was right. So they set Selna's corpse into the withy burial basket and brought her into the infirmarer's room. There they washed and dressed her body, brushed her hair until it shone, then twined the top withes of the basket closed.

It took six of them, one at each corner of the basket, and two at head and foot, to carry the burden up Holy Hill to the great mazed cave, Alta's Rock, where the bodies of generations of sisters lay wrapped and preserved, under blazing torches.

Though they went up to Alta's Rock at noon, they waited until night for the ceremony, eating sparingly of the fruits they had brought with them. They spoke quietly of Selna's life, of her hunting skills and her fearlessness, her quick temper and her quicker smile. And they spoke as often of Marjo, not the pale shadow, but the hearty, laughing companion.

Kadreen remarked that it was Alta's luck that had led them to find Selna's body.

"No, sister, it was the skill of my sisters and me. We trailed her through several nights, and if she had not been out of her mind, we would never have picked up her trail, for she was the best of us," said Amalda.

Kadreen shook her head and placed her hand on Amalda's shoulder. "I mean, sister, that it was Alta's gracious gift that we have her body with us at Holy Hill, for how many of our own lie far away in unmarked graves?"

When the moon rose, the group on the Hill was almost doubled, the children alone without dark sisters.

Marjo's body appeared in its own basket by Selna's side, the withy latticework as finely done as her sister's.

Then the priestess, her voice ragged with sorrow, began. "For our sisters who are united even in death," she said, then breaking a moment out of the ritual whispered to the two corpses, "There is nothing wrong between you now."

Donya drew a loud, groaning breath, and the two kitchen maids burst into tears.

The priestess sang the first of the Seven praises, with the others quickly joining in, singing the parts they had known from childhood.

> In the name of Alta's cave,
> The dark and lonely grave . . .

When the seventh was done, and only the last lovely echo lingered in the air, they picked up the baskets and carried Selna and Marjo into the cave.

Donya and her dark sister were the last, Donya carrying the white-haired babe who was so full of ewe's milk, she slept peacefully on the kitchener's ample breast.

THE MYTH:

Then Great Alta said, "There shall be one of you, my only daughter, who shall be thrice born and thrice orphaned. She shall lie by a dead mother's side three times yet shall herself live. She shall be queen above all things, yet queen she will not be. She shall carry a babe in her womb for each mother, yet mother them not. The three shall be as one and begin the world anew. So I say and so shall it be."

And then Great Alta picked out of the light a weeping child as white as snow, as red as blood, as black as night, and suckled her until the child was still.

THE HOMESICK CHICKEN

EDWARD D. HOCH

W hy did the chicken cross the road?

To get on the other side, you'd probably answer, echoing an old riddle that was popular in the early years of the last century.

But my name is Barnabus Rex, and I have a different answer.

I'd been summoned to the Tangaway Research Farms by the director, an egg-headed old man named Professor Mintor. After parking my car in the guarded lot and passing through the fence—it was an EavesStop, expensive, but sure protection against all kinds of electronic bugging—I was shown into the presence of the director himself. His problem was simple. The solution was more difficult.

"One of the research chickens pecked its way right through the security fence, then crossed an eight-lane belt highway to the other side. We want to know why."

"Chickens are a bit out of my line," I replied.

"But your specialty is the solution of scientific riddles, Mr. Rex, and this certainly is one." He led me out of the main research building to a penned-in area where the test animals were kept. We passed a reinforced electric cage in which he pointed out the mutated turkeys being bred for life in the domes of the colonies of the moon. Further along were some leggy-looking fowl destined for Mars. "They're particularly well adapted to the Martian terrain and environment," Professor Mintor explained. "We've had to do very little development work; we started from desert roadrunners."

"What about the chickens?"

"The chickens are something else again. The strain, called ZIP-1000, is being developed for breeding purposes on Zipoid, the second planet of Barnard's star. We gave them extra-strength beaks—something like a parrot's—to crack the extra-tough seed hulls used for feed. The seed hulls in turn were developed to withstand the native fauna like the space-lynx and the ostroid, so that—"

"Aren't we getting a little off course?" I asked.

"Ah—yes. The problem. What *is* a problem is the chicken that crossed the road. It used its extra-strength beak to peck its way right through this security fence. But the puzzling aspect is its motivation. It crossed that belt highway—a dangerous undertaking even for a human—and headed for the field as if it were going home. And yet the chicken was hatched right here within these walls. How could it be homesick for something it had never known?"

"How indeed?" I stared bleakly through the fence at the highway and the deserted field opposite. What was there to attract a chicken—even one of Professor Mintor's super-chickens—to that barren bit of land? "I should have a look at it," I decided. "Can you show me the spot where the chicken crossed the highway?"

He led me around a large pen to a spot in the fence where a steel plate temporarily blocked a jagged hole. I knelt to examine the shards of complex, multiconductor mesh, once more impressed by the security precautions. "I'd hate to meet your hybrid chickens on a dark night, Professor."

"They would never attack a human being, or even another creature," Mintor quickly assured me. "The beak is used only for cracking seed hulls, and perhaps in self-defense."

"Was it self-defense against the fence?"

He held up his hands. "I can't explain it."

I moved the steel plate and stooped to go through the hole. In that moment I had a chicken's-eye view of the belt highway and the barren field beyond, but they offered no clues. "Be careful crossing over," Mintor warned. "Don't get your foot caught!"

Crossing a belt highway on foot—a strictly illegal practice—could be dangerous to humans and animals alike. With eight lanes to traverse it meant hopping over eight separate electric power guides—any one of which could take off a foot if you misstepped. To imagine a chicken with the skill to accomplish it was almost more than I could swallow. But then I'd never before been exposed to Professor Mintor's super-chickens.

The empty lot on the other side of the belt highway held nothing of interest to human or chicken, so far as I could see. It was barren of grass or weeds, and seemed nothing more than a patch of dusty earth dotted with a few pebbles. In a few sunbaked depressions I found the tread of auto tires, hinting that the vacant lot was sometimes used for parking.

I crossed back over the belt highway and reentered the Tangaway compound through the hole in the fence. "Did you find anything?" Mintor asked.

"Not much. Exactly what was the chicken doing when it was recovered?"

"Nothing. Pecking at the ground as if it were back home."

"Could I see it? I gather it's no longer kept outside."

"After the escape we moved them all to the interior pens. There was some talk of notifying Washington since we're under government contract, but I suggested we call you in first. You know how the government is about possible security leaks."

"Is Tangaway the only research farm doing this sort of thing?"

"Oh, no! We have a very lively competitor named Beaverbrook Farms. That's part of the reason for all this security. We just managed to beat them out on the ZIP-1000 contract."

I followed him into a windowless room lit from above by solar panes. The clucking of the chickens grew louder as we passed into the laboratory proper. Here the birds were kept in a large enclosure, constantly monitored by overhead TV. "This one," Mintor said, leading me to a pen that held but a single chicken with its oddly curved beak. It looked no different from the others.

"Are they identified in any way? Laser tattoo, for instance?"

"Not at this stage of development. Naturally when we ship them out for space use they're tattooed."

"I see." I gazed down at the chicken, trying to read something in those hooded eyes. "It was yesterday that it crossed the highway?"

"Yes."

"Did it rain here yesterday?"

"No. We had a thunderstorm two days ago, but it passed over quickly."

"Who first noticed the chicken crossing the road?"

"Granley—one of our gate guards. He was checking security in the parking lot when he spotted it, about halfway across. By the time he called me and we got over there it was all the way to the other side."

"How did you get it back?"

"We had to tranquilize it, but that was no problem."

"I must speak to this guard, Granley."

"Follow me."

The guard was lounging near the gate. I'd noticed him when I arrived and parked my car. "This is Barnabus Rex, the scientific investigator," Mintor announced. "He has some questions for you."

"Sure," Granley replied, straightening up. "Ask away."

"Just one question, really," I said. "Why didn't you mention the car that was parked across the highway yesterday?"

"What car?"

"A parked car that probably pulled away as soon as you started after the chicken."

His eyes widened. "My God, you're right! I'd forgotten it till now! Some kids; it was painted all over stripes, like they're doing these days. But how did you know?"

"Sunbaked tire tracks in the depressions where water would collect. They told me a car had been there since your rain two days ago. Your employees use the lot here, and no visitors would park over there when they had to cross the belt highway to reach you."

"But what does it mean?" Professor Mintor demanded.

"That your mystery is solved," I said. "Let me have a tranquilizer gun and I'll show you."

I took the weapon he handed me and led the way back through the research rooms to the penned-up chickens. Without hesitation I walked up to the lone bird and tranquilized it with a single shot.

"Why did you do that?" Mintor asked.

"To answer your riddle."

"All right. Why *did* the chicken cross the road?"

"Because somebody wanted to play back the contents of a tape recorder implanted in its body. For some time now you've been spied upon, Professor Mintor—I imagine by your competitor, Beaverbrook Farms."

"Spied upon! By that—*chicken?*"

"Exactly. It seemed obvious to me from the first that the fence-pecking chicken was not one of your brood. It was much too strong and much too homesick. But if it wasn't yours it must have been added to your flock surreptitiously, and that could only have been for the purposes of industrial espionage. Since you told me Beaverbrook was doing similar work, this has to be their chicken. I think an X-ray will show a micro-miniaturized recorder for listening in on your secret conversations."

"Damnedest thing I ever heard," Professor Mintor muttered, but he issued orders to have the sleeping chicken X-rayed.

"It was a simple task for them to drop the intruding chicken over your fence at night, perhaps lassoing one of your birds and removing it so the count would be right. Those fences are all right for detecting any sort of bugging equipment, but they aren't very good at stopping ordinary intrusion—otherwise that wandering chicken would have set off alarms when it started to cut a hole there. Beaverbrook has been recording your conversations, probably trying to stay one jump ahead on the next government contract. They couldn't use a transmitter in the chicken because of your electronic fence, so they had to recover the bird itself to read out the recording. At the right time, the chicken pecked its way through the fence and started across the highway, but when the guard spotted it the waiting driver panicked and took off. The chicken was left across the road without any way to escape."

"But how did the chicken know when to escape?" asked Mintor. "Could they have some kind of electronic honing device . . . ?"

I smiled, letting the Professor's puzzlement stretch out for a moment. "That was the easiest part," I said at last. "Imprinting."

"But . . ."

"Exactly. The highly distinctive stripes on the car. The Beaverbrook people evidently trained the chicken from—ah—hatching to associate that pattern with home and food and so on."

A technician trotted up to the professor, waving a photographic negative. "The X-rays—there *was* something inside that chicken!"

"Well, Mr. Rex, you were right," the professor conceded.

"Of course, in a sense the chicken *did* cross the road to get to the other side," I admitted. "They always do."

"Have you solved many cases like this one?"

I merely smiled. "Every case is different, but they're always a challenge. I'll send you my bill in the morning—and if you ever need me again, just call."

EMPIRE STATE

KEITH MINNION

n the year of our Lord 2238 the frigate *Huguenot*, of forty-two guns and over three hundred souls, set forth from the Catskill Archipelago in search of the Empire State. I was a raw thirteen when we sailed, but of good family and certain wealth, so it was my lot (and my privilege) to hold the station of captain's cabin boy and personal yeoman. And though many years have passed between the adventure itself and this, its sorely delinquent chronicle, my memories of both its wonders and its horrors have remained with me, as sharp as the Westchester sea breezes, as fresh as the Stockbridge surf. In keeping with current custom (and a still freshly inked contract) this will not merely be a collection of log entries; even *I* would find that boring. No, this shall be a *story,* a *tale,* the manuscript of which shall be left in the care of Messrs. Dubois and Lefebre of the Lefebre Trading Company, Mohonk, our financial backers who live for the scribbled word, the totaled column, the balanced book. Indulge me, reader. And watch the boy; he may for all the good wide world be *me.*

The sounds and silences of the sailing ship filled the air even as the stars filled the evening sky. Tobe, the boy, leaned out over the frothing, phosphorescent bow wake, his hands fast in the sprit rigging, and listened: to the creaking voices of timber and plank, to the groans of rope and line, the steady rushing of the wind, and below it all, to the constant, hurrying hiss of the sea as the ship cut ponderously through it.

He was less than a shadow, all but invisible against the black and glittering waves. The woman slave and the free seaman, crouching together just forward of the fo'c's'le, could not see him and therefore spoke freely, if only in rough whispers:

". . . He'll be on you after quarters for missing that brass and the que-deck teak," said the seaman. "It's the little things that catch Hasbrouck's eye."

"But who is on *him,*" the slave named Loundes said, with some heat, "for such a little thing as getting us lost?"

Lost? Tobe's shoulders tightened; his brow creased. They couldn't be lost; not two weeks from last sight of land . . . how could they actually think the ship had lost its way? He held his breath. . . .

"He's the captain," Hawkins, the seaman, said. "He doesn't need anyone knocking *his* head, least of all the likes of you and yours."

Loundes grunted. She said, "Well, I for one am blood puked being kept from knowing what is going on. I may be bound to follow this ship to hell and back, but I still have the right to know the where and the when and the why of it. We all do."

"Slaves or freebooters," Hawkins replied, shrugging, "make no difference to Captain Hasbrouck. We all pull pay every day we sail this godforsaken ship, same as he. The Lefebre Company wants metals, and you can be sure Hasbrouck will do his damnedest to bring them back a hold full. He'll let his wardroom know the details of his plans soon enough, and then the freemen, and then you. He's just waiting for some sign to tell him he's *right.*"

"But what if we've left this 'Empire State' of his in our wake already and are now bow-on toward Spain? You've heard the stories; God knows what crawls on *those* shores." She spread her arms wide, embracing the night. "No one has ever been this far out, two weeks from our last landfall, chasing rumors and legends centuries old . . ."

Hawkins looked at her with no little amusement. "What's the

use worrying, eh? *Huguenot* was built for such a voyage. No trust in those sails of yours?"

Loundes grunted again, and spat, windward; Tobe caught a little. She turned into the new moonlight now flooding the horizon, and her cheek gleamed like wet silver. "There's a lot of sea beneath us," she said, so quietly Tobe barely heard her. "That's all."

Hawkins only nodded.

Later, with a steaming pot of turned cider in one hand and a basket of sandwiches in the other, Tobe kicked respectfully at Captain Hasbrouck's sea-cabin door. It opened immediately; golden light streamed out; the captain stood silhouetted in it, holding forth his hands, taking the basket from the boy and motioning him in. His was a small cabin, and filled to overflowing with charts, navigational tools, and other exotic devices. Still, the captain, small of frame and wiry, seemed lost in it. He looked Tobe up and down with his shrewd blue eyes, and his orange hair, on fire in the lamplight, shook its curls with his quick laughter. "So, lad," he said, "what is it they are whispering tonight?"

"The same, sir," Tobe said, filling a mug. "But this time the slave belonging to Hawkins—Loundes is her name—was complaining that we were lost." He managed to control the question in his voice, but his eyes, he knew, betrayed him.

"Ahh" was all the captain said, however. He took the mug and drank, then gestured with it to the charts at the same moment the ship took an unexpected roll. Cider on the charts, Tobe thought as he grabbed wildly for balance, but nothing spilled. The Captain winked, took another drink, then put the mug down to flatten a chart curl. "We have time for another lesson tonight, I think."

Tobe flushed with quiet excitement, and his eyes jumped to the silver, glass, and brass instruments strewn about. Which one would it be? What mysteries would the captain allow him to glimpse, however complex, however incomprehensible, however *wonderful,* this time?

Captain Hasbrouck reached for his sextant. "I think tonight we will allay your fears as to whether *Huguenot* is or isn't lost. Here," and he placed the instrument firmly into Tobe's hands, "you remember how to use this, I expect?"

"Yes, sir," Tobe whispered.

The captain laughed and clapped the boy on his back. "We shall make a pilot of you yet, lad, I think. Come, up on deck with you to shoot your stars."

"Can I—?"

"Carry the axe up yourself? Of course, lad." He held the cabin door for Tobe. "A pilot always carries his own tools. Don't forget the log, quill, and ink, now . . ."

Master Whaley, *Huguenot*'s sailing master, was on the bridge. Jumping from the ladder, the captain waved him to his ease. "Keep the deck and the con, Edward," he said. "Tonight I am only an observer."

Master Whaley noticed Tobe then, following the captain off the ladder. "Another lesson for the boy, sir?"

Hasbrouck nodded. "One can never get too much celestial navigation, I think. What stars do you have for us tonight, Edward? We require only three."

Master Whaley duly pointed them out, and Tobe set to his task. He checked each sight and reading several times before he felt comfortable enough to attempt the final set he would use. Captain Hasbrouck watched him in the darkness, smiling slightly.

I wonder, Tobe thought, feeling the captain's eyes on him, does he see himself in me? Does he see the cabin boy he once was, wishing to be a pilot, hoping someday to be commander of his own ship? Tobe redoubled his concentration, determined to be perfect, determined to make the captain proud of him. Someday, he thought, I too shall have a ship. Someday I too will lead great adventures. Someday.

"Soundings are erratic, sir," Master Whaley was saying. "Rough bottom as well; we lost three lines today alone."

"I know." The captain turned to look forward. "We are close, I think," he said.

Tobe's heart skipped, and he almost missed a sighting. He took in a long breath and regripped the sextant.

"You don't need to hear it from me, sir, I'm sure," Whaley said, "but I've noticed a general feeling of uneasiness among the slaves this past week. Ours are an excitable lot, as a rule. And most of them have never sailed beyond sight of land."

"And lucky they are," the captain replied, "to have the opportunity! Damn *squids;* lucky they are to be here at *all,* eh, Edward?"

"To be sure, sir."

"Have you your figures yet, lad?"

Tobe laid aside his quill. "Yes, sir; I've just noted them down."

"Good. Let's go below and plot them, then."

As he passed the sailing master, Hasbrouck said, "Tomorrow," and Tobe's heart skipped once more. Tomorrow . . .

He found Deb still awake in his rack.

Her eyes, bright in the shuttered lamp he carried, blinked widely. Tobe extinguished the flame and slid in next to her warmth.

"Another lesson?"

He kissed her. "Celestial navigation."

She kissed him back. "Sounds religious."

"It's fun . . . like *this.*"

She gasped. "Hey, I'm not ready yet. . . ."

Regardless, he slid into her warmth, and covered her protest with another kiss.

Presently, he whispered, "It's tomorrow, I think."

Deb yawned, and snuggled close. "What are you babbling about?"

"The captain told Master Whaley 'tomorrow.' "

"Tomorrow what?"

"Just 'tomorrow.' But I know what he meant."

"And . . . ?"

"Can't you guess?"

"Listen, yeoman, I don't hob with the commanding officer of this tub every waking moment, like you; we slaves scrub decks; see?" And she held up hands he couldn't see in the darkness. He grabbed for them anyway, put them around his neck, and they lay together quietly for a moment.

"The Empire State," he said then. "He was talking about the Empire State. We must be arriving tomorrow."

"Let's just say we'd *better* arrive tomorrow. The senior squids have been talking seriously about desertion, you know. Or if not that, maybe even mutiny."

Tobe stifled a laugh. "Mutiny? How?"

"You think they'd tell me? Everybody on *Huguenot* knows who I sleep with."

"They should all be so lucky—"

She punched his arm. "Really, Tobe, I've never heard talk this bad before. The captain should listen to the protests, not brush them aside. We slaves make up nearly a third of the crew, after all."

"But you're . . . they're *squids*!"

She punched him again. "Goodnight, little boy," she hissed, and turned over.

"Hey, wait a—"

"Doors are closed, Tobe. See you second watch."

Tobe scowled a little, but left her alone. In the dark and pitching night his thoughts turned back to visions of the Empire State . . . and these led him quickly to the stairs of sleep, where his visions just as quickly became dreams . . .

The bells for colors the next evening were still echoing through the passageways when there was a firm rap on Captain Hasbrouck's door.

The captain didn't even look up from his meal. "See who it is, lad," he said, his mouth full.

Tobe opened it a crack and saw three slaves, one female, two male, standing at attention beyond. The increasingly heavy seas that *Huguenot* had been meeting throughout the day caused the two men to lose their balance and grab the bulkhead for support, but the third stepped defiantly forward. Tobe saw then that it was Loundes.

He glanced back. "Sir?"

"For Christ's sake," the captain cried, spraying food, "first this damn storm coming and now *squids*!" He shoved his plate away. "How many, then?"

"Three, sir."

"Well, I only have the stomach for one. Bring her forward and —*damn these seas*!" for at that moment his mug had tipped and spilled hot cider into his crotch.

Loundes was in the cabin before Tobe could stop her, however, and came to attention again in front of the captain's table. Wiping his pants with the tablecloth, Captain Hasbrouck glanced up once, then continued cleaning himself.

The slave, staring, was silent.

"And what is your pleasure tonight?" the captain demanded finally, throwing aside the cloth and bringing both fists down on the table.

The ship rolled and Loundes stumbled, but did not fall; she regained her balance even as the ship did, and said, "I represent the eighty-three servile landsmen and landswomen of *Huguenot*'s crew, and—"

"Sir," Tobe prompted.

"—and I would like to—"

"Of *Huguenot*'s crew, *sir,*" Tobe repeated.

The slave flushed; the captain smiled; Tobe grinned behind his hand.

"Very well," Loundes said, *"sir.* As spokeswoman for one third of the crew I have come, *sir,* to ask some important questions."

There was faraway thunder, then, gently tearing the night.

"Well, be quick about it," the captain said. "This damned storm will be upon us sooner than I'd feared."

"First and foremost, *sir,* we want to know when we will reach the Empire State."

Captain Hasbrouck stood, went to the cabin's only hull port, and looked out. "All too soon," he replied, and gestured outside. "Weather permitting, of course."

"With all due respect, *sir,* we've been given evasive answers like that for the past week. I would hate to return to the others with nothing more than that to—"

A blue-white glare momentarily silhouetted the captain against the port glass, then a great peal of thunder sounded, shivering the very timbers of the ship. *Huguenot* took a particularly long and sickening roll at that moment and all three in the cabin lost their footing and ended up in a tangle against the hull bulkhead.

"Madam," Captain Hasbrouck said, extricating himself, "this meeting, however brief, however unfulfilling, must now come to an end. It seems I have a storm that begs my undivided attention. Tobe, escort her below."

"But—" Loundes began again.

"Enough."

The two matched glares for a moment, eye to eye, then Loundes cursed and looked away.

The captain brushed past her. "Tobe," he said over his shoulder as he exited, "the bridge, five minutes," and stumbled headlong into the two slaves still waiting in the passageway. "God *damn* these squids!" he roared, and then was gone.

It took only those scant five minutes for the storm to hit in force. When Tobe emerged topside the rain immediately and completely drenched him; the wind, shrieking, grabbed at him with great and powerful hands, threatening to toss him into the ragged darkness. Tobe shielded his eyes and looked wildly about, and saw the captain at the port rail. He was shouting orders to the seamen and slaves aloft in the rigging as they attempted to clear the remaining canvas.

Tobe struggled through the lashing sheets of rain and frothing sea spray to a secure position at the railing close enough to the captain to hear any order given. Hasbrouck gave him a wink in welcome, spat out a mouthful of seawater, and gestured to the heart of the storm.

Tobe looked, but saw the sky and sea in mingled blackness only, at once mere inches, then unaccountable miles, it seemed, from the ship. Then lightning flashed and the sky lifted into rolling, roiling, snakelike cloud banks, and standing against the glare of the lightning bolt Tobe saw a massive island rising sheer from the crashing seas.

"THERE!" the captain cried, above the screaming wind and deafening thunderclap.

Darkness again rushed the ship, drowning it once more, but the lightning's afterimage remained before Tobe, burning brightly. "The Empire State," he whispered, his voice charged with sudden incredulous wonder. *The Empire State. . . .*

Those of the crew who had missed the sight of it at the previous flash certainly saw it at the next, for now the island was twice as large, twice as tall, twice as ominous. . . .

"By God," Tobe heard on the wind, "it's a *building!*"

Another lightning flash, and its thunderclap ripped the air. Now all could see that this "island" before them was indeed a man-made structure, a huge and terribly old building, or at least the topmost portion of one, standing alone against the stormy sea. Hundreds of empty windows gaped at the crew, limned in green slime, before darkness once again plunged the structure into obscurity and deadly proximity.

The captain leaped to the helm. "Hard to port, Master Whaley! Hard over!" Both he and the sailing master put their weight to the wheel, and *Huguenot,* protesting mightily, slowly came about.

The Empire State Building moved past with nightmarish slowness, but the ship cleared it with no damage.

"Dear Christ!" the captain shouted then. "There's another!"

It was indeed another wreck of a building, rising up from the furious sea, another obstacle for the ship, however slowly, to dance around. And beyond that building, emerging from the rain like wraiths, were still more buildings. . . .

New orders were shouted to the crew in the rigging; more sail was cleared; *Huguenot* came about once more, this time heeling to such a degree that Tobe's only choices were to marry the railing or drop into the black waves. He chose the former.

Taking a wave head-on he swallowed a bellyful of seawater, then promptly heaved both it and his supper. The next wave cleaned his clothes, but not his pride. *Children* do this, he thought wretchedly, little *boys,* not *him.* Still, he vomited again.

Hasbrouck noticed the condition of his seasick yeoman and promptly ordered him below.

"But, sir, I—"

"BELOW!"

Tobe went.

Deb, he found, had preceded him. She lay shivering in his rack, thoroughly soaked, and seasick herself. Seeing her condition only made Tobe more disgusted with his own. He flung his clothes under the rack and crawled in with her; they clung together and shared what little warmth the wind and sea had not already robbed from them.

Tobe wanted desperately to share his misery, his shame, but found he could not. The shame of disgracing himself in front of the captain was too much to admit to a *woman;* it was enough to leave him silent.

Deb said only, "Can you sleep?"

He found, only after some time, that he finally could.

*   *   *

The news that the Empire State was inhabited spread quickly through the crew. In the clearing dawn mists, tier after tier of soldiers were revealed, as well as other figures crossing spidery bridges between exposed sections of the massive ancient building. The majority of the inhabitants, however, could be seen leaning out of the hundreds of windows overlooking *Huguenot,* apparently as curious as the crew.

At midmorning Tobe saw a boat with six oarsmen round the building's western corner. Captain Hasbrouck saw it, too, and climbed to the bridge to watch its approach.

After some minutes the boat stationed itself within hailing distance, and two figures in colorful dress stood, easily riding the swells, and raised hands in greeting.

The captain crossed his arms; the crew, taking the hint, was silent.

"Shall I have a boat lowered to meet them?" Master Whaley asked, after a moment.

Hasbrouck shook his head calmly. "Let's wait," he said.

More minutes passed, and Tobe found himself acutely aware of just how heavy the silence was; the rising tension was almost palpable; he wanted to *do* something, *anything.* . . .

Enough, he told himself then; you have shamed yourself enough for one voyage. Bide; *learn* from this. The captain will know what to do.

After several minutes had gone by one of the persons standing in the boat called out, "Hail!"

The captain leaned out on the railing. "I'm listening!" He bellowed back.

"Will you parley?"

Hasbrouck hesitated, glanced at Master Whaley who shrugged. "Where?" He replied finally.

"At your convenience, sir!"

"Convenience," the captain murmured, smiling slightly. "We'll see." He raised his voice again. "Come ahead!," and turned to Tobe. "Meet the master-at-arms at the accom ladder and have the two of them brought to the wardroom. Tell the jailer I want the rest kept topside. Understood?"

"Yes, sir."

"Then make it so. Master Whaley? You're relieved; I'll need you below. Mr. Walkill? You have the deck." With one final, calculating look to the approaching boat, Captain Hasbrouck left the bridge.

Tobe entered the wardroom after knocking. The captain, seated before the stern ports, looked up and winked.

"We have them in the passageway, sir," the boy said.

"Is the master-at-arms with you, lad?"

"Yes, sir."

"Jailer!"

The warrant officer leaned in past the door. "Sir?"

"Stand easy in the p-way, will you? And send in our envoys."

"Yes, sir."

The door opened fully; Tobe stepped out of the way as the representatives from the Empire State swept through. The otherwise utilitarian wardroom was instantly transformed by their gaudy robes and heavy perfumes. Tobe blinked; this was his first real chance to observe them fully; he blinked again, and then realized that his mouth was open.

Both Captain Hasbrouck and Master Whaley rose, their own faces impassive, but Tobe was certain that they, too, were surprised. Though perhaps surprised, he thought, was too mild a word.

Both of the representatives wore heavy, elaborate, painstakingly feminine makeup. Like harlots.

And one of them was even a woman.

Women were forbidden access to the wardroom.

The woman said, "We are agents for the director, sir."

The captain, of course, ignored her. He spoke instead to the man. "My name is Sammael Hasbrouck, captain of the free ship *Huguenot,* from the island of Mohonk in the Catskill Archipelago. We have come to open a trade route, mutually agreeable to—"

"Captain," the woman interrupted, "I am the representative of the Skyscraper. All initial communications must be with me."

Tobe's mouth dropped open again. She had actually dared to interrupt? And the impertinence!

The captain, however, only frowned. "Must *she* do all the talking?" he asked of the male representative.

The man smiled, and shrugged. "She's my superior," he said.

In a corner now, Tobe cringed; the master-at-arms peeked his head into the compartment again, but Hasbrouck waved him back out. "Take over, Edward," he whispered to the sailing master at his side. "I suddenly have no stomach for this; my next words to these . . . people . . . I will certainly regret."

Master Whaley nodded, his face a perfect mask, and said, "As our captain just mentioned, ma'am, we have come on a mission of peace from an island group to the north and west of your—" He groped momentarily for the term she had used.

"It's the Skyscraper," the woman said, with no small note of pride. "And the Skyscraper is part of the City."

Master Whaley bowed his head slightly, and continued. "We have come to the Skyscraper in hopes of establishing a mutually profitable trade agreement. We are not an official diplomatic mission, of course, but merely agents for a trading company whose sole purpose is to find—"

"Clients," the woman said. "It is a concept and practice we are familiar with. We trade with many lands, many nations. There is much that we require, but also much that we offer."

"Excellent. Might a delegation of no more than six men be welcome to parley with your leaders, ma'am?"

"Certainly." And the woman smiled. "I will arrange it. Does tomorrow noon suit you?"

Master Whaley turned to the captain. "Sir . . . ?"

"Fine," Hasbrouck said, tightly. "Fine. Our master-at-arms will show you back to your boat. Tobe?" And he gestured stiffly toward the door.

The two envoys rose, then bowed deeply. "It has been a pleasure, sir," the woman said.

Hasbrouck only nodded.

After he had delivered the envoys to the master-at-arms in the passageway and had closed the wardroom door behind him, Tobe could still hear the captain exclaiming, ". . . and open the ports, by God, I'm *gagging* from their stench!"

*   *   *

Deb dropped out of a passing work party and cornered Tobe at the weather deck rail. "They say the captain practically kicked the envoys off the ship," she whispered, glancing around.

Tobe glanced too. "One of them was a *woman*," he whispered back.

Deb whistled. "In the wardroom? So it's *true*," and she grinned broadly.

Over Tobe's shoulder the Empire State Building was blue and mute in the afternoon haze. She looked at it for a long moment, her grin lingering. Tobe found he didn't like what he saw in her eyes. "You'd better follow your working party," he said. "I can't bail you out with the mates every time, you know."

Her grin softened, and she touched his cheek gently, then, "See you!" and she was gone.

Tobe turned to look at the building himself. Things must be very different there, he thought. Different, certainly, and maybe dangerously so. A sudden shiver of nervous dread went through him, and he wondered: *What is going to happen next?*

That night he awoke only slightly when Deb left his rack. "Wha—" he said, blinking in the darkness.

"Shhh, I'm only going to pee," she said, and stepped out into the passageway.

Tobe next awoke to the clamoring of the ship's bell. In the dawn light, swinging to his feet, he realized he was still alone in his rack; Deb, apparently, had never returned.

As he pulled on his clothes a seaman ran by his compartment. "The squids deserted ship last night," he panted, and continued on his way. Impossible, Tobe thought. They'd be crazy to—

"Christ," he muttered, "where the hell is Deb?"

The captain's cabin was empty. Tobe ran next to the bridge, where he found Hasbrouck by the wheel, surrounded by his officers. ". . . but just how many are actually gone?" he was demanding.

The master-at-arms spread his hands. "Fifty at least," he said, "maybe more. It's most of the female slaves and some of the male ones as well. We'll have to muster the lot of them to get an accurate count."

The burly deck officer said, "I can count the bitching squids I have left on one hand." He spat toward the railing. "Better they all went, if you were asking me."

"Perhaps, William," Captain Hasbrouck said, "perhaps someday I shall."

Uneasy, lifeless laughter. Then the master-at-arms spoke again. "We know they went over the side within an hour after the four-to-eight watch turnover. No later than five. And they swam rather than wake us all by lowering boats. Still, we had two men on anchor watch, one on stern watch, ten Marines patrolling, one duty cook, and two here on the bridge."

"And all of them," broke in the master corpsman, "are in sickbay with bashed skulls. I expect to lose a few by noon."

"So this desertion," the captain said, "was well planned. Obviously. Hell, I slept through it like a baby, as did you all."

"Damn squids," said the deck officer. "Sneaky as cats."

Then the captain noticed Tobe. "Ah, lad, go warn the galley. The wardroom, gentlemen? First a plan, then a full stomach, and then we *act.*"

The thunder of several cannon—short and wide, but eloquent—still echoed in Tobe's ears as the whaleboat was lowered into the water. Captain Hasbrouck's parting instructions echoed there as well: "Take copious notes; remember everything; I want to know what they think as much as what they say. I'm counting on you, lad."

Master Whaley, leading the whaleboat crew, favored Tobe with a smile. "Nervous?"

Tobe shook his head importantly, then looked out across the waves to the Empire State Building. He gestured to it. "I have a score to settle."

"Hah. Don't we all."

The coxswain loosed the stern line. "Clear!" he called, and they were away.

With every slow, steady oarsbeat the Empire State loomed. Tobe took in every window, every stone, every rusted girder and metal panel. Never in his brief life among the islands of the Catskills had he seen anything so huge, so ancient, so alien. All of *this* world lay under the sea, buried in the ooze of the past. Yet . . .

Master Whaley ordered the oars pulled in when they reached hailing distance. Hundreds of inhabitants crowded every available vantage point. Tobe, his heart racing, strained to make out individual faces. Where were they? he thought. Where is *she*?

The sailing master raised his megaphone. "I wish to speak with someone in charge!"

"Green light!" came the reply, floating across the water on a breeze.

"That means 'go,' " said someone from the stern.

"Are you certain, Mr. Hawkins?"

The seaman nodded. "Something my old Dad told me once. Old talk."

Master Whaley raised his megaphone once more. "We will come ahead, then!" And aside, to the boat crew, "Into the jaws, gentlemen, steady as she goes."

They rowed unopposed toward a large, rough maw cut into the side of the building. As they neared it Tobe could hear the echoing crash of the sea swells riding one after the other into the cavernous darkness. Going to their death, he thought. And then: As we are?

Above them, as if in answer, the soldiers of the Empire State manning the lower windows and walls lowered their bows and spears, and sheathed their swords.

After Tobe's eyes became accustomed to the dark of the enclosed harbor he looked about, almost frantic to take it all in. He saw numerous stone buttresses on all sides topped by ledges and balconies of all sizes, and punctuated by shadowed arches leading into the bowels of the building. And on every balcony and ledge, at every archway he saw more people, talking, gesturing, regarding them as though they were little animals caught in a firmly sprung trap.

A gaily dressed group standing at the end of a quay that extended almost to the center of the enclosed harbor raised their arms, and the population quieted. The continued steady rush of the sea through the entrance and against the pilings of the quay was the only sound until Master Whaley spoke.

"We come in peace," he said in a voice loud and clear enough for all to hear.

A woman with long, golden hair replied, "That is most wise, sir."

Whaley smiled. "Can you tell me the condition of my fellow crewmembers?"

"They are well."

"May I speak with them?"

The woman turned to the others and spoke quietly, then she turned back and shook her head. "It is not possible, sir."

Hawkins grumbled something that Tobe missed, but Master Whaley heard it and silenced him with a look.

"Our captain cannot deal in good faith," he said to the woman, "until the question at hand is resolved. We must have our crewmembers back."

"Your crew came to us freely," the woman said, choosing her words carefully, "just as you have."

"Their act of desertion was unlawful. Surely, madam, you can understand our position."

The group on the quay conferred again, and then the woman said, "We understand your position and we sympathize, if only in principle. We must, however, ask that you understand our position as well. Anyone who comes to us with good intentions from any vessel, from any nation, is welcome in the Skyscraper, or in our sister buildings of the City. The bloodlines must remain clear, and without new citizens it cannot."

Master Whaley made to speak, but the woman continued, "It is our wish that you leave the City. Much can be avoided by your swift and peaceful departure."

"We cannot leave with our questions unanswered. We require a guarantee that our people are alive and well." Master Whaley's voice exposed a sharp edge. "We need to know that it is their wish that we leave, and that they stay."

The woman turned again to her companions. Their conversation was animated, and lasted several minutes. Then the woman said, "We do not condone violence, sir."

"And neither do we," Master Whaley replied immediately.

"We have . . . heard differently."

"You have only heard one side. Allow us to moor and we can both decide what is true and what is not."

The woman gazed at Master Whaley for a long moment. Then she said, "With you they were slaves. Here, they are free. This meeting is ended. I wish you fair seas, sir. Goodbye."

They turned as one and left the quay. Tobe watched them walk through an arch and disappear in the darkness there. Then he looked about, searching again for a familiar face in the crowds around them before turning to the sailing master. "Is it over?" he asked. "Is this all?"

Whaley shook his head, his expression somber. "It is far from over, lad." He also looked about, taking in the hundreds of people still watching them from the walls. "Far from over," he said again. Then he looked out to where *Huguenot* rode at anchor, and his eyes blazed. "And the first thing we must do is tell the captain."

"What kind of defenses can they have? Spears? Flaming arrows?" Captain Hasbrouck paced furiously, hands clasped behind his back, his scowling face downcast.

"We saw only bows, spears, and swords," Master Whaley said. "And ceremonial ones at that."

"They can't have the powder for cannon, sir," contributed Master Eyck, the gunnery officer. "Catapults, maybe, but no serious firepower. Their limited range will cripple them."

"*We* will cripple them, gunner," the captain said. "We will make them wish we never popped over their cozy little horizon in the first place." He looked out a port to the Empire State, now a respectful distance away, and studied it through squinted eyes.

Tobe, from a corner, spoke up. "Sir?"

Hasbrouck turned. "Yes, lad?"

"You plan to bombard them?"

"I plan to *destroy* them."

"But what about . . . what about the people?"

The captain grinned coldly. "Hopefully we will murder the lot of them, eh, gunner?"

"Yes, sir," replied Eyck. "My boys are primed."

"We'll run port side first with full broadsides from both decks to show them at the outset what *Huguenot* is capable—"

"But, sir!" Tobe interrupted, his eyes wide, his mind in turmoil. "Do they have to die? Can't we, can't we—"

The deck officer cuffed him. "Is our little squid losing his nerve *before* the damned battle? Save it, lad, for when a sword aims to shove down your throat. Then you've my permission to crap your pants."

The wardroom erupted in hearty laughter, and Tobe's protests were drowned out. He fled the compartment red-faced and ashamed, but angry as well. He ran until he found himself on the weatherdeck so far forward that the jib rigging snagged him. One more step and the gray ocean crested, ready to swallow him whole with the commonest of ripples.

He couldn't get an image of Deb out of his mind, an image of her cut and bleeding, lying in a tumbled, grotesque heap. And standing over her, laughing as he sheathed his bloody sword, was Captain Hasbrouck. . . .

The words rang out again: ". . . We'll make them wish we never came . . . we'll murder the lot of them. . . ."

And with that a brand new feeling surfaced within him, a feeling so new that he gasped as though struck: "I'll *hate you*!" He screamed into the wind. "I'll hate you *forever*!"

And he knew in his heart that he would.

One hour before sunset, *Huguenot* attacked.

Because of the crew shortage Tobe was assigned to one of the ammo gangs bringing the smooth round stones up from the ballast voids. He had to work furiously to keep pace with the men on either side of him as broadside after broadside thundered from the ship. He didn't have time to think, to despair at what was happening, nor to be angry about it. There was only the stones, and the rhythm, and the death being dealt above.

Huguenot made three passes, successful ones judging from the cheers of the crew manning the cannon. Their jubilance infected the crew below; the ammo gangs began a victory chanty in time with their labor, loud, strong and bawdy. Tobe found himself singing along with the rest, caught in the moment, forgetting in the new, raw thrill of it where the stones he was passing up were being shot, and who lay in their terrible path. *I am the killer*, said his hands as they gripped a stone and passed it on. *I am the killer, I am the killer. . . .*

His momentary exhilaration turned just as quickly to horror and disgust, but he was caught fast in the rhythm, the breath of death as he fed it, stone by stone. *I am the killer, I am the killer. . . .*

On the fourth pass someone yelled down, "The cowards are finally returning fire!"

With what, Tobe wondered miserably. He imagined their little spears and arrows slicing into the sea, hopelessly and ludicrously short of their mark. Take a lesson from the *real* killers, you poor people, he thought; look closely and see how it is done. . . .

Suddenly he was aware of a different note in the cheering above; cries of concern were beginning to mingle in, then gain in numbers. Then a voice above the rest shrieked, *"They're GODDAMN WHALES!"*

The ship lurched as something massive collided with it. Tobe was flung off his feet and sent sprawling into a ladder well. Several others piled in after him, cursing, thrashing about; Tobe could smell their fear, and he crouched at the bottom of the well until they extricated themselves. This has to stop, he thought, his anger feeding on panic and blossoming into rage. This is madness, madness. . . .

When he saw his opportunity to get out himself he took it, running up through the confused, shouting crowds of ammo handlers to find the source of the madness; he went to find his captain.

He found instead a weatherdeck awash with soldiers of the Empire State. They all wore scarlet, and they swung huge curved swords. The ship's Marines met them blade to blade, and blood flew as freely as rain.

Tobe grabbed a barrel cover for a shield and ran aft. "This has to stop!" he yelled through the din of battle. "This has to stop!" He saw the sea full of pilot whales and dolphins; some were saddled and harnessed; indeed, there were still soldiers riding in, leaping from their mounts and swarming up the side of the ship to reinforce the soldiers already on board.

More than once the barrel cover took a shove or a sword blow, but Tobe, perhaps because he was young, perhaps because he held no weapon, or perhaps simply because he ducked and dodged at all the proper moments, made it alive to the aft topdeck where, shielded by his personal marine guard, Captain Hasbrouck was about to dispatch one of the scarlet soldiers lying at his feet.

"Ah, lad!" Hasbrouck motioned him into the relative safety behind the marine. "Come watch a slave die!"

Tobe looked down and saw that the soldier was Loundes, the deserter.

"I could have killed you in your sleep, captain," she said, defiant even in defeat. "I could have cut your balls off, but I didn't."

Hasbrouck pointed his sword at her belly, at Seaman Hawkins's brand there. "For that possibility, bitch," he said, "I grant you a clean thrust." And he ran her through. "But nothing more." He pulled his blade free, and blood cascaded from her mouth. She jerked twice, then was still.

"Make a note, lad," the captain said, "to buy Hawkins another when we return home."

With a cry of uncontrollable fury Tobe flung himself at Hasbrouck, striking at him, kicking, scratching and screaming. Taken completely by surprise, Hasbrouck fell back to the stern railing, his sword caught between them. Just as the Marine began to react the two tumbled over the railing and into the shadow of the air between the ship and the sea. And before they hit the water Tobe grasped the swordblade in both hands and thrust it up under his captain's chin, burying it in his brain.

"*There!*" he cried, "*there!*" as he tumbled into the sea. *There* . . . as the cool bitter water enveloped him . . . you bastard . . . and finally, as he lost consciousness . . . oh God, what have I done? . . .

The blinding white light that he saw when he first opened his eyes took several moments to resolve itself into a window. The view through it came next: of a clear morning sky over a calm blue sea . . . and of a three-masted frigate riding at anchor, swinging with the current. After several more moments he realized it was *Huguenot.*

"Tobe?"

He turned his eyes away from the brightness and focused them on a person seated beside his bed. "Deb . . ." he whispered, the word grating on a sore, raw throat.

She leaned over him, put her hand to his forehead, then touched his cheek with her lips.

"Where are we?" He asked. "Where—?"

"In the Empire State, only they call it the Skyscraper here. One of the Sea Riders fished you out of the water and brought you to safety. How do you feel?"

"Tired," he said, "very tired. And sore." His palms, too, were throbbing, and itching terribly. He raised his hands only with effort, and found that both of them were bandaged.

"They say you were cut deeply, probably by grabbing a sword. Do you remember?"

Tobe did, then, in a rush of memories, and a soft groan escaped his lips. "I . . . killed someone."

Deb's eyes widened. "Who? One of the soldiers?"

He shook his head. She really didn't know. And if she didn't, perhaps no one did. Perhaps any witnesses were as dead as . . . *he* was. Could this be justice? He wondered. "It doesn't matter," he said. "The battle . . . it's over?"

She nodded. "You've been bedridden for nearly a week; your fever only broke last night. Tobe, I thought you were going to die, too . . . I thought I was going to lose you."

He looked at her. "Then why did you go, that night?"

She hung her head.

He touched her arm with a bandaged hand. "Who is dead?"

Looking up again, but not at him, she wiped a streak of tears away. "All of the marines; they fought to the last man, as usual. And nearly half of the remaining crew, including the captain, though his body was never found. And Loundes—"

"I know; I saw her die."

"Bravely?"

"Yes, and quickly. But what of Master Whaley?"

"Alive. I saw him only yesterday, at the conclusion of the negotiations. He commands *Huguenot* now."

"There is peace, then?"

She nodded. "The ship departs soon. You . . . are to go back with them."

Tobe knew that that was how it must be. A tear of his own welled up, hesitated, but in the end did not fall. "When?"

Deb rose. "When you say you are strong enough. When you feel up to it." She ran her hand through his hair. "You rest, now. You'll need all of your strength. . . ."

At the door she suddenly turned back. "You don't have to go back with them, you know. You can stay if you want to."

He shook his head slowly. "I have to go, Deb. That part of me hasn't changed, even after all of this. You could come back, too, if you want."

She managed a shadow of a smile. "I'm not as brave as Loundes," she said.

He smiled too. "Oh, yes you are."

"Something," she said, "keeps telling me that we will be together, somehow, sometime." She opened the door. "I will probably wait for you, Tobe," she said, and then closed the door behind her.

On either side of the ship the sea parted, and the mottled backs of two sperm whales breached. From the bridge Tobe heard them spit and gasp, and their plumes hung in the air like smoke.

"Our escorts," Master Whaley murmured.

Tobe said nothing.

It was a gray day, and the sea was the color of slate, meeting the sky blurrily in veils of mist and fog. In their wake the Empire State was already lost to view.

The sailing master looked at the boy. "You have done a little growing up on this voyage," he said.

"A bit," Tobe agreed bitterly.

Master Whaley nodded slowly. "I think," he said then, "we should be frank with one another. Ever since your return you have been wearing your feelings on your sleeve. That can be a very dangerous thing to do, these days."

Tobe glanced up. "What do you mean?"

The sailing master drew him close, and whispered, "Listen to me; if nothing else, hear this: hate him if you need to; hate him with everything that is in you, but never let anyone see your hatred; never let anyone else know." He winked solemnly. "If you let it show here, now, you can count the days till you are a meal for the trailing sharks, and believe me, no one will notice you are gone."

Tobe hesitated, then said, "Do you hate him, Master Whaley?"

"Ahh." The sailing master stood away from the railing. "That would be telling." He put his hand on Tobe's shoulder. "Now off with you. Scrub that look from your face and *mourn your captain.* He is the hero of this godforsaken adventure, after all."

He winked again, and Tobe, after a moment, winked back.

It was a long, a very long, voyage home.

My hand is now cramped, reader, my pile of paper used, and my pot of ink nearly dry. This story, no—this prologue to the true story yet to be, is now complete. My mind is clear; I am, I think, ready.

My yeoman promises fair winds tomorrow. She is young and eager to please; she treats me with bemused, yet I suspect genuine, respect. She will make a fine captain someday.

Of her respect I only hope I am worthy, for on the morning tide we sail for the Empire State.

Aye, reader; old Captain Hasbrouck has lain rotting in his sea grave these past twenty years, with his legends and his prejudices gone with him. Times have changed, and I am captain now.

"I will probably wait for you," Deb said.

I only pray she has.

PROFESSION

ISAAC ASIMOV

George Platen could not conceal the longing in his voice. It was too much to suppress. He said, "Tomorrow's the first of May. Olympics!"

He rolled over on his stomach and peered over the foot of his bed at his roommate. Didn't he feel it, too? Didn't *this* make some impression on him?

George's face was thin and had grown a trifle thinner in the nearly year and a half that he had been at the House. His figure was slight but the look in his blue eyes was as intense as it had ever been, and right now there was a trapped look in the way his fingers curled against the bedspread.

George's roommate looked up briefly from his book and took the opportunity to adjust the light-level of the stretch of wall near his chair. His name was Hali Omani and he was a Nigerian by birth. His dark brown skin and massive features seemed made for calmness, and mention of the Olympics did not move him.

He said, "I know, George."

George owed much to Hali's patience and kindness when it was needed, but even patience and kindness could be overdone. Was this a time to sit there like a statue built of some dark, warm wood?

George wondered if he himself would grow like that after ten years here and rejected the thought violently. No!

He said defiantly, "I think you've forgotten what May means."

The other said, "I remember very well what it means. It means nothing! You're the one who's forgotten that. May means nothing to you, George Platen, and," he added softly, "it means nothing to me, Hali Omani."

George said, "The ships are coming in for recruits. By June, thousands and thousands will leave with millions of men and women heading for any world you can name, and all that means nothing?"

"Less than nothing. What do you want me to do about it, anyway?" Omani ran his finger along a difficult passage in the book he was reading and his lips moved soundlessly.

George watched him. Damn it, he thought, yell, scream; you can do that much. Kick at me, do anything.

It was only that he wanted not to be so alone in his anger. He wanted not to be the only one so filled with resentment, not to be the only one dying a slow death.

It was better those first weeks when the Universe was a small shell of vague light and sound pressing down upon him. It was better before Omani had wavered into view and dragged him back to a life that wasn't worth living.

Omani! He was old! He was at least thirty. George thought: Will I be like that at thirty? Will I be like that in twelve years?

And because he was afraid he might be, he yelled at Omani, "Will you stop reading that fool book?"

Omani turned a page and read on a few words, then lifted his head with its skullcap of crisply curled hair and said, "What?"

"What good does it do you to read the book?" He stepped forward, snorted "More electronics," and slapped it out of Omani's hands.

Omani got up slowly and picked up the book. He smoothed a crumpled page without visible rancor. "Call it the satisfaction of curiosity," he said. "I understand a little of it today, perhaps a little more tomorrow. That's a victory in a way."

"A victory. What kind of a victory? Is that what satisfies you in life? To get to know enough to be a quarter of a Registered Electronician by the time you're sixty-five?"

"Perhaps by the time I'm thirty-five."

"And then who'll want you? Who'll use you? Where will you go?"

"No one. No one. Nowhere. I'll stay here and read other books."

"And that satisfies you? Tell me! You've dragged me to class. You've got me to reading and memorizing, too. For what? There's nothing in it that satisfies me."

"What good will it do you to deny yourself satisfaction?"

"It means I'll quit the whole farce. I'll do as I planned to do in the beginning before you dovey-lovied me out of it. I'm going to force them to—to—"

Omani put down his book. He let the other run down and then said, "To what, George?"

"To correct a miscarriage of justice. A frame-up. I'll get that Antonelli and force him to admit he—he—"

Omani shook his head. "Everyone who comes here insists it's a mistake. I thought you'd passed that stage."

"Don't call it a stage," said George violently. "In my case, it's a fact. I've told you—"

"You've told me, but in your heart you know no one made any mistake as far as you were concerned."

"Because no one will admit it? You think any of them would admit a mistake unless they were forced to?—Well, I'll force them."

It was May that was doing this to George; it was Olympics month. He felt it bring the old wildness back and he couldn't stop it. He didn't want to stop it. He had been in danger of forgetting.

He said, "I was going to be a Computer Programmer and I *can* be one. I could be one today, regardless of what they say analysis shows." He pounded his mattress. "They're wrong. They *must* be."

"The analysts are never wrong."

"They *must* be. Do you doubt my intelligence?"

"Intelligence hasn't one thing to do with it. Haven't you been told that often enough? Can't you understand that?"

George rolled away, lay on his back, and stared somberly at the ceiling.

"What did you want to be, Hali?"

"I had no fixed plans. Hydroponicist would have suited me, I suppose."

"Did you think you could make it?"

"I wasn't sure."

George had never asked personal questions of Omani before. It struck him as queer, almost unnatural, that other people had had ambitions and ended here. Hydroponicist!

He said, "Did you think you'd make *this*?"

"No, but here I am just the same."

"And you're satisfied. Really, really satisfied. You're happy. You love it. You wouldn't be anywhere else."

Slowly, Omani got to his feet. Carefully, he began to unmake his bed. He said, "George, you're a hard case. You're knocking yourself out because you won't accept the facts about yourself. George, you're here in what you call the House, but I've never heard you give it its full title. Say it, George, say it. Then go to bed and sleep this off."

George gritted his teeth and showed them. He choked out, "No!"

"Then I will," said Omani, and he did. He shaped each syllable carefully.

George was bitterly ashamed at the sound of it. He turned his head away.

For most of the first eighteen years of his life, George Platen had headed firmly in one direction, that of Registered Computer Programmer. There were those in his crowd who spoke wisely of Spationautics, Refrigeration Technology, Transportation Control, and even Administration. But George held firm.

He argued relative merits as vigorously as any of them, and why not? Education Day loomed ahead of them and was the great fact of their existence. It approached steadily, as fixed and certain as the calendar—the first day of November of the year following one's eighteenth birthday.

After that day, there were other topics of conversation. One could discuss with others some detail of the profession, or the virtues of one's wife and children, or the fate of one's space-polo team, or one's experiences in the Olympics. Before Education Day, how-

ever, there was only one topic that unfailingly and unwearyingly
held everyone's interest, and that was Education Day.

"What are you going for? Think you'll make it? Heck, that's no
good. Look at the records; quota's been cut. Logistics, now—"

Or Hypermechanics, now— Or Communications, now— Or
Gravitics, now—

Especially Gravitics at the moment. Everyone had been talking
about Gravitics in the few years just before George's Education Day
because of the development of the Gravitic power engine.

Any world within ten light-years of a dwarf star, everyone said,
would give its eyeteeth for any kind of Registered Gravitics Engineer.

The thought of that never bothered George. Sure it would; all
the eyeteeth it could scare up. But George had also heard what had
happened before in a newly developed technique. Rationalization
and simplification followed in a flood. New models each year; new
types of gravitic engines; new principles. Then all those eyeteeth
gentlemen would find themselves out of date and superseded by
later models with later educations. The first group would then have
to settle down to unskilled labor or ship out to some backwoods
world that wasn't quite caught up yet.

Now Computer Programmers were in steady demand year after
year, century after century. The demand never reached wild peaks;
there was never a howling bull market for Programmers; but the
demand climbed steadily as new worlds opened up and as older
worlds grew more complex.

He had argued with Stubby Trevelyan about that constantly. As
best friends, their arguments had to be constant and vitriolic and, of
course, neither ever persuaded or was persuaded.

But then Trevelyan had had a father who was a Registered Metallurgist and had actually served on one of the Outworlds, and a
grandfather who had also been a Registered Metallurgist. He himself
was intent on becoming a Registered Metallurgist almost as a matter
of family right and was firmly convinced that any other profession
was a shade less than respectable.

"There'll always be metal," he said, "and there's an accom-
plishment in molding alloys to specification and watching structures
grow. Now, what's a Programmer going to be doing? Sitting at a
coder all day long, feeding some fool mile-long machine."

Even at sixteen, George had learned to be practical. He said simply, "There'll be a million Metallurgists put out along with you."

"Because it's good. A good profession. The best."

"But you get crowded out, Stubby. You can be way back in line. Any world can tape out its own Metallurgists, and the market for advanced Earth models isn't so big. And it's mostly the small worlds that want them. You know what percent of the turnout of Registered Metallurgists get tabbed for worlds with a Grade A rating. I looked it up. It's just 13.3 per cent. That means you'll have seven chances in eight of being stuck in some world that just about has running water. You may even be stuck on Earth; 2.3 percent are."

Trevelyan said belligerently, "There's no disgrace in staying on Earth. Earth needs technicians, too. Good ones." His grandfather had been an Earth-bound Metallurgist, and Trevelyan lifted his finger to his upper lip and dabbed at an as yet nonexistent mustache.

George knew about Trevelyan's grandfather and, considering the Earth-bound position of his own ancestry, was in no mood to sneer. He said diplomatically, "No intellectual disgrace. Of course not. But it's nice to get into a Grade A world, isn't it?

"Now, you take Programmers. Only the Grade A worlds have the kind of computers that really need first-class Programmers, so they're the only ones in the market. And Programmer tapes are complicated and hardly anyone fits. They need more Programmers than their own population can supply. It's just a matter of statistics. There's one first-class Programmer per million, say. A world needs twenty and has a population of ten million, they have to come to Earth for five to fifteen Programmers. Right?

"And you know how many Registered Computer Programmers went to Grade A planets last year? I'll tell you. Every last one. If you're a Programmer, you're a picked man. Yes, sir."

Trevelyan frowned. "If only one in a million makes it, what makes you think *you'll* make it?"

George said guardedly, "I'll make it."

He never dared tell anyone; not Trevelyan; not his parents; of exactly what he was doing that made him so confident. But he wasn't worried. He was simply confident (that was the worst of the memories he had in the hopeless days afterward). He was as blandly confident as the average eight-year-old kid approaching Reading Day—that childhood preview of Education Day.

Of course, Reading Day had been different. Partly, there was the simple fact of childhood. A boy of eight takes many extraordinary things in stride. One day you can't read and the next day you can. That's just the way things are. Like the sun shining.

And then not so much depended upon it. There were no recruiters just ahead, waiting and jostling for the lists and scores on the coming Olympics. A boy or girl who goes through the Reading Day is just someone who has ten more years of undifferentiated living upon Earth's crawling surface; just someone who returns to his family with one new ability.

By the time Education Day came, ten years later, George wasn't even sure of most of the details of his own Reading Day.

Most clearly of all, he remembered it to be a dismal September day with a mild rain falling. (September for Reading Day; November for Education Day; May for Olympics. They made nursery rhymes out of it.) George had dressed by the wall lights, with his parents far more excited than he himself was. His father was a Registered Pipe Fitter and had found his occupation on Earth. This fact had always been a humiliation to him, although, of course, as anyone could see plainly, most of each generation must stay on Earth in the nature of things.

There had to be farmers and miners and even technicians on Earth. It was only the late-model, high-specialty professions that were in demand on the Outworlds, and only a few million a year out of Earth's population of eight billion could be exported. Every man and woman on Earth couldn't be among that group.

But every man and woman could hope that at least one of his children could be one, and Platen, Senior, was certainly no exception. It was obvious to him (and, to be sure, to others as well) that George was notably intelligent and quick-minded. He would be bound to do well and he would have to, as he was an only child. If George didn't end on an Outworld, they would have to wait for grandchildren before a next chance would come along, and that was too far in the future to be much consolation.

Reading Day would not prove much, of course, but it would be the only indication they would have before the big day itself. Every parent on Earth would be listening to the quality of reading when his child came home with it; listening for any particularly easy flow of words and building that into certain omens of the future. There were few families that didn't have at least one hopeful who, from Reading Day on, was the great hope because of the way he handled his trisyllabics.

Dimly, George was aware of the cause of his parents' tension, and if there was any anxiety in his young heart that drizzly morning, it was only the fear that his father's hopeful expression might fade out when he returned home with his reading.

The children met in the large assembly room of the town's Education hall. All over Earth, in millions of local halls, throughout that month, similar groups of children would be meeting. George felt depressed by the grayness of the room and by the other children, strained and stiff in unaccustomed finery.

Automatically, George did as all the rest of the children did. He found the small clique that represented the children on his floor of the apartment house and joined them.

Trevelyan, who lived immediately next door, still wore his hair childishly long and was years removed from the sideburns and thin, reddish mustache that he was to grow as soon as he was physiologically capable of it.

Trevelyan (to whom George was then known as Jawjee) said, "Bet you're scared."

"I am not," said George. Then, confidentially, "My folks got a hunk of printing up on the dresser in my room, and when I come home, I'm going to read it for them." (George's main suffering at the moment lay in the fact that he didn't quite know where to put his hands. He had been warned not to scratch his head or rub his ears or pick his nose or put his hands into his pockets. This eliminated almost every possibility.)

Trevelyan put *his* hands in his pockets and said, "My father isn't worried."

Trevelyan, Senior, had been a Metallurgist on Diporia for nearly seven years, which gave him a superior social status in his neighborhood even though he had retired and returned to Earth.

Earth discouraged these re-immigrants because of population

problems, but a small trickle did return. For one thing the cost of living was lower on Earth, and what was a trifling annuity on Diporia, say, was a comfortable income on Earth. Besides, there were always men who found more satisfaction in displaying their success before the friends and scenes of their childhood than before all the rest of the Universe besides.

Trevelyan, Senior, further explained that if he stayed on Diporia, so would his children, and Diporia was a one-spaceship world. Back on Earth, his kids could end anywhere, even Novia.

Stubby Trevelyan had picked up that item early. Even before Reading Day, his conversation was based on the carelessly assumed fact that his ultimate home would be in Novia.

George, oppressed by thoughts of the other's future greatness and his own small-time contrast, was driven to belligerent defense at once.

"My father isn't worried either. He just wants to hear me read because he knows I'll be good. I suppose your father would just as soon not hear you because he knows you'll be all wrong."

"I will not be all wrong. Reading is *nothing.* On Novia, I'll *hire* people to read to me."

"Because *you* won't be able to read yourself, on account of you're *dumb!*"

"Then how come I'll be on Novia?"

And George, driven, made the great denial, "Who says you'll be on Novia? Bet you don't go anywhere."

Stubby Trevelyan reddened. "I won't be a Pipe Fitter like your old man."

"Take that back, you dumbhead."

"You take *that* back."

They stood nose to nose, not wanting to fight but relieved at having something familiar to do in this strange place. Furthermore, now that George had curled his hands into fists and lifted them before his face, the problem of what to do with his hands was, at least temporarily, solved. Other children gathered round excitedly.

But then it all ended when a woman's voice sounded loudly over the public address system. There was instant silence everywhere. George dropped his fists and forgot Trevelyan.

"Children," said the voice, "we are going to call out your

names. As each child is called, he or she is to go to one of the men waiting along the side walls. Do you see them? They are wearing red uniforms so they will be easy to find. The girls will go to the right. The boys will go to the left. Now look about and see which man in red is nearest to you—"

George found his man at a glance and waited for his name to be called off. He had not been introduced before this to the sophistications of the alphabet, and the length of time it took to reach his own name grew disturbing.

The crowd of children thinned; little rivulets made their way to each of the red-clad guides.

When the name "George Platen" was finally called, his sense of relief was exceeded only by the feeling of pure gladness at the fact that Stubby Trevelyan still stood in his place, uncalled.

George shouted back over his shoulder as he left, "Yay, Stubby, maybe they don't want you."

That moment of gaiety quickly left. He was herded into a line and directed down corridors in the company of strange children. They all looked at one another, large-eyed and concerned, but beyond a snuffling "Quitcher pushing" and "Hey, watch out" there was no conversation.

They were handed little slips of paper which they were told must remain with them. George stared at his curiously. Little black marks of different shapes. He knew it to be printing but how could anyone make words out of it? He couldn't imagine.

He was told to strip; he and four other boys who were all that now remained together. All the new clothes came shucking off and four eight-year-olds stood naked and small, shivering more out of embarrassment than cold. Medical technicians came past, probing them, testing them with odd instruments, pricking them for blood. Each took the little cards and made additional marks on them with little black rods that produced the marks, all neatly lined up, with great speed. George stared at the new marks, but they were no more comprehensible than the old. The children were ordered back into their clothes.

They sat on separate little chairs then and waited again. Names were called again and "George Platen" came third.

He moved into a large room, filled with frightening instruments with knobs and glassy panels in front. There was a desk in the very center, and behind it a man sat, his eyes on the papers piled before him.

He said, "George Platen?"

"Yes, sir," said George, in a shaky whisper. All this waiting and all this going here and there was making him nervous. He wished it were over.

The man behind the desk said, "I am Dr. Lloyd, George. How are you?"

The doctor didn't look up as he spoke. It was as though he had said those words over and over again and didn't have to look up any more.

"I'm all right."

"Are you afraid, George?"

"N-no, sir," said George, sounding afraid even in his own ears.

"That's good," said the doctor, "because there's nothing to be afraid of, you know. Let's see, George. It says here on your card that your father is named Peter and that he's a Registered Pipe Fitter and your mother is named Amy and is a Registered Home Technician. Is that right?"

"Y-yes, sir."

"And your birthday is February thirteenth, and you had an ear infection about a year ago. Right?"

"Yes, sir."

"Do you know how I know all these things?"

"It's on the card, I think, sir."

"That's right." The doctor looked up at George for the first time and smiled. He showed even teeth and looked much younger than George's father. Some of George's nervousness vanished.

The doctor passed the card to George. "Do you know what all those things there mean, George?"

Although George knew he did not he was startled by the sudden request into looking at the card as though he might understand now through some sudden stroke of fate. But they were just marks as before and he passed the card back. "No, sir."

"Why not?"

George felt a sudden pang of suspicion concerning the sanity of this doctor. Didn't he know why not?

George said, "I can't read, sir."

"Would you like to read?"

"Yes, sir."

"Why, George?"

George stared, appalled. No one had ever asked him that. He had no answer. He said falteringly, "I don't know, sir."

"Printed information will direct you all through your life. There is so much you'll have to know even after Education Day. Cards like this one will tell you. Books will tell you. Television screens will tell you. Printing will tell you such useful things and such interesting things that not being able to read would be as bad as not being able to see. Do you understand?"

"Yes, sir."

"Are you afraid, George?"

"No, sir."

"Good. Now I'll tell you exactly what we'll do first. I'm going to put these wires on your forehead just over the corners of your eyes. They'll stick there but they won't hurt at all. Then, I'll turn on something that will make a buzz. It will sound funny and it may tickle you, but it won't hurt. Now if it does hurt, you tell me, and I'll turn it off right away, but it won't hurt. All right?"

George nodded and swallowed.

"Are you ready?"

George nodded. He closed his eyes while the doctor busied himself. His parents had explained this to him. They, too, had said it wouldn't hurt, but then there were always the older children. There were the ten- and twelve-year-olds who howled after the eight-year-olds waiting for Reading Day, "Watch out for the needle." There were the others who took you off in confidence and said, "They got to cut your head open. They use a sharp knife that big with a hook on it," and so on into horrifying details.

George had never believed them but he had had nightmares, and now he closed his eyes and felt pure terror.

He didn't feel the wires at his temple. The buzz was a distant thing, and there was the sound of his own blood in his ears, ringing hollowly as though it and he were in a large cave. Slowly he chanced opening his eyes.

The doctor had his back to him. From one of the instruments a strip of paper unwound and was covered with a thin, wavy purple line. The doctor tore off pieces and put them into a slot in another machine. He did it over and over again. Each time a little piece of film came out, which the doctor looked at. Finally, he turned toward George with a queer frown between his eyes.

The buzzing stopped.

George said breathlessly, "Is it over?"

The doctor said, "Yes," but he was still frowning.

"Can I read now?" asked George. He felt no different.

The doctor said, "What?" then smiled very suddenly and briefly. He said, "It works fine, George. You'll be reading in fifteen minutes. Now we're going to use another machine this time and it will take longer. I'm going to cover your whole head, and when I turn it on you won't be able to see or hear anything for a while, but it won't hurt. Just to make sure, I'm going to give you a little switch to hold in your hand. If anything hurts, you press the little button and everything shuts off. All right?"

In later years, George was told that the little switch was strictly a dummy; that it was introduced solely for confidence. He never did know for sure, however, since he never pushed the button.

A large smoothly curved helmet with a rubbery inner lining was placed over his head and left there. Three or four little knobs seemed to grab at him and bite into his skull, but there was only a little pressure that faded. No pain.

The doctor's voice sounded dimly. "Everything all right, George?"

And then, with no real warning, a layer of thick felt closed down all about him. He was disembodied, there was no sensation, no universe, only himself and a distant murmur at the very ends of nothingness telling him something—telling him—telling him—

He strained to hear and understand but there was all that thick felt between.

Then the helmet was taken off his head, and the light was so bright that it hurt his eyes while the doctor's voice drummed at his ears.

The doctor said, "Here's your card, George. What does it say?"

George looked at his card again and gave out a strangled shout. The marks weren't just marks at all. They made up words. They were words just as clearly as though something were whispering them in his ears. He could *hear* them being whispered as he looked at them.

"What does it say, George?"

"It says—it says—'Platen, George. Born 13 February 6492 of Peter and Amy Platen in . . .'" He broke off.

"You can read, George," said the doctor. "It's all over."

"For good? I won't forget how?"

"Of course not." The doctor leaned over to shake hands gravely. "You will be taken home now."

It was days before George got over this new and great talent of his. He read for his father with such facility that Platen, Senior, wept and called relatives to tell the good news.

George walked about town, reading every scrap of printing he could find and wondering how it was that none of it had ever made sense to him before.

He tried to remember how it was not to be able to read and he couldn't. As far as his feeling about it was concerned, he had always been able to read. Always.

At eighteen, George was rather dark, of medium height, but thin enough to look taller. Trevelyan, who was scarcely an inch shorter, had a stockiness of build that made "Stubby" more than ever appropriate, but in this last year he had grown self-conscious. The nickname could no longer be used without reprisal. And since Trevelyan disapproved of his proper first name even more strongly, he was called Trevelyan or any decent variant of that. As though to prove his manhood further, he had most persistently grown a pair of sideburns and a bristly mustache.

He was sweating and nervous now, and George, who had himself grown out of "Jaw-jee" and into the curt monosyllabic gutturability of "George," was rather amused by that.

They were in the same large hall they had been in ten years before (and not since). It was as if a vague dream of the past had come to sudden reality. In the first few minutes George had been distinctly surprised at finding everything seem smaller and more cramped than his memory told him; then he made allowance for his own growth.

The crowd was smaller than it had been in childhood. It was exclusively male this time. The girls had another day assigned them.

Trevelyan leaned over to say, "Beats me the way they make you wait."

"Red tape," said George. "You can't avoid it."

Trevelyan said, "What makes *you* so damned tolerant about it?"

"I've got nothing to worry about."

"Oh, brother, you make me sick. I hope you end up Registered Manure Spreader just so I can see your face when you do." His somber eyes swept the crowd anxiously.

George looked about, too. It wasn't quite the system they used on the children. Matters went slower, and instructions had been given out at the start in print (an advantage over the pre-Readers). The names Platen and Trevelyan were well down the alphabet still, but this time the two knew it.

Young men came out of the education rooms, frowning and uncomfortable, picked up their clothes and belongings, then went off to analysis to learn the results.

Each, as he came out, would be surrounded by a clot of the thinning crowd. "How was it?" "How'd it feel?" "Whacha think ya made?" "Ya feel any different?"

Answers were vague and noncommittal.

George forced himself to remain out of those clots. You only raised your own blood pressure. Everyone said you stood the best chance if you remained calm. Even so, you could feel the palms of your hands grow cold. Funny that new tensions came with the years.

For instance, high-specialty professionals heading out for an Outworld were accompanied by a wife (or husband). It was important to keep the sex ratio in good balance on all worlds. And if you were going out to a Grade A world, what girl would refuse you? George had no specific girl in mind yet; he wanted none. Not now! Once he made Programmer; once he could add to his name, Registered Computer Programmer, he could take his pick, like a sultan in a harem. The thought excited him and he tried to put it away. Must stay calm.

Trevelyan muttered, "What's it all about anyway? First they say it works best if you're relaxed and at ease. Then they put you through this and make it impossible for you to be relaxed and at ease."

"Maybe that's the idea. They're separating the boys from the men to begin with. Take it easy, Trev."

"Shut up."

George's turn came. His name was not called. It appeared in glowing letters on the notice board.

He waved at Trevelyan. "Take it easy. Don't let it get you."

He was happy as he entered the testing chamber. Actually happy.

The man behind the desk said, "George Platen?"

For a fleeting instant there was a razor-sharp picture in George's mind of another man, ten years earlier, who had asked the same question, and it was almost as though this were the same man and he, George, had turned eight again as he had stepped across the threshold.

But the man looked up and, of course, the face matched that of the sudden memory not at all. The nose was bulbous, the hair thin and stringy, and the chin wattled as though its owner had once been grossly overweight and had reduced.

The man behind the desk looked annoyed. "Well?"

George came to Earth. "I'm George Platen, sir."

"Say so, then. I'm Dr. Zachary Antonelli, and we're going to be intimately acquainted in a moment."

He stared at small strips of film, holding them up to the light owlishly.

George winced inwardly. Very hazily, he remembered that other doctor (he had forgotten the name) staring at such film. Could these be the same? The other doctor had frowned and this one was looking at him now as though he were angry.

His happiness was already just about gone.

Dr. Antonelli spread the pages of a thickish file out before him now and put the films carefully to one side. "It says here you want to be a Computer Programmer."

"Yes, doctor."

"Still do?"

"Yes, sir."

"It's a responsible and exacting position. Do you feel up to it?"

"Yes, sir."

"Most pre-Educates don't put down any specific profession. I believe they are afraid of queering it."

"I think that's right, sir."

"Aren't you afraid of that?"

"I might as well be honest, sir."

Dr. Antonelli nodded, but without any noticeable lightening of his expression. "Why do you want to be a Programmer?"

"It's a responsible and exacting position, as you said, sir. It's an important job and an exciting one. I like it and I think I can do it."

Dr. Antonelli put the papers away, and looked at George sourly. He said, "How do you know you like it? Because you think you'll be snapped up by some Grade A planet?"

George thought uneasily: He's trying to rattle you. Stay calm and stay frank.

He said, "I think a Programmer has a good chance, sir, but even if I were left on Earth, I know I'd like it." (That was true enough. I'm not lying, thought George.)

"All right, how do you know?"

He asked it as though he knew there was no decent answer and George almost smiled. He had one.

He said, "I've been reading about Programming, sir."

"You've been *what*?" Now the doctor looked genuinely astonished and George took pleasure in that.

"Reading about it, sir. I bought a book on the subject and I've been studying it."

"A book for Registered Programmers?"

"Yes, sir."

"But you couldn't understand it."

"Not at first. I got other books on mathematics and electronics. I made out all I could. I still don't know much, but I know enough to know I like it and to know I can make it." (Even his parents never found that secret cache of books or knew why he spent so much time in his own room or exactly what happened to the sleep he missed.)

The doctor pulled at the loose skin under his chin. "What was your idea in doing that, son?"

"I wanted to make sure I would be interested, sir."

"Surely you know that being interested means nothing. You could be devoured by a subject and if the physical makeup of your brain makes it more efficient for you to be something else, something else you will be. You know that, don't you?"

"I've been told that," said George cautiously.

"Well, believe it. It's true."

George said nothing.

Dr. Antonelli said, "Or do you believe that studying some subject will bend the brain cells in that direction, like that other theory that a pregnant woman need only listen to great music persistently to make a composer of her child. Do you believe that?"

George flushed. That had certainly been in his mind. By forcing his intellect constantly in the desired direction, he had felt sure that he would be getting a head start. Most of his confidence had rested on exactly that point.

"I never—" he began, and found no way of finishing.

"Well, it isn't true. Good Lord, youngster, your brain pattern is fixed at birth. It can be altered by a blow hard enough to damage the cells or by a burst blood vessel or by a tumor or by a major infection —each time, of course, for the worse. But it certainly can't be affected by your thinking special thoughts." He stared at George thoughtfully, then said, "Who told you to do this?"

George, now thoroughly disturbed, swallowed and said, "No one, doctor. My own idea."

"Who knew you were doing it after you started?"

"No one. Doctor, I meant to do no wrong."

"Who said anything about wrong? Useless is what I would say. Why did you keep it to yourself?"

"I—I thought they'd laugh at me." (He thought abruptly of a recent exchange with Trevelyan. George had very cautiously broached the thought, as of something merely circulating distantly in the very outermost reaches of his mind, concerning the possibility of learning something by ladling it into the mind by hand, so to speak, in bits and pieces. Trevelyan had hooted, "George, you'll be tanning your own shoes next and weaving your own shirts." He had been thankful then for his policy of secrecy.)

Dr. Antonelli shoved the bits of film he had first looked at from position to position in morose thought. Then he said, "Let's get you analyzed. This is getting me nowhere."

The wires went to George's temples. There was the buzzing. Again there came a sharp memory of ten years ago.

George's hands were clammy; his heart pounded. He should never have told the doctor about his secret reading.

It was his damned vanity, he told himself. He had wanted to show how enterprising he was, how full of initiative. Instead, he had showed himself superstitious and ignorant and aroused the hostility of the doctor. (He could tell the doctor hated him for a wise guy on the make.)

And now he had brought himself to such a state of nervousness, he was sure the analyzer would show nothing that made sense.

He wasn't aware of the moment when the wires were removed from his temples. The sight of the doctor, staring at him thoughtfully, blinked into his consciousness and that was that; the wires were gone. George dragged himself together with a tearing effort. He had quite given up his ambition to be a Programmer. In the space of ten minutes, it had all gone.

He said dismally, "I suppose no?"

"No what?"

"No Programmer?"

The doctor rubbed his nose and said, "You get your clothes and whatever belongs to you and go to room 15-C. Your files will be waiting for you there. So will my report."

George said in complete surprise, "Have I been Educated already? I thought this was just to—"

Dr. Antonelli stared down at his desk. "It will all be explained to you. You do as I say."

George felt something like panic. What was it they couldn't tell him? He wasn't fit for anything but Registered Laborer. They were going to prepare him for that; adjust him to it.

He was suddenly certain of it and he had to keep from screaming by main force.

He stumbled back to his place of waiting. Trevelyan was not there, a fact for which he would have been thankful if he had had enough self-possession to be meaningfully aware of his surroundings. Hardly anyone was left, in fact, and the few who were looked as though they might ask him questions were it not that they were too worn out by their tail-of-the-alphabet waiting to buck the fierce, hot look of anger and hate he cast at them.

What right had *they* to be technicians and he, himself, a Laborer? Laborer! He was *certain*!

He was led by a red-uniformed guide along the busy corridors lined with separate rooms each containing its groups, here two, there five: the Motor Mechanics, the Construction Engineers, the Agronomists—There were hundreds of specialized Professions and most of them would be represented in this small town by one or two anyway.

He hated them all just then: the Statisticians, the Accountants, the lesser breeds and the higher. He hated them because they owned their smug knowledge now, knew their fate, while he himself, empty still, had to face some kind of further red tape.

He reached 15-C, was ushered in, and left in an empty room. For one moment, his spirits bounded. Surely, if this were the Labor classification room, there would be dozens of young people present.

A door sucked into its recess on the other side of a waist-high partition and an elderly, white-haired man stepped out. He smiled and showed even teeth that were obviously false, but his face was still ruddy and unlined and his voice had vigor.

He said, "Good evening, George. Our own sector has only one of you this time, I see."

"Only one?" said George blankly.

"Thousands over the Earth, of course. Thousands. You're not alone."

George felt exasperated. He said, "I don't understand, sir. What's my classification? What's happening?"

"Easy, son. You're all right. It could happen to anyone." He held out his hand and George took it mechanically. It was warm and it pressed George's hand firmly. "Sit down, son. I'm Sam Ellenford."

George nodded impatiently. "I want to know what's going on, sir."

"Of course. To begin with, you can't be a Computer Programmer, George. You've guessed that, I think."

"Yes, I have," said George bitterly. "What will I be, then?"

"That's the hard part to explain, George." He paused, then said with careful distinctness, "Nothing."

"What!"

"Nothing!"

"But what does that mean? Why can't you assign me a profession?"

"We have no choice in the matter, George. It's the structure of your mind that decides that."

George went a sallow yellow. His eyes bulged. "There's something wrong with my mind?"

"There's *something* about it. As far as professional classification is concerned, I suppose you can call it wrong."

"But why?"

Ellenford shrugged. "I'm sure you know how Earth runs its Educational program, George. Practically any human being can absorb practically any body of knowledge, but each individual brain pattern is better suited to receiving some types of knowledge than others. We try to match mind to knowledge as well as we can within the limits of the quota requirements for each profession."

George nodded. "Yes, I know."

"Every once in a while, George, we come up against a young man whose mind is not suited to receiving a superimposed knowledge of any sort."

"You mean I can't be Educated?"

"That is what I mean."

"But that's crazy. I'm intelligent. I can understand—" He looked helplessly about as though trying to find some way of proving that he had a functioning brain.

"Don't misunderstand me, please," said Ellenford gravely. "You're intelligent. There's no question about that. You're even above average in intelligence. Unfortunately that has nothing to do with whether the mind ought to be allowed to accept superimposed knowledge or not. In fact, it is almost always the intelligent person who comes here."

"You mean I can't even be a Registered Laborer?" babbled George. Suddenly even that was better than the blank that faced him. "What's there to know to be a Laborer?"

"Don't underestimate the Laborer, young man. There are dozens of subclassifications and each variety has its own corpus of fairly detailed knowledge. Do you think there's no skill in knowing the proper manner of lifting a weight? Besides, for the Laborer, we must select not only minds suited to it, but bodies as well. You're not the type, George, to last long as a Laborer."

George was conscious of his slight build. He said, "But I've never heard of anyone without a profession."

"There aren't many," conceded Ellenford. "And we protect them."

"Protect them?" George felt confusion and fright grow higher inside him.

"You're a ward of the planet, George. From the time you walked through that door, we've been in charge of you." And he smiled.

It was a fond smile. To George it seemed the smile of ownership; the smile of a grown man for a helpless child.

He said, "You mean, I'm going to be in prison?"

"Of course not. You will simply be with others of your kind."

Your kind. The words made a kind of thunder in George's ear.

Ellenford said, "You need special treatment. We'll take care of you."

To George's own horror, he burst into tears. Ellenford walked to the other end of the room and faced away as though in thought.

George fought to reduce the agonized weeping to sobs and then to strangle those. He thought of his father and mother, of his friends, of Trevelyan, of his own shame—

He said rebelliously, "I learned to read."

"Everyone with a whole mind can do that. We've never found exceptions. It is at this stage that we discover—exceptions. And when you learned to read, George, we were concerned about your mind pattern. Certain peculiarities were reported even then by the doctor in charge."

"Can't you try Educating me? You haven't even tried. I'm willing to take the risk."

"The law forbids us to do that, George. But look, it will not be bad. We will explain matters to your family so they will not be hurt. At the place to which you'll be taken, you'll be allowed privileges. We'll get you books and you can learn what you will."

"Dab knowledge in by hand," said George bitterly. "Shred by shred. Then, when I die I'll know enough to be a Registered Junior Office Boy, Paper-Clip Division."

"Yet I understand you've already been studying books."

George froze. He was struck devastatingly by sudden understanding. "That's it . . ."

"What is?"

"That fellow Antonelli. He's knifing me."

"No, George. You're quite wrong."

"Don't tell me that." George was in an ecstasy of fury. "That lousy bastard is selling me out because he thought I was a little too wise for him. I read books and tried to get a head start toward programming. Well, what do you want to square things? Money? You won't get it. I'm getting out of here and when I finish broadcasting this—"

He was screaming.

Ellenford shook his head and touched a contact.

Two men entered on catfeet and got on either side of George. They pinned his arms to his sides. One of them used an air-spray hypodermic in the hollow of his right elbow and the hypnotic entered his vein and had an almost immediate effect.

His screams cut off and his head fell forward. His knees buckled and only the men on either side kept him erect as he slept.

They took care of George as they said they would; they were good to him and unfailingly kind—about the way, George thought, he himself would be to a sick kitten he had taken pity on.

They told him that he should sit up and take some interest in life; and then told him that most people who came there had the same attitude of despair at the beginning and that he would snap out of it.

He didn't even hear them.

Dr. Ellenford himself visited him to tell him that his parents had been informed that he was away on special assignment.

George muttered, "Do they know—"

Ellenford assured him at once, "We gave no details."

At first George had refused to eat. They fed him intravenously.

They hid sharp objects and kept him under guard. Hali Omani came to be his roommate and his stolidity had a calming effect.

One day, out of sheer desperate boredom, George asked for a book. Omani, who himself read books constantly, looked up, smiling broadly. George almost withdrew the request then, rather than give any of them satisfaction, then thought: What do I care?

He didn't specify the book and Omani brought one on chemistry. It was in big print, with small words and many illustrations. It was for teenagers. He threw the book violently against the wall.

That's what he would be always. A teenager all his life. A pre-Educate forever and special books would have to be written for him. He lay smoldering in bed, staring at the ceiling, and after an hour had passed, he got up sulkily, picked up the book, and began reading.

It took him a week to finish it and then he asked for another.

"Do you want me to take the first one back?" asked Omani.

George frowned. There were things in the book he had not understood, yet he was not so lost to shame as to say so.

But Omani said, "Come to think of it, you'd better keep it. Books are meant to be read and reread."

It was that same day that he finally yielded to Omani's invitation that he tour the place. He dogged at the Nigerian's feet and took in his surroundings with quick hostile glances.

The place was no prison certainly. There were no walls, no locked doors, no guards. But it was a prison in that the inmates had no place to go outside.

It was somehow good to see others like himself by the dozen. It was so easy to believe himself to be the only one in the world so— maimed.

He mumbled, "How many people here anyway?"

"Two hundred and five, George, and this isn't the only place of the sort in the world. There are thousands."

Men looked up as he passed, wherever he went; in the gymnasium, along the tennis courts; through the library (he had never in his life imagined books could exist in such numbers; they were stacked, actually stacked, along long shelves). They stared at him curiously and he returned the looks savagely. At least *they* were no better than he; no call for *them* to look at him as though he were some sort of curiosity.

Most of them were in their twenties. George said suddenly, "What happens to the older ones?"

Omani said, "This place specializes in the younger ones." Then, as though he suddenly recognized an implication in George's question that he had missed earlier, he shook his head gravely and said, "They're not put out of the way, if that's what you mean. There are other Houses for older ones."

"Who cares?" mumbled George, who felt he was sounding too interested and in danger of slipping into surrender.

"You might. As you grow older, you will find yourself in a House with occupants of both sexes."

That surprised George somehow. "Women, too?"

"Of course. Do you suppose women are immune to this sort of thing?"

George thought of that with more interest and excitement than he had felt for anything since before that day when . . . He forced his thought away from that.

Omani stopped at the doorway of a room that contained a small closed-circuit television set and a desk computer. Five or six men sat about the television. Omani said, "This is a classroom."

George said, "What's that?"

"The young men in there are being educated. Not," he added, quickly, "in the usual way."

"You mean they're cramming it in bit by bit."

"That's right. This is the way everyone did it in ancient times."

This was what they kept telling him since he had come to the House, but what of it? Suppose there had been a day when mankind had not known the diatherm-oven. Did that mean he should be satisfied to eat meat raw in a world where others ate it cooked?

He said, "Why do they want to go through that bit-by-bit stuff?"

"To pass the time, George, and because they're curious."

"What good does it do them?"

"It makes them happier."

George carried that thought to bed with him.

The next day he said to Omani ungraciously, "Can you get me

into a classroom where I can find out something about programming?"

Omani replied heartily, "Sure."

It was slow and he resented it. Why should someone have to explain something and explain it again? Why should he have to read and reread a passage, then stare at a mathematical relationship and not understand it at once? That wasn't how other people had to be.

Over and over again, he gave up. Once he refused to attend classes for a week.

But always he returned. The official in charge, who assigned reading, conducted the television demonstrations, and even explained difficult passages and concepts, never commented on the matter.

George was finally given a regular task in the gardens and took his turn in the various kitchen and cleaning details. This was represented to him as being an advance, but he wasn't fooled. The place might have been far more mechanized than it was, but they deliberately made work for the young men in order to give them the illusion of worthwhile occupation, of usefulness. George wasn't fooled.

They were even paid small sums of money out of which they could buy certain specified luxuries or which they could put aside for a problematical use in a problematical old age. George kept his money in an open jar, which he kept on a closet shelf. He had no idea how much he had accumulated. Nor did he care.

He made no real friends though he reached the stage where a civil good day was in order. He even stopped brooding (or almost stopped) on the miscarriage of justice that had placed him there. He would go weeks without dreaming of Antonelli, of his gross nose and wattled neck, of the leer with which he would push George into a boiling quicksand and hold him under, till he woke screaming with Omani bending over him in concern.

Omani said to him on a snowy day in February, "It's amazing how you're adjusting."

But that was February, the thirteenth to be exact, his nineteenth birthday. March came, then April, and with the approach of May he realized he hadn't adjusted at all.

The previous May had passed unregarded while George was still
in his bed, drooping and ambitionless. This May was different.

All over Earth, George knew, Olympics would be taking place
and young men would be competing, matching their skills against
one another in the fight for a place on a new world. There would be
the holiday atmosphere, the excitement, the news reports, the self-
contained recruiting agents from the worlds beyond space, the glory
of victory or the consolations of defeat.

How much of fiction dealt with these motifs; how much of his
own boyhood excitement lay in following the events of Olympics
from year to year; how many of his own plans—

George Platen could not conceal the longing in his voice. It was
too much to suppress. He said, "Tomorrow's the first of May. Olympics!"

And that led to his first quarrel with Omani and to Omani's
bitter enunciation of the exact name of the institution in which
George found himself.

Omani gazed fixedly at George and said distinctly, "A House for
the Feebleminded."

George Platen flushed. Feebleminded!

He rejected it desperately. He said in a monotone, "I'm leaving." He said it on impulse. His conscious mind learned it first from
the statement as he uttered it.

Omani, who had returned to his book, looked up. "What?"

George knew what he was saying now. He said it fiercely, "I'm
leaving."

"That's ridiculous. Sit down, George, calm yourself."

"Oh, no. I'm here on a frame-up, I tell you. This doctor, Antonelli, took a dislike to me. It's the sense of power these petty bu-
reaucrats have. Cross them and they wipe out your life with a stylus
mark on some file card."

"Are you back to that?"

"And staying there till it's all straightened out. I'm going to get
to Antonelli somehow, break him, force the truth out of him."
George was breathing heavily and he felt feverish. Olympics month
was here and he couldn't let it pass. If he did, it would be the final
surrender and he would be lost for all time.

Omani threw his legs over the side of his bed and stood up. He was nearly six feet tall and the expression on his face gave him the look of a concerned Saint Bernard. He put his arm about George's shoulder, "If I hurt your feelings—"

George shrugged him off. "You just said what you thought was the truth, and I'm going to prove it isn't the truth, that's all. Why not? The door's open. There aren't any locks. No one ever said I couldn't leave. I'll just walk out."

"All right, but where will you go?"

"To the nearest air terminal, then to the nearest Olympics center. I've got money." He seized the open jar that held the wages he had put away. Some of the coins jangled to the floor.

"That will last you a week maybe. Then what?"

"By then I'll have things settled."

"By then you'll come crawling back here," said Omani earnestly, "with all the progress you've made to do over again. You're mad, George."

"Feebleminded is the word you used before."

"Well, I'm sorry I did. Stay here, will you?"

"Are you going to try to stop me?"

Omani compressed his full lips. "No, I guess I won't. This is your business. If the only way you can learn is to buck the world and come back with blood on your face, go ahead. . . . Well, go ahead."

George was in the doorway now, looking back over his shoulder. "I'm going"—he came back to pick up his pocket grooming set slowly— "I hope you don't object to my taking a few personal belongings."

Omani shrugged. He was in bed again reading, indifferent.

George lingered at the door again, but Omani didn't look up. George gritted his teeth, turned and walked rapidly down the empty corridor and out into the night-shrouded grounds.

He had expected to be stopped before leaving the grounds. He wasn't. He had stopped at an all-night diner to ask directions to an air terminal and expected the proprietor to call the police. That didn't happen. He summoned a skimmer to take him to the airport and the driver asked no questions.

Yet he felt no lift at that. He arrived at the airport sick at heart.

He had not realized how the outer world would be. He was surrounded by professionals. The diner's proprietor had had his name
inscribed on the plastic shell over the cash register. So and so,
Registered Cook. The man in the skimmer had his license up, Registered Chauffeur. George felt the bareness of his name and experi-
enced a kind of nakedness because of it; worse, he felt skinned. But
no one challenged him. No one studied him suspiciously and demanded proof of professional rating.

George thought bitterly: Who would imagine any human being
without one?

He bought a ticket to San Francisco on the three A.M. plane. No
other plane for a sizable Olympics center was leaving before morning and he wanted to wait as little as possible. As it was, he sat
huddled in the waiting room, watching for the police. They did not
come.

He was in San Francisco before noon and the noise of the city
struck him like a blow. This was the largest city he had ever seen
and he had been used to silence and calm for a year and a half now.

Worse, it was Olympics month. He almost forgot his own pre-
dicament in his sudden awareness that some of the noise, excitement, confusion was due to that.

The Olympics boards were up at the airport for the benefit of
the incoming travelers, and crowds jostled around each one. Each
major profession had its own board. Each listed directions to the
Olympics Hall where the contest for that day for that profession
would be given; the individuals competing and their city of birth;
the Outworld (if any) sponsoring it.

It was a completely stylized thing. George had read descriptions
often enough in the newsprints and films, watched matches on television, and even witnessed a small Olympics in the Registered
Butcher classification at the county seat. Even that, which had no
conceivable Galactic implication (there was no Outworlder in atten-
dance, of course) aroused excitement enough.

Partly, the excitement was caused simply by the fact of competition, partly by the spur of local pride (oh, when there was a hometown boy to cheer for, though he might be a complete stranger),
and, of course, partly by betting. There was no way of stopping the
last.

George found it difficult to approach the board. He found himself looking at the scurrying, avid onlookers in a new way.

There must have been a time when they themselves were Olympic material. What had *they* done? Nothing!

If they had been winners, they would be far out in the Galaxy somewhere, not stuck here on Earth. Whatever they were, their professions must have made them Earth-bait from the beginning; or else they had made themselves Earth-bait by inefficiency at whatever high-specialized professions they had had.

Now these failures stood about and speculated on the chances of newer and younger men. Vultures!

How he wished they were speculating on him.

He moved down the line of boards blankly, clinging to the outskirts of the groups about them. He had eaten breakfast on the strato and he wasn't hungry. He was afraid, though. He was in a big city during the confusion of the beginning of Olympics competition. That was protection, sure. The city was full of strangers. No one would question George. No one would care about George.

No one would care. Not even the House, thought George bitterly. They cared for him like a sick kitten, but if a sick kitten up and wanders off, well, too bad, what can you do?

And now that he was in San Francisco, what did he do? His thoughts struck blankly against a wall. See someone? Whom? How? Where would he even stay? The money he had left seemed pitiful.

The first shamefaced thought of going back came to him. He could go to the police—He shook his head violently as though arguing with a material adversary.

A word caught his eye on one of the boards, gleaming there: *Metallurgist.* In smaller letters, *nonferrous.* At the bottom of a long list of names, in flowing script, *sponsored by Novia.*

It induced painful memories: himself arguing with Trevelyan, so certain that he himself would be a Programmer, so certain that a Programmer was superior to a Metallurgist, so certain that he was following the right course, so certain that he was clever—

So clever that he had to boast to that small-minded, vindictive Antonelli. He had been so sure of himself that moment when he had been called and had left the nervous Trevelyan standing there, so cocksure.

George cried out in a short, incoherent high-pitched gasp. Someone turned to look at him, then hurried on. People brushed past impatiently pushing him this way and that. He remained staring at the board, openmouthed.

It was as though the board had answered his thought. He was thinking "Trevelyan" so hard that it had seemed for a moment that of course the board would say "Trevelyan" back at him.

But that *was* Trevelyan, up there. And *Armand* Trevelyan (Stubby's hated first name; up in lights for everyone to see) and the right hometown. What's more, Trev had wanted Novia, aimed for Novia, insisted on Novia; and this competition was sponsored by Novia.

This had to be Trev; good old Trev. Almost without thinking, he noted the directions for getting to the place of competition and took his place in line for a skimmer.

Then he thought somberly: Trev made it! He wanted to be a Metallurgist, and he made it!

George felt colder, more alone than ever.

There was a line waiting to enter the hall. Apparently, Metallurgy Olympics was to be an exciting and closely fought one. At least, the illuminated sky sign above the hall said so, and the jostling crowd seemed to think so.

It would have been a rainy day, George thought, from the color of the sky, but San Francisco had drawn the shield across its breadth from bay to ocean. It was an expense to do so, of course, but all expenses were warranted where the comfort of Outworlders was concerned. They would be in town for the Olympics. They were heavy spenders. And for each recruit taken, there would be a fee both to Earth, and to the local government from the planet sponsoring the Olympics. It paid to keep Outworlders in mind of a particular city as a pleasant place in which to spend Olympics time. San Francisco knew what it was doing.

George, lost in thought, was suddenly aware of a gentle pressure on his shoulder blade and a voice saying, "Are you in line here, young man?"

The line had moved up without George's having noticed the widening gap. He stepped forward hastily and muttered, "Sorry, sir."

There was the touch of two fingers on the elbow of his jacket and he looked about furtively.

The man behind him nodded cheerfully. He had iron-gray hair, and under his jacket he wore an old-fashioned sweater that buttoned down the front. He said, "I didn't mean to sound sarcastic."

"No offense."

"All right, then." He sounded cozily talkative. "I wasn't sure you might not simply be standing there, entangled with the line, so to speak, only by accident. I thought you might be a—"

"A what?" said George sharply.

"Why, a contestant, of course. You look young."

George turned away. He felt neither cozy nor talkative, and bitterly impatient with busybodies.

A thought struck him. Had an alarm been sent out for him? Was his description known, or his picture? Was Gray-hair behind him trying to get a good look at his face?

He hadn't seen any news reports. He craned his neck to see the moving strip of news headlines parading across one section of the city shield, somewhat lackluster against the gray of the cloudy afternoon sky. It was no use. He gave up at once. The headlines would never concern themselves with him. This was Olympics time and the only news worth headlining was the comparative scores of the winners and the trophies won by continents, nations, and cities.

It would go on like that for weeks, with scores calculated on a per capita basis and every city finding some way of calculating itself into a position of honor. His own town had once placed third in an Olympics covering Wiring Technician; third in the whole state. There was still a plaque saying so in Town Hall.

George hunched his head between his shoulders and shoved his hands in his pocket and decided that made him more noticeable. He relaxed and tried to look unconcerned, and felt no safer. He was in the lobby now, and no authoritative hand had yet been laid on his shoulder. He filed into the hall itself and moved as far forward as he could.

It was with an unpleasant shock that he noticed Gray-hair next to him. He looked away quickly and tried reasoning with himself. The man had been right behind him in line, after all.

Gray-hair, beyond a brief and tentative smile, paid no attention to him and, besides, the Olympics was about to start. George rose in his seat to see if he could make out the position assigned to Trevel-yan and at the moment that was all his concern.

The hall was moderate in size and shaped in the classical long oval, with the spectators in the two balconies running completely about the rim and the contestants in the linear trough down the center. The machines were set up, the progress boards above each bench were dark, except for the name and contest number of each man. The contestants themselves were on the scene, reading, talking together; one was checking his fingernails minutely. (It was, of course, considered bad form for any contestant to pay any attention to the problem before him until the instant of the starting signal.)

George studied the program sheet he found in the appropriate slot in the arm of his chair and found Trevelyan's name. His number was twelve and, to George's chagrin, that was at the wrong end of the hall. He could make out the figure of Contestant Twelve, stand-ing with his hands in his pockets, back to his machine, and staring at the audience as though he were counting the house. George couldn't make out the face.

Still, that was Trev.

George sank back in his seat. He wondered if Trev would do well. He hoped, as a matter of conscious duty, that he would, and yet there was something within him that felt rebelliously resentful. George, professionless, here, watching. Trevelyan, Registered Metal-lurgist, Nonferrous, there, competing.

George wondered if Trevelyan had competed in his first year. Sometimes men did, if they felt particularly confident—or hurried. It involved a certain risk. However efficient the Educative process, a preliminary year on Earth ("oiling the stiff knowledge," as the ex-pression went) insured a higher score.

If Trevelyan was repeating, maybe he wasn't doing so well. George felt ashamed that the thought pleased him just a bit.

He looked about. The stands were almost full. This would be a well-attended Olympics, which meant greater strain on the contes-tants—or greater drive, perhaps, depending on the individual.

Why Olympics, he thought suddenly? He had never known. Why was bread called bread?

Once he had asked his father: "Why do they call it Olympics, Dad?"

And his father had said: "Olympics means competition."

George had said: "Is when Stubby and I fight an Olympics, Dad?"

Platen, Senior, had said: "No. Olympics is a special kind of competition and don't ask silly questions, You'll know all you have to know when you get Educated."

George, back in the present, sighed and crowded down into his seat.

All you have to know!

Funny that the memory should be so clear now. "When you get Educated." No one ever said, *"If* you get Educated."

He always had asked silly questions, it seemed to him now. It was as though his mind had some instinctive foreknowledge of its inability to be Educated and had gone about asking questions in order to pick up scraps here and there as best it could.

And at the House they encouraged him to do so because they agreed with his mind's instinct. It was the only way.

He sat up suddenly. What the devil was he doing? Falling for that lie? Was it because Trev was there before him, an Educee, competing in the Olympics that he himself was surrendering?

He *wasn't* feedleminded! No!

And the shout of denial in his mind was echoed by the sudden clamor in the audience as everyone got to his feet.

The box seat in the very center of one long side of the oval was filling with an entourage wearing the colors of Novia, and the word "Novia" went up above them on the main board.

Novia was a Grade A world with a large population and a thoroughly developed civilization, perhaps the best in the Galaxy. It was the kind of world that every Earthman wanted to live in someday; or, failing that, to see his children live in. (George remembered Trevelyan's insistence on Novia as a goal—and there he was competing for it.)

The lights went out in that section of the ceiling above the audience and so did the wall lights. The central trough, in which the contestants waited, became floodlit.

Again George tried to make out Trevelyan. Too far.

The clear, polished voice of the announcer sounded. "Distinguished Novian sponsors. Ladies. Gentlemen. The Olympics competition for Metallurgist, Nonferrous, is about to begin. The contestants are—"

Carefully and conscientiously, he read off the list in the program. Names. Home towns. Educative years. Each name received its cheers, the San Franciscans among them receiving the loudest. When Trevelyan's name was reached, George surprised himself by shouting and waving madly. The gray-haired man next to him surprised him even more by cheering likewise.

George could not help but stare in astonishment and his neighbor leaned over to say (speaking loudly in order to be heard over the hubbub), "No one here from my home town; I'll root for yours. Someone you know?"

George shrank back. "No."

"I noticed you looking in that direction. Would you like to borrow my glasses?"

"No. Thank you." (Why didn't the old fool mind his own business?)

The announcer went on with other formal details concerning the serial number of the competition, the method of timing and scoring and so on. Finally, he approached the meat of the matter and the audience grew silent as it listened.

"Each contestant will be supplied with a bar of nonferrous alloy of unspecified composition. He will be required to sample and assay the bar, reporting all results correctly to four decimals in per cent. All will utilize for this purpose a Beeman Microspectrograph, Model FX-2, each of which is, at the moment, not in working order."

There was an appreciative shout from the audience.

"Each contestant will be required to analyze the fault of his machine and correct it. Tools and spare parts are supplied. The spare part necessary may not be present, in which case it must be asked for, and time of delivery thereof will be deducted from final time. Are all contestants ready?"

The board above Contestant Five flashed a frantic red signal.

Contestant Five ran off the floor and returned a moment later. The audience laughed good-naturedly.

"Are all contestants ready?"

The boards remained blank.

"Any questions?"

Still blank.

"You may begin."

There was, of course, no way anyone in the audience could tell how any contestant was progressing except for whatever notations went up on the notice board. But then, that didn't matter. Except for what professional Metallurgists there might be in the audience, none would understand anything about the contest professionally in any case. What was important was who won, who was second, who was third. For those who had bets on the standings (illegal, but unpreventable), that was all-important. Everything else might go hang.

George watched as eagerly as the rest, glancing from one contestant to the next, observing how this one had removed the cover from his microspectrograph with deft strokes of a small instrument; how that one was peering into the face of the thing; how still a third was setting his alloy bar into its holder; and how a fourth adjusted a vernier with such small touches that he seemed momentarily frozen.

Trevelyan was as absorbed as the rest. George had no way of telling how he was doing.

The notice board over Contestant Seventeen flashed: Focus plate out of adjustment.

The audience cheered wildly.

Contestant Seventeen might be right and he might, of course, be wrong. If the latter, he would have to correct his diagnosis later and lose time. Or he might never correct his diagnosis and be unable to complete his analysis or, worse still, end with a completely wrong analysis.

Never mind. For the moment, the audience cheered.

Other boards lit up. George watched for Board Twelve. That came on finally: "Sample holder off-center. New clamp depresser needed."

An attendant went running to him with a new part. If Trevelyan was wrong, it would mean useless delay. Nor would the time elapsed in waiting for the part be deducted. George found himself holding his breath.

Results were beginning to go up on Board Seventeen, in gleaming letters: aluminum, 41.2649; magnesium, 22.1914; copper, 10.1001.

Here and there, other boards began sprouting figures.

The audience was in bedlam.

George wondered how the contestants could work in such pandemonium, then wondered if that were not even a good thing. A first-class technician should work best under pressure.

Seventeen rose from his place as his board went red-rimmed to signify completion. Four was only two seconds behind him. Another, then another.

Trevelyan was still working, the minor constituents of his alloy bar still unreported. With nearly all contestants standing, Trevelyan finally rose, also. Then, tailing off, Five rose, and received an ironic cheer.

It wasn't over. Official announcements were naturally delayed. Time elapsed was something, but accuracy was just as important. And not all diagnoses were of equal difficulty. A dozen factors had to be weighed.

Finally, the announcer's voice sounded, "Winner in the time of four minutes and twelve seconds, diagnosis correct, analysis correct within an average of zero point seven parts per hundred thousand, Contestant Number—*Seventeen,* Henry Anton Schmidt of—"

What followed was drowned in the screaming. Number Eight was next and then Four, whose good time was spoiled by a five part in ten thousand error in the niobium figure. Twelve was never mentioned. He was an also-ran.

George made his way through the crowd to the Contestants' Door and found a large clot of humanity ahead of him. There would be weeping relatives (joy or sorrow, depending) to greet them, newsmen to interview the top-scorers, or the hometown boys, autograph hounds, publicity seekers and the just plain curious. Girls, too, who might hope to catch the eye of a top-scorer, almost certainly headed for Novia (or perhaps a low-scorer who needed consolation and had the cash to afford it).

George hung back. He saw no one he knew. With San Francisco

so far from home, it seemed pretty safe to assume that there would be no relatives to condole with Trev on the spot.

Contestants emerged, smiling weakly, nodding at shouts of approval. Policemen kept the crowds far enough away to allow a lane for walking. Each high-scorer drew a portion of the crowd off with him, like a magnet pushing through a mound of iron filings.

When Trevelyan walked out, scarcely anyone was left. (George felt somehow that he had delayed coming out until just that had come to pass.) There was a cigarette in his dour mouth and he turned, eyes downcast, to walk off.

It was the first hint of home George had had in what was almost a year and a half and seemed almost a decade and a half. He was almost amazed that Trevelyan hadn't aged, that he was the same Trev he had last seen.

George sprang forward. *"Trev!"*

Trevelyan spun about, astonished. He stared at George and then his hand shot out. "George Platen, *what* the devil—"

And almost as soon as the look of pleasure had crossed his face, it left. His hand dropped before George had quite the chance of seizing it.

"Were you in there?" A curt jerk of Trev's head indicated the hall.

"I was."

"To see me?"

"Yes."

"Didn't do so well, did I?" He dropped his cigarette and stepped on it, staring off to the street, where the emerging crowd was slowly eddying and finding its way into skimmers, while new lines were forming for the next scheduled Olympics.

Trevelyan said heavily, "So what? It's only the second time I missed. Novia can go shove after the deal I got today. There are planets that would jump at me fast enough— But, listen, I haven't seen you since Education Day. Where did you go? Your folks said you were on special assignment but gave no details and you never wrote. You might have written."

"I should have," said George uneasily. "Anyway, I came to say I was sorry the way things went just now."

"Don't be," said Trevelyan. "I told you. Novia can go shove—

At that I should have known. They've been saying for weeks that the Beeman machine would be used. All the wise money was on Beeman machines. The damned Education tapes they ran through me were for Henslers and who uses Henslers? The worlds in the Goman Cluster, if you want to call them worlds. Wasn't *that* a nice deal they gave me?"

"Can't you complain to—"

"Don't be a fool. They'll tell me my brain was built for Henslers. Go argue. *Everything* went wrong. I was the only one who had to send out for a piece of equipment. Notice that?"

"They deducted the time for that, though."

"Sure, but I lost time wondering if I could be right in my diagnosis when I noticed there wasn't any clamp depresser in the parts they had supplied. They don't deduct for that. If it had been a Hensler, I would have *known* I was right. How could I match up then? The top winner was a San Franciscan. So were three of the next four. And the fifth guy was from Los Angeles. They get big-city Educational tapes. The best available. Beeman spectrographs and all. How do I compete with them? I came all the way out here just to get a chance at a Novian-sponsored Olympics in my classification and I might just as well have stayed home. I knew it, I tell you, and that settles it. Novia isn't the only chunk of rock in space. Of all the damned—"

He wasn't speaking to George. He wasn't speaking to anyone. He was just uncorked and frothing. George realized that.

George said, "If you knew in advance that the Beemans were going to be used, couldn't you have studied up on them?"

"They weren't in my tapes, I tell you."

"You could have read—books."

The last word had tailed off under Trevelyan's suddenly sharp look.

Trevelyan said, "Are you trying to make a big laugh out of this? You think this is funny? How do you expect me to read some book and try to memorize enough to match someone else who *knows*."

"I thought—"

"You try it. You try—" Then, suddenly, "What's your profession, by the way?" He sounded thoroughly hostile.

"Well—"

"Come on, now. If you're going to be a wise guy with me, let's see what you've done. You're still on Earth, I notice, so you're not a Computer Programmer and your special assignment can't be much."

George said, "Listen, Trev, I'm late for an appointment." He backed away, trying to smile.

"No you don't." Trevelyan reached out fiercely, catching hold of George's jacket. "You answer my question. Why are you afraid to tell me? What is it with you? Don't come here rubbing a bad showing in my face, George, unless you can take it, too. Do you hear me?"

He was shaking George in frenzy and they were struggling and swaying across the floor, when the Voice of Doom struck George's ear in the form of a policeman's outraged call.

"All right now. *All* right. Break it up."

George's heart turned to lead and lurched sickeningly. The policeman would be taking names, asking to see identity cards, and George lacked one. He would be questioned and his lack of profession would show at once; and before Trevelyan, too, who ached with the pain of the drubbing he had taken and would spread the news back home as a salve for his own hurt feelings.

George couldn't stand that. He broke away from Trevelyan and made to run, but the policeman's heavy hand was on his shoulder. "Hold on, there. Let's see your identity card."

Trevelyan was fumbling for his, saying harshly, "I'm Armand Trevelyan, Metallurgist, Nonferrous. I was just competing in the Olympics. You better find out about him, though, officer."

George faced the two, lips dry and throat thickened past speech.

Another voice sounded, quiet, well-mannered. "Officer. One moment."

The policeman stepped back. "Yes, sir?"

"This young man is my guest. What is the trouble?"

George looked about in wild surprise. It was the gray-haired man who had been sitting next to him. Gray-hair nodded benignly at George.

Guest? Was he mad?

The policeman was saying, "These two were creating a disturbance, sir."

"Any criminal charges? Any damages?"

"No, sir."

"Well, then, I'll be responsible." He presented a small card to the policeman's view and the latter stepped back at once.

Trevelyan began indignantly, "Hold on, now—" but the policeman turned on him.

"All right, now. Got any charges?"

"I just—"

"On your way. The rest of you—move on." A sizable crowd had gathered, which now, reluctantly, unknotted itself and raveled away.

George let himself be led to a skimmer but balked at entering.

He said, "Thank you, but I'm not your guest." (Could it be a ridiculous case of mistaken identity?)

But Gray-hair smiled and said, "You weren't, but you are now. Let me introduce myself, I'm Ladislas Ingenescu, Registered Historian."

"But—"

"Come, you will come to no harm, I assure you. After all, I only wanted to spare you some trouble with a policeman."

"But why?"

"Do you want a reason? Well, then, say that we're honorary towns-mates, you and I. We both shouted for the same man, remember, and we townspeople must stick together, even if the tie is only honorary. Eh?"

And George, completely unsure of this man, Ingenescu, and of himself as well, found himself inside the skimmer. Before he could make up his mind that he ought to get off again, they were off the ground.

He thought confusedly: The man has some status. The policeman deferred to him.

He was almost forgetting that his real purpose here in San Francisco was not to find Trevelyan but to find some person with enough influence to force a reappraisal of his own capacity of Education.

It could be that Ingenescu was such a man. And right in George's lap.

Everything could be working out fine—fine. Yet it sounded hollow in his thought. He was uneasy.

*   *   *

During the short skimmer-hop, Ingenescu kept up an even flow of small-talk, pointing out the landmarks of the city, reminiscing about past Olympics he had seen. George, who paid just enough attention to make vague sounds during the pauses, watched the route of flight anxiously.

Would they head for one of the shield-openings and leave the city altogether?

The skimmer landed at the roof-entry of a hotel and, as he alighted, Ingenescu said, "I hope you'll eat dinner with me in my room?"

George said, "Yes," and grinned unaffectedly. He was just beginning to realize the gap left within him by a missing lunch.

Ingenescu let George eat in silence. Night closed in and the wall lights went on automatically. (George thought: I've been on my own almost twenty-four hours.)

And then over the coffee, Ingenescu finally spoke again. He said, "You've been acting as though you think I intend you harm."

George reddened, put down his cup and tried to deny it, but the older man laughed and shook his head.

"It's so. I've been watching you closely since I first saw you and I think I know a great deal about you now."

George half rose in horror.

Ingenescu said, "But sit down. I only want to help you."

George sat down but his thoughts were in a whirl. If the old man knew who he was, why had he not left him to the policeman? On the other hand, why should he volunteer help?

Ingenescu said, "You want to know why I should want to help you? Oh, don't look alarmed. I can't read minds. It's just that my training enables me to judge the little reactions that give minds away, you see. Do you understand that?"

George shook his head.

Ingenescu said, "Consider my first sight of you. You were waiting in line to watch an Olympics, and your microreactions didn't match what you were doing. The expression of your face was wrong, the action of your hands was wrong. It meant that something, in general, was wrong, and the interesting thing was that, whatever it was, it was nothing common, nothing obvious. Perhaps, I thought, it was something of which your own conscious mind was unaware.

"I couldn't help but follow you, sit next to you. I followed you again when you left and eavesdropped on the conversation between your friend and yourself. After that, well, you were far too interesting an object of study—I'm sorry if that sounds cold-blooded—for me to allow you to be taken off by a policeman. Now tell me, what is it that troubles you?"

George was in an agony of indecision. If this was a trap, why should it be such an indirect, roundabout one? And he *had* to turn to someone. He had come to the city to find help and here was help being offered. Perhaps what was wrong was that it was being offered. It came too easy.

Ingenescu said, "Of course, what you tell me as a Social Scientist is a privileged communication. Do you know what that means?"

"No, sir."

"It means, it would be dishonorable for me to repeat what you say to anyone for any purpose. Moreover no one has the legal right to compel me to repeat it."

George said, with sudden suspicion, "I thought you were a Historian."

"So I am."

"Just now you said you were a Social Scientist."

Ingenescu broke into loud laughter and apologized for it when he could talk. "I'm sorry, young man, I shouldn't laugh, and I wasn't really laughing at you. I was laughing at Earth and its emphasis on physical science, and the practical segments of it at that. I'll bet you can rattle off every subdivision of construction technology or mechanical engineering and yet you're a blank on social science."

"Well, then what *is* social science?"

"Social science studies groups of human beings, and there are many high-specialized branches to it, just as there are to zoology, for instance. For instance, there are Culturists, who study the mechanics of cultures, their growth, development, and decay. Cultures," he added, forestalling a question, "are all the aspects of a way of life. For instance it includes the way we make our living, the things we enjoy and believe, what we consider good and bad and so on. Do you understand?"

"I think I do."

"An Economist—not an Economic Statistician, now, but an Economist—specializes in the study of the way a culture supplies the bodily needs of its individual members. A psychologist specializes in the individual member of a society and how he is affected by the society. A Futurist specializes in planning the future course of a society, and a Historian . . . that's where I come in, now."

"Yes, sir."

"A Historian specializes in the past development of our own society and of societies with other cultures."

George found himself interested. "Was it different in the past?"

"I should say it was. Until a thousand years ago, there was no Education; not what we call Education, at least."

George said, "I know. People learned in bits and pieces out of books."

"Why, how do you know this?"

"I've heard it said," said George cautiously. Then, "Is there any use in worrying about what's happened long ago? I mean, it's all done with, isn't it?"

"It's never done with, my boy. The past explains the present. For instance, why is our Educational system what it is?"

George stirred restlessly. The man kept bringing the subject back to that. He said snappishly, "Because it's best."

"Ah, but why is it best? Now you listen to me for one moment and I'll explain. Then you can tell me if there is any use in history. Even before interstellar travel was developed—" He broke off at the look of complete astonishment on George's face. "Well, did you think we always had it?"

"I never gave it any thought, sir."

"I'm sure you didn't. But there was a time, four or five thousand years ago, when mankind was confined to the surface of Earth. Even then, his culture had grown quite technological and his numbers had increased to the point where any failure in technology would have meant mass starvation and disease. To maintain the technological level and advance it in the face of an increasing population, more and more technicians and scientists had to be trained, and yet, as science advanced, it took longer and longer to train them.

"As first interplanetary and then interstellar travel was developed, the problem grew more acute. In fact, actual colonization of extra-Solar planets was impossible for about fifteen hundred years because of lack of properly trained people.

"The turning point came when the mechanics of the people storage of knowledge within the brain was worked out. Once that had been done, it became possible to devise Educational tapes that would modify the mechanics in such a way as to place within the mind a body of knowledge ready-made, so to speak. But you know about *that*.

"Once that was done, trained men could be turned out by the thousands and millions, and we could begin what someone has since called the 'Filling of the Universe.' There are now fifteen hundred inhabited planets in the Galaxy and there is no end in sight.

"Do you see all that is involved? Earth exports Education tapes for low-specialized professions and that keeps the Galactic culture unified. For instance, the Reading tapes insure a single language for all of us. Don't look so surprised, other languages are possible, and in the past were used. Hundreds of them.

"Earth also exports high-specialized professionals and keeps its own population at an endurable level. Since they are shipped out in a balanced sex ratio, they act as self-reproductive units and help increase the populations on the Outworlds where an increase is needed. Furthermore, tapes and men are paid for in material which we much need and on which our economy depends. *Now* do you understand why our Education is the best way?"

"Yes, sir."

"Does it help you to understand, knowing that without it, interstellar colonization was impossible for fifteen hundred years?"

"Yes, sir."

"Then you see the uses of history." The Historian smiled. "And now I wonder if you see why I'm interested in you?"

George snapped out of time and space back to reality. Ingenescu, apparently, didn't talk aimlessly. All this lecture had been a device to attack him from a new angle.

He said, once again withdrawn, hesitating, "Why?"

"Social Scientists work with societies and societies are made up of people."

"All right."

"But people aren't machines. The professionals in physical science work with machines. There is only a limited amount to know about a machine and the professionals know it all. Furthermore, all machines of a given sort are just about alike so that there is nothing to interest them in any given individual machine. But people, ah— they are so complex and so different one from another that a Social Scientist never knows all there is to know or even a good part of what there is to know. To understand his own specialty, he must always be ready to study people; particularly unusual specimens."

"Like me," said George tonelessly.

"I shouldn't call you a specimen, I suppose, but you are un- usual. You're worth studying, and if you will allow me that privilege then, in return, I will help you if you are in trouble and if I can."

There were pinwheels whirring in George's mind. All this talk about people and colonization made possible by Education. It was as though caked thought within him were being broken up and strewn about mercilessly.

He said, "Let me think," and clamped his hands over his ears.

He took them away and said to the Historian, "Will you do something for me, sir?"

"If I can," said the Historian amiably.

"And everything I say in this room is a privileged communica- tion. You said so."

"And I meant it."

"Then get me an interview with an Outworld official, with— with a Novian."

Ingenescu looked startled. "Well, now—"

"You can do it," said George earnestly. "You're an important official. I saw the policeman's look when you put that card in front of his eyes. If you refuse, I—I won't let you study me."

It sounded a silly threat in George's own ears, one without force. On Ingenescu, however, it seemed to have a strong effect.

He said, "That's an impossible condition. A Novian in Olym- pics month—"

"All right, then, get me a Novian on the phone and I'll make my own arrangements for an interview."

"Do you think you can?"

"I know I can. Wait and see."

Ingenescu stared at George thoughtfully and then reached for the visiphone.

George waited, half drunk with this new outlook on the whole problem and the sense of power it brought. It couldn't miss. It *couldn't* miss. He would be a Novian yet. He would leave Earth in triumph despite Antonelli and the whole crew of fools at the House for the (he almost laughed aloud) Feebleminded.

George watched eagerly as the visiplate lit up. It would open up a window into a room of Novians, a window into a small patch of Novia transplanted to Earth. In twenty-four hours, he had accomplished that much.

There was a burst of laughter as the plate unmisted and sharpened, but for the moment no single head could be seen but rather the fast passing of the shadows of men and women, this way and that. A voice was heard, clear-worded over a background of babble. "Ingenescu? He wants me?"

Then there he was, staring out of the plate. A Novian. A genuine Novian. (George had not an atom of doubt. There was something completely Outworldly about him. Nothing that could be completely defined, or even momentarily mistaken.)

He was swarthy in complexion with a dark wave of hair combed rigidly back from his forehead. He wore a thin black mustache and a pointed beard, just as dark, that scarcely reached below the lower limit of his narrow chin, but the rest of his face was so smooth that it looked as though it had been depilated permanently.

He was smiling. "Ladislas, this goes too far. We fully expect to be spied on, within reason, during our stay on Earth, but mind reading is out of bounds."

"Mind reading, Honorable?"

"Confess! You knew I was going to call you this evening. You knew I was only waiting to finish this drink." His hand moved up into view and his eye peered through a small glass of a faintly violet liqueur. "I can't offer you one, I'm afraid."

George, out of range of Ingenescu's transmitter, could not be seen by the Novian. He was relieved at that. He wanted time to compose himself and he needed it badly. It was as though he were made up exclusively of restless fingers, drumming, drumming—

But he was right. He hadn't miscalculated. Ingenescu *was* important. The Novian called him by his first name.

Good! Things worked well. What George had lost on Antonelli, he would make up, with advantage, on Ingenescu. And someday, when he was on his own at last, and could come back to Earth as powerful a Novian as this one who could negligently joke with Ingenescu's first name and be addressed as "Honorable" in turn— when he came back, he would settle with Antonelli. He had a year and a half to pay back and he—

He all but lost his balance on the brink of the enticing daydream and snapped back in sudden anxious realization that he was losing the thread of what was going on.

The Novian was saying, "—doesn't hold water. Novia has a civilization as complicated and advanced as Earth's. We're not Zeston, after all. It's ridiculous that we have to come here for individual technicians."

Ingenescu said soothingly, "Only for new models. There is never any certainty that new models will be needed. To buy the Educational tapes would cost you the same price as a thousand technicians and how do you know you would need that many?"

The Novian tossed off what remained of his drink and laughed. (It displeased George, somehow, that a Novian should be this frivolous. He wondered uneasily if perhaps the Novian ought not to have skipped that drink and even the one or two before that.)

The Novian said, "That's typical pious fraud, Ladislas. You know we can make use of all the late models we can get. I collected five Metallurgists this afternoon—"

"I know," said Ingenescu. "I was there."

"Watching me! Spying!" cried the Novian. "I'll tell you what it is. The new-model Metallurgists I got differed from the previous model only in knowing the use of Beeman Spectrographs. The tapes couldn't be modified that much, not that much" (he held up two fingers close together) "from last year's model. You introduce the new models only to *make* us buy and spend and come here hat in hand."

"We don't *make* you buy."

"No, but you sell late-model technicians to Landonum and so we have to keep pace. It's a merry-go-round you have us on, you

pious Earthmen, but watch out, there may be an exit somewhere."
There was a sharp edge to his laugh, and it ended sooner than it
should have.

Ingenescu said, "In all honesty, I hope there is. Meanwhile, as
to the purpose of my call—"

"That's right, *you* called. Oh, well, I've said my say and I suppose next year there'll be a new model of Metallurgist anyway for us
to spend goods on, probably with a new gimmick for niobium as-
says and nothing else altered, and the next year— But go on, what is
it you want?"

"I have a young man here to whom I wish you to speak."

"Oh?" The Novian looked not completely pleased with that.
"Concerning what?"

"I can't say. He hasn't told me. For that matter he hasn't even
told me his name and profession."

The Novian frowned. "Then why take up my time?"

"He seems quite confident that you will be interested in what he
has to say."

"I dare say."

"And," said Ingenescu, "as a favor to me."

The Novian shrugged. "Put him on and tell him to make it
short."

Ingenescu stepped aside and whispered to George, "Address
him as 'Honorable.' "

George swallowed with difficulty. This was it.

George felt himself going moist with perspiration. The thought
had come so recently, yet it was in him now so certainly. The begin-
nings of it had come when he had spoken to Trevelyan, then everything had fermented and billowed into shape while Ingenescu had
prattled, and then the Novian's own remarks had seemed to nail it
all into place.

George said, "Honorable, I've come to show you the exit from
the merry-go-round." Deliberately, he adopted the Novian's own
metaphor.

The Novian stared at him gravely. "What merry-go-round?"

"You yourself mentioned it, Honorable. The merry-go-round
that Novia is on when you come to Earth to—to get technicians."

(He couldn't keep his teeth from chattering; from excitement, not
fear.)

The Novian said, "You're trying to say that you know a way by
which we can avoid patronizing Earth's mental supermarket. Is that
it?"

"Yes, sir. You can control your own Educational system."

"Umm. Without tapes?"

"Y-yes, Honorable."

The Novian, without taking his eyes from George, called out,
"Ingenescu, get into view."

The Historian moved to where he could be seen over George's
shoulder.

The Novian said, "What is this? I don't seem to penetrate."

"I assure you solemnly," said Ingenescu, "that whatever this is
it is being done on the young man's own initiative, Honorable. I
have not inspired this. I have nothing to do with it."

"Well, then, what is the young man to you? Why do you call me
on his behalf?"

Ingenescu said, "He is an object of study, Honorable. He has
value to me and I humor him."

"What kind of value?"

"It's difficult to explain; a matter of my profession."

The Novian laughed shortly. "Well, to each his profession." He
nodded to an invisible person or persons outside plate range.
"There's a young man here, a protégé of Ingenescu or some such
thing, who will explain to us how to Educate without tapes." He
snapped his fingers, and another glass of pale liqueur appeared in
his hand. "Well, young man?"

The faces on the plate were multiple now. Men and women,
both, crammed in for a view of George, their faces molded into
various shades of amusement and curiosity.

George tried to look disdainful. They were all, in their own
ways, Novians as well as the Earthman, "studying" him as though
he were a bug on a pin. Ingenescu was sitting in a corner, now,
watching him owl-eyed.

Fools, he thought tensely, one and all. But they would have to
understand. He would *make* them understand.

He said, "I was at the Metallurgist Olympics this afternoon."

"You, too?" said the Novian blandly. "It seems all Earth was there."

"No, Honorable, but I was. I had a friend who competed and who made out very badly because you were using the Beeman machines. His education had included only the Henslers, apparently an older model. You said the modification involved was slight." George held up two fingers close together in conscious mimicry of the other's previous gesture. "And my friend had known some time in advance that knowledge of the Beeman machines would be required."

"And what does that signify?"

"It was my friend's lifelong ambition to qualify for Novia. He already knew the Henslers. He had to know the Beemans to qualify and he knew that. To learn about the Beemans would have taken just a few more facts, a bit more data, a small amount of practice perhaps. With a life's ambition riding the scale, he might have managed this—"

"And where would he have obtained a tape for the additional facts and data? Or has Education become a private matter for home study here on Earth?"

There was dutiful laughter from the faces in the background.

George said, "That's why he didn't learn, Honorable. He thought he needed a tape. He wouldn't even try without one, no matter what the prize. He refused to try without a tape."

"Refused, eh? Probably the type of fellow who would refuse to fly without a skimmer." More laughter and the Novian thawed into a smile and said, "The fellow is amusing. Go on. I'll give you another few moments."

George said tensely, "Don't think this is a joke. Tapes are actually bad. They teach too much; they're too painless. A man who learns that way doesn't know how to learn any other way. He's frozen into whatever position he's been taped. Now if a person *weren't* given tapes but were forced to learn by hand, so to speak, from the start; why, then he'd get the habit of learning, and continue to learn. Isn't that reasonable? Once he has the habit well developed he can be given just a small amount of tape-knowledge, perhaps, to fill in gaps or fix details. Then he can make further progress on his own. You can make Beeman Metallurgists out of your own Hensler

Metallurgists in that way and not have to come to Earth for new models."

The Novian nodded and sipped at his drink. "And where does everyone get knowledge without tapes? From interstellar vacuum?"

"From books. By studying the instruments themselves. By *thinking*."

"Books? How does one understand books without Education?"

"Books are in words. Words can be understood for the most part. Specialized words can be explained by the technicians you already have."

"What about reading? Will you allow reading tapes?"

"Reading tapes are all right, I suppose, but there's no reason you can't learn to read the old way, too. At least in part."

The Novian said, "So that you can develop good habits from the start?"

"Yes, yes," George said gleefully. The man was beginning to understand.

"And what about mathematics?"

"That's the easiest of all, sir—Honorable. Mathematics is different from other technical subjects. It starts with certain simple principles and proceeds by steps. You can start with nothing and learn. It's practically designed for that. Then, once you know the proper types of mathematics, other technical books become quite understandable. Especially if you start with easy ones."

"Are there easy books?"

"Definitely. Even if there weren't, the technicians you now have can try to write easy books. Some of them might be able to put some of their knowledge into words and symbols."

"Good Lord," said the Novian to the men clustered about him. "The young devil has an answer for everything."

"I have. I have," shouted George. "Ask me."

"Have you tried learning from books yourself? Or is this just theory with you?"

George turned to look quickly at Ingenescu, but the Historian was passive. There was no sign of anything but gentle interest in his face.

George said, "I have."

"And do you find it works?"

"Yes. Honorable," said George eagerly. "Take me with you to Novia. I can set up a program and direct—"

"Wait, I have a few more questions. How long would it take, do you suppose, for you to become a Metallurgist capable of handling a Beeman machine, supposing you started from nothing and did not use Educational tapes?"

George hesitated. "Well—years, perhaps."

"Two years? Five? Ten?"

"I can't say. Honorable."

"Well, there's a vital question to which you have no answer, have you? Shall we say five years? Does that sound reasonable to you?"

"I suppose so."

"All right. We have a technician studying metallurgy according to this method of yours for five years. He's no good to us during that time, you'll admit, but he must be fed and housed and paid all that time."

"But—"

"Let me finish. Then when he's done and can use the Beeman, five years have passed. Don't you suppose we'll have modified Beemans then which he *won't* be able to use?"

"But by then he'll be expert on learning. He could learn the new details necessary in a matter of days."

"So you say. And suppose this friend of yours, for instance, had studied up on Beemans on his own and managed to learn it; would he be as expert in its use as a competitor who had learned it off the tapes?"

"Maybe not—" began George.

"Ah," said the Novian.

"Wait, let *me* finish. Even if he doesn't know something as well, it's the ability to learn further that's important. He may be able to think up things, new things that no tape-Educated man would. You'll have a reservoir of original thinkers—"

"In your studying," said the Novian, "have you thought up any new things?"

"No, but I'm just one man and I haven't studied long—"

"Yes. Well, ladies, gentlemen, have we been sufficiently amused?"

"Wait," cried George, in sudden panic. "I want to arrange a personal interview. There are things I can't explain over the visiphone. There are details—"

The Novian looked past George. "Ingenescu! I think I have done you your favor. Now, really, I have a heavy schedule tomorrow. Be well!"

The screen went blank.

George's hands shot out toward the screen, as though in a wild impulse to shake life back into it. He cried out, "He didn't believe me. He didn't believe me."

Ingenescu said, "No, George. Did you really think he would?"

George scarcely heard him. "But why not? It's all true. It's all so much to his advantage. No risk. I and a few men to work with—a dozen men training for years would cost less than one technician. He was drunk! Drunk! He didn't understand."

George looked about breathlessly. "How do I get to him? I've got to. This was wrong. Shouldn't have used the visiphone. I need time. Face to face. How do I—"

Ingenescu said, "He won't see you, George. And if he did, he wouldn't believe you."

"He will, I tell you. When he isn't drinking. He—" George turned squarely toward the Historian and his eyes widened. "Why do you call me George?"

"Isn't that your name? George Platen?"

"You know me?"

"All about you."

George was motionless except for the breath pumping his chest wall up and down.

Ingenescu said, "I want to help you, George. I told you that. I've been studying you and I want to help you."

George screamed, "I don't need help. I'm not feebleminded. The whole world is, but I'm not." He whirled and dashed madly for the door.

He flung it open and two policemen roused themselves suddenly from their guard duty and seized him.

For all George's straining, he could feel the hypo-spray at the fleshy point just under the corner of his jaw, and that was it. The last thing he remembered was the face of Ingenescu, watching with gentle concern.

George opened his eyes to the whiteness of a ceiling. He remembered what had happened. He remembered it distantly as though it had happened to somebody else. He stared at the ceiling till the whiteness filled his eyes and washed his brain clean, leaving room, it seemed, for new thought and new ways of thinking.

He didn't know how long he lay there so, listening to the drift of his own thinking.

There was a voice in his ear. "Are you awake?"

And George heard his own moaning for the first time. Had he been moaning? He tried to turn his head.

The voice said, "Are you in pain, George?"

George whispered, "Funny. I was so anxious to leave Earth. I didn't understand."

"Do you know where you are?"

"Back in the—the House." George managed to turn. The voice belonged to Omani.

George said, "It's funny I didn't understand."

Omani smiled gently, "Sleep again—"

George slept.

And woke again. His mind was clear.

Omani sat at the bedside reading, but he put down the book as George's eyes opened.

George struggled to a sitting position. He said, "Hello."

"Are you hungry?"

"You bet." He stared at Omani curiously. "I was followed when I left, wasn't I?"

Omani nodded. "You were under observation at all times. We were going to maneuver you to Antonelli and let you discharge your aggressions. We felt that to be the only way you could make progress. Your emotions were clogging your advance."

George said, with a trace of embarrassment, "I was all wrong about him."

"It doesn't matter now. When you stopped to stare at the Metallurgy notice board at the airport, one of our agents reported back the list of names. You and I had talked about your past sufficiently so that I caught the significance of Trevelyan's name there. You asked for directions to the Olympics; there was the possibility that this might result in the kind of crisis we were hoping for; we sent Ladislas Ingenescu to the hall to meet you and take over."

"He's an important man in the government, isn't he?"

"Yes, he is."

"And you had him take over. It makes me sound important."

"You *are* important, George."

A thick stew had arrived, steaming, fragrant. George grinned wolfishly and pushed his sheets back to free his arms. Omani helped arrange the bed-table. For a while, George ate silently.

Then George said, "I woke up here once before just for a short time."

Omani said, "I know. I was here."

"Yes, I remember. You know, everything was changed. It was as though I was too tired to feel emotion. I wasn't angry any more. I could just think. It was as though I had been drugged to wipe out emotion."

"You weren't," said Omani. "Just sedation. You had rested."

"Well, anyway, it was all clear to me, as though I had known it all the time but wouldn't listen to myself. I thought: What was it I had wanted Novia to let me do? I had wanted to go to Novia and take a batch of un-Educated youngsters and teach them out of books. I had wanted to establish a House for the Feebleminded— like here—and Earth already has them—many of them."

Omani's white teeth gleamed as he smiled. "The Institute of Higher Studies is the correct name for places like this."

"Now I see it," said George, "so easily I am amazed at my blindness before. After all, who invents the new instrument models that require new-model technicians? Who invented the Beeman spectrographs, for instance? A man called Beeman, I suppose, but he couldn't have been tape-Educated or how could he have made the advance?"

"Exactly."

"Or who makes Educational tapes? Special tape-making technicians? Then who makes the tapes to train *them*? More advanced technicians? Then who makes the tapes—You see what I mean.

Somewhere there has to be an end. Somewhere there must be men and women with capacity for original thought."

"Yes, George."

George leaned back, stared over Omani's head, and for a moment there was the return of something like restlessness to his eyes.

"Why wasn't I told all this at the beginning?"

"Oh, if we could," said Omani, "the trouble it would save us. We can analyze a mind, George, and say this one will make an adequate architect and that one a good woodworker. We know of no way of detecting the capacity for original, creative thought. It is too subtle a thing. We have some rule-of-thumb methods that mark out individuals who may possibly or potentially have such a talent.

"On Reading Day, such individuals are reported. You were, for instance. Roughly speaking, the number so reported comes to one in ten thousand. By the time Education Day arrives, these individuals are checked again, and nine out of ten of them turn out to have been false alarms. Those who remain are sent to places like this."

George said, "Well, what's wrong with telling people that one out of—of a hundred thousand will end at places like these? Then it won't be such a shock to those who do."

"And those who don't? The ninety-nine thousand nine hundred and ninety-nine that don't? We can't have all those people considering themselves failures. They aim at the professions and one way or another they all make it. Everyone can place after his or her name: Registered something-or-other. In one fashion or another every individual has his or her place in society and this is necessary."

"But we?" said George. "The one in ten thousand exception?"

"You can't be told. That's exactly it. It's the final test. Even after we've thinned out the possibilities on Education Day, nine out of ten of those who come here are not quite the material of creative genius, and there's no way we can distinguish those nine from the tenth that we want by any form of machinery. The tenth one must tell us himself."

"How?"

"We bring you here to a House for the Feebleminded and the man who won't accept that is the man we want. It's a method that can be cruel, but it works. It won't do to say to a man, 'You can create. Do so.' It is much safer to wait for a man to say, 'I can create, and I will do so whether you wish it or not.' There are ten thousand men like you, George, who support the advancing technology of fifteen hundred worlds. We can't allow ourselves to miss one recruit to that number or waste our efforts on one member who doesn't measure up."

George pushed his empty plate out of the way and lifted a cup of coffee to his lips.

"What about the people here who don't—measure up?"

"They are taped eventually and become our Social Scientists. Ingenescu is one. I am a Registered Psychologist. We are second echelon, so to speak."

George finished his coffee. He said, "I still wonder about one thing."

"What is that?"

George threw aside the sheet and stood up. "Why do they call them Olympics?"

THE BAND FROM THE PLANET ZOOM

ANDREW WEINER

They didn't really come from the planet Zoom, of course, but I could never get my tongue around where they did come from, and Zoom was close enough. Better, really. It sounded so much like a put-on that hardly anyone ever dreamed that we were serious. I had a hard time believing it myself, most of the time, and I was their manager.

Originally they had called themselves the Blueberries, not that any of them had ever seen or tasted a blueberry. It was my idea to call them the Band from the Planet Zoom. Well, not exactly an idea. It just sort of slipped out. I was at least half-drunk at the time, or I would have been more careful, but as it turned out it was all for the best.

It happened at one of our early club dates. I had invited some of my former colleagues from the rock press to take in the action. They lined themselves up skeptically at the bar while I bought the drinks, a transaction perhaps even more disconcerting for them than it was for me.

The rock hacks, as usual, were drinking too much because the drinks were free. I was drinking too much partly out of habit, but mainly because I was nervous. I was wondering what they would think of my protégés. The last few gigs had been just wonderful, but I was concerned that I might be pushing them along too fast.

I needn't have worried. The band started out with their Vanilla Fudge arrangement of "Eve of Destruction," slipped in an original that sounded like an outtake from *Beatles for Sale,* and then moved into their Mamas and Papas–style "Wild Thing." By the time they got to their Four Tops version of the Left Banke's "Pretty Ballerina," the hacks were staring openmouthed, drinks forgotten.

The Left Banke, I should perhaps explain, were an obscure two-hit wonder dating back to the mid-1960s. Their biggest claim to fame was that the Four Tops had covered the first and biggest of these hits, "Walk Away, Renee." The Tops had never gotten around to the second. Not until now, at least. As the band played their instruments, the video screen behind them on the tiny stage showed them doing a perfect replica of a Four Tops dance routine. It was one of the silliest sights that could be imagined.

And the hits just kept on coming. Teri put down her bass guitar and stepped up to the microphone to do her eerily good early Marianne Faithfull impersonation on the Stones' "Satisfaction." It helped, of course, that she looked quite a lot like early Marianne Faithfull, but she had the voice down too. Then Frank switched from lead guitar to organ and led the band into their Bob Dylan/ *Blonde on Blonde*–style reworking of "She Don't Care About Time," a glorious but utterly obscure old Byrds b-side. And so it went on.

"Who are these guys?" asked Chuck Rickert, a staff writer over at *Record Universe.* "Where do they come from?"

I had prepared a stack of press releases that told the story of the Blueberries and their nostalgic pilgrimage from Bloomington, Indiana, to once-swinging London, England. I had even sprung for a bunch of black-and-white glossies showing them taking in the sights on Carnaby Street. But I had left all that stuff in the truck, and I had forgotten most of the imaginary details. So I winged it. As I say, I was at least half-drunk.

"They're the band from the planet Zoom," I said. "Come two thousand light years to save the spirit of rock 'n' roll." It was a pretty good line, I thought, but I didn't mind giving it to Rickert. I was out of the rockcrit business myself, at least for a while.

Two thousand light years was pushing things a little, though.

Two thousand light years and they would never have picked up our radio and TV signals and heard our rock 'n' roll in the first place. The way I figured it—and they were never very clear on this point— it was more like fifteen. If they had been much closer than fifteen light years, they would have been able to track what had happened to rock 'n' roll since the early 1970s—and they probably wouldn't have bothered to come. I wouldn't have, anyway.

"That's a good one," Rickert said, nodding his head in admiration as he scribbled in his notebook.

"The planet Zoom," I continued, "is situated in the Crab Nebula, I don't have the exact coordinates to hand. The inhabitants live in enormous sentient trees, which act as giant radio antennae in picking up radio transmissions from other star systems . . ."

It was a slow week for news, and the English pop press were hungry, as ever, for new sensations, no matter how idiotic. My story was certainly idiotic enough. And as for the Band from the Planet Zoom (as they would henceforth become known), they were . . . well, not *good* exactly. It wasn't a matter of good or bad. But they were certainly sensational, and even my jaded former colleagues could see it. Even *I* could see it, for that matter, and there were few rock hacks more jaded than myself.

So we got full-page spreads in two of the five leading pop weeklies, and a mention in a couple of others. Rickert did quite well for us, headlining his piece "Out of the Interstellar Garage" and dropping phrases like "cosmic cover band."

Over at *Music Nova,* the paper that catered to the rock intelligentsia, Nicky Far did even better, turning in an admirably impenetrable piece titled "The Alien Viewpoint," which leaned heavily on Barthes, Levi-Strauss, and Wittgenstein. He was especially taken with their version of "Pretty Ballerina," calling it "a new high in punk structuralism. Decomposing and recomposing the text the Zoomers explode our codes of sign and meaning . . . creating and destroying complex new mythologies at will."

I could hardly have done better myself. He would, I thought, be a good man to write the liner notes on our first Greatest Hits package.

And even before the papers hit the streets, the word-of-mouth had spread, and the record company A & R people came crowding around. And from there, of course, it was ever onward and upward.

It is hard for me, even now, to comprehend just how much my life has changed since the day I met the Band from the Planet Zoom.

I put down my paintbrush and take a sip of my Campari-and-soda and gaze out of the window at the picture-perfect wilds of the southern Italian countryside. I call my accountant in London and he confirms that, as usual, my funds have continued to multiply, flowing hither and thither across the globe in search of ever-higher returns, from T-bills to yen to Swiss francs to orange juice futures and back again. Sometimes, in the night, I think I can hear my money, rushing onward like a mighty river flowing.

Things did not work out exactly as I might have wanted them to, but the money is at least somewhat consoling. Certainly I have come a long way from twenty pounds per thousand words.

Yet it did not start out as such a wonderful day, the day I met the Band from the Planet Zoom. As soon as I opened my eyes, in fact, I immediately regretted it. The hangover was quite as awful as I had anticipated, and my attempts to ward it off—several aspirins and much water, on staggering home the night before—had proved entirely futile.

I cursed Righteous Records and their cheap Italian wine and their dreadful new heavy metal band. Power Drill. That was one album I yearned to reduce to vinyl dust.

I became aware that my front doorbell was ringing, had been doing so insistently for the past minute, had indeed awoken me from my restless slumber at the repulsively early hour of ten in the morning.

Groaning, I climbed out of bed and picked my way toward the door through the chaos of clothes and record albums and ashtrays and empty cigarette packs and beer cans and other debris that covered the floor.

The man at the door was holding a record-shaped package, but he was not a postman. The uniform was the wrong color, and in any case no postman would have bothered to ring the bell for so long. He was a courier.

Furious, I grabbed the package, scrawled my signature on the delivery slip, and slammed the door in his face.

That was the problem with being a free-lance rock writer. People were always bombarding you with free records and T-shirts and all sorts of crap. The records, at least, had some value. The going rate down at the local secondhand store was one pound fifty pence. The T-shirts made okay dish towels.

I made myself some tea and took another couple of aspirins. Then I considered opening the package. It was possible that it held records sent for review by *Fast!*, the rock monthly to which I contributed many of my pearls of wisdom. Possible, but unlikely. *Fast!* was not much given to using couriers. Actually, it was a big day when they put on enough stamps to cover the full cost of the postage. More likely it was some record company with more money than sense, flacking every rock hack in town.

How could I have known that I, Rick Haas, had been selected from the thousands of swarming, striving rock critics to receive the only copy in existence, but for the master tape, of that astonishing missive? How could I have known that I, Rick Haas, was the favorite rock critic of a bunch of eccentric aliens?

Not that the competition was so terrific.

As I ripped open the cardboard packaging, a handwritten note fell to the floor.

Dear Rick, it read.

This record is not yet commercially available. This is a preview copy. We have much admired your writing, and would appreciate hearing your opinion on this.

That was all, except for an indecipherable signature and a phone number.

The record itself had a plain white cardboard sleeve. Inside were two single-sided acetates, labeled only "Side One" and "Side Two," and, in smaller print, "The Blueberries."

I groaned. I cursed. A demo. Not even worth a quid down at the record exchange.

And that note. So modest, so obeisant. Just what I needed: being asked to act as an unpaid PR man for a bunch of amateurs. No doubt they were expecting a full-length feature in *Fast!*

I considered dumping record and note into the trash. But I had misplaced the garbage can, and in any case morbid curiosity got the better of me. I put on side one, track one. And was immediately enthralled.

What I was listening to, I later discovered, was their Jimi Hendrix–style arrangement of an old Fairport Convention song called "Meet on the Ledge," and I suppose I did recognize it on some level. The next track was immediately familiar as an old Rolling Stones song, circa 1964, except that to my knowledge it was no song that the Rolling Stones had ever sung. Then came Manfred Mann doing P. F. Sloan's "Sins of a Family" the way they used to do Dylan, except that they never had. And so it went on.

As I rode on the tube to Notting Hill, I wondered who exactly I was going to meet. My suspicion was that it would be a bunch of polite but thoroughly inscrutable Japanese kids. No one else, I thought, could copy so many different rock 'n' roll styles so perfectly, yet in such bizarre combinations. No one else would want to.

They turned out, however, to be boringly Caucasian and otherwise quite unremarkable, except for the matter of their hair and dress. The three male members of the band, who introduced themselves as Bill, Frank, and Tom, were dressed in mid-Sixties style suits with velvet collars and thin ties, and they affected the short-long hairstyle of the period, complete with fringes. Their one female member, Teri, the one who bore the more than passing resemblance to mid-Sixties Marianne Faithfull, was wearing a rather stunning purple miniskirt which stimulated in me immediate nostalgia for times past, along with other emotions.

They told me that they had come from Bloomington, Indiana, but I could detect no trace of accent in their voices, none at all. They looked to be in their early twenties.

Their apartment was in a well-kept building at the fashionable end of the Portobello Road. It was large and tidy but almost completely devoid of furnishings. In the living room there were only a few cushions, scattered on the floor. The walls, however, were covered with old rock posters, a mammoth collage of Barry McGuire and Diana Ross, Bob Dylan and Geno Washington, and on and on. The choice was nothing if not eclectic.

They were anxious, of course, to hear my verdict.

"It's brilliant," I said, "except . . ."

I realized that I had not thought through my exception. I tried to marshal my critical faculties. What was the fatal flaw here? There always was at least one such flaw, it was simply a matter of putting your finger on it. I was operating on too little sleep, and with a still-raging hangover, but a good hack can work with even the most intractable material under the most adverse of circumstances.

"It lacks character," I said, finally. "There's no distinctive *voice*. That could be said, of course, of a lot of music. But you've taken matters to extremes. It's all style and no meaning at all. It misses the whole point of rock 'n' roll."

"What would that be?" asked the one who called himself Bill, and who looked a little like the younger John Fogerty. "What *is* the point?"

There was a definite eagerness in his voice.

"Well . . ." I began.

I realized, suddenly, that I had forgotten the point, if indeed I have ever known it. I racked my brains, thumbing mentally through miles of yellowed newsprint.

"Rebellion," I said, groping. "Teen sexuality. Sense of community. Of shared identity. Like that . . ."

They stared at me, clearly waiting to hear more.

"Defining the frontier," I said, "in the intergenerational war. Developing a politics of everyday life. A shared code . . ."

I rubbed my eyes. What exactly had Greil Marcus said in *Creem* back in 1968? I had misquoted it often enough. Or had it been Jon Landau?

"The hell with it," I said finally. "You guys are going to make a million."

"You mean," Bill said, "that people would buy our records?"

"Yes," I said, feeling a little like Santa Claus handing out the presents. "Lots of them."

Except for the part about Bloomington, Indiana, almost everything they told me about themselves at that first meeting was true. They were all long-term, hard-core rock fans with a particular affection for the music of the 1960s. They had decided to form a band to play the kind of music they liked, and had financed the demo from their own funds. They had no management, and almost no knowledge of the music business, other than what they had gleaned from their reading of the rock press. They had yet to approach a record company.

Even then, though, there were parts of the story that did not quite compute. These kids had an encyclopedic knowledge of music made while they were still in nappies. They were also well-informed about the current scene, although they held it in fairly low esteem. But when the conversation turned to some of the developments in the industry between then and now, they were surprisingly ignorant.

"The Sex Pistols?" Frank asked me at one point. "Who were the Sex Pistols?"

Finally, they got around to asking me to be their manager. I had almost no qualifications for the job, and had never even contemplated such a career move in the past. Indeed, I hardly thought of what I did as being in any sense a career.

Yet it was time for a change, long past time. And besides, I was already a little in love with Teri, no doubt because she brought into play long suppressed adolescent Marianne Faithfull fantasies. Later, of course, I would come to love her for herself, or at least to think that I did so.

I was easily persuaded.

I decided that the band would start up by playing a few club dates before approaching the record companies. I found that they could play their instruments well, but they had as much stage presence as a frozen dinner. And so we hired a rehearsal hall and worked to develop a stage act. I advised on the order of the songs, and made suggestions for new material.

Money appeared not to be a problem for them. They owned first-rate equipment. They paid me a regular salary from the start. They paid cash for a truck, and hired a full road crew. They were not your usual beginners band.

They were as vague about their source of funding as they were about their previous lives in Bloomington, Indiana.

Their ignorance of British history and culture was startling even for Americans.

"This Queen," Tom asked me, "do you elect her, or what?"

There were also strange gaps in their knowledge about their

own supposed homeland. They had only the vaguest notion, for example, of the geographical relationship of New York to Los Angeles. Jimmy Carter was a mystery to them, and so was Stephen King. Yet they knew who had played bass on every Tamla record ever issued.

Finally I had decided to ask Teri. Our relationship had not yet developed in a romantic direction, but already I felt closer to her than to the other members of the band. For all their unfailing politeness, there was something a bit impenetrable, a bit remote, about Frank, Bill, and Tom, although of course I could not have suspected how remote.

I took her out for lunch at a small Italian restaurant in Soho—I had told her that it was once a favorite of the Beatles—and for all I know it might have been—and posed the question directly.

"Where are you guys *from*?"

And so she told me.

It was perhaps a little better than my own worst-case scenario, that they were escapees from a mental institution. Yet I was not really prepared to accept her answer.

"You're putting me on," I told her, although I had never known any of them to lie about anything else, except, as it turned out, about Bloomington, Indiana.

"We thought it would make things simpler to pretend we were from around here," she said.

"New Zealand," I said. "Perhaps you should say you're from New Zealand. People might believe that."

"Actually," she said, "probably no one would believe we were from the planet Zoom."

Except she didn't say "Zoom."

"You're right," I said. "I'm not sure I do."

Believe it or not—and at this point I suppose I *do* believe it—that was where they claimed to be from. Earth rock, they told me, was very big on the planet Zoom. They'd been tuning in to our radio signals since the 1920s, and there were some Zoomers who still grooved to the Glenn Miller sound. But it was rock 'n' roll that had really taken hold. All the kids loved it. If they were kids . . . I was never exactly clear on that point. There was, at least, some phase in the life cycle of the Zoomer at which they could really relate to the big beat, but whether at that point they were kids or senior citizens or something else again I could never really grasp, no matter how many times they tried to explain it to me.

The Zoomers, it seemed, had had faster-than-light interstellar travel for millennia, but they weren't big on tourism. They much preferred to stay home and tune in on the rest of the galaxy. They used some form of instrumentation to do this, by the way. I made up the part about the trees. They could pick up signals from several dozen planets, but Earth was the clear favorite. Reception was better, too.

So they listened and they watched. But somehow it wasn't enough. They craved more rock 'n' roll. And so they started to make it for themselves, just like rock fans right here on Earth. A bunch of kids would get together in a basement, or whatever passed for a basement on Zoom, and the beat would go on. As a species the Zoomers had never been great innovators. They hadn't invented much of anything, beyond a certain point. Even their space drive was given to them by visiting aliens. But they were terrific mimics.

And the Band from the Planet Zoom were the most terrific of all. They were, in fact, the biggest entertainment stars on their entire home world. If I understood them correctly, they were bigger than even the Beatles had been on Earth. Yet they regarded all that as small potatoes. They yearned to compete in the big league. And so they did.

To cut a long story short, the Band from the Planet Zoom was a wild success. The first album chased up the English charts, then did the same in the States even before we hit Shea Stadium. Shea was their idea, by the way, kind of a nostalgic pilgrimage.

The bigger they got, of course, the more media attention they received, and not just from the rock press. Yet for all the inevitable discussion of where they had *really* come from, no one tried that hard to find out. They took it all at face value, a funny put-on, good copy.

As for me, I was having the time of my life. I was managing the best little rock 'n' roll band in the world, maybe even the universe.

And I was doing a pretty good job of it too. I hardly even drank anymore.

I was also romantically involved with an alien bass player and early Marianne Faithfull look-alike, although after a while I didn't think of her in those terms. She was just Teri.

"I'm not sure if I should be doing this," she had said, after we had kissed for the first time, even though she had seemed just as enthusiastic as I was. We were in the backseat of the limo taking us back from a club. Bill, Frank, and Tom had gone their own ways that night, fortunately for me.

"Don't people do this on Zoom?" I had asked.

"Well, yes. And no. It's a bit hard to explain."

"Is it Bill, then?" I asked. "Or Frank? Or Tom?"

I had often wondered about the exact nature of the relationship between the four of them.

She laughed out loud at the thought.

"Oh, no," she said. "We're a . . ." She said an unpronounceable word. "Like brothers and sisters. Or anyway, something like that."

"Then I don't see the problem."

And for a while there had been no problem, none at all.

Of course it was too good to last.

Bill had sounded agitated on the phone. When he arrived at the office he was holding the latest issue of *Music Nova*. He passed it over to me silently, pointing to a review of their latest album. I hadn't read it yet, but I had a good idea of what it would say. It said that the Band from the Planet Zoom were merely skilled mimics, regurgitating tired old rock clichés in apparently new forms, and that while this had once been amusing it had now become tiresome. It concluded by suggesting that they should just go stick their heads down the toilet and flush themselves away.

Except for the last line, which struck me as a bit unimaginative, I could have written that review myself. Probably I *would* have written it myself, if I was still in that line of work.

Lately they had been getting a lot of reviews like this one.

"I don't understand it," Bill said. "The critics used to love us."

"Critics have a very short attention span," I said. "They bore easily. If they can't build you up, they start pulling you down. It's normal. Don't worry about it. Screw the critics. Look at the charts."

At that very moment, the Band from the Planet Zoom stood at the top of both the album and singles charts on both sides of the Atlantic. They had even topped the U.S. country charts, with their cross-over folk-rock version of Woody Guthrie's "Grand Coulee Dam." They were on top of the world.

"It's not enough," he said.

"What's not enough?"

"Our success," he said. "It's empty. Hollow."

"I would say that it seems pretty solid."

"But it's not *creative*," he said. "We're not creative. We're not adding one iota of originality to the sum of rock 'n' roll. We're just refining and recombining things that other people have done."

"I suppose that's true," I said. "But it never bothered you before."

"It's not enough," he said again. "It's not creative, it's not authentic, there's no distinctive voice, no character. You were right from the start."

"A lot of bands," I said, "are like that. Either they start like that, or end up like that. Lose connection along the way. Run out of songs to play. But they keep on playing anyway, most of them."

"Creedence Clearwater Revival, 1968, 'Lodi,' " Bill said, automatically. "But the point is, we were never connected in the first place. Never had any genuine roots."

Obviously he was serious about this. But I really didn't know what to suggest.

"Maybe," I said, "you could go back to your roots. Inject something of your background into your music. Something of Zoom."

"Zoom," Bill said, "is boring. Zoom is nowhere."

Despite my protests, the Band from the Planet Zoom canceled their forthcoming Far East tour. They built their own 16-track studio in a house in Beverly Hills and withdrew into total seclusion. No one was allowed in there, not even me.

I missed Teri horribly.

"I'm sorry," she told me. "This was a group decision. This is something we really have to work out for ourselves."

I spent some time in London, and some more time in Italy. Out of sheer boredom I began to paint again, for the first time in ten years. I spoke to the band on the phone from time to time, but they were evasive when I asked how things were going.

"All right," Frank would say, or Bill, or Tom, "I think it's going all right."

Teri was no more forthcoming, although we talked a lot about other things. I told her about the house I had found in Italy, and she said she was looking forward to seeing it.

This went on for months. And then finally they summoned me to L.A. to hear the masterwork. They sat around me in the huge living room as it boomed from the speakers, watching my reactions. Reactions I was trying very hard to mask. Almost from the first note it was wretched. Really rotten. Boring, pointless, pretentious drivel.

Oh, there were flashes here and there of the old Zoomers. Even a potential chart single, if you pared out the five-minute instrumental passage and cleaned up the vocals. But these were mostly accidental. They had set out determined to create something entirely original, something completely new under this or any other sun, and for the most part they had succeeded. It was just unfortunate that it was virtually unlistenable.

When the tape ended I asked to hear it again. It was, if anything, worse the second time around. Finally came the moment I dreaded.

"Well," Frank asked. "What do you think?"

"It's interesting," I said. "Courageous . . ." I trailed off. "What the hell. It stinks."

Frank nodded. "That's what we thought."

"You tried too hard," I said. "Tried to be something you're not. You are who you are."

"Clever copyists," Bill said. "A cosmic cover band."

"But there's nothing really new in rock," I said. "Not really new. What is rock 'n' roll anyway? Just the same chords and riffs and stuff rotated endlessly. You could make a pretty good argument to that effect."

I was straining, though, and they could hear it.

"There's always something new in the music," Bill said. "Something of the performer. If you're going to leave a real mark."

"You've already made a mark."

"Five years from now, who will remember?"

"Five years from now you can still be at the top," I said. "You've barely scratched the surface so far."

"I'm sorry, Rick," Teri told me, from across the room. "That isn't going to happen. You see, we've decided. We're going home."

"When?" I asked. "When did you decide? You only just heard my opinion."

They looked from one to another, but no one offered to explain. Somehow they didn't need to. I had always thought they had an uncanny ability to communicate with one another, one which went beyond words, and now I knew that for sure.

"Don't be so hasty," I said. "We should talk about this some more."

But Frank shook his head.

"It's like Teri told you," he said. "We all decided. I'm sorry, Rick, but we can't go on with this. It just isn't . . . *fun* any more."

Teri did come to stay with me in my house in Italy before they left.

"It's charming," she told me. "Wonderful. We have nothing like this."

"Stay here," I told her. "Stay with me. You can be a solo act. Or we can just give up the business altogether. Christ knows we can afford to."

"I can't," she said. "Please don't ask me that."

"What will I do?" I asked. "What am I going to do without you?"

"You'll get over it," she said. "You'll find something else to do with your life. Find another band. Or paint, perhaps." She indicated the half-finished painting sitting on the easel. "I think that's really quite good."

"I'm not talking about the band," I said. "I'm talking about you and me."

"I can't stay," she said. "I just can't, even if I wanted to. Me and Bill and Frank and Tom, we're a . . ." And she used the same unpronounceable word I had heard in that little Soho café. I realized now that its meaning was a little stronger than "brothers and sisters."

"We have to stay together," she told me. "That takes precedence always, even over—over bonding relationships."

"But you're on Earth now," I said. "We do things differently here. You can adjust, adapt. You're like us in every other way already, after all."

"Not really," she said. "You see, this isn't really me. This is just the form I've taken here. Back home I don't look like this at all. Except when we perform, of course."

I realized, then, that I had suspected something like this all along, but had done a very good job of repressing the idea. She had seemed entirely human to me in every way that counted.

"What do you look like?" I asked.

"I knew this was a mistake," she said. "I knew I shouldn't have allowed myself . . ."

"What do you look like?" I asked, again.

"It doesn't matter," she said. "The point is, you think you love me but you don't really. You love only what you think you see."

"That's true in any relationship," I said. "We all have illusions about other people. That's part of being in love."

"I wouldn't know about that," she said. "But I do know about us. It's like the music, really, our relationship. It's all style, all appearance, and we should keep it that way. You wouldn't love the real me. You couldn't possibly."

"How terrible could it be?" I asked. "After all, you were able to love me. Or at least, you said you did. If we're as different as you're suggesting, how could that be possible?"

"We're more cognitively flexible," she said. "We've been exposed to a greater variety of life forms, and we're able to imitate many of them. We have a much greater capacity for aesthetic appreciation even of very different morphologies."

"But I couldn't handle it, is that what you're saying?"

"No," she said. "You couldn't."

"Yes I could," I said, desperate. "Try me."

She resisted, but I persisted. Finally, at the end of that last week together, she gave in.

"This is another mistake," she warned me. "This is not how you want to remember me."

And so she showed me her real form. And, sad to say, she was right, and I was wrong. I could not handle it. I could not love the real her, it was all I could do to stay in the same room. Sad, and despicable, but true all the same.

Let me leave it at that. I see no point in going into prurient and still painful detail.

They were indeed very clever copyists.

So the Band from the Planet Zoom packed their bags, such as they were, and returned to their native world. Or at least, I have no reason to believe otherwise. And these days nobody much thinks about them, except maybe to wonder whatever happened to them.

I remember them, of course, and particularly Teri, the way I knew her and the way I last saw her. It took me a long time to get over Teri, and in a certain sense I never did.

But even I hardly play their records anymore. For that matter, I hardly ever listen to rock 'n' roll.

I'm retired from the business, you see. I don't manage rock bands and I certainly don't write about them. I made a good deal of money from my involvement with the Band from the Planet Zoom, and I got good advice on investing it. I don't have to work another day in my life, and almost certainly I won't.

Instead, I paint. It was something I always wanted to do, but never had the time for before. Back in school the art teachers always said that I had talent, at least as a draftsman, although I was a little lacking in imagination.

I paint in my villa in southern Italy. I paint very much in the style of my idols, de Chirico and Magritte. I'm getting pretty good at doing de Chirico, but I'm still having trouble with Magritte.

One of these days, I tell myself, I'm going to paint something really original. One of these days.

But I would not call it a burning ambition, and I will not be deeply disappointed if I fail. There are worse things, after all, than being a stylish and clever copyist.

Much worse things.

THE WEB
DANCER
SOMTOW SUCHARITKUL

he was poised in the pause on a leap's edge, toes nudging the rope-slack in the tight circlet of glare, pressed between a breath and its release—a girl of eleven, alone under a billion unseen eyes.

This time—

Nika flexed her toes swiftly for the first triple somersault of her career. She gathered in all the strands of tension and compressed them, *hard,* into a knot of neutronium deep within herself, then released it all at once, exploded outward at the ends of her limbs, *gave* into the perfect curve of the movement—

And slipped!

There was a moment between falling and fallen. A moment drawn out and still. A moment of cutting clarity. In that moment her gray eyes saw—

—image boxes slamming to the ground, lens-jewels splintering, fire cartwheeling over instrument banks, doorways dominoing over monitors and shelfstands, and—

(It wasn't my fault I slipped! she thought. *Something collided with the show satellite! There's a war going on in this system and we should never have chosen to record here but they said we were neutral and*

performers can't be touched because they come under the protection of the Inquest!)

—technicians were running amok, alien uniforms of different sides flashed across the floor, bodies cascaded like flocks of birds, someone in a booming voice declaring this quadrant of space now occupied, performers with mouths open staring at the slaughter, screaming—

(She closed her eyes then. *I'm going to die!* she thought, not caring anymore. *I'm just going to be a chance victim of someone else's war . . .* and then she wished her hair was streaming above her, not cropped to a centimeter's length, but then she remembered why she had cut it off, and she felt a yawning emptiness inside her and wanted to die.)

—rope flopping snakelike, writhing, tangling her feet, and—

(I don't care! she thought fiercely. *I'm Nika of the clan of Rax and the show never stops, never never never—)*

The vault of the show satellite cracked. Through the airshield the stars shone . . . and another ship, huge, with none of the gaudy local markings, was growing rapidly, blacking out the starlight.

Who could they be? she wondered, in the split second before the forceshield slapped her into blackness.

Nika opened her eyes. (*Why am I still alive?* she thought.)

"They're all dead." The voice was gravelly, the accent strange. "Don't think of them anymore. Be at peace with yourself."

Silhouettes of two men; and behind them . . . She could not tell where the room ended and where the wild dance of laser-bright lights began. Flametongues whipped against blackness! And darting between them, neckerchief swirls of purple, crimson, cerulean, cadmium-yellow, ultramarine, bursting out and fading into darkness.

. . . *We're in a starship!* For they were in the overcosm then: that *other* space, of strange dimensions, where *far* becomes *near.*

"Dead?" She faced her captors. *How much time had passed?* She could still feel the tightrope slipping from her feet and the utter helplessness. . . .

"Dead," the gravelly voice echoed. "We won't harm you, girl. We saved your life."

He was good looking, bland, overdressed; his body-jewels gleamed in the rainbow fire of outside. She disliked him at once. The other one, though: severe, old, dressed from head to foot in a single shimmercloak.

An Inquestor! So somehow, power was involved. A lot of power.

It wasn't the first time Nika had been whisked away from everything she knew. *I'm so tired,* she thought . . . she wanted to cry. But she knew she would not. She had vowed never to cry again.

"They are all dead, your friends," said the Inquestor, not unkindly. "Some might have survived a month or two . . . but time dilation has taken care of *them*. We intercepted a local battle to pluck you out."

"But the Inquest doesn't interfere in local wars!" she said. When that evoked no response, she cried out, "I could have *done* it!"

"Done what?" said the first man.

"The triple somersault!" she said. "The climax of my career, recorded on crystals for a billion eyes."

"Career!" the young man scoffed.

"Don't mock her," said the Inquestor sharply. "Kaz Amar, go back to your astrogating." The man bowed, departed quickly. "You're a child yet," the Inquestor said when they were alone. "Let's not hear talk of crowning moments of careers, Nika, not for another century yet."

Nika felt rage gathering inside her. *I'm not a child!* How dare they patronize her! They had taken away everything: her homeworld, her friends, the nomadic life of the show-satellites, flicking from system to system . . . and they had plucked her away from her supreme achievement.

(She felt the rope slipping beneath her feet again. She would have struck out in fury—)

Then she heard inside herself the voice of Iliash, who had trained her: *Push your rage inward! Let it collapse like the aftermath of a nova, into a ball of neutronium! Harder, harder* . . . the voice pounded at her memory. . . .

"Nikkyeh—" the other began, consolingly.

"Nika. I'm not a child." How dare he presume to address her by a diminutive, when he was neither lover nor friend.

"Good, you have personal dignity, spirit," said the Inquestor, appraising her.

"Take me *home*!"

The Inquestor stood impassive. He towered over her, a darkened doorway set into the wall of light-swirls. "Nika—"

"I won't stay here! I have to get back to homeworld. If I train hard I can make the panhuman games. You don't have the right to kidnap me." But she felt her past slipping away, she saw that she no longer believed in homeworld or in herself. . . .

"Nika," said the Inquestor. "You are a Rax, and we have need of a Rax. You've grown up thinking you're nothing special, just fit for the circus; your body too small for a warrior, your intellect too unschooled for a thinker. But you are one of the most valuable people in the Dispersal of Man. You're not ready for all this yet. You should have had more time, more training. But we're desperate."

"For what?"

"Listen. I am Ton Exkandar z Vangyvel K'Ning, Inquestor and Kingling."

"Ruler of my homeworld . . ." Blurred images of infancy whirlpooled.

"Yes. Don't say I didn't have the right to kidnap you." He paused. Behind, fireworks burst from a sea of ink. Fire-ripples laced the darkness. *Why is he trying to justify himself?* Nika thought. Then: *He's vulnerable.* She wanted to trust him, but—

"It is incredible that we should need you!" he burst out. "That I should gatecrash a petty war, like a space pirate, a common kidnapper—"

"But why do you need me?" She was bewildered, angry, frightened. "Did you destroy the show-satellite just to get *me*?"

"No," said Ton Exkandar, "we intercepted the local war. You *had* to be saved."

Am I that important? I'm only a girl! What sort of game am I a pawn in?

"And now I'll never do it. . . ."

"Do what?"

But Nika had shut him out of her thoughts. She had turned away from him; and now she watched the shifting, soundless patterns, letting them soothe her, hypnotize her. . . .

She imagined an infinite rope stretched all the way across the overcosm, and infinite Nikas, reflections of herself, leaping, upending themselves in a swift tight arc of movement, whirling down to touch the rope with the gentlest of touches. . . .

And slipping.

It was closed-loop holotape of the memory, each time no less terrifying.

How could she fight these people? She didn't know who they were and what they wanted. And she had fought too many people already to become what she was. She was tired! Drained!

"And now I'll never do it," she said, shuddering.

She would not let them put her into stasis. So there would be three subjective months in the overcosm, and there was nothing to do.

In her quarters there was one curved gray wall which could be blanked and which gave a view of the madness outside. When she was awake she lay on her pallet and watched.

They had put up a series of ranked transverse bars for her to practice on. But she wouldn't touch them. She didn't even look at them. Because they made her suspect her whole childhood had been manipulated, had been drawn toward . . . something no one would tell her about.

There was nothing to do but remember. And this she did, in the moments before sleep, or after staring herself into a trance while the colors danced. . . .

She was six and the children had all gone to war. She had run all the way from the orphanage to watch them, to stand by the wall and see the ships rise like a flock of silverdoves and cross the faces of the far, cold suns of Vangyvel.

Mother found her weeping under a whispertree. It reached out a furcoated metal hand to the child's brow; and the tree sang as the breezes of Vangyvel touched its flutelike leaves, a soft random counterpoint . . . "Don't cry," said Mother in its consoling mode.

"I want to go, too!"

"So you shall, so you shall . . . but right now you're too small. Too precious, too special," it said, increasing its sympathy-tones in a steep gradient with each word.

"There's something wrong with me! I know it, I know it!" She began sobbing again, with the utter, end-of-the-universe hopelessness that only children know. For a while now she had not grown at all, and her bones were thin and hollow. "I'm a mutant or something! Isn't that why I'm in an orphanage?"

"Of course not, child, you're very special, only I can't tell you why yet. . . ."

And the froglet will become a Kingling! thought Nika, bitter. Mother was programmed to lie to her. After all, it was only a machine. The tree seemed to copy her sobs, mocking them, the way the other children always did. . . .

"I'll never cry again!" she said passionately. "I'll do something with my tiny body that no one else will be able to do!"

"That's my girl."

"All right, Mother. Nikkyeh will go home now." They stepped toward the displacement plate and commanded the coordinates.

That was the day she had first felt the emptiness inside, yearning to be filled. And had thrown anger into it.

Later she threw herself into dancing the rope. She had to be good at *something*! And she was. Her sense of balance was *unnatural,* everyone said. Which was true.

She could spin like a gyroscope down half the length of a slackrope. She could do it slowly, making them blue from holding their collective breath, stretch out the tension to its elastic limits, then reverse in a flash, stifling the gasps of relief.

Rax Iliash was her teacher. They brought him in, encouraging her. He was older, about twelve or so, she judged, but small, too, like her. Two years he spent pushing her. He knew so much, he who seemed just a child.

The moments when she released all her anger at being different, all her frustration at not being normal, perhaps—into achingly beautiful parabolas of motion across emptiness—these were her moments of joy. Finally they made crystals of her dancing, and they became nomads. The homeless life of the show-satellites pleased Nika—what had home meant but children's mocking laughter?

On initiation, she, too, had received the clan title of Rax. She and Iliash were the only two either of them had ever heard of. She never took part in the initiation; the Inquestor of Judgment had merely handed the title to her. . . .

"But am I not to be tested?" She was suspicious as always, of everyone except Iliash.

Worried, overworked, the eyes had looked right through her and he said: "Daughter, you are Rax. We cannot waste you." *What did that mean?*

Once she and Iliash had gone to the zoo world and wandered around like tourists, gaping at the pseudoenvironments: the fire-snows of Ont, the methane fogs of Brekekekex, the rivermountains of Ellory, the amber skies of Lalaparalla; and the beasts: lobster-things, fire-things, cloud-things, balloon-things . . .

Two innocents, they walked hand in hand. Between the force-shielded habitats were corridors of a manworld environment.

They came to a cave where a crystal creature slept. The crowd lurched forward as it woke.

Suddenly a burst of anguish issued from the cave and hit Nika, almost physically. "Did you *feel* that?"

"Yes. Yes." His gray eyes, so like hers, were troubled. The crowd was unaware of anything; they bent down, almost touching the forceshield, murmuring, "Oh, how cute. . . ."

Iliash's hands almost squashed Nika's. Waves of pain crested and ebbed. "I can't stand it!" she said. Then, crying out: "It's a mistake! That's a sentient creature! You can't cage him!"

Curious stares, laughter. She was being mocked again! She was almost fainting with the pain. Iliash pulled her and dragged her along the path, away from the crowd.

Now they reached a field, with ten-meter-high cornstalks under an ink-blue sky. Iliash was saying, "Nikkyeh, you and I have this empathy. It's one of our special things, an empathy with alien beings. You and I are *tailored,* Nikkyeh! The Inquest has some purpose for us."

She clutched him to her. But they were just two children, and nothing came of it.

Soon after the show-satellite left for another system, Nika began to train for the triple somersault in 0.5 gravity. No rope dancer had ever done it before. She worked with a fierceness not usually found

in children. She had to fill the void inside her! She was hungry for
training. . . .

And so she forgot all about the Inquest's special purpose. It
seemed so irrelevant. She was far from Vangyvel now; and the Dispersal of Man comprised a respectable percentage of the galaxy.

But when she was nine Iliash left the troupe.

She went to say goodbye to him. They were on a desert planet, a
dreary planet of endless red sand under a sapphire sky. Iliash stood
. . . strange how he had never grown at all . . . beside two tall
figures in shimmercloaks. Inquestors! And behind the three—

It was a sphere. It was totally black, featureless, perhaps ten
meters in diameter. It appeared to have no substance. It was as if a
portion of the sandscape and sky had been blotted out, had simply
ceased to exist. It was a tachyon bubble, of course. Inquestors used
them to travel instantly through space. Never ordinary people. The
overcosm still required subjective time of the traveler, even though it
was, in effect, faster than light. The overcosm had its own overcosm,
and it was through these highest planes that the tachyon devices
traveled, short-cutting the short-cuts.

It was black because it was not even part of the universe. And
only the Inquest could use them, because of the devastating energy
waste, and because it might lend too much power to the lower clans.

Nika was afraid. *Two* Inquestors! A tachyon bubble! So Iliash
had to be important, somehow.

But he was just a kid!

She looked at the boy whose gray eyes so resembled her own,
who shared her clan name, whom she was about to lose forever.
Would they come for her, too?

"You're all I have, Ilyeh!"

The two Inquestors moved impatiently. There was not much
time.

"Ilyeh." She held his hand tight.

"Nikkyeh," he said, "I've learned what the Inquest made us for.
Now I'm going away to do what I have to do. . . ."

She raged impotently. *Push it inside yourself, the neutronium ball!*
"I love you, Ilyeh," she said. (*Do I?* she asked herself.) "When we're
older, if time dilation hasn't made us too far apart in age—"

"Don't talk about what can't be!" he said. His eyes looked wistful, yet hopeless.

"What do you mean?"

"You and I—" He stopped suddenly, turning to see whether they were watching him. "We don't have puberty. We don't grow. How old am I, Nikkyeh? How old do you think? I'm *eighty-seven*!"

Nika chose to ignore this; she could not believe it. "You can refuse to go," she pleaded.

"They made us too well," said Iliash. "They made us so we'll *want* to do this, they put the love of it in our bones. . . ."

"Of *what*?" she said sullenly. "There's nothing I love more than you!"

"There is, there is!" He turned to go. The two Inquestors had faded into the tachyon bubble, and one of his feet had already vanished into the blob. She felt abandoned, lied to. He was like Mother after all.

"What do you mean?" she shouted. "What is there that I love more than you?"

"That triple somersault!" he said. He blew her a kiss, wrenched himself around and leaped into the bubble. It winked out. There was no trace of it on the sand, only three sets of footprints that led to the same spot and vanished . . . she turned away and began to walk toward the landing craft.

Now she felt truly empty. Even Iliash, whom she had trusted, had finally betrayed her.

The triple somersault! The cruelty of it! How could he make fun of her like this?

But it was true.

That was the day she cut off all her hair, disgusted with herself. And determined to think of nothing at all but the triple somersault, to feed all her anger to the triple somersault!

"Why don't you use the bars?" Exkandar asked, gently. It had been two months; and—abandoning her past in despair—Nika had grown her hair again. It was long now, and fiery as a bursting star.

"When the birds aren't happy, they don't sing."

"As you wish."

"Why do they all treat me so condescendingly here?" she said, sounding suddenly frail.

Exkandar said: "You're indispensable; they're not. They're afraid of you, really."

"But why?"

"You'll see."

She watched one swirl of green flame as it slowly transformed into a crazy spiral and melded into the blackness. *"You'll see! You'll see!* Do you people never tell anyone anything?"

"Nika, I don't know that you could take it yet. You're too young. I counseled against all this—"

"Well, give me a clue!"

"All right," he said heavily. "We need more starships. There is to be a war, a war with aliens . . ."

"That has nothing to do with me. Performers are neutral."

"Wait, listen to me!" *How tired he sounds!* Nika thought. "How do starships work? You should know that."

Nika laughed. "They're navigated through the overcosm," she said, "by an astrogator who is in communion with a delphinoid shipmind—" When Exkandar did not answer, she went on, "Delphinoids are giant creatures who are all brain. They're captured on . . . some planet, I don't know. They perceive the overcosm directly. They're cybernetically implanted into ships by means of . . . some crystal or other . . ."

"Yes," said Exkandar. "There are semisentient crystals that can concentrate and focus particle streams into the overcosm."

"But," Nika said, "they never told us, in school, where the crystals come from."

"And there is your clue," said Exkandar, and would say no more.

Nika thought it over. She had been tailored—gene-tailored—for empathy with alien minds, for minimal physical development. They needed starships. The ships needed crystals. *It doesn't make any sense!*

Exkandar said, "I want you to keep practicing. Use the bars, Nika." She saw them, light finger-thin poles of some flexible polymer, stretched from wall to wall in ranks of increasing height. For a moment only she wanted to rush up to them and spring into action, leaping from one to the other till she could dance on the highest pole . . .

"No," she said. *Am I punishing them or myself?* Exkandar took this as a dismissal and left. And Nika wondered at this, that her word could command a Kingling and Inquestor.

Then, making sure she was unobserved, she flashed up in an easy bound onto the first rung, then from one ranked bar to the next as though they were steps in a pyramid. When she reached the highest one, she tiptoed swiftly along the bar, her weight hardly flexing it at all. Her mind wandered. . . .

She caught her balance. *Out of practice!* She remembered how she had fallen, and then the bar slithered from under her; quickly she grabbed with her hands and pulled herself up again. . . .

Oh, no. They've ruined me.

There was a new kind of queasiness in her stomach. *I'm afraid!* she thought, startled by the new emotion.

In a few days they reached a nameless planet that intersected a nexus in the tachyon universe. It was a blizzard-swept place, without inhabitants save for the nexus station crew, all of the clan of Nartak, another one Nika had never encountered.

The two of them came down in a lander to await their tachyon bubble. High overhead, it materialized, blotting out more and more of the snowburst as it descended, sinking through the domeroof as though it were thin air. There was a humming; another Inquestor, also in a plain shimmercloak, emerged from the black blot.

Disappointment showed on the stranger's face. "Only one?"

"We could trace no others," said Exkandar quickly. "And this is a youngling of eleven."

"It's a catastrophe!" said the visitor. "Come, both of you." To Exkandar: "Is she prepared?" He toyed with his shimmercloak.

"She doesn't know anything," said Exkandar. "The circumstances of her presence with us were . . . traumatic; I thought it best—"

"Yes, yes." He blotted out. Exkandar pushed the girl ahead into the bubble; once inside she could not tell she was *inside* at all. They moved, suddenly, into the air, and Nika felt no excitement or wonder, only the same deadness she had felt since her capture. But just before they blinked out—

This is where they took Iliash!

She closed her eyes and remembered his face, as though she were looking into a mirror: the eyes that reflected her own, the boyishness that, she now knew, concealed long experience.

She smiled . . . for the first time since the attack on the satellite . . . and clutched the memory of his face to her, determined never to let it slip.

Bleak. Gray. Bleak. Gray.

It was an impossibly tiny planet, with a horizon that dropped too soon, like an asteroid's: its diameter was only fifty kilometers. There was a core of neutronium, the size of a wine-goblet perhaps, denser even than the degenerate matter of white dwarfs, they said. Or perhaps a seething soup of quarks, or perhaps compressed all the way into a black hole . . . whatever it was, it gave the planet a surface gravity of 0.78.

She hated the planet!

It had crazy naked crags, gray and featureless, that erupted out of gray, mirror-still lakes. The sky was gray, too, an even, impenetrable gray like Iliash's eyes, like Nika's eyes.

Nika and Exkandar hovered in the floater over the mountains. "It's artificial, this planet," she said. It was obvious. But instead of wondering at it, she detested it.

"Yes," said Exkandar, "but not built by us. Not by humans. By a race long extinct. A world built to order, built for the breeding of the tarn crystals. We haven't worked out every variable. We can't duplicate what this world does! The neutronium core, for instance—we don't know how vital that is. If it is, we can't replicate it at all."

The floater swooped toward the frighteningly close horizon, whipping aside to avoid the crag. Nika heard a quiet rumbling, almost beneath the threshold of hearing. "What's that sound?" she asked. And felt herself *drawn* to the sound somehow, attracted by it. . . .

"The mountains are in heat."

"Oh." The two days she had spent here had only compounded

her bewilderment. Something brushed her face. She started to strike out at it in annoyance. . . .

She looked up to see a monstrous butterfly, with a wingspan of perhaps a meter, hovering ahead. She let out a little scream, more in surprise than fright.

The animal hovered. The resemblance to a butterfly was only superficial, she saw. It had uncountable tiers of wings, each paper-thin and translucent, refracting light into a thousand colors. There were two legs, crystalline and muscular at the same time . . . and a small, oval head with six or seven eyelike organs. From the head sprouted paper fans—they looked like fans—that glittered intermittently as they caught the light . . . the wings moved, vibrated faster than the eye could see; and then were suddenly still as a wind sprang up to support the creature. The fans rotated nervously, catching at sunlight; there was little of it here, for the sun was perpetually hidden in veils of gray cloud.

The creature watched the floater and its occupants for a long time. They were buoyed up by the same air current.

Angel, thought Nika, *faery, creature of myth* . . . her heart almost stopped beating. Something in the void inside her responded to it . . .

Suddenly the creature shivered all over, spread its wings, vibrated them, a shimmering aurora of lights splashed across the grayness, a whir of wings, a dazzling soaring into the cloudbanks that left an after image like the ghost of a rainbow. . . .

So beautiful! "If only I were like it," she said, "and not trapped the way I am."

"It is a farfal," said Exkandar. "The farfellor are the larval forms. . . ."

"Of what?" she said as they rounded another precipice and skimmed a lake of deathly stillness.

"Of the tarn creatures."

"There are beasts, then, living in the mountains?" She tried not to sound too interested, but in spite of herself . . .

"No. They *are* the mountains."

Nika whipped around in panic, upsetting the floater for a moment. She saw the torturous crags, straddling the horizon, twisted shapes that strained toward the ash-gray cloudveils. . . .

"Whoever built this planet was far superior to us, in technology, in bioengineering . . . tarn crystals, the things that focus the minds of delphinoid ships, are the unfertilized ova of these mountains," said Exkandar. "The adult forms are static, vast, silicon-based; photosynthesizing silicon chains from the gray sunlight and from the silicate-rich crust, the salts dissolved in the lakewater. Perhaps their roots even reach down to the neutronium core—there are unsolved anomalies in its particle emissions—and draw on its energy. We don't know exactly how it works, just that it's a very lucky thing for the Dispersal of Man, a secret stumbled on many millennia ago which has kept the human race in contact with itself, which has stabilized and enriched our culture. . . ."

So that's how the Inquest keeps control of the Dispersal of Man, thought Nika. *And it's such a precarious secret, too. They're so* vulnerable. *Without the crystals, war and commerce would both cease.*

But what does it have to do with me?

"The clan of Rax . . . we are collectors of tarn crystals, then?" she said. *It's humiliating!* she thought. *To scrabble in the rocks, when I could have been the Dispersal's greatest rope dancer.* It didn't sound possible.

"Let's float onward." He blinked, and Nika knew that he was keying the floater by means of a brain-implant. Soon they soared above the lake and swerved around a peak, with the horizon gaining on them. . . .

They reached a plateau encircled by a wall of stubbier mountains. A flock of farfellor swooped by the mountain-face and swung upward, in a perfect arc, like a necklace drawn up by an unseen hand.

The floater came to rest near the edge of the plateau and they stepped down. The rumbling came again. "Is that what you meant, when you said the mountain was *in heat*?"

"They have cycles. Now look ahead of you."

Nika obeyed him. For a moment she had forgotten she was a prisoner, destined for an unknown and probably unpleasant fate.

Gray statues of farfellor stood on the plateau's edge, staring out over the emptiness at the ring of tarn creatures. Nika went up and touched one, tentatively; its touch was cold as marble. Now two or three farfellor, circling overhead, swooped down in a wild glittering and landed beside them, and stopped moving. As she watched, veins of grayness grew and spread across the color-lattice of wings, across the crystalline legs—

"They're dying!" she gasped.

"No, metamorphosing . . . in a few years, a century perhaps, another tarn creature will grow here. There is an active phase of reproduction. After that the mountain is quiet, and never moves again; it might be dead or dormant, we don't know. Are they sentient, Nika? You were bred for empathy with aliens. . . ."

She listened for the cries of other minds. But she could not tell. There could have been a voice, but it was a murmur so distant that it might have come from another world. "I don't know."

"None of you ever know, for sure."

What an alien world! And she was so alone in it. She pushed ever harder at her fear, hoping it would contract to nothing. "But where are the other Rax? Where is Iliash?" She knew he was withholding something. "Why us? Do we have to die to get your precious crystals out of the mountains, is that it?" For a moment Nika longed for the touch of Mother's fur-covered iron hand . . . *but I mustn't be a child!* she thought. *Must fight* . . .

"It's hard for me to tell you, little one. We Inquestors," Exkandar paused, choosing his words, "are above all compassionate; at initiation we are selected for this trait. I can't bring myself to—"

What could it be that upset him so? Nika could imagine only death. Panic pounded at her. She sprang up and bolted for the floater. When she reached it he had already caught her.

"No, it's not what you think!" he shouted. "Come, let me finish what I have to show you." And again he seemed so vulnerable that Nika felt for him; though she knew that she was the victim, not he.

Some forty kilometers on there was a peak, especially huge, going right up through the clouds. They flew into a small building, open on three sides, built into the foot of the mountain; steps were carved into it, and there were other houses, a small village. People— guards or workmen—in blinding bright tunics, were milling around the hallway. When they saw Exkandar they bowed; when they saw Nika they gaped.

At the end of the hall there was a tiny passageway, circular, maybe a meter wide. It led to total darkness.

It's a tunnel! she thought. *They're going to force me in there and make me dig around for the eggs. . . .* "You can't make me go in there!" she said, hysterically. "The other Rax are lost in the tunnels, aren't they? You bred us small to make us live out our lives in there? I won't do it! I'm a rope dancer, I need the open—"

Exkandar stared at her incredulously, then burst out laughing, for the first time since she'd known him.

One of the workers said quickly: "Lord Inquestor, she doesn't know?"

The mountain rumbled a little. The workers fell on their knees and seemed to be deep in prayer.

"They don't know the truth," Exkandar whispered to Nika. "They worship the tarn creatures. They're the egg-collectors, they gather them as they roll down the oviducts—that's what the tunnels are—and they'll worship you, too! We've set it up as a religion to conceal what the eggs really are. . . ."

"Then what *is* my role?" Nika was exasperated beyond endurance. "What happened to Iliash? Didn't you bring a Rax named Iliash here?"

Exkandar took her by the hand. "I'll show you now."

At the entrance they boarded the floater and wafted upward, following the gradient of the tarn, hugging the surface. Nika strained to see some crack, some irregularity of color or texture. There was none; it was all one gray.

They glided onto a perch of the cliff-face. The Inquestor jumped off and motioned her to look. At first she saw nothing—

Then—

Growing out of the cliff edge, flung out taut over the chasm till it disappeared into the grayness, was a tightrope. Nika ran to the edge, got down on her knees and leaned over to touch it. It felt . . . made for her. The slackness of it was just right, the pressure just enough. A stadium out in the wilderness, on an unnamed planet!

Something inside her responded at last. She yearned to walk the strand. . . .

Her eye ran along the rope, and she saw faint lines alongside it, crossing over it, above and below . . . mostly, the lines were invisible, until the light fell just right, until the wind tugged gently on them.

She put one foot forward, and remembered—

(Rope slipping from under her, wild vertigo of burning machinery and people aflame, whirling—*I've been kidnapped! I should be
angry! I shouldn't do anything they want me to do!*)

And fear. The fear that had come to her for the first time, unbid-
den, when she had tried to practice again on the ship. She tried to
swallow it up, kneeling down and caressing the rope, pulling at the
tension. . . .

Exkandar explained. "These strands are the tarn creature's nervous system. When it is in heat, the larval forms . . . and you . . .
will feel it calling you; the farfellor fly over and dance lightly on the
strands, stimulating the sleeping mountain . . . after a while,
sometimes half an hour, sometimes half a day or more, the eggs are
released, one by one, sliding down the tunnels to the oviduct-
mouths. The dancing farfal sends out empathy-signals all over the
planet, and thousands of farfellor flock to the tunnel mouth to fertilize the eggs, making tempests with their wings, breaking the sides of
the mountain in their urgency. . . .

"And after, they are too exhausted. They have spent everything;
their fertilizing fluid, their reserves of energy—for farfellor do not
ingest—and with their last strength they fly to a plateau, become
rooted and dormant, await the next stage of their cycle. Thousands
of them will eventually merge into a single mountain—"

And suddenly, Nika saw what he was driving at. "*I* have to
dance on the webstrands!" she cried out. And it came to her at once,
how she had been manipulated at every stage in her life.

"Don't blame us, Nika!" Exkandar said, anguished. "If there
were another way we would have found it. But we need *unfertilized*
ova! And if the dancer does not send out signals to the other farfellor, the eggs are not fertilized. We tried using robots and androids
and altered animals . . . but nothing works except a human being,
reacting to impulses given off by the alien mind, small, perfectly in
control of his body—"

"Can't you slaughter them as they attack the mountain? Can't
you set up forceshields?"

"The mountain senses if there are any obstacles to the eggs
reaching the air freely. That's why the temple is open on three sides.
We tried braving it out, assaulting the storm with missiles and pro-

jectiles. But often the eggs would be damaged, their crystalline alignments warped; and usually one farfal would get through. And one is enough to fertilize them all."

Bitterly, Nika said, "And when we've danced on the ropes, and given you your priceless eggs—what then? Do we die? One day, do we fall off? Do we slip?"

"Accidents are common. I won't lie to you. And it is necessary to keep the number of Rax small and separated from one another, until they are needed . . . and now you are the only one. You see, the farfellor . . . *compete* with the web dancers—"

"I have to fight them off?"

Those beautiful creatures were deadly, then! They were her enemies. . . .

Exkandar was silent.

"And what happens afterward . . . ?"

Nika saw that he was disturbed; she knew that there would be more, and not pleasant, information. Furiously, she turned away from him. How cleverly they had trapped her!

She looked over the precipice. Now that she knew what to look for, she could see many of the strands, silvery-white, crisscrossing one another in strange, irregular grids, stretching out to invisibility.

"I won't do it! You can't force me!"

("There *is* something that you love more than me!" Iliash had said.) The ropes shifted and swayed in the soundless breeze. *I want to! I want to!* her mind cried out. *I could tiptoe out, ever so lightly, I could press my feet in and spring up, high, high, high, do the triple somersault, here, hovering over the emptiness—*

"Curse you, Inquestors!" she said. "You made me too well!" And she trembled with longing and revulsion.

"Yes," Exkandar said.

Built on stilts over the largest lake, the House of Rax must have been able to house a hundred or more web dancers. Nika was lost in it. Even her private room was as large as a moonhopper.

She threw herself into practice, which was in a varigrav gymnasium larger than the whole show-satellite had been, with silklike strands stretched over a protective forceshield. She was too immersed to notice the empty corridors hung with imagesongs and lightmobiles, the tape libraries smelling of overscrubbed disuse. But she had time to ask questions.

To become angrier.

She needed that anger, as fuel for the web dance. She had no love, no hope. Anger was all she could dredge up from inside the great emptiness.

She learned that the Rax were cloned (in both sexes, purely a cosmetic difference) from a centuries-old blueprint tissue, and that they were released into orphanages one at a time in worlds as distant as possible from one another; that a recent radical mutation of the tissue culture had almost wrecked the system, that samples had been taken from her in her sleep to rectify and perpetrate the system. That explained partly why she was the only one there now; also, there had been a rash of accidents. The Inquest was desperate indeed.

The mountain god took its toll in human sacrifice.

She learned that replacements for her were being tracked down all over the Dispersal of Man, and that after this breeding season she would be free to leave. Not because of charity.

She would be burned out. Her empathy-circuits would be ruined. Web dancing made a ruin of the mind and the body . . . but they would let her go. She could be a dancer still . . . with a different set of memories.

They would destroy her memories completely—not just the planet, the web dancing; but everything, just in case. Yes, she would truly be free.

Or dead.

But perhaps Iliash was out there among the stars, a ghost of himself with a different personality . . . and Nika became angrier. *I'll dance for him!* she thought. *I'll make him see me!*

If I'm angry enough I won't be afraid.

In her mind she tumbled again from the rope, she heard the screaming and saw the fire flash. Iliash had told her: *Anger is good. It's the next best thing to courage. But push it all inside you, coil it up so it'll rush out when you need it most.*

She tumbled in the gymnasium, too, onto the springy forceshield. *It's hopeless, I'm not ready.*

She learned that they had tried to set up a forceshield under the tarnweb, but the mountain had not been fooled. It had sensed an irritation in the environment, and the ova had not come.

She became angrier.

They implanted fingerlasers on both her hands and keyed them to subvocalized syllables. Now there were sounds she could never even *think* again. For hours she danced the high ropes, flicking death at farfal-robots. She learned very fast. Of course: she was made that way.

In her room she lay and gashed the walls with the fingerlasers, and when she came back the walls would always be repaired, unblemished as before. She grew angrier then, and in between practicing she lay and brooded.

Beyond her fear of slipping, beyond the anger—she saw herself, running free on the highrope, whirling against the wind, her body a perfect song of curves and arches, a still hurricane-eye of the wild elements. . . .

It's not just the thought of slipping, she told herself in the darkness before sleep. *I'm not a cog in their machine! I hate them for making me want this, for manipulating me this way! I want it to be just me!*

But she had sworn never to cry again, that time so many years ago. And she had never broken that oath. So she swallowed everything and woke up knotted with anger.

A few weeks later she found a holosculpture library in a circular room where half the wall could be deopaqued to show the lake that curved and dipped so abruptly into the mountainpeaks. They were both so gray, she thought, the landscape outside and the silver walls inside. No wonder the workers wore such dazzling colors. She watched the lake; it never rippled, but cast a perfect echo of the gray sky.

I'm almost angry enough—

A worker, in crimson-and-blue swirled tunic, was waiting deferentially. "May I help you, little miss? I am Ynnither, librarian of the House of Rax. The computer indicated you were here."

Nika was annoyed that her solitude had been broken so callously. "I have to be alone! I'm going to break my skull on the rocks, for the sake of the universe or something, and I can't be alone!"

"Is there something you would like to see, a particular holo-sculpture? Before there was so much work—"

Perhaps he could tell her something. "What about *before*? You have holosculptures of the others, of the Rax before me? Of a Rax named Iliash?" For a moment she panicked, dreading what the answer might be.

There was a rumble—

"There now, miss, that'll be the big one calling for his mate," said the worker. "It'll be your time soon."

". . . Iliash?" She was adamant.

Ynnither said, "I remember him all right. He was the daringest of them all. To the last he was daring. Cocky. A legend to us."

"Show me."

Nika heard the hum of machinery, and the view-walls opaqued. He appeared in midair, about a meter from her face, suspended in midleap. His hair floated above him, caught in that moment.

She walked closer to the holosculpture, ran her hand through emptiness. How she longed to be part of that frozen moment. . . .

The gray eyes looked back, full of defiance.

"We have the sculpture in kinetic, too, miss," said the worker, and turned to adjust the machinery.

All at once Iliash finished his leap, in the middle of the emptiness, in one impetuous curve. Nika thought, *Not as refined as I would be. But how achingly beautiful!*

He vanished, leaped again, vanished, leaped again—with the playback in the kinetic mode, there was wind in the picture, ruffling the waves of hair; and as he landed the face broke into a smile at once triumphant and fragile.

"He was your friend, miss?"

Was? Realization shot through her, and she felt outrage . . . outrage. . . .

"He was the greatest web dancer we have had. You should have seen him in life! We often watched on the monitors in the eggroom. He's dead now."

She stared at the leaping figure till her eyes burned.

"A farfal got him, miss, on the very day he was scheduled to return to his homeworld. He needn't have danced the web that day; they'd told him it was enough. But he was wilder than usual, ran like an animal across the ropes—how we mere mortals envy your powers!—and then he shouted, *'I'm going to try for that triple somersault!'* And he stood on the rope and steadied himself for a tremendous leap. The farfal swooped down and dislodged him. They never found all the pieces."

So you're dead! she thought. Blood was on her hands and she realized how hard she had clenched them. *Control your anger, roll it into a secret place inside you so you can throw it into your leap—*

And Nika knew that she was ready. The rage had built up inside and was ready to explode. The void inside her was full.

The rumbling came again, and Exkandar was standing beside her. "You must come now, Nika. The mountain is calling for you. . . ."

In the back of her mind she felt an alien presence, tugging at her, hungry and passionate. She did not have to be told what it was. She had been bred for empathy with aliens' minds. It was the call of the tarn-creature to all the farfellor. Then they deopaqued the wall and she saw the mountain peaks jutting out over the lakeface, and her heart gave a funny leap and she let out a cry. And understood the ugly, dissonant rumbling . . . it was a song!

And she felt tears rushing. Choking them back, she said, "I can't help what I am, after all. Even after what you did to Iliash, the only person I've ever loved, and the others."

"Come!"

"Did you think this would make me feel like a superhero in a kid's holoplay, rushing in to save the Galaxy from the evil aliens?" she said, exulting. "I'll dance the webs—but not for your precious ships. I'll dance for Iliash, who died for my somersault. I'll dance for the perfect leap! I'll dance for ME!" And she was proud of what she was, and of her importance.

And she looked the Inquestor—a Lord of the Dispersal—full in the face, and saw . . . humility. And pitied him at last.

The rumbling called her, thrilling her. She saw flocks of farfellor, responding likewise, flashing across the sky.

And, against the mountain peaks and the steel sky, the ghost of the boyfigure with the bright gray eyes tumbled and leaped, tumbled and leaped, over and over, with consummate grace.

*   *   *

After about twenty meters Nika opened her eyes.

She had been testing the web's tautness. With every cautious step she had felt the strand bend itself, accommodate itself to her weight. It was a thing alive, that strand. Not like the lifeless ropes of the show-satellite, which her own body gave life to. Here was a rope she was almost in communion with . . . but she did not trust it, not quite yet.

She looked. Below was Exkandar on his floater: if she tumbled, he would catch her if he could. There were other webstrands, their ends lost in the grayness. The grayness was overpowering. Space and distance were swallowed up by it, so that she seemed suspended in midnothingness.

Love me. Love me. Leap for me. Dance for me.

It was a voice not quite sentient that sang in the back of her mind, more the voice of an animal in need, broadcasting distress signals. "You poor mountain," Nika whispered. "You're just a pawn in their game, like me. Yes, I'll dance for you. . . ."

She took a tentative leap forward, landed lightly on her right foot, spun around.

Love me more! More!

The voice tugged at her, yearned for her . . . she whirled once, twice, each time leaning harder into the silkstrand, catching herself miraculously just at the instant she would have tumbled.

"That's right, Nika, slowly, cautiously," prompted Exkandar's voice, reaching her via a head implant. She shrugged the voice off contemptuously. They didn't know anything, these people who used the tarn-creature's eggs to control the Galaxy. Right now there was only her and the mountain, alone together.

A light wind sprang up. She took four more steps, then narrowly avoided a tumble, overcompensated for the wind, almost tripped again, flung out her arms wildly and steadied herself in a moment. Above the rumble came a high whistling, mixing with the wind sounds.

She looked up, pushing down harder with her toes and keeping her arms outstretched for the balance. A flock of farfellor broke through the cloudveils, a dozen or more of them, swooping, converging on her—

Mustn't panic—

(She remembered the rope slipping from under her over and over but the whisper of the mountain touched her, calmed her. . . .)

Dance more, dance more, why do you stop?

The fighter convoy moved in to cut them off. About fifty meters above her head, a projectile volley exploded the flock into wild flurries of color. The farfellor screamed, a heartrending highpitched keening that became part of the whistling wind. *Poor creatures,* Nika thought for a moment. *Sacrifices.*

But I'm going to ignore Exkandar and the farfellor and the Inquest and the fate of the Galaxy now. I'm just going to leap high, leap perfect, leap, she thought.

Leap for me, love me!

Impetuously, she cartwheeled across to the next strand, ran swiftly along it, leaping back to the first strand, making singing arcs in the air.

("For the sake of all of us, play it safe, girl!" she heard Exkandar say. And laughed at him. . . .)

One of the farfellor had not been killed. It hovered over her, vulturelike, waiting. Nika ignored it, until it swooped down and knocked against her face. Angrily she whirled round and bisected it with her fingerlasers, watching the iridescent pieces fall forever into grayness. . . . She turned back to the web dancing, feeling the pull of the mountain, *loving* the mountain.

Suddenly the sky was alive with the flapping of farfal wings! A sea of colors crashed across the sky, and the convoys were everywhere, slaughtering. Farfal bodies plummeted like rain. Projectiles zinged and boomed.

Nika closed her eyes, reaching for the strands with her nerves, with her mind—

And leaped up, somersaulting! In her mind's eye Iliash turned with her. Her feet touched the strand and she steadied herself with relief. She laughed again, feeling the mountain's joyous response. And whirled again, arms out, like a top, with the wind flushing her face and her hair flying.

I think I can do it—

A shudder went through her, a release of rapture, thrilling her. . . .

The mountain was giving birth! She knew it, she could feel with it, she could feel the eggs falling down the long tunnels toward the foot of the mountains.

"You've done it!" Exkandar cried. "We'll come and get you now—"

"No!" she cried. "I think I can do it."

"Do what?" She saw the floater climbing up after her. She ran along the web, farther out into the emptiness, using the bounce of the web to propel her even faster. . . .

And then, in a moment when she found herself quite alone, she wound up all her anger and all her love, everything that was ever pent up in her slight body, and *compressed* it into a core of neu-tronium and then exploded, hurled herself upward—

Iliash! You should see me now!

—defying the planet's pull, higher than she could have thought possible, and somersaulted, with the world and the farfel colors kaleidoscoping about her eyes and the windstream burning her—

One—

Two—

Three—

And touched the web, giddy with triumph and joy.

". . . all right," Exkandar's voice was saying. "Don't move, we'll come for you. It was a fantastic crop. You've done well by the Gal-axy. . . ."

She laughed again, a peal of laughter that scorned Exkandar and all his kind. "I've done well by me!" she shouted, her face flushed. "I've done the first triple somersault on a rope *ever*! I've danced free under the open sky with the wind singing and the mountain loving me. And I'll never forget this! I'll show you! You can erase my memory, you can discard me like another used-up tool, but I won't forget! Not ever, not if I live a thousand years!

She had come to the arena again, a grown woman still shaped like a girl, to dance the rope dance. It was the Highfest of Vangyvel —which, they had told her, was once her homeworld—and it was the nameday of the Kingling Exkandar, who would actually deign to attend. But this meant nothing to her. She stepped onto the slackrope.

There was no forceshield. She despised safety. . . .

The tiers of crowd rose to the roof of the dome. In a breath darkness fell, and she was alone in a pool of light.

She danced. She danced with a kind of crazy joy, a wildness that always drove her audience to a frenzy. But all this was routine; the climax was yet to come.

She did some dazzling footwhirls; and then, suspended only by her feet, twisted her body up the length of the rope, accelerating to the music. The crowd was deafening now, the waves of sound egging her on, pounding at her. . . .

And then she stood in the middle of the nothingness, prevented by a thread from abrupt death. She stood frozen for a long while, while the crowd grew silent, pondering.

Her eyes fell on the royal pew, and met the eyes of Kingling Exkandar, aloof, his Inquestral shimercloak topped by the iridium crown.

Odd, she thought, *that face* . . .

And she closed her eyes in the ritual of the triple somersault, imagining herself away, far away, on some made-up, impossible planet:

Gray lakes, still as mirrors . . .
Colors, sluicing the gray sky, threatening . . .
Wind, caressing her . . .
Mountain peaks, jutting from a too-near horizon . . .

(What was the memory? From what scene in her sketchy past had it come? It would always come to her before the great leap. She seemed to remember that once, ages ago, she had filled the void inside her with anger, not love. . . .)

And she pressed her body like an arrow into the bowstring and sprang upward, as the wind whistled and the creatures like butterflies flashed against the alien sky—

She landed. The crowd's silence broke into thunder. The strange planet retreated into her unconscious. She had been perfect.

Perfect!

As she looked out at the crowd, only a trace of the phantom memory lingered, a voice not human, crying out for her compassion—

Love me. Dance for me. Leap for me. Love me.

THE HOB
JUDITH MOFFETT

Elphi was the first of them to wake that spring, which meant he was the first to catch, almost at once, the faint whiff of corruption. Feeling ghastly, as always upon just emerging from hibernation, he dragged himself out of his bunk to go and see which of the remnant of elderly hobs had died during the winter.

He tottered round the den in darkness, unable as yet to manage the coordination required to strike a light. Nor did he really require one. Hobs were nocturnal. Besides, this group had been overwintering in the same den for nearly a hundred years.

Tarn Hole and Hasty Bank lay together, deep in sleep. Hodge Hob seemed all right . . . and Broxa . . . and Scugdale. . . . Ah. Woof Howe Hob was the dead one. Elphi checked on Hart Hall, just to make sure there had been only one death, then wobbled back to his own bed to think.

They would have to get Woof Howe out of the den: he thrust that thought, and the necessity for fast action, into the forefront of his mind to blank out the yawning hollowness, the would-be grief. Every decade or two, now, another of them was lost. The long exile seemed to be coming inexorably to an end, not by rescue as they had gone on expecting for so long, but by slow attrition. Only seven

were left of the fifteen stranded in this place, and soon there would
be none.

Elphi rolled out again; these thoughts were unproductive, as
they had ever been. He needed a drink and a meal.

The great stone that had sealed the den all winter posed a problem. By human standards the hobs were prodigiously strong for
their size, even in great age, but Elphi—feeble after his months-long
fast—would ordinarily not have attempted to move the stone un-
aided. But he managed it, finally, and poked his head with due
caution out into the world.

Outside it was early April on the heather moors of North Yorkshire. Weak as he was, Elphi shuddered with pleasure as the fresh
moorland wind blew into his face. The wind was strong, and fiercely
cold, but cold had never bothered the hobs and it was not for
warmth's sake that Elphi doubled back down the ladder to fetch
forth something to wrap around himself, something that would de-
ceive the eyes of any unlikely walker still on the tops in the last few
hours of light. That done, he dragged the heavy stone back across
the hole, sealing in the scent of death, and set off on all fours stiffly
through the snow-crusted heather.

He followed a sheep-track, keeping a weather eye out as he
trotted along for any farmer who might be gathering his moor ewes
to bring them down "inside" for lambing now. Those years when
the hobs slept a bit later than usual they sometimes found their
earliest forays cramped by the presence of farmers and dogs, neither
of which could be easily fooled by their disguise. When that happened they were forced to be nocturnal indeed.

But the sheep Elphi saw had a week to go at least before they
would be gathered in, and he began to relax. Walkers were always
fairly few at this uncomfortable season, and the archeologists who
had been working at the prehistoric settlement sites on Danby Rigg
the previous summer were not in evidence there now. Perhaps getting rid of old Woof Howe would not be quite so difficult as he had
feared—not like the year they had woken in mid-April to find
Kempswithen dead and the tops acrawl with men and dogs for days.
The only humans he was at all likely to encounter this late afternoon
would be hauling hay up to their flocks, and since their tractors and

pickups made a din that carried for miles in the open landscape he had no fear of being caught napping.

The local dogs all knew about the hobs, of course, as they knew about the grouse and hares, but they rarely came on the tops unless they were herding sheep, and when they were herding sheep they generally stuck to business. The problem dogs were those the walkers allowed to run loose, whether under good voice control or no. *They* could be really troublesome. In August and September, when the heather turned the moorland into a shag carpet of purple flowers forty miles wide and a tidal wave of tourists came pouring up to see and photograph them, the hobs never showed their noses aboveground by day at all. But it was a bother, despite their perfect ease at getting about in the dark; for except from November to April hobs didn't do a lot of sleeping, and they always had more than enough essential work to see to. Then there was the grouse shooting, which started every year on August twelfth and went on till long after Elphi and his companions had gone to ground for the winter. . . .

Of course, the horde of August visitors was also a great boon. All summer the hobs picked up a stream, steady but relatively thin, of useful stuff dropped or forgotten by visitors. August brought the flood, and the year's bonanza: bandanas, wool socks, chocolate bars, granola bars, small convenient pads of paper, pencils and pens, maps, rubber bands, safety pins, lengths of nylon cord, fourteen Swiss Army knives in fifteen years, guidebooks, comic books, new batteries for the transistors (three) and the electric torches (five). Every night in summer they would all be out scavenging the courses of the long-distance footpaths, the Lyke Wake Walk and the Cleveland Way, each with a big pouch to carry home the loot in.

Earlier and later in the year, however, they were forced to spend more time hunting, and hunting a meal was Elphi's first priority now. Luckily he and his people could digest just about anything they could catch (or they would not have been able to survive here at all). They were partial to dale-dwelling rabbit and spring lamb, and had no objection to road-killed ewe when they could get it; but as none of these was available at the moment, Elphi settled for a grouse he happened to start: snapped its neck, dismembered it, and ate it raw on the spot, hungrily but neatly, arranging the feathers to look like a fox kill (and counting on a real fox to come and polish off the bones he left behind).

Satisfied, his head clearer, Elphi trotted another mile to a stream, where he washed the blood off his hands and had his first drink in more than four months. He had begun to move better now. His hands and broad feet shod in sheepskin with the fleece side out settled into their long habit of brushing through the old snow without leaving identifiable tracks. Still on all fours, he picked up speed.

Now then: what were they to do with Woof Howe Hob so that no human could possibly discover that he had ever existed?

Burning would be best. But fire on the moors in April was a serious thing; a fire would be noticed and investigated. The smoke could be seen a long way, and the park rangers were vigilant. Unless a convenient mist were to cover the signs . . . but the hobs almost never, on principle, risked a fire, and in any case there were far too few stored peats in the den to burn a body, even a hob's small body. Elphi suddenly *saw* Woof Howe on a heap of smoldering peats and his insides shriveled. He forced the picture away.

They would have to find someplace to bury Woof Howe where nobody would dig him up. But where? He cursed himself and all the rest, his dead friend included, for having failed to work out in advance a strategy for dealing with a problem so certain to occur. Their shrinking from it had condemned one of their number—himself, as it turned out—to solving it alone, if none of the others woke up before something had to be done.

Elphi thought resentfully of the past century and a half—of the increasing complications the decades had added to his life. In the old days nobody would have fussed over a few odd-looking bones, unless they'd been human bones. In the old days people hadn't insisted on figuring everything out. People had accepted that the world was full of wonders and mysteries; but nowadays the living hobs' continued safety depended on making the remains of their dead comrades disappear absolutely. They'd managed it with Kempswithen, rather gruesomely, by cutting him into very small bits quite unrecognizable as humanoid, and distributing these by night over four hundred square miles of open moorland. None of them would care to go through that again, unless there were positively no other way.

Elphi thought about that while he gazed out above the stream bed and the afternoon wore gradually on. The air was utterly clear. Far off to northwestward the peak of Roseberry Topping curled down like the tip of a soft ice-cream cone (Elphi knew this, having seen a drawing of one in a newspaper a hiker had thrown away); and all between Roseberry Topping and Westerdale Moor, where he now risked standing upright for a moment to look, swept the bristly, shaggy, snowy heath, mile after mile of it, swelling and falling, a frozen sea of bleakness that was somehow at the same time achingly beautiful. White snow had powdered over an underlayer of russet— that was dead bracken at the moor's edge—and the powdered bracken lent a pinkish tint to the whole wide scene. The snow ended roughly where the patchwork fields and pastures of Danby Dale and Westerdale began, and among these, scattered down the dales, were tiny clumps of stone farm buildings.

Elphi had spent the first, best two centuries of his exile down there, on a couple of farms in Danby Dale and Great Fryup Dale. These dales, and the sweep of bleakness above them, made up the landscape of most of his extremely long life; he could scarcely re-member, anymore, when he had had anything else to look at. How-ever truly he yearned for rescue with one facet of his soul, he beheld these dales with a more immediate yearning, and the moors them-selves he loved with a surprising passion. All the hobs did or had, except Hob o' t' Hurst and Tarn Hole Hob. Woof Howe had loved them, too, as much as any.

Elphi drew in the pure icy air, and turned once around com-pletely to view the whole great circle of which he was the center, noting without concern as he turned that a wall of mist had begun to drift toward him off the sea. Then he dropped down, and was again a quadruped with a big problem.

They might *expose* Woof Howe, he thought suddenly—scatter the pieces in that way. It would be risky, but possible if the right place could be found, and if the body could be hidden during the day. Elphi set off northwestward, moving very rapidly now that the kinks were out of his muscles, instinctively finding a way of least resistance between stiff scratchy twigs of heather. He meant to check out a place or three for suitability before getting on back to the den to see if anybody else was awake.

*   *   *

Jenny Shepherd, as she tramped along, watched the roke roll toward her with almost as little concern. Years ago on her very first walking tour of Yorkshire, Jenny, underequipped and uncertain of her route, had lost her way in a thick dripping fog long and late enough to realize exactly how much danger she might have been in. But the footpath across Great and Little Hograh Moors was plain, though wetter than it might have been, a virtual gully cut through the slight snow and marked with cairns, and having crossed it more than once before Jenny knew exactly where she was. Getting to the hostel would not be too difficult even in the dark, and anyway she was equipped today to deal with any sort of weather.

In order to cross a small stone bridge the path led steeply down into a stream bed. Impulsively Jenny decided to take a break there, sheltered somewhat from the wind's incessant keening, before the roke should swallow her up. She shrugged off her backpack, leaned it upright against the bridge, and pulled out one insulating pad of blue foam to sit on and another to use as a backrest, a Thermos, a small packet of trail gorp, half a sandwich in a Baggie, a space blanket, and a voluminous green nylon poncho. She was dressed already in coated nylon rain pants over pile pants over soft woolen longjohns, plus several thick sweaters and a parka, but the poncho would help keep out the wet and wind and add a layer of insulation.

Jenny shook out the space blanket and wrapped herself up in it, shiny side inward. Then she sat, awkward in so much bulkiness, and adjusted the foam rectangles behind and beneath her until they felt right. The Thermos was still half full of tea; she unscrewed the lid and drank from it directly, replacing the lid after each swig to keep the cold out. There were ham and cheese in the sandwich and unsalted peanuts, raisins, and chunks of plain chocolate in the gorp.

Swathed in her space blanket, propped against the stone buttress of the bridge, Jenny munched and guzzled, one glove off and one glove on, in a glow of the well-being that ensues upon vigorous exercise in the cold, pleasurable fatigue, solitude, simple creature comforts, and the smug relish of being on top of a situation that would be too tough for plenty of other people (her own younger self, for one). The little beck poured noisily beneath the bridge's span and down toward the dale and the trees below; the wind blew, but not on Jenny. She sat there tucked into the landscape, in a daze of pure contentment.

The appearance overhead of the first wispy tendrils of mist merely deepened her sense of comfort, and she sat on, knowing it would very soon be time to pack up and go but reluctant to bring the charm of the moment to a close.

A sheep began to come down the stream bed above where Jenny sat, a blackface ewe, one of the mountain breeds—Swaledale, would it be? Or Herdwick? No, Herdwicks were a Lake District breed. With idle interest she watched it scramble down jerkily, at home here, not hurrying and doubtless as cozy in its poncho of dirty fleece as Jenny was herself in her Patagonia pile. She watched it lurch toward her, knocking the stones in its descent—and abruptly found herself thinking of the albino deer in the park at home in Pennsylvania: how when glimpsed it had seemed half-deer, half-goat, with a deer's tail that lifted and waved as it walked or leaped away, and a prick-eared full-face profile exactly like the other deer's; yet it had moved awkwardly on stubby legs and was the wrong color, grayish-white with mottling on the back.

This sheep reminded her somehow of the albino deer, an al-most-but-not-quite right sort of sheep. Jenny had seen a lot of sheep, walking the English uplands. Something about this one was definitely funny. Were its legs too *thick?* Did it move oddly? With the fog swirling more densely every second it was hard to say just *what* the thing looked like. She strained forward, trying to see.

For an instant the mist thinned between them, and she perceived with a shock that the sheep was *carrying something in its mouth.*

At Jenny's startled movement the ewe swung its dead flat eyes upon her—froze—whirled and plunged back up the way it had come. As it wheeled it emitted a choked high wheeze, perhaps sheeplike, and dropped its bundle.

Jenny pushed herself to her feet, dis-cocooned herself from the space blanket, and clambered up the steep streambed. The object the sheep had dropped had rolled into the freezing water; she thrust in her ungloved right hand—gritting her teeth—and pulled it out. The thing was a dead grouse with a broken neck.

Now Jenny Shepherd, despite her name, was extremely ignorant of the personal habits of sheep. But they were grazing animals, not carnivores—even a baby knew that. Maybe the sheep had found the dead grouse and picked it up. Sheep might very well do that sort of thing, pick up carrion and walk around with it, for all Jenny knew. But she shivered, heaved the grouse back into the water and stuck her numb wet hand inside her coat. Maybe sheep *did* do that sort of thing; but she had the distinct impression that something creepy had happened, and her mood was spoiled.

Nervously now she looked at her watch. Better get a move on. She slipped and slid down to the bridge and repacked her pack in haste. There were four or five miles of open moor yet to be crossed before she would strike a road, and the fog was going to slow her down some. Before heaving the pack back on Jenny unzipped one of its outside pockets and took out a flashlight.

Elphi crashed across the open moor, beside himself. How *could* he have been so careless? Failing to spot the walker was bad enough, yet if he had kept his head all would have been well; nobody can swear to what they see in a fog with twilight coming on. But dropping the grouse, that was unpardonable. For a hundred and fifty years the success of the concealment had depended on unfaltering vigilance and presence of mind, and he had demonstrated neither. That he had just woken up from the winter's sleep, that his mind was burdened with trouble and grief, that walkers on the moors were scarcer than sunshine at this month and hour—none of it excused his incredible clumsiness. Now he had not one big problem to deal with, but two.

The old fellow groaned and swung his head from side to side, but there was no help for what he had to do. He circled back along the way he'd come so as to intersect the footpath half a mile or so east of the bridge. The absence of boot tracks in the snow there had to mean that the walker was heading in this direction, toward Westerdale, and would presently pass by.

He settled himself in the heather to wait; and minutes later, when the dark shape bulked out of the roke, he stepped upright into the path and blocked it. Feeling desperately strange, for he had not spoken openly to a human being in nearly two centuries, Elphi said hoarsely: "Stop reet theear, lad, an' don't tha treea ti run," and when a loud, startled *Oh!* burst from the walker, "Ah'll deea thee nae ho't, but thoo mun cum wiv me noo." His Yorkshire dialect was as thick as clotted cream.

The walker in its flapping garment stood rigid in the path before him. "What—I don't—I can't understand what you're *saying!*"

A woman! And an American! Elphi knew an American accent when he heard one, from the wireless, but he had *never* spoken with an American in all his life—nor with *any* sort of woman, come to that. What would an American woman be *doing* up here at this time of year, all on her own? But he pulled his wits together and replied carefully, "Ah said, ye'll have to cum wiv me. Don't be frighted, an' don't try to run off. No harm will cum ti ye."

The woman, panting and obviously badly frightened despite his words, croaked, "What in God's name *are* you?"

Elphi imagined the small, naked, elderly, hair-covered figure he presented, with his large hands and feet and bulging, knobby features, the whole wrapped up in a dirty sheepskin, and said hastily, "Ah'll tell ye that, aye, but nut noo. We's got a fair piece of ground ti kivver."

Abruptly the walker unfroze. She made some frantic movements beneath her huge garment and a bulky pack dropped out onto the ground, so that she instantly appeared both much smaller and much more maneuverable. Elphi made himself ready to give chase, but instead of fleeing she asked, "Have you got a gun?"

"A *gun* saidst 'ee?" It was Elphi's turn to be startled. "Neea, but iv thoos's na—if ye won't gang on yer own feet Ah'll bring thee along masen. Myself, that's to say. But Ah'd rather not, t'would be hard on us both. Will ye cum then?"

"This is *crazy! No,* dammit!" The woman eyed Elphi blocking the trail, then glanced down at her pack, visibly figuring the relative odds of getting past him with or without it. Suddenly, dragging the pack by one shoulder strap, she was advancing upon him. "Get out of the way!"

At this Elphi groaned and swung his head. "Mistress, tha mun cum, and theear's an end," he exclaimed desperately, and darting forward he gripped her wrist in his large knobbly sheepskin-padded hand. "Noo treea if tha can break loose."

But the woman refused to struggle, and in the end Elphi had no choice but to yank her off her feet and along the sloppy footpath for a hundred yards or so, ignoring the noises she made. He left her sitting in the path rubbing her wrist, and went back for the pack, which he shouldered himself. Then, without any more talk, they set off together into the fog.

By the time they arrived at the abandoned jet mine which served the hobs for a winter den, Jenny's tidy mind had long since shut itself down. Fairly soon she had stopped being afraid of Elphi, but the effort of grappling with the disorienting strangeness of events was more than her brain could manage. She was hurt and exhausted, and more than exhausted. Already, when Elphi in his damp fleece had reared up before her in the fog and blocked her way, she had had a long day. These additional hours of bushwhacking blindly through the tough mist-soaked heather in the dark had drained her of all purpose and thought beyond that of surviving the march.

Toward the end, as it grew harder and harder for her to lift her peat-clogged boots clear of the heather, she'd kept tripping and falling down. Whenever that happened her odd, dangerous little captor would help her up quite gently, evidently with just a tiny fraction of his superhuman strength.

Earlier, she had remembered seeing circus posters in the Middlesbrough station while changing from her London train; maybe, she'd thought, the little man was a clown or "circus freak" who had run off into the hills. But that hadn't seemed very probable; and later, when another grouse exploded under their feet like a feathered grenade, and the dwarf had pounced in a flash upon it and broken its neck—a predator that efficient—she'd given the circus idea up for a more terrifying one: maybe he was an escaped inmate of a mental hospital. Yet Elphi himself, in spite of everything, was somehow unterrifying.

But Jenny had stopped consciously noticing and deciding things about him quite a long while before they got where they were going; and when she finally heard him say "We's heear, lass," and saw him bend to ease back the stone at the entrance to the den, her knees gave way, and she flopped down sideways into the vegetation.

She awoke to the muted sound of a radio.

She lay on a hard surface, wrapped snugly in a sheepskin robe, smelly and heavy but marvelously warm. For some moments she basked in the comforting warmth, soothed by the normalness of the radio's voice; but quite soon she came fully awake and knew—with a sharp jolt of adrenaline—what had happened and where she must be now.

Jenny lay in what appeared to be a small cave, feebly lit by a stubby white "emergency" candle—one of her own, in fact. The enclosure was stuffy but not terribly so, and the candle burned steadily where it stood on a rough bench or table, set in what looked to be (and was) an aluminum pie-plate of the sort snack pies are sold in. The radio was nowhere in sight.

Someone had undressed her; she was wearing her sheep sleeping bag for a nightie and nothing else.

Tensely Jenny turned her head and struggled to take mental possession of the situation. The cave was lined with bunks like the one in which she lay, and in each of these she could just make out . . . forms. Seven of them, all evidently deep in sleep (or cold storage?) and, so far as she could tell, all creatures like the one that had kidnapped her. As she stared Jenny began to breathe in gasps again, and the fear which had faded during the march returned in full strength. *What was this place? What was going to happen to her? What the hell was it all about?*

The first explanation that occurred to her was also the most menacing: that she had lost her own mind, that her unfinished therapeutic business had finally caught up with her. If the little man had not escaped from an institution, then maybe she was on her own way to one. In fact Jenny's record of mental stability, while not without an average number of weak points, contained no hint of anything like hallucinations or drug-related episodes. But in the absence of a more obvious explanation her confidence on this score was just shaky enough to give weight and substance to such thoughts.

To escape them (and the panic they engendered) Jenny applied herself desperately to solving some problems both practical and pressing. It was cold in the cave; she could see her breath. Her bladder was bursting. A ladder against one wall disappeared into a hole in the ceiling, and as the cave appeared to have no other entryway she supposed the ladder must lead to the outside world, where now for several reasons she urgently wished to be. She threw off the robe and wriggled out of the sleeping-bag—catching her breath at the pain from dozens of sore muscles and bruises—and crippled across the stone floor barefoot; but the hole was black as night and airless, not open, at the top. Jenny was a prisoner, naked and in need.

Well, then, find something—a bucket, a pan, anything! Poking about, in the nick of time she spotted her backpack in the shadows of the far wall. In it was a pail of soft plastic meant for carrying water, which Jenny frantically grubbed out and relieved herself into. Half-full, the pail held its shape and could be stood, faintly steaming, against the wall. Shuddering violently, she then snatched bundles of clothes and food out of the pack and rushed back into bed. In point of fact there wasn't all that much in the way of extra clothing: one pair of woolen boot socks, clean underwear, slippers, a cotton turtleneck, and a spare sweater. No pants, no shoes, no outerwear; she wouldn't get far over the open moor without any of those. Still, she gratefully pulled on what she found and felt immensely better; nothing restores a sense of confidence in one's mental health, and some sense of control over one's situation, like dealing effectively with a few basic needs. Thank God her kidnapper had brought the pack along!

Next Jenny got up again and climbed to the top of the ladder; but the entrance was closed by a stone far too heavy to move.

The radio sat in a sort of doorless cupboard, a tiny transistor in a dimpled red plastic case. BOOTS THE CHEMIST was stamped on the front in gold, and a wire ran from the extended tip of its antenna along one side of the ladder, up the hole. Jenny brought it back into bed with her, taking care not to disconnect the wire.

She was undoing the twisty on her plastic bag of food when there came a scraping, thumping noise from above and a shaft of daylight shot down the hole. Then it was dark again, and legs—whitish hair-covered legs—and the back of a gray fleece came into view. Frozen where she sat, Jenny waited, heart thumping.

The figure that turned to face her at the bottom of the ladder looked by candlelight exactly like a very old, very small gnome of a man, covered with hair—crown, chin, body and all—save for his large hands and feet in pads of fleece. But this was a superficial impression. The arms were longer and the legs shorter than they should have been; and Jenny remembered how this dwarf had ranged before her on four limbs in the fog, looking as much like a sheep as he now looked like a man. She thought again of the albino deer.

They contemplated one another. Gradually, outlandish as he looked, Jenny's fear drained away again and her pulse rate dropped back to normal. Then the dwarf seemed to smile. "It's a bright morning, the roke's burned off completely," he said, in what was almost BBC English with only the faintest trace of Yorkshire left in the vowels.

Jenny said, calmly enough, "Look: I don't understand any of this. First of all I want to know if you're going to let me go."

She got an impression of beaming and nodding. "Oh, yes, indeed!"

"When?"

"This afternoon. Your clothes should be dry in time, I've put them out in the sun. It's a rare bit of luck, our getting a sunny morning." He unfastened the sheepskin as he spoke and hung it from a peg next to a clump of others, then slipped off his moccasins and mitts and put them on the shelf where the radio had stood. Except for his hair he wore nothing.

Abruptly Jenny's mind skittered away, resisting this strangeness. She shut her eyes, unafraid of the hairy creature but overwhelmed by the situation in which he was the central figure. "Won't you please explain to me what's going on? Who are you? Who are *they*? What is this place? Why did you make me come here? Just—what's going *on*?" Her voice went up steeply, near to breaking.

"Yes, I'll tell you all about it now, and when you've heard me out I hope you'll understand what happened yesterday—why it was necessary." He dragged a stool from under the table and perched on it, then quickly hopped up again. "Now, have you enough to eat? I'm afraid we've nothing at all to offer a guest at this time of year, apart from the grouse—but we can't make any sort of fire in this clear weather and I very much doubt you'd enjoy eating her raw. I brought her back last night in case anyone else was awake and hungry, which they're unfortunately not . . . but let me see: I've been through your pack quite thoroughly, I'm afraid, and I noticed some packets of dehydrated soup and tea and so forth; now suppose we were to light several more of these excellent candles and bunch them together, couldn't we boil a little pot of water over the flames? I expect you're feeling the cold." As he spoke the old fellow bustled about—rummaged in the pack for pot and candles, filled the pot half full of water from Jenny's own canteen, lit the candles from the burning one, and arranged supports for the pot to rest on while the water heated. He moved with a speed and economy that were so remarkable as to be almost funny, a cartoon figure whisking about the cave. "There, now! You munch a few biscuits while we wait, and I'll do my best to begin to clear up the mystery."

Jenny had sat mesmerized while her abductor rattled on, all the time dashing to and fro. Now she took tea, sugar, dried milk, two envelopes of Knorr's oxtail soup, and a packet of flat objects called Garibaldis here in England but raisin cookies by Nabisco (and squashed-fly biscuits by the children in *Swallows and Amazons*). She was famished, and lulled into calmness as the old fellow contrived to sound more and more like an Oxbridge don providing a student with fussy hospitality in his rooms in college. She had not forgotten the sensation of being dragged as by a freight train along the footpath, but was willing to set the memory aside. "What became of your accent? Last night I could barely understand you—or are you the same one that brought me in?"

"Oh, aye, that was me. As I said, none of the others is awake." He glanced rather uneasily at the row of shadowy cots. "Though it's getting to be high time they were. Actually, what's happened is that most of the time you were sleeping, I've been swotting up on my Standard English. I used the wireless, you see. Better switch it off now, actually, if you don't mind," he added. "Our supply of batteries is very, ah, irregular and where should *we* be now if there hadn't been any left last night, eh?" Silently Jenny clicked off the red radio and handed it to him, and he tucked it carefully back into its cubby. Then he reseated himself upon the stool, looking expectant.

Jenny swallowed half a biscuit and objected, "How can you totally change your accent and your whole style of speaking in one night, just by listening to the radio? It's not possible."

"Not for you, of course not, no, no. But we're *good* at languages, you see. Very, very good; it's the one thing in us that our masters valued most."

At this Jenny's wits reeled again, and she closed her eyes and gulped hard against nausea, certain that unless some handle on all this weirdness were provided *right away* she might start screaming helplessly and not be able to stop. She *could not* go on chatting with this Santa's elf for another second. Jenny Shepherd was a person who was never comfortable unless she felt she understood things; to understand is, to some extent, to have control over. "Please," she pleaded, "just tell me who or what you are and what's happening here. Please."

At once the old fellow jumped up again. "If I may—" he murmured apologetically and peered again into the treasure trove of Jenny's backpack. "I couldn't help noticing that you're carrying a little book I've seen before—yes, here it is." He brought the book back to the table and the light: the Dalesman paperback guide to the Cleveland Way. Swiftly finding the page he wanted he passed the book over to Jenny, who got up eagerly from the bed, holding the robe around her, to read by candlelight:

> The Cleveland area is extremely rich in folklore which goes
> back to Scandinavian sources and often very much further.
> Perhaps the hobs, those strange hairy little men who did great
> deeds—sometimes mischievous, sometimes helpful—were in
> some way a memory of those ancient folk who lingered on in
> parts of the moors almost into historic times. In the years
> between 1814 and 1823 George Calvert gathered together sto-
> ries still remembered by old people. He lists twenty-three
> "Hobmen that were commonly held to live hereabout," includ-
> ing the famous Farndale Hob, Hodge Hob of Bransdale, Hob
> of Tarn Hole, Dale Town Hob of Hawnby, and Hob of Hasty
> Bank. Even his list misses out others which are remembered,
> such as Hob Hole Hob of Runswick who was supposed to cure
> the whooping cough. Calvert also gives a list of witches. . . .

But this was no help, it made things worse! "You're telling me you're a *hob*?" she blurted, aghast. What nightmarish fantasy was this? "Hob . . . as in hobbit?" However dearly Jenny might love Tolkien's masterpiece, the idea of having spent the night down a hobbit-hole—in the company of seven dwarves!—was completely

unacceptable. In the real world hobbits and dwarves must be strictly
metaphorical, and Jenny preferred to live in the real world all the
time.

The odd creature continued to watch her. "Hob as in hobbit?
Oh, very likely. Hob as in hobgoblin, most assuredly—but as to
whether *we* are hobs, the answer is yes and no." He took the book
from her and laid it on the table. "Sit down, my dear, and bundle up
again; and shall I pour out?" for the water had begun to sizzle
against the sides of the little pot.

"What did you mean, yes *and* no?" Jenny asked a bit later,
sitting up in bed with a steaming Sierra Club cup of soup balanced
in her lap and a plastic mug of tea in her hands, and thinking: This
better be good.

"First, may I pour myself a cup? It's a long story," he said, "and
it's best to begin at the beginning. My name is Elphi, by the way.

"At least the dale folk called me Elphi until I scarcely remembered my true name, and it was the same with all of us—we took
the names they gave us and learned to speak their language so well
that we spoke no other even amongst ourselves.

"This is the whole truth, though you need not believe it. My
friends and myself were in service aboard an exploratory vessel from
another star. Hear me out," for Jenny had made an impatient movement, "I said you need not believe what I tell you. The ship called
here, at Earth, chiefly for supplies but also for information. Here, of
course, we knew already that only one form of life had achieved
mastery over nature. Often that is the case, but on my world there
were two, and one subordinate to the other. Our lords the Gafr were
physically larger than we, and technologically gifted as we were not,
and also they did not hibernate; that gave them an advantage,
though their lives were shorter (and that gave *us* one). We think the
Gafr had been with us, and over us, from the first, when we both
were still more animal than thinking thing. Our development, you
see, went hand in hand with theirs but their gift was mastery and
ours was service—always, from our prehistory.

"And from our prehistory our lives were intertwined with theirs,
for we were of great use to one another. As I've said, we Hefn are
very good with languages, at speaking and writing them—and also
we are stronger for our size than they, and quicker in every way,

though I would have to say less clever. I've often thought that if the Neanderthal people had lived on into modern times their relations with *you* might have developed in a similar way . . . but the Gafr are far less savage than you, and never viewed us as competitors, so perhaps I'm wrong. We are very much less closely related than you and the Neanderthal people."

"How come you know so much about the Neanderthalers?" Jenny interrupted to ask.

"From the wireless, my dear! The wireless keeps us up to date. We would be at a sad disadvantage without it, don't you agree?

"So the Gafr—"

"How would you spell that?"

"G-A-F-R. One *F,* not two, and no *E.* The Gafr built the starships and we went to work aboard them. It was our life, to be their servants and dependents. You should understand that they never were cruel. Neither we nor they could imagine an existence without the other, after so many eons of relying upon one another.

"Except that aboard my ship, for no reason I can now explain, a few of us became dissatisfied, and demanded that we be given responsibilities of our own. Well, you know, it was as if the sheepdogs hereabouts were one day to complain to the farmers that from now on they wanted flocks of their own to manage, with the dipping and tupping and shearing and lambing and all the rest. Our lords were as dumbfounded as these farmers would be—a talking dog, you see. When we couldn't be reasoned or scolded out of our notion, and it began to interfere with the smooth functioning of the ship, the Gafr decided to put us off here for a while to think things over. They were to come back for us as soon as we'd had time to find out what running our own affairs without them would be like. That was a little more than three hundred and fifty years ago."

Jenny's mouth fell open; she had been following intently. "Three hundred and fifty of your years, you mean?"

"No, of yours. We live a *long* time. To human eyes we appeared very old men when still quite young, but now we are old indeed—and look it, too, I fear.

"Well, they put fifteen of us off here, in Yorkshire, and some dozen others in Scandinavia somewhere. I often wonder if any of

that group has managed to keep alive, or whether the ship came
back for them but not for us—but there's no knowing.

"It was early autumn; we supposed they meant to fetch us off
before winter, for they knew the coming of hard winter would put us
to sleep. They left us well supplied and went away, and we all had
plenty of time to find life without the Gafr as difficult—psychologi-
cally, I suppose you might say—as they could possibly have wished.
Oh, yes! We waited, very chastened, for the ship to return. But the
deep snows came and finally we had to go to earth, and when we
awoke the following spring we were forced to face the likelihood
that we were stranded here.

"A few found they could not accept a life in this alien place
without the Gafr to direct their thoughts and actions; they died in
the first year. But the rest of us, though nearly as despairing, preferred life to death—and we said to one another that the ship might
yet return.

"When we awoke from our first winter's sleep, the year was
1624. In those days the high moors were much as you see them
now, but almost inaccessible to the world beyond them. The villages
were linked by a few muddy cart tracks and stone pannier trods
across the tops. No one came up here but people that had business
here, or people crossing from one dale into another: farmers, poach-
ers, panniermen, Quakers later on . . . the farmers would come up
by turf road from their own holdings to gather bracken for stock
bedding, and to cut turf and peat for fuel, and ling—that's what they
call the heather hereabouts, you know—for kindling and thatching.
They burned off the old ling to improve the grazing, and took away
the burned stems for kindling. And they came after bilberries in late
summer, and to bring hay to their sheep on the commons in winter,
as some still do. But nobody came from outside, passing through
from one distant place to another, and the local people were an
ignorant, superstitious lot as the world judges such things, shut away
up here. They would sit about the hearth of an evening, whole
families together, and retell the old tales. And we would hang about
the eaves, listening.

"All that first spring we spied out the dales farms, learned the
language and figured our chances. Some of us wanted to go to the
dalesmen with our story and ask to be taken into service, for it

would have comforted us to serve a good master again. But others—
I was one—said such a course was as dangerous as it was useless,
for we would not have been believed and the Church would have
had us hunted down for devil's spawn.

"Yet we all yearned and hungered so after direction and com-
panionship that we skulked about the farms despite the risk, watching how the men and milkmaids worked. We picked up the knack
of it easily enough, of milking and churning and threshing and
stacking—the language of farm labor, as you might say!—and by
and by we began to lend a hand, at night, when the house was
sleeping—serving *in secret,* you see. We asked ourselves, would the
farmers call us devil's spawn for *that?* and thought it a fair gamble.
We'd thresh out the corn, and then we'd fill our pouches with barley
and drink the cat's cream off the doorstep for our pay.

"At least we thought it was the cat's cream. But one night in
harvest-time, one of us—Hart Hall it was—heard the farmer tell his
wife, 'Mind tha leaves t'bate o' cream for t' hob. He deeas mair i'
yah neet than a' t'men deea iv a day.' That's how we learnt that the
people were in no doubt about who'd been helping them.

"We could scarcely believe our luck. Of course we'd heard talk
of witches and fairies, very superstitious they were in those days,
and now and again one would tell a tale of little men called
hobmen, part elf, part goblin as it seemed, sometimes kind and
sometimes tricksy. They'd put out a bowl of cream for the hob, for if
they forgot, the hob would make trouble for them, and if they remembered he would use them kindly."

"That was a common practice in rural Scandinavia too—to set
out a bowl of porridge for the *tomte,"* Jenny put in.

"Aye? Well, well . . . no doubt the cats and foxes got the
cream, before *we* came! Well, we put together every scrap we could
manage to overhear about the hobmen, and the more we heard the
more our way seemed plain. By great good fortune we looked the
part. We *are* manlike, more or less, though we go as readily upon
four feet as two, and stood a good deal smaller than the ordinary
human even in those days when men were not so tall as now, and
that meant no great harm would come of it should we happen to be
seen. That was important. There hadn't been so many rumors of
hobbish helpfulness in the dales for a very long time, and as curios-

ity grew we were spied upon in our turn—but I'm getting ahead of my tale.

"By the time a few years had passed we'd settled ourselves all through these dales. Certain farmsteads and local spots were spoken of as being 'haunted bi t'hob'; well, one way and another we found out where they were and one of us would go and live there, and carry on according to tradition. Not all of us did that, now—some just found a farm they liked and moved in. But for instance it was believed that a certain hob, that lived in a cave at Runswick up on the coast, could cure what they called t'kink-cough, so one of us went on up there to be Hob Hole Hob, and when the mothers would bring their sick children and call to him to cure them, he'd do what he could."

"What *could* he do, though?"

"Not a great deal, but more than nothing. He could make them more comfortable, and unless a child was very ill, he could make it more likely that they would recover."

"How? Herbs and potions?"

"No, not at all—merely the power of suggestion. But quite effective, oh, aye.

"There was a tradition, too, of a hob in Farndale that was the troublesome sort, and as it seemed wisest not to neglect that mischievous side of our ledger altogether, once in a while we would send somebody over there to let out the calves and spill the milk and put a cart on the barn roof, and generally make a nuisance of himself. It kept the old beliefs alive, you see. It wouldn't have done for people to start thinking the hobs had all got good as gold, we had the sense to see that. The dalesfolk used to say, 'Gin t'hobman takes ti yan, ya'r yal reet i' t'lang run, but deea he tak agin' 'ee 'tis anither story!' We wanted them to go right on saying that.

"But we did take to them—aye, we did indeed, though the Gafr and the dalesmen were so unlike. The Yorkshire farmer of those times for all his faults was what they call the salt of the earth. They made us good masters, and we served them well for nigh on two hundred years."

Jenny wriggled and leaned toward Elphi, raptly attending. "Did any of you ever *talk* with humans, face to face? Did you ever have any human friends, that you finally told the truth to?"

"No, my dear. We had no friends among humans in the sense you mean, though we befriended a few in particular. Nor did we often speak with humans. We thought it vital to protect and preserve their sense of us as magical and strange—supernatural, in fact. But now and again it would happen.

"I'll tell you of one such occasion. For many and many a year my home was at Hob Garth near Great Fryup Dale, where a family called Stonehouse had the holding. There was a Thomas Stonehouse once, that lived there and kept sheep.

"Now, the time I'm speaking of would have been about 1760 or thereabouts, when Tommy was beginning to get on a bit in years. Somehow he fell out with a neighbor of his called Matthew Bland, an evil-tempered fellow he was, and one night I saw Bland creep along and break the hedge, and drive out Tommy's ewes. Tommy was out all the next day in the wet, trying to round them up, but without much luck for he only found five out of the forty, and so I says to myself: here's a job for Hob. The next morning all forty sheep were back in the field and the hedge patched up with new posts and rails.

"Well! but that wasn't all: when I knew Tommy to be laid up with a cold, and so above suspicion himself, I nipped along and let Bland's cattle loose. A perfectly hobbish piece of work that was! Old Bland, he was a full fortnight rounding them up. Of course, at the time the mischief was done Tommy had been in his bed with chills and a fever, and everybody knew it; but Bland came and broke the new fence anyway and let the sheep out again—he was that furious, he had to do something.

"As Tommy was still too ill to manage, his neighbors turned out to hunt the sheep for him. But the lot of 'em had wandered up onto the tops in a roke like the one we had yesterday evening, and none could be found at all. All the same, that night Hob rounded them up and drove them home, and repaired the fence again. Bear in mind, my dear, that such feats as the farmers deemed prodigious were simple enough for us, for we have excellent sight in the dark, and great strength in the low gravity here, and are quick on our feet, whether four or two.

"Now, four of Tommy's ewes had fallen into a quarry in the roke and broken their necks, and never came home again. When he was well enough he walked out to the field to see what was left of the flock and cut some hay for it—this was early spring, I remember, just about this time. We'd waked sooner than usual that year, which was a bit of luck for Tommy. I saw him heading up there, and followed. And when I knew him to be grieving over the four lost ewes I accosted him in the road and said not to fret any more, that the sheep would be accounted for and then some at lambing time— for I knew that most were carrying twins, and I meant to help with the lambing as well, to see that as many as possible would live.

"He took me then for an old man, a bit barmy though kindly intentioned. But later, when things turned out the way I'd said, it was generally talked of—how there was no use Matthew Bland trying to play tricks on Tommy Stonehouse, for the hobman had befriended him, and when t'hobman taks ti yan . . . aye, it was a bit of luck for Tommy that we woke early that spring.

"But to speak directly to a farmer so, that was rare. More often the farmer took the initiative upon himself, or his wife or children or servants did, by slipping out to spy upon us at work, or by coming to beg a cure. There was talk of a hob that haunted a cave in the Mulgrave Woods, for instance. People would put their heads in and shout 'Hob-thrush Hob! Where is thoo?' and the hob was actually meant to reply—and the dear knows how *this* tradition began— 'Ah's tyin' on mah lef' fuit shoe, An' Ah'll be wiv thee—noo!' Well, we didn't go as far as that, but once in a while one of us might slip up there for a bit so's to be able to shout back if anyone called into the cave. Most often it was children.

"Mostly, people weren't frightened of t'hob. But as I've said, we thought it as well to keep the magic bright. There was one old chap, name of Gray, with a farm over in Bransdale; he married himself a new wife who couldn't or wouldn't remember to put out the jug of cream at bedtime as the old wife had always done. Well, Hodge Hob, that had helped that family for generations, he pulled out of there and never went back. And another time a family called Oughtred, that farmed over near Upleatham, lost *their* hob because he died. That was Hob Hill Hob, that missed his step and broke his neck in a mine shaft, the first of us all to go out since the very beginning. Well, Kempswithen overheard the Oughtreds discussing it—whyever had the hob gone away?—and they agreed it must have

been because one of the workmen had hung his coat on the win-
nowing machine and forgot it, and the hobman had thought it was
left there for *him*—for everyone knew you mustn't offer clothes to
fairies and such or they'll take offense.

"Well! We'd been thinking another of us might go and live at
Hob Hill Farm, but after that we changed our minds. And when a
new milkmaid over at Hart Hall spied on Hart Hall Hob and saw
him flailing away at the corn one night without a stitch on, and
made him a shirt to wear, and left it in the barn, we knew he'd have
to leave there too, and he did. One curious thing: the family at Hart
Hall couldn't decide whether the hob had been offended because
he'd been given the shirt at all, or because it had been cut from
coarse cloth instead of fine linen! We know, because they fretted
about it for months, and sacked the girl.

"At all events we'd make the point now and then that you
mustn't offend the hob or interfere with him or get too close and
crowd him, and so we made out pretty well. Still hoping for rescue,
you know, but content enough on the whole. We were living all
through the dales, north and south, the eleven of us who were left
alive—at Runswick, Great Fryup, Commondale, Kempswithen,
Hasty Bank, Scugdale, Farndale, Hawnby, Broxa . . . Woof Howe
. . . and we'd visit a few in-between places that were said to be
haunted by t'hob, like the Mulgrave Cave and Obtrush Rook above
Farndale. It was all right.

"But after a longish time things began to change.

"This would be perhaps a hundred and fifty years ago, give or
take a couple of decades. Well, I don't know just how it was, but bit
by bit the people hereabouts began to be less believing somehow,
less sure their grandfathers had really seen the fairies dance on Fairy
Cross Plain, or that Obtrush Rook was really and truly haunted by
the hobman. And by and by we began to feel that playing hob i'
t'hill had ceased to be altogether safe. Even in these dales there were
people now that wanted explanations for things, and that weren't
above poking their noses into our affairs.

"And so, little by little, we began to withdraw from the farms.
For even though we were no longer afraid of being taken for Satan's
imps and hunted down, concealment had been our way of getting by
for such a very long time that we preferred to go on the same way.

But for the first time in many long years we often found ourselves thinking of the ship again and wishing for its return. But I fear the ship was lost.

"Gradually, then, we drew back out of the dales to the high moortops, moved into the winter dens we'd been using right along, and set ourselves to learning how to live up here entirely—to catch grouse and hares, and find eggs and berries, instead of helping ourselves to the farmer's stores. Oh, we were good hunters and we loved these moors already, but still it was a hard and painful time, almost a second exile. I remember how I once milked a ewe— thinking to get some cream—only to find that it was the jug set out for me by the farmer's wife that I wanted and missed, for that was a symbol of my service to a master that respected what I did for him; but a worse time was coming.

"There were mines on the moors since there were people in the land at all, but not so very long after we had pulled back up out of the dales altogether, ironstone began to be mined in Rosedale on a larger scale than ever before, and they built a railroad to carry the ore right round the heads of Rosedale and Farndale and down to Battersby Junction. I daresay you know the right of way now as a footpath, my dear, for part of it lies along the route of the Lyke Wake Walk. But in the middle of the last century men came pouring onto the high moors to build the railroad. Some even lived up here, in shacks, while the work was ongoing. And more men poured across the moors from the villages all round about, to work in the Rosedale pits, and then there was no peace at all for us, and no safety.

"That was when we first were forced to go about by day in sheepskin.

"It was Kempswithen's idea, he was a clever one! The skins weren't too difficult to get hold of, for sheep die of many natural causes, and also they are easily killed, though we never culled more than a single sheep from anyone's flock, and then always an old ewe or a lame one, of little value. It went against the grain to rob the farmers at all, but without some means of getting about by daylight we could not have managed. The ruse worked well, for nearly all the railroad workers and miners came here from outside the dales, and were unobservant about the ways of sheep, and we were careful.

"But the noise and smoke and peacelessness drove us away

from our old haunts onto the bleakest part of the high moors where the fewest tracks crossed. We went out there and dug ourselves in.

"It was a dreary time. And the mines had scarcely been worked out and the railroad dismantled when the Second War began, and there were soldiers training on Rudland Rigg above Farndale, driving their tanks over Obtrush Rook till they had knocked it to bits, and over Fylingdales Moor, where we'd gone to escape the miners and the trains."

"Fylingdales, where the Early Warning System is now?"

"Aye, that's the place. During the war a few planes made it up this far, and some of the villages were hit. We slept through a good deal of that, luckily—we'd found this den by then, you see, an old jet working that a fox had opened. But it was uneasy sleep, it did us little good. Most particularly, it was not good for us to be of no use to any master—that began to do us active harm, and we were getting old. Two of us died before the war ended, another not long after. And still the ship did not return."

Something had been nagging at Jenny. "Couldn't you have reproduced yourselves after you came up here? You know—formed a viable community of hobs in hiding. Kept your spirits up."

"No, my dear. Not in this world. It wasn't possible, we knew it from the first, you see."

"Why wasn't it possible?" But Elphi firmly shook his head; this was plainly a subject he did not wish to pursue. Perhaps it was too painful. "Well, so now there are only eight of you?"

"Seven," said Elphi. "When I woke yesterday Woof Howe was dead. I'd been wondering what in the world to do with him when I so stupidly allowed you to see me."

Jenny threw the shadowed bunks a startled glance, wondering which contained a corpse. But something else disturbed her more. "You surely can't mean to say that in the past hundred and fifty years not one of you has ever been caught off-guard, until yesterday!"

Elphi gave the impression of smiling, though he did not really smile. "Oh, no, my dear. One or another of us has been caught napping a dozen times or more, especially in the days since the Rosedale mines were opened. Quite a few folk have sat just where you're sitting and listened, as you've been listening, to much the same tale I've been telling *you*. Dear me, yes! Once we rescued eight people from a train stalled in a late spring snowstorm, and we've revived more than one walker in the last stages of hypothermia— that's besides the ones who took us by surprise."

His ancient face peered up at her through scraggly white hair, and Jenny's apprehension grew. "And none of them ever told? It's hard to believe."

"My dear, none of them has ever remembered a thing about it afterward! Would we take such trouble to keep ourselves hidden, only to tell the whole story to any stranger that happens by? No indeed. It passes the time and entertains our guests, but they always forget. As will you, I promise—but you'll be safe as houses. Your only problem will be accounting for the lost day."

Jenny had eaten every scrap of her emergency food and peed the plastic pail nearly full, and now she huddled under her sheepskin robe by the light of a single fresh candle, waiting for Elphi to come back. He had refused to let her climb up to empty her own slops and fetch back her own laundry. "I'm sorry, my dear, but there's no roke today—that's the difficulty. If ever you saw this place again you would remember it—and besides, you know, it's no hardship for me to do you a service." So she waited, a prisoner beneath the heavy doorway stone, desperately trying to think of a way to prevent Elphi from stealing back her memories of him.

Promising not to tell anybody, ever, had had no effect. ("They all promise, you know, but how can we afford the risk? Put yourself in my place.") She cudgeled her wits: what could she offer him in exchange for being allowed to remember all this? Nothing came. The things the hobs needed—a different social order on Earth, the return of the Gafr ship, the Yorkshire of three centuries ago—were all beyond her power to grant.

Jenny found she believed Elphi's tale entirely: that he had come to Earth from another world, that he would not harm her in any way, that he could wipe the experience of himself from her mind— as effortlessly as she might wipe a chalkboard with a wet rag—by "the power of suggestion," just as Hob Hole Hob had "cured" the whooping cough by the power of suggestion. Somewhere in the course of the telling both skepticism and terror had been neutralized by a conviction that the little creature was speaking the unvarnished truth. She had welcomed this conviction. It was preferable to the fear that she had gone stark raving mad; but above and beyond all that she did believe him.

And all at once she had an idea that just might work. At least it seemed worth trying; she darted across the stone floor and scrabbled frantically in a pocket of her pack. There was just enough time. She burrowed back beneath the sheepskin robe where Elphi had left her with only seconds to spare.

The old hob backed down the ladder with her pail flopping from one hand and her bundle of clothes clutched in the opposite arm, and this time he left the top of the shaft open to the light and cold and the wuthering of the wind. He had tied his sheepskin on again. "Time to suit up now, I think—we want to set you back in the path at the same place and time of day." He scanned the row of sleepers anxiously and seemed to sigh.

Jenny's pile pants and wool socks were nearly dry, her sweaters, longjohns, and boots only dampish. She threw off the sheepskins and began to pull on the many layers of clothing one by one. "I was wondering," she said as she dressed, "I wanted to ask you, how could the hobs just *leave* a farm where they'd been in secret service for maybe a hundred years?"

Elphi's peculiar flat eyes peered at her mildly. "Our bond was to the serving, you see. There were always other farms where extra hands were needed. What grieved us was to leave the dales entirely."

No bond to the people they served, then; no friendship, just as he had said. But all the same— "Why couldn't you come out of hiding now? I know it could be arranged! People all over the world would give anything to know about you!"

Elphi seemed both amused and sad. "No, my dear. Put it out of your mind. First, because we must wait here so long as any of us is left alive, in case the ship should come. Second, because we love these moors and would not leave them. Third, because here on Earth we have always served in secret, and have got too old to care to change our ways. Fourth, because if people knew about us we would never again be given a moment's peace. Surely you know that's so."

He was right about the last part anyway; people would never leave them alone, even if the other objections could be answered. Jenny herself didn't want to leave Elphi alone. It was no use.

As she went to mount the ladder the old hob moved to grasp her arm. "I'm afraid I must ask you to wear this," he said apologetically. "You'll be able to see, but not well. Well enough to walk. Not well enough to recognize this place again." And reaching up he slipped a thing like a deathcap over her head and fastened it loosely but firmly around her neck. "The last person to wear this was a shopkeeper from Bristol. Like you, he saw more than he should have seen, and was our guest for a little while one summer afternoon."

"When was that? Recently?"

"Between the wars, my dear."

Jenny stood, docile, and let him do as he liked with her. As he stepped away, "Which was the hob that died?" she asked through the loose weave of the cap.

There was a silence. "Woof Howe Hob."

"What *will* you do with him?"

Another silence, longer this time. "I don't quite know . . . I'd hoped some of the rest would wake up, but the smell . . . it's beginning to trouble me too much to wait. I don't imagine you can detect it."

"Can't you just wake them up?"

"No, they must wake in their own time, more's the pity."

Jenny drew a deep breath. "Why not let *me* help you, then, since there's no one else?"

An even longer silence ensued, and she began to hope. But "You can help me *think* if you like, as we walk along," Elphi finally said. "I don't deny I should be grateful for a useful idea or two, but I must have you on the path by late this afternoon, come what may." And he prodded his captive up the ladder.

Above ground, conversation was instantly impossible. After the den's deep silence the incessant wind seemed deafening. This time Jenny was humping the pack herself, and with the restricted sight and breathing imposed by the cap she found just walking quite difficult enough; she was too sore (and soon too winded) to argue anymore.

After a good long while Elphi said this was far enough, that the cap could come off now and they could have a few minutes' rest. There was nothing to sit on, only heather and a patch of bilberry, so Jenny took off her pack and sat on that, wishing she hadn't eaten every last bit of her supplies. It was a beautiful day, the low sun brilliant on the shaggy, snowy landscape, the sky deep and blue, the tiers of hills crisp against one another.

Elphi ran on a little way, scouting ahead. From a short distance, with just his back and head showing above the vegetation, it was astonishing how much he really did move and look like a sheep. She said as much when he came back. "Oh, aye, it's a good and proven disguise, it's saved us many a time. Mind you, the farmers are hard to fool. They know their own stock, and they know where theirs and everyone else's ought to be—the flocks are heafed on the commons and don't stray much. 'Heafed,' that means they stick to their own bit of grazing. So we've got to wear a fleece with a blue mark on the left flank if we're going one way and a fleece with red on the shoulder if we're going another, or we'll call attention to ourselves and that's the last thing we want."

"Living or dead," said Jenny meaningfully.

"Aye." He gave her a sharp glance. "You've thought of something?"

"Well, all these abandoned mines and quarries, what about putting Woof Howe at the bottom of one of those, under a heap of rubble?"

Elphi said, "There's fair interest in the old iron workings. We decided against mines when we lost Kempswithen."

"What did you do with him? You never said."

"Nothing we should care to do again." Elphi seemed to shudder.

"Haven't I heard," said Jenny slowly, "that fire is a great danger up here in early spring? There was a notice at the station, saying that when the peat gets really alight it'll burn for weeks."

"We couldn't do that!" He seemed truly shocked. "Nay, such fires are dreadful things! Nothing at all will grow on the burned ground for fifty years and more."

"But they burn off the old heather, you told me so yourself."

"Controlled burning that is, closely watched."

"Oh." They sat silent for a bit, while Jenny thought and Elphi

waited. "Well, what about this: I know a lot of bones and prehistoric animals, cave bears and Irish elk and so on—*big* animals—
were found in a cave at the edge of the Park somewhere, but there
haven't been any finds like that on the moors because the acid in the
peat completely decomposes everything. I was reading an article
about it. Couldn't you bury your friend in a peat bog?"

Elphi pondered this with evident interest. "Hmmm. It might be
possible at that—nowadays it might. Nobody cuts the deep peat for
fuel anymore, and bog's poor grazing land. Walkers don't want to
muck about in a bog. About the only chaps who like a bog are the
ones that come to look at wildflowers, and it's too early for them to
be about."

"Are there any bogs inside the fenced-off part of Fylingdales,
the part that's closed to the public?"

Elphi groaned softly, swinging his head. "Ach, Woof Howe did
hate it so, skulking in that dreary place. But still, the flowers would
have pleased him."

"Weren't there some rare plants found recently inside the fence,
because the sheep haven't been able to graze them down in there?"

"Now, that's true," Elphi mused. "They wouldn't disturb the
place where the bog rosemary grows. I've heard them going on
about the bog rosemary and the marsh andromedas around
May Moss." He glanced at the sun. "Well, I'm obliged to you, my
dear. And now we'd best be off. Time's getting on. And I want you
to get out your map, and put on your rain shawl now."

"My what?"

"The green hooded thing you were wearing over your other
clothes when I found you."

"Oh, the poncho." She dug this out, heaved and hoisted the
pack back on and belted it, then managed to haul the poncho on
and down over pack and all despite the whipping of the wind, and
to snap the sides together. All this took time, and Elphi was fidget-
ing before she finished. She faced him, back to the wind. "Since I
helped solve your problem, how about helping me with mine?"

"And what's that?"

"I want to remember all this, and come back and see you
again."

This sent Elphi off into a great fit of moaning and head-swinging. Abruptly he stopped and stood, rigidly upright. "Would you force me to lie to you? What you ask cannot be given, I've told you why."

"I *swear* I wouldn't tell anybody!" But when this set off another groaning fit Jenny gave up. "All right. Forget it. Where is it you're taking me?"

Elphi sank to all fours, trembling a little, but when he spoke his voice sounded ordinary. "To the track across Great Hograh, where we met. Just over there, do you see? The line of cairns?" And sure enough, there on the horizon was a row of tiny cones. "You walk before me now, straight as you can, till you strike the path."

Jenny, map in hand and frustration in heart, obediently started to climb toward the ridge, lifting her boots high and clear of the snow-dusted heather. The wind was now at her back. Where a sheep-track went the right way she followed it until it wandered off-course, then cast about for another; and in this way she climbed at last onto the narrow path. She stopped to catch her breath and admire the view, then headed east, toward the Youth Hostel at Westerdale Hall, with the sun behind her.

For a couple of miles after that Jenny thought of nothing at all except the strange beauty of the scenery, her general soreness and tiredness, and the hot, bad dinner she would get in Westerdale. Then, with a slight start, she wondered when the fog had cleared, and why she hadn't noticed. She pulled off the flapping poncho—dry already!—rolled it up, reached behind to stuff it under the pack flap, then retrieved her map in its clear plastic cover from between her knees and consulted it. If that slope directly across the dale was Kempswithen, then she must be about *here,* and so would strike the road into Westerdale quite soon. She would be at the hostel in, oh, maybe an hour, and have a hot bath—hot wash, anyway, the hostel probably wouldn't have such a thing as a bathtub, they hardly ever did—and the biggest dinner she could buy.

"This is our off-season. You're in luck," said the hostel warden. "We were expecting you yesterday. In summer there wouldn't have been a bed in the place, but we're not fully booked tonight so not to worry. Will you be wanting supper?"

"I booked for the fifth," said Jenny a bit severely. "I'm quite sure, because the fifth is my sister's birthday."

"Right. But the fifth was yesterday; this is the sixth." He put his square finger on a wall calendar hanging behind him. "Thursday, April the sixth. All right?"

"It's Wednesday the fifth," said Jenny patiently, wondering how this obvious flake had convinced the Youth Hostel Association to hire him for a position of responsibility. She held out her wrist so he could read the day and date.

He glanced at the watch. "As a matter of fact it says Thursday the sixth. But it's quite all right, you'll get a bed. Now, what about supper, yes or no? There's people waiting to sign in."

Jenny stared at the little squares on the face of her watch and felt her own face begin to burn. "Sorry, I guess I made a mistake. Ah —yes, please, I definitely do want supper." A couple of teenage boys, waiting in the queue behind her, were looking at her strangely; she fumbled out of her boots, slung them into the bootrack, hoisted up her pack, and with all the dignity she could summon up proceeded toward the dormitory she'd been assigned to.

Safe in the empty dorm she picked a bed and sat on it, dumping her pack on the floor beside her. "I left Cambridge on the third," she said aloud. "I stayed two nights in York. I got on the Middlesbrough train this morning, changed there for Whitby, got off at Kildale, and walked over the tops to Westerdale. How and where in tarnation did I manage to lose a day?"

On impulse she got out her seat ticket for the Inter-City train. The seat had been booked for the third. The conductor had looked at and punched the ticket. Nobody else had tried to sit in the same seat. There could be no reasonable likelihood of a mistake about the day.

Yet her watch, which two days ago had said Monday, April third, now said Thursday, April sixth. Where could the missing day have gone?

But there was no one to tell her, and the room was cold. Jenny came back to the present: she needed hot water, food, clean socks, her slippers, and (for later) several more blankets on her bed. She wrestled her pack around, opened it, and pulled out her towel and soap box; but her spare pair of boot socks was no longer clean. In fact, it had obviously been worn hard. Both socks were foot-shaped, stuck full of little twiglets of heather, and just slightly damp.

The prickly bits of heather made Jenny realize that the socks she was wearing were prickly as well. She stuck a finger down inside the prickliest sock to work the bits of heather loose, giving this small practical problem all her attention so as to hold panic at bay.

The prickle in her right sock was not heather, but a small piece of paper folded up tight. Hands shaking, Jenny opened the scrap of paper and spread it flat on her thigh. It was a Lipton teabag wrapper, scribbled over with a pen on the nonprinted side, in her own handwriting. The scribble said:

> hob called ELFY (?)—caught me in fog, made me come home with him—disguised as *sheep*—lives in hole with 6 others—*hobs are aliens*—he'll make me forget but TRY TO REMEMBER—Danby High Moor?/Bransdale?/Farndale?— KEEP TRYING, DON'T GIVE UP!!!

These words, obviously penned in frantic haste, meant nothing whatever to Jenny. What was a hob? Yet she had written this herself, no question.

Her mind did a slow cartwheel. The sixth of April. Thursday, not Wednesday.

Jenny folded up the scrap of paper and stowed it carefully in her wallet. Methodically then she went through the pack. The emergency food packet had gone, vanished. So had the flashlight, and the candles. The spare shirt and underwear that ought to have been fresh were not. Her little aluminum mess-kit pot, carefully soaped for easy cleaning through so many years of camping trips, had been blackened with smoke on the bottom.

Something inexplicable had happened and Jenny had forgotten what it was—been made to forget, apparently; and to judge by this message from out of the lost day she had considered it well worth remembering.

All right then, she decided, hunched aching and grubby on a hard bed in that cold, empty room, the thing to do was to follow instructions and not give up. Trust her own judgment. Keep faith with herself, even if it took years.

*   *   *

It did take years, but Jenny never gave up. She returned as often to the North York Moors National Park as summers, semester breaks, and sabbaticals permitted, coming to know Danby High Moor, and Bransdale and Farndale, and *their* moors, as well as a foreign visitor could possibly know them in every season; and each visit made her love that rugged country better. In time she became a regular guest at a farm in Danby Dale that did bed-and-breakfast for people on holiday, and never again needed to sleep in Westerdale Hall.

The wish to unriddle the mystery of the missing April fifth retained its strength and importance without, luckily, becoming obsessive, and this fact confirmed Jenny's instinctive sense that when she had scribbled that note to herself she had been afraid only of forgetting, not of the thing to be forgotten. She wanted the lost memories back, not in order to confront and exorcise them, but to repossess something of value that rightfully belonged to her.

But Elphi's powers of suggestion were exceptional. Try as she might, Jenny could not recapture what had happened. Diligent research did uncover a great deal of information about hobs (including the correct spelling of Elphi's name, for he had been famous in his day). And Jenny also made it her business to learn what she could about people who believed themselves to have been captured and examined by aliens (for instance, they are drawn back again and again to the scene of the close encounter). Many of these people had clearly been traumatized, and were afterwards tormented by their inability to remember what had happened to them. Following their example, in case it might help, Jenny eventually sat through a few sessions with a hypnotist; but whether because her participation was half-hearted or because Elphi's skills were of a superior sort, she could remember nothing.

None of Jenny's efforts, in fact, produced the results she actively desired and sought. They did have the wholly unlooked-for result of finding her a husband, and a new and better home.

Frank Flintoft at forty-eight had flyaway white hair and a farmer's stumping gait, but also wide-awake blue eyes in a curiously innocent face. His parents were very old friends of John and Rita Dowson, whose farm in Danby Dale had become Jenny's hob-hunting base in Yorkshire. Frank had grown up on his family's farm in

Westerdale, gone off to Cambridge on a scholarship, then returned to take a lease on a place near Swainby, just inside the Park boundary, and settle down to breeding blackface sheep.

The Dowsons had spoken of this person to Jenny with a mixture of admiration and dubiety. A local boy that went away to University rarely came back. Frank *had* come back—but with Ideas, and also with a young bride who had left for London before the first year was out; and the Dowsons frowned upon divorce. Frank would use no chemicals, not even to spray his bracken, which put John Dowson's back up. For another thing, he went in for amateur archeology —with the blessing of the County Archeologists for half the North Riding—and was known to the Archeology Departments at the Universities of York and Leeds. And with it all, more often than not Frank's Swaledale gimmer lambs took Best of Breed at the annual Danby Show.

This paragon and Jenny were introduced on one of her summer junkets. The two hit it off immediately, saw a lot of each other whenever Jenny was in Yorkshire, but were not quick to marry. Frank had first to convince himself that Jenny truly loved the moor country for its own sake, and could be trusted not to leave it, before he was prepared to risk a second marriage; but Jenny, to her own surprise, felt wholly willing to exchange her old life for Frank, a Yorkshire sheep farm at the moors' edge, with a two hundred-year-old stone farmhouse, and part-time teaching at York University.

Not until six months after the wedding did Jenny tell her husband about the hob named Elphi. They had finished their evening meal and were sitting at the kitchen table before the electric fire, and at a certain point in the bizarre narrative Frank put his thick hand over hers. "I've heard of Elphi myself," he said thoughtfully when she had finished. "Well, and so that's what really brought you back here, year after year . . . you've still got the note you wrote yourself, I expect." Jenny had had the teabag wrapper laminated, years before. Wordless she went to her room to fetch it, and wordless he read what she had written there.

"Can *you* suggest an explanation?" she finally asked.

Frank shook his head. "But I know one thing. Ancient places have got lives of their own. There's 3,500 years of human settlement on these moors, love. When I'm working on one of the ancient sites

I often feel anything at all might happen up there. Almost anything," he amended; "I'm not happy thinking of the hobs as spacemen from somewhere else—I've been hearing tales of Hob all my life, you know. He belongs to our own folklore. I'd prefer to find an explanation closer to home."

"Well anyway, then, you won't think me barmy to go on trying to solve the mystery? It's the one *truly* extraordinary thing that ever happened to me," she added apologetically.

Frank grinned and shook his head again. "You didn't by any chance marry me for convenience, did you—in order to get on with the search?"

"Not *only* for that," said Jenny in relief, and hugged her tolerant and broad-minded husband.

But more years went by, and gradually she forgot to think about Elphi at all. Her quest had brought her a life which suited her so perfectly, and absorbed her so entirely, that in the end there was too little dissatisfaction left in Jenny to fuel the search for a solution to the puzzle.

One early summer morning, five years after she had come to live with Frank, the two of them—as they frequently did—took the Land-Rover and a hamper of sandwiches up to the tops, for a day of archeology and botanizing. Over a period of several months Frank had been surveying several minor Bronze Age sites between Nab Farm and Blakey Topping, just outside the southern boundary of the four-square-mile forbidden zone of the Early Warning System on Fylingdales Moor. Private land within the Park was thickly strewn with these ancient sites, mostly cairns and field systems. Many had still not been officially identified, and quite a few of the landowners were unaware of their existence. The Park Committee were only too happy to accept Frank's skilled, and free, assistance with the mapping and recording of the less important sites, and Frank enjoyed the work. But the painstaking patience it required was more in his line than Jenny's; she preferred to poke about in the bogland of Nab Farm and nearby May Moss.

On this day she left Frank setting up his equipment under a gray ceiling of cloud, and hiked off briskly through a spur of afforested land to see whether the marsh andromeda had bloomed. An hour and a half later she reappeared, stumbling and panting, to drag a startled Frank away from his work, back through the narrow bit of pine plantation to the stretch of bog she had been scanning for rare plants. Something—perhaps a dog, or a trail bike—had gouged a large messy hole in the peat; and inside the hole, just visible above dark water, what looked like a hand and part of an arm had been exposed. The arm appeared to be covered with long hair.

Frank stepped back hastily, yanking his Wellington boot out of the muck with a rude noise. "One of us had better go after the police."

"No," said Jenny, still panting. *"We've* got to dig him out. Never mind why, just help me do it." Already she was pulling her anorak over her head and rolling up her sleeves.

There were no flies on Frank Flintoft. After one hard look at his wife he began unbuttoning his own jacket.

Apart from a few sheep scattered across the long slopes of moor there was no one to see them delving in the bog. In twenty minutes, using a pocketknife, a plastic trowel, and their bare hands, they had exposed a small body. The body had been laid on its back in a shallow grave, not shrouded or even clothed except in the long, shaggy hair, stained a dark brown by the peaty water, that covered him completely.

While they labored to clear the face, scooping up double handfuls of mucky peat and throwing them out of the hole, Jenny abruptly began to cry silently; and when the body lay wholly uncovered, and they had poured a canteen of water over it to wash it a little cleaner, Frank stood and gazed soberly, then put his arm around Jenny and said gently, "Elphi, I presume."

Jenny took no notice of the tears that continued to streak her filthy face, except to wipe her nose on her sleeve. "No, it's another hob, called Woof Howe." And there at the graveside she began to tell Frank the story which had fallen upon her, entire and clear in every detail, as soon as their digging had revealed the corpse's form. "I'm pretty sure he meant to bury Woof Howe in the bog over there, on the grounds of the EWS," she finished. "The fence must have been too much for him—imagine trying to get in there carrying a body, all by yourself, no matter *how* strong you were." The moor wind blew upon them, stirring the reeds around the grave; Jenny shivered and leaned against Frank.

"Or I suppose this could be one of the other hobs, that died later on—Elphi himself, possibly."

"Un-uh, not Elphi," said Jenny. She spoke in a dazed way, obviously somewhat in shock, and Frank gave her a concerned look. "I really thought the acid in the peat would decompose soft tissue fast—that's what I told him, I'd actually read it somewhere—but I hadn't heard then about the bog people of Ireland and Denmark that were preserved for thousands of years in peat bogs."

"Ah. And so the result was just the opposite of what you intended."

"It looks that way, doesn't it." She stared down at the dead face. "I'm glad and sorry both."

"But mostly glad?"

"I guess so."

"Well," said Frank, "what shall we do about it then? Notify the police after all, or the Moors Centre?"

"No." Jenny roused herself and stood on her own feet. "We'll just bury him again, and try to make it look like this spot had never been touched."

Frank started, but swallowed his objections. "Sure that's what you want?"

Jenny stated flatly, "Elphi wouldn't trust me to keep his secret. I'm going to prove he was wrong. We'll just cover Woof Howe up again, and smooth out the mud, and leave him in peace."

"It's been over fifteen years, love," Frank could not help protesting. "The other hobs could all be dead by now."

"I know, but what if they're not?"

Sighing, Frank gave in. "But we'll take his picture first at least, all right? *I'd* quite like to have one."

"Okay, I guess that can't do any harm." So, having wiped the mud off his hands as best he could, Frank snapped several pictures with Jenny's camera, with its close-up lens for photographing wildflowers, before beginning to push the peat back into the hole containing the perfectly preserved body of Woof Howe Hob.

In a fortnight's time the reeds had reestablished themselves upon the grave; in another month nobody could have said for certain just where the bog at May Moss had been disturbed. No one's curiosity was aroused and no inquiries were made; and that would have been the end of the matter, except for this:

About the time the sedge was growing tall again above Woof Howe, Frank stood in the kitchen door and called to Jenny, "What in the name of sanity possessed you to try mucking out the chicken coop all on your own?" He sounded quite cross, for him.

Jenny came into the kitchen carrying a book. "Is this a clever way of shaming me into action? You know I've had the bloody chicken coop on my conscience for weeks, but if anybody's been mucking it out it wasn't me."

"Come and see." Frank led her through the gathering dusk, across the barnyard. There stood the coop, its floor scraped down to the wood and spread with clean straw. The hens clucked about contentedly in their yard. The manure-filled rubbish had been raked into a tidy heap for composting. Jenny stared flabbergasted.

"Do you actually mean to say," said Frank, "that this isn't your doing?"

"It ought to be, but it's not."

They walked slowly back toward the house, arms about each other, trying to puzzle it out.

"Maybe Billy Davies dropped by after school, thinking to earn a few pounds and surprise us," Frank suggested. "I've paid him to muck out the pigs, and the barn, and he knows about composting . . . but it doesn't seem his style somehow."

"I guess it could have been John, or Peter," Jenny said doubtfully. "Though why either of them would take it upon himself . . . and the only person I've actually *spoken* to about wanting to get around to the job is you. Did you mention it to anybody?"

The thought struck each of them at the same instant.

"Waaaaaaait a minute—" said Frank, and "Good God, you don't think—" said Jenny; and both were speechless, staring at one another.

Frank found his voice first. "Now, if they're *not* all dead—"

Jenny interrupted: "Frank! What if one of the sheep on the commons, that day at May Moss—wasn't a sheep!"

His eyes opened wide. "Wasn't a sheep? You mean—and followed us here somehow, found out who you were, and where we lived?"

"Is that possible? Could they do it? What if they could!"

"You said it wasn't him in the grave, you were sure of it."

"I still am. It wasn't him."

"Well then, who else would muck out a chicken coop without being asked, tell me that!"

By now they were laughing and clutching at each other, almost dancing. Abruptly Jenny broke free and ran up the kitchen steps. She snatched a stoneware jug down from a shelf, filled it to the brim with cream from the crock in the fridge, and set the jug on the top step, careful not to spill a drop.

WHY I LEFT HARRY'S ALL-NIGHT HAMBURGERS

LAWRENCE WATT-EVANS

Harry's was a nice place—probably still is. I haven't been back lately. It's a couple of miles off I-79, a few exits north of Charleston, near a place called Sutton. Used to do a pretty fair business until they finished building the Interstate out from Charleston and made it worthwhile for some fast-food joints to move in right next to the cloverleaf; nobody wanted to drive the extra miles to Harry's after that. Folks used to wonder how old Harry stayed in business, as a matter of fact, but he did all right even without the Interstate trade. I found out when I worked there.

Why did I work there, instead of at one of the fast-food joints? Because my folks lived in a little house just around the corner from Harry's, out in the middle of nowhere—not in Sutton itself, just out there on the road. Wasn't anything around except our house and Harry's place. He lived out back of his restaurant. That was about the only thing I could walk to in under an hour, and I didn't have a car.

This was when I was sixteen. I needed a job, because my dad was out of work again and if I was gonna do anything I needed my own money. Mom didn't mind my using her car—so long as it came back with a full tank of gas and I didn't keep it too long. That was the rule. So I needed some work, and Harry's All-Night Hamburgers was the only thing within walking distance. Harry said he had all the help he needed—two cooks and two people working the counter, besides himself. The others worked days, two to a shift, and Harry did the late-night stretch all by himself. I hung out there a little, since I didn't have anywhere else, and it looked like pretty easy work—there was hardly any business, and those guys mostly sat around telling dirty jokes. So I figured it was perfect.

Harry, though, said that he didn't need any help.

I figured that was probably true, but I wasn't going to let logic keep me out of driving my mother's car. I did some serious begging, and after I'd made his life miserable for a week or two, Harry said he'd take a chance and give me a shot, working the graveyard shift, midnight to eight A.M., as his counterman, busboy, and janitor all in one.

I talked him down to seven-thirty, so I could still get to school, and we had us a deal. I didn't care about school so much myself, but my parents wanted me to go, and it was a good place to see my friends, y'know? Meet girls and so on.

So I started working at Harry's nights. I showed up at midnight the first night, and Harry gave me an apron and a little hat, like something from a diner in an old movie, same as he wore himself. I was supposed to wait tables and clean up, not cook, so I don't know why he wanted me to wear them, but he gave them to me, and I needed the bucks, so I put them on and pretended I didn't notice that the apron was all stiff with grease and smelled like something nasty had died on it a few weeks back. And Harry—he's a funny old guy, always looked fiftyish, as far back as I can remember. Never young, but never getting really old, either, you know? Some people do that, they just seem to go on forever. Anyway, he showed me where everything was in the kitchen and back room, told me to keep busy cleaning up whatever looked like it wanted cleaning, and told me, over and over again, like he was really worried that I was going to cause trouble, "Don't bother the customers. Just take their orders, bring them their food, and don't bother them. You got that?"

"Sure," I said, "I got it."

"Good," he said. "We get some funny guys in here at night, but they're good customers, most of them, so don't you screw up with anyone. One customer complains, one customer stiffs you for the check, and you're out of work, you got that?"

"Sure," I said, though I've gotta admit I was wondering what to do if some cheapskate skipped without paying. I tried to figure how much of a meal would be worth paying for in order to keep the job, but with taxes and all it got too tricky for me to work out, and I decided to wait until the time came, if it ever did.

Then Harry went back in the kitchen, and I got a broom and swept up out front a little until a couple of truckers came in and ordered burgers and coffee.

I was pretty awkward at first, but I got the hang of it after a little bit. Guys would come in, women, too, one or two at a time, and they'd order something, and Harry'd have it ready faster than you can say "cheese," practically, and they'd eat it, and wipe their mouths, and go use the john, and drive off, and none of them said a damn thing to me except their orders, and I didn't say anything back except "Yes, sir," or "Yes, ma'am," or "Thank you, come again." I figured they were all just truckers who didn't like the fast-food places.

That was what it was like at first, anyway, from midnight to about one, one-thirty, but then things would slow down. Even the truckers were off the roads by then, I guess, or they didn't want to get that far off the Interstate, or they'd all had lunch, or something. Anyway, by about two that first night I was thinking it was pretty clear why Harry didn't think he needed help on this shift, when the door opened and the little bell rang.

I jumped a bit; that bell startled me, and I turned around, but then I turned back to look at Harry, 'cause I'd seen him out of the corner of my eye, you know, and he'd got this worried look on his face, and *he* was watching *me;* he wasn't looking at the customer at all.

About then I realized that the reason the bell had startled me was that I hadn't heard anyone drive up, and who the hell was going to be out walking to Harry's place at two in the morning in the West Virginia mountains? The way Harry was looking at me, I knew this must be one of those special customers he didn't want me to scare away.

So I turned around, and there was this short little guy in a really

heavy coat, all zipped up, made of that shiny silver fabric you see
race-car drivers wear in the cigarette ads, you know? And he had on
padded ski pants of the same stuff, with pockets all over the place,
and he was just putting down a hood, and he had on big thick
goggles like he'd been out in a blizzard, but it was April and there
hadn't been any snow in weeks and it was about fifty, sixty degrees
out.

He looked at me funny and said, "I suppose so."

Well, I didn't want to blow it, so I pretended I didn't notice, I
just said, "Hello, sir; may I take your order?"

He looked at me funny and said, "I suppose so."

"Would you like to see a menu?" I said, trying to be on my best
behavior—hell, I was probably overdoing it; I'd let the truckers find
their own menus.

"I suppose so," he said again, and I handed him the menu.

He looked it over, pointed to a picture of a cheeseburger that
looked about as much like anything from Harry's grill as Sly Stallone
looks like me, and I wrote it down and passed the slip back to
Harry, and he hissed at me, "Don't bother the guy!"

I took the hint, and went back to sweeping until the burger was
up, and as I was handing the plate to the guy there was a sound out
front like a shotgun going off, and this green light flashed in through
the window, so I nearly dropped the thing, but I couldn't go look
because the customer was digging through his pockets for money, to
pay for the burger.

"You can pay after you've eaten, sir," I said.

"I will pay first," he said, real formal. "I may need to depart
quickly. My money may not be good here."

The guy hadn't got any accent, but with that about the money I
figured he was a foreigner, so I waited, and he hauled out a handful
of weird coins, and I told him, "I'll need to check with the manager." He gave me the coins, and while I was taking them back to
Harry and trying to see out the window, through the curtain, to see
where that green light came from, the door opened and these three
women came in, and where the first guy was all wrapped up like an
Eskimo, these people weren't wearing anything but jeans. Women,
remember, and it was only April.

Hey, I was just sixteen, so I tried real hard not to stare and I
went running back to the kitchen and tried to tell Harry what was

going on, but the money and the green light and the half-naked women all got tangled up and I didn't make much sense.

"I *told* you I get some strange customers, kid," he said. "Let's see the money." So I gave him the coins, and he said, "Yeah, we'll take these," and made change—I don't know how, because the writing on the coins looked like Russian to me, and I couldn't figure out what any of them were. He gave me the change, and then looked me in the eye and said, "Can you handle those women, boy? It's part of the job; I wasn't expecting them tonight, but we get strange people in here, I told you that. You think you can handle it without losing me any customers, or do you want to call it a night and find another job?"

I really wanted that paycheck; I gritted my teeth and said, "No problem!"

When you were sixteen, did you ever try to wait tables with six bare boobs right there in front of you? Those three were laughing and joking in some foreign language I'd never heard before, and I think only one of them spoke English, because she did all the ordering. I managed somehow, and by the time they left Harry was almost smiling at me.

Around four things slowed down again, and around four-thirty or five the breakfast crowd began to trickle in, but between two and four there were about half a dozen customers, I guess; I don't remember who they all were any more, most of them weren't that strange, but that first little guy and the three women, them I remember. Maybe some of the others were pretty strange, too, maybe stranger than the first guy, but he was the *first,* which makes a difference, and then those women—well, that's gonna really make an impression on a sixteen-year-old, y'know? It's not that they were particularly beautiful or anything, because they weren't, they were just women, and I wasn't used to seeing women with no shirts.

When I got off at seven-thirty, I was all mixed up; I didn't know what the hell was going on. I was beginning to think maybe I imagined it all.

I went home and changed clothes and caught the bus to school, and what with not really having adjusted to working nights, and being tired, and having to think about schoolwork, I was pretty much convinced that the whole thing had been some weird dream.

So I came home, slept through until about eleven, then got up and went to work again.

And damn, it was almost the same, except that there weren't any half-naked women this time. The normal truckers and the rest came in first, then they faded out, and the weirdos started turning up.

At sixteen, you know, you think you can cope with anything. At least, I did. So I didn't let the customers bother me, not even the ones who didn't look like they were exactly human beings to begin with. Harry got used to me being there, and I did make it a lot easier on him, so after the first couple of weeks it was pretty much settled that I could stay on for as long as I liked.

And I liked it fine, really, once I got used to the weird hours. I didn't have much of a social life during the week, but I never had, living where I did, and I could afford to do the weekends up in style with what Harry paid me and the tips I got. Some of those tips I had to take to the jewelers in Charleston, different ones so nobody would notice that one guy was bringing in all these weird coins and trinkets, but Harry gave me some pointers—he'd been doing the same thing for years, except that he'd gone through every jeweler in Charleston and Huntington and Wheeling and Washington, Pa., and was halfway through Pittsburgh.

It was fun, really, seeing just what would turn up there and order a burger. I think my favorite was the guy who walked in, no car, no lights, no nothing, wearing this electric blue hunter's vest with wires all over it, and these medieval tights with what Harry called a codpiece, with snow and some kind of sticky goop all over his vest and in his hair, shivering like it was the Arctic out there, when it was the middle of July. He had some kind of little animal crawling around under that vest, but he wouldn't let me get a look at it; from the shape of the bulge it made it might have been a weasel or something. He had the strangest damn accent you ever heard, but he acted right at home and ordered without looking at the menu.

Harry admitted, when I'd been there awhile, that he figured anyone else would mess things up for him somehow. I might have thought I was going nuts, or I might have called the cops, or I might have spread a lot of strange stories around, but I didn't, and Harry appreciated that.

Hey, that was easy. If these people didn't bother Harry, I figured, why should they bother me? And it wasn't anybody else's business, either. When people asked, I used to tell them that sure, we got weirdos in the place late at night—but I never said just how weird.

And I never got as cool about it as Harry was; I mean, a flying saucer in the parking lot wouldn't make Harry blink. *I* blinked, when we got 'em—we did, but not very often, and I had to really work not to stare at them. Most of the customers had more sense; if they came in something strange they hid it in the woods or something. But there were always a few who couldn't be bothered. If any state cops ever cruised past there and saw those things, I guess they didn't dare report them. No one would've believed them anyway.

I asked Harry once if all these guys came from the same place.

"Damned if I know," he said. He'd never asked, and he didn't want me to, either.

Except he was wrong about thinking that would scare them away. Sometimes you can tell when someone wants to talk, and some of these people did. So I talked to them.

I think I was seventeen by the time someone told me what was really going on, though.

Before you ask any stupid questions, no, they weren't any of them Martians or monsters from outer space or anything like that. Some of them were from West Virginia, in fact. Just not *our* West Virginia. Lots of different West Virginias, instead. What the science fiction writers called "parallel worlds." That's one name, anyway. Other dimensions, alternate realities, they had lots of different names for it.

It all makes sense, really. A couple of them explained it to me. See, everything that ever could possibly have happened, in the entire history of the universe right from the Big Bang up until now, *did* happen—somewhere. And *every* possible difference means a different universe. Not just if Napoleon lost at Waterloo, or won, or whatever he didn't do here; what does Napoleon matter to the *universe,* anyway? Betelgeuse doesn't give a flying damn for all of Europe, past, present, or future. But every single atom or particle or whatever, whenever it had a chance to do something—break up or stay together, or move one direction instead of another, whatever—it did *all* of them, but all in different universes. They didn't branch off, either—all the universes were always there, there just wasn't any difference between them until this particular event came along. And that means that there are millions and millions of identical universes, too, where the differences haven't happened yet. There's an infinite number of universes—more than that, an infinity of infinities. I mean, you can't really comprehend it; if you think you're close, then multiply that a few zillion times. *Everything* is out there.

And that means that in a lot of those universes, people figured out how to travel from one to another. Apparently it's not that hard; there are lots of different ways to do it, too, which is why we got everything from guys in street clothes to people in spacesuits and flying saucers.

But there's one thing about it—with an infinite number of universes, I mean really infinite, how can you find just one? Particularly the first time out? Fact is, you can't. It's just not possible. So the explorers go out, but they don't come back. Maybe if some *did* come back, they could look at what they did and where it took them and figure out how to measure and aim and all that, but so far as any of the ones I've talked to know, nobody has ever done it. When you go out, that's it, you're out there. You can go on hopping from one world to the next, or you can settle down in one forever, but like the books say, you *really* can't go home again. You can get close, maybe —one way I found out a lot of this was in exchange for telling this poor old geezer a lot about the world outside Harry's. He was pretty happy about it when I was talking about what I'd seen on TV, and naming all the presidents I could think of, but then he asked me something about some religion I'd never heard of that he said he belonged to, and when I said I'd never heard of it he almost broke down. I guess he was looking for a world like his own, and ours was, you know, close, but not close enough. He said something about what he called a "random walk principle"—if you go wandering around at random you keep coming back close to where you started, but you'll never have your feet in *exactly* the original place, they'll always be a little bit off to one side or the other.

So there are millions of these people out there drifting from world to world, looking for whatever they're looking for, sometimes millions of them identical to each other, too, and they run into each other. They know what to look for, see. So they trade information, and some of them tell me they're working on figuring out how to *really* navigate whatever it is they do, and they've figured out some of it already, so they can steer a little.

I wondered out loud why so many of them turn up at Harry's, and this woman with blue-gray skin—from some kind of medication, she told me—tried to explain it. West Virginia is one of the best places to travel between worlds, particularly up in the mountains around Sutton, because it's a pretty central location for eastern North America, but there isn't anything there. I mean, there aren't any big cities, or big military bases, or anything, so that if there's an atomic war or something—and apparently there have been a *lot* of atomic wars, or wars with even worse weapons, in different worlds —nobody's very likely to heave any missiles at Sutton, West Virginia. Even in the realities where the Europeans never found America and it's the Chinese or somebody building the cities, there just isn't any reason to build anything near Sutton. And there's something in particular that makes it an easy place to travel between worlds, too; I didn't follow the explanation. She said something about the Earth's magnetic field, but I didn't catch whether that was part of the explanation or just a comparison of some kind.

The mountains and forests make it easy to hide, too, which is why our area is better than out in the desert someplace.

Anyway, right around Sutton it's pretty safe and easy to travel between worlds, so lots of people do.

The strange thing, though, is that for some reason that nobody really seemed very clear on, Harry's, or something like it, is in just about the same place in millions of different realities. More than millions; infinities, really. It's not always exactly Harry's All-Night Hamburgers; one customer kept calling Harry Sal, for instance. It's *there,* though, or something like it, and one thing that doesn't seem to change much is that travelers can eat there without causing trouble. Word gets around that Harry's is a nice, quiet place, with decent burgers, where nobody's going to hassle them about anything, and they can pay in gold or silver if they haven't got the local money, or in trade goods or whatever they've got that Harry can use. It's easy to find, because it's in a lot of universes, relatively—as I said, this little area isn't one that varies a whole lot from universe to universe, unless you start moving long distances. Or maybe not *easy* to find, but it can be found. One guy told me that Harry's seems to be in more universes than Washington, D.C. He'd even seen one of my doubles before, last time he stopped in, and he thought he might have actually gotten back to the same place until I swore I'd never seen him before. He had these really funny eyes, so I was sure I'd have remembered him.

We never actually got repeat business from other worlds, y'know, not once, not ever; nobody could ever find the way back to exactly our world. What we got were people who had heard about Harry's from other people, in some other reality. Oh, maybe it wasn't exactly the same Harry's they'd heard about, but they'd heard that there was usually a good place to eat and swap stories in about that spot.

That's a weird thought, you know, that every time I served someone a burger a zillion of me were serving burgers to a zillion others—not all of them the same, either.

So they come to Harry's to eat, and they trade information with each other there, or in the parking lot, and they take a break from whatever they're doing.

They came there, and they talked to me about all those other universes, and I was seventeen years old, man. It was like those Navy recruiting ads on TV, see the world—except it was see the *worlds,* all of them, not just one. I listened to everything those guys said. I heard them talk about the worlds where zeppelins strafed Cincinnati in a Third World War, about places the dinosaurs never died out and mammals never evolved any higher than rats, about cities built of colored glass or dug miles underground, about worlds where all the men were dead, or all the women, or both, from biological warfare. Any story you ever heard, anything you ever read, those guys could top it. Worlds where speaking aloud could get you the death penalty—not what you said, just saying *anything* out loud. Worlds with spaceships fighting a war against Arcturus. Beautiful women, strange places, everything you could ever want, out there *somewhere,* but it might take forever to find it.

I listened to those stories for months. I graduated from high school, but there wasn't any way I could go to college, so I just stayed on with Harry—it paid enough to live on, anyway. I talked to those people from other worlds, even got inside some of their ships, or time machines, or whatever you want to call them, and I thought about how great it would be to just go roaming from world to world. Any time you don't like the way things are going, just pop! And the whole world is different! I could be a white god to the Indians in a world where the Europeans and Asians never reached America, I figured, or find a world where machines do all the work and people just relax and party.

When my eighteenth birthday came and went without any sign I'd ever get out of West Virginia, I began to really think about it, you know? I started asking customers about it. A lot of them told me not to be stupid; a lot just wouldn't talk about it. Some, though, some of them thought it was a great idea.

There was one guy, this one night—well, first, it was September, but it was still hot as the middle of summer, even in the middle of the night. Most of my friends were gone—they'd gone off to college, or gotten jobs somewhere, or gotten married, or maybe two out of the three. My dad was drinking a lot. The other kids were back in school. I'd started sleeping days, from eight in the morning until about four P.M., instead of evenings. Harry's air conditioner was busted, and I really wanted to just leave it all behind and go find myself a better world. So when I heard these two guys talking at one table about whether one of them had extra room in his machine, I sort of listened, when I could, when I wasn't fetching burgers and Cokes.

Now, one of these two I'd seen before—he'd been coming in every so often ever since I started working at Harry's. He looked like an ordinary guy, but he came in about three in the morning and talked to the weirdos like they were all old buddies, so I figured he had to be from some other world originally himself, even if he stayed put in ours now. He'd come in about every night for a week or two, then disappear for months, then start turning up again, and I had sort of wondered whether he might have licked the navigation problem all those other people had talked about. But then I figured, probably not, either he'd stopped jumping from one world to the next, or else it was just a bunch of parallel people coming in, and it probably wasn't ever the same guy at all, really. Usually, when that happened, we'd get two or three at a time, looking like identical twins or something, but there was only just one of this guy, every time, so I figured, like I said, either he hadn't been changing worlds at all, or he'd figured out how to navigate better than anyone else, or something.

The guy he was talking to was new; I'd never seen him before. He was big, maybe six-four and heavy. He'd come in shaking snow and soot off a plastic coverall of some kind, given me a big grin, and ordered two of Harry's biggest burgers, with everything. Five minutes later the regular customer sat down across the table from him, and now he was telling the regular that he had plenty of room in his ship for anything anyone might want him to haul cross-time.

I figured this was my chance, so when I brought the burgers I said something real polite, like, "Excuse me, sir, but I couldn't help overhearing; d'you think you'd have room for a passenger?"

The big guy laughed and said, "Sure, kid! I was just telling Joe here that I could haul him and all his freight, and there'd be room for you, too, if you make it worth my trouble!"

I said, "I've got money; I've been saving up. What'll it take?"

The big guy gave me a big grin again, but before he could say anything Joe interrupted.

"Sid," he said, "could you excuse me for a minute? I want to talk to this young fellow for a minute, before he makes a big mistake."

The big guy, Sid, said, "Sure, sure, I don't mind." So Joe got up, and he yelled to Harry, "Okay if I borrow your counterman for a few minutes?"

Harry yelled back that it was okay. I didn't know what the hell was going on, but I went along, and the two of us went out to this guy's car to talk.

And it really was a car, too—an old Ford van. It was customized, with velvet and bubble windows and stuff, and there was a lot of stuff piled in the back, camping gear and clothes and things, but no sign of machinery or anything. I still wasn't sure, you know, because some of these guys did a really good job of disguising their ships, or time machines, or whatever, but it sure *looked* like an ordinary van, and that's what Joe said it was. He got into the driver's seat, and I got into the passenger seat, and we swiveled around to face each other.

"So," he said. "Do you know who all these people are? I mean people like Sid?"

"Sure," I said. "They're from other dimensions, parallel worlds and like that."

He leaned back and looked at me hard, and said, "You know that, huh? Did you know that none of them can ever get home?"

"Yes, I knew that," I told him, acting pretty cocky.

"And you still want to go with Sid to other universes? Even when you know you'll never come home to this universe again?"

"That's right, mister," I told him. "I'm sick of this one. I don't have anything here but a nothing job in a diner; I want to *see* some of the stuff these people talk about, instead of just hearing about it."

"You want to see wonders and marvels, huh?"

"Yes!"

"You want to see buildings a hundred stories high? Cities of strange temples? Oceans thousands of miles wide? Mountains miles high? Prairies, and cities, and strange animals and stranger people?"

Well, that was just exactly what I wanted, better than I could have said it myself. "Yes," I said. "You got it, mister."

"You lived here all your life?"

"You mean this world? Of course I have."

"No, I meant here in Sutton. You lived here all your life?"

"Well, yeah," I admitted. "Just about."

He sat forward and put his hands together, and his voice got intense, like he wanted to impress me with how serious he was. "Kid," he said, "I don't blame you a bit for wanting something different; I sure as hell wouldn't want to spend my entire life in these hills. But you're going about it the wrong way. You don't want to hitch with Sid."

"Oh, yeah?" I said. "Why not? Am I supposed to build my own machine? Hell, I can't even fix my mother's carburetor."

"No, that's not what I meant. But kid, you can see those buildings a thousand feet high in New York, or in Chicago. You've got oceans here in your own world as good as anything you'll find anywhere. You've got the mountains, and the seas, and the prairies, and all the rest of it. I've been in your world for eight years now, checking back here at Harry's every so often to see if anyone's figured out how to steer in no-space and get me home, and it's one hell of a big, interesting place."

"But," I said, "what about the spaceships, and—"

He interrupted me, and said, "You want to see spaceships? You go to Florida and watch a shuttle launch. Man, that's a spaceship. It may not go to other worlds, but that *is* a spaceship. You want strange animals? You go to Australia or Brazil. You want strange people? Go to New York or Los Angeles, or almost anywhere. You want a city carved out of a mountaintop? It's called Machu Picchu, in Peru, I think. You want ancient, mysterious ruins? They're all over Greece and Italy and North Africa. Strange temples? Visit India; there are supposed to be over a thousand temples in Benares alone. See Angkor Wat, or the pyramids—not just the Egyptian ones, but the Mayan ones, too. And the great thing about all of these places, kid, is that afterwards, if you want to, you can come home. You don't *have* to, but you *can.* Who knows? You might get homesick some day. Most people do. *I* did. I wish to hell I'd seen more of my own world before I volunteered to try any others."

I kind of stared at him for a while. "I don't know," I said. I mean, it seemed so easy to just hop in Sid's machine and be gone forever, I thought, but New York was five hundred miles away—and then I realized how stupid that was.

"Hey," he said, "don't forget, if you decide I was wrong, you can always come back to Harry's and bum a ride with someone. It won't be Sid, he'll be gone forever, but you'll find someone. Most world-hoppers are lonely, kid; they've left behind everyone they ever knew. You won't have any trouble getting a lift."

Well, that decided it, because, you know, he was obviously right about that, as soon as I thought about it. I told him so.

"Well, good!" he said. "Now, you go pack your stuff and apologize to Harry and all that, and I'll give you a lift to Pittsburgh. You've got money to travel with from there, right? These idiots still haven't figured out how to steer, so I'm going back home—not my *real* home, but where I live in your world—and I wouldn't mind a passenger." And he smiled at me, and I smiled back, and we had to wait until the bank opened the next morning, but he didn't really mind. All the way to Pittsburgh he was singing these hymns and war-songs from his home world, where there was a second civil war in the nineteen-twenties because of some fundamentalist preacher trying to overthrow the Constitution and set up a church government; he hadn't had anyone he could sing them to in years, he said.

That was six years ago, and I haven't gone back to Harry's since.

So that was what got me started traveling. What brings *you* to Benares?

A FINAL NOTE
TO THE
READER

Not long ago I attended a lecture by the astronaut Michael Collins. Mr. Collins spoke eloquently about what it was like to orbit the moon and about suggested plans for space stations, return trips to the moon, and voyages to Mars. Perhaps the most memorable topic of his speech was his discussion of the attention NASA could focus on a planet which may be the most valuable and the most interesting body in the solar system: our own planet, Earth.

Michael Collins's concern and appreciation for our homeworld are echoed by other astronauts, who have also talked about how fragile Earth appears to them as it hangs suspended against the velvet blackness of space.

Earth is the only body in this solar system that supports and encourages life, and like any other living creature it must be nourished to survive. However, people today are deeply concerned about the effects of toxic wastes, the destruction of rain forests and the ozone layer and the warming trend that could ensue, and what would happen to Earth in a nuclear war.

Science fiction writers, who often wonder where we all may be tomorrow, have long been aware of how important it is to look after our planet properly. Because their first goal is usually to entertain their readers, their work is often associated with robots and faster-than-light spaceships. These stories may be set as far away in time and space as we can possibly imagine. But, as we've seen in this anthology, some of the most adventurous SF tales can also be set on Earth.

An author's inspiration for an earthbound story may develop out of concern for a particular issue. He or she may mull over an idea such as the greenhouse effect—Is Earth really warming up? How will this affect the climate? How will that affect my characters? —or he might wonder about what could happen if the arms race continued unchecked. What if no one brought any pressure to bear on our presidents and our premiers? What if our differences are resolved on our battlefields and not through discussion and cooperation?

The best stories don't moralize. They simply leave us thinking. The stories in this anthology all offer something more than just an entertaining tale. One makes us think about displacement and loneliness, another about the nature of fairy tales, and some make us think about the Earth itself. James Patrick Kelly's "Still Time," one of the most exciting tales I've ever read, is an excellent example of this. The story is a breathless adventure tale about one man's reaction to the onset of nuclear war. Throughout the story, we hope the characters will make it, and when we finally put it down we are thankful there is "still time" to resolve our conflicts peacefully.

Keith Minnion's "Empire State" is a rousing tale of adventure on the high seas. Yet the islands in this watery story are the office buildings of New York City! We aren't sure where the water came from, and the characters don't speculate, but we are left with a set of questions to ponder. Just how much coastal area will we lose if Earth warms up and the icebergs start to melt . . . ?

In "The Hob," Judith Moffett does not worry us with the threat of nuclear war or of a massive warming trend. She does transport us, though, to a Yorkshire moor so enchanting and so realistic we could swear we'd gone along with Jenny for the hike. It is a brilliant reminder of how much we have to lose.

Science fiction has always caused people to reflect, and some say that reading SF helped them decide which direction in life to take. Astronauts and NASA scientists have remarked that the ideas and optimism prevalent in science fiction were part of what convinced them that humankind could get into orbit, reach the moon, and perhaps go even farther. Tomorrow's environmental scientists, geologists, agronomists, and people who are simply involved in protecting Earth may say that they, too, were partly inspired by science fiction. After all, since we are most likely to have our own real-life adventures here on Earth, we will have to take care of our planet. Astronauts, scientists, and science fiction writers will continue to remind us that our beautiful blue world, suspended breathtakingly against the void, should not be treated lightly.

Sheila Williams,
September 1989

ABOUT THE
CONTRIBUTORS

Kim Stanley Robinson ("Glacier"):
In 1988 Kim Stanley Robinson received the Nebula award for his novella "The Blind Geometer." That same year, the readers of *Isaac Asimov's Science Fiction Magazine* declared his novella "Mother Goddess of the World" their favorite in *IAsfm's* annual poll. Both stories went on to be finalists for the Hugo Award. An earlier, eloquent tale of a boy impressed into service on the Spanish Armada, "Black Air," won a World Fantasy Award for the author. While "Glacier" is set slightly in our future, it is an equally touching tale of a boy who must adapt to an unfriendly environment. Mr. Robinson lives in Chevy Chase, Maryland, with his wife and their infant son.

Connie Willis ("And Who Would Pity a Swan?"):
So what happens after the fairy tale ends? That's a question which has intrigued Connie Willis since childhood, and it's the one that inspired "And Who Would Pity a Swan?" Ms. Willis is a three-time winner of the Nebula award, a two-time Hugo Award winner, and a World Fantasy Award finalist. She lives in Greeley, Colorado.

Barry B. Longyear ("The Tryouts"):
In 1978, Barry B. Longyear's first published science fiction story appeared in *IAsfm*. A year later, *IAsfm* published Mr. Longyear's "Enemy Mine," which went on to win the Nebula award for Best Novella. Four years after that, "Enemy Mine" became a movie starring Dennis Quaid and Louis Gossett, Jr. In the meantime, Mr. Longyear wrote more than two dozen stories for *IAsfm,* becoming one of the magazine's most prolific and popular authors. "The Tryouts" is the story that started it all. He lives in Farmington, Maine.

James Patrick Kelly ("Still Time"):
James Patrick Kelly has been a finalist for both the Nebula and Hugo awards. He is a full-time writer who lives in Durham, New Hampshire, with his nine-year-old daughter Maura. Mr. Kelly is also a part-time teacher of the art of writing science fiction, to high-school and junior-high-school students. He often uses his own fiction in his classes, and he's found "Still Time" to be his students' favorite tale.

Jane Yolen ("The White Babe"):
Jane Yolen is the author of more than one hundred books. She's a past president of the Science Fiction Writers of America and she's served on the board of directors of the Society of Children's Book Writers since that organization's inception. The prestigious honors bestowed on Ms. Yolen include the Christopher Medal, the Jewish Book Council Award, the World Fantasy Award, and the Daedalus Award. She lives in Hatfield, Massachusetts.

Edward D. Hoch ("The Homesick Chicken"):
Ed Hoch is best known as a mystery writer. For more than fifteen years he has had a story featured in every issue of *Ellery Queen's Mystery Magazine*—more than two hundred stories so far, and he's still going strong. In 1968 Mr. Hoch won the Edgar Allan Poe Award for Best Short Story for "The Oblong Room." "The Homesick Chicken" is one of his rare and delightful forays into science fiction. Mr. Hoch lives in Rochester, New York.

Keith Minnion ("Empire State"):
The author, his wife, and their two children live in Philadelphia in a house that closely resembles a haunted mansion. Mr. Minnion has been an art teacher and an officer in the navy. He's a civilian now but he still does technical writing and book design for the navy.

Isaac Asimov ("Profession"):
Isaac Asimov is the author of more than 430 books. It is hard to say whether he is better known for his science or his science fiction; but even outside these fields he has built a huge following with his works on such subjects as Shakespeare, Gilbert and Sullivan, and the Bible. Certainly his most famous stories are science fiction, and they include "Nightfall," "Foundation," "The Ugly Little Boy," "The Last Question," and many other classics. Dr. Asimov lives in New York City with his wife, Janet, and is probably writing another book as you read this.

Andrew Weiner ("The Band from the Planet Zoom"):
Andrew Weiner is a Canadian author whose stories have appeared in a number of science fiction magazines, and on the television show *Tales from the Darkside.* Mr. Weiner's career as a writer began with free-lance articles on rock music and other nonfiction subjects. He assures us, though, that "The Band from the Planet Zoom" is in no way autobiographical. Mr. Weiner lives in Toronto.

Somtow Sucharitkul ("The Web Dancer"):
Originally from Thailand, currently living in Sun Valley, California, Somtow Sucharitkul has had one of the most diverse careers in (and out of) science fiction. In addition to the many short stories and novels he has published under his own name and as "S. P. Somtow," Mr. Sucharitkul is a musical composer, a screenwriter, and an actor, of sorts: he recently had a role as an evil deity in a comic horror film titled *The Laughing Dead. The New Encyclopedia of Science Fiction* lists among his strengths "a splendid lyricism, sensitive characterizations, and outrageous inventiveness," all of which are very much evident in "The Web Dancer."

Judith Moffett ("The Hob"):

Judith Moffett, whose first science fiction story was also her first nominee for the Nebula Award, received the 1988 John W. Campbell Award for Best New Author. Ms. Moffett is now at work on a novel set in the same world as her second Nebula nominee, "The Hob." She and her husband live in Wallingford, Pennsylvania.

Lawrence Watt-Evans ("Why I Left Harry's All-Night Hamburgers"):

"Why I Left Harry's All-Night Hamburgers" is a tale that reveals just how exciting science fiction and the Earth itself can be. One of the most popular stories ever published in *IAsfm,* it placed first in our annual readers' poll, was a finalist for the Nebula award, and brought home the Hugo. Lawrence Watt-Evans lives in Gaithersburg, Maryland, with his wife and two children.

ABOUT THE
EDITORS

Sheila Williams has worked extensively in the field of science fiction. She is the managing editor of *Isaac Asimov's Science Fiction Magazine,* and has also edited science fiction novels. *Why I Left Harry's All-Night Hamburgers and Other Stories from Isaac Asimov's Science Fiction Magazine* is the second anthology she has coedited for young adults. She lives in New York City with her husband.

Charles Ardai is the subsidiary rights associate at Davis Publications, Inc.—the publishers of *IAsfm.* Mr. Ardai has been involved in the creation of a comic book series, books, calendars, and a line of mystery cassettes. He is also a free-lance writer who first appeared in print in the New York *Daily News* at age eleven. Charles Ardai lives in New York City.

SC
WHY

Why I left Harry's
all-night hamburgers,
and other stories
from Isaac Asimov's
science fiction
magazine.

11315

$14.95